Piers Anthony was born in Oxford in 1934, moved with his family to Spain in 1939 and finally to the United States in 1940, after his father was expelled from Spain by Franco's government. He became an American citizen in 1958, and before devoting himself full-time to writing worked as a technical writer for a communications company and taught English. He has made a name for himself as a writer of original, inventive stories whose imaginative, mind-twisting style is full of extraordinary, and often poetic, images and bizarre flights of cosmic fancy.

Chaining the Lady is the second part of his brilliant new SF adventure, The *Cluster* Series, which chronicles the history of our Galaxy over a long mythical period and ranges over the full extent of the galactic cluster. The series starts with *Vicinity Cluster*, and is continued in *Kirlian Quest*.

Also by Piers Anthony

Piers Anthony

Chaining the Lady

PANTHER
GRANADA PUBLISHING
London Toronto Sydney New York

Published by Granada Publishing Limited
in Panther Books 1979

ISBN 0 586 04838 3

First published in Great Britain by
Millington Ltd 1978
Copyright © Piers Anthony 1978

Granada Publishing Ltd
Frogmore, St Albans, Herts AL2 2NF
and
3 Upper James Street, London W1R 4BP
1221 Avenue of the Americas, New York, NY 10020, USA
117 York Street, Sydney, NSW 2000, Australia
100 Skyway Avenue, Toronto, Ontario, Canada M9W 3A6
110 Northpark Centre, 2193 Johannesburg, South Africa
CML Centre, Queen & Wyndham, Auckland 1, New Zealand

Set, printed and bound in Great Britain by
Cox & Wyman Ltd, London., Reading and Fakenham
Set in Intertype Times

Granada Publishing ®

Contents

Part Three – MASTER OF ANDROMEDA

Prologue

The security guard was young, fresh from the most rigorous academy, and human. That, virtually by definition, meant trouble. As the acolytes of the Cluster Tarot Temple put it, the Suit of Gas equated with both the Sphere of Sol and the condition of Trouble for excellent reason. No wonder that suit's symbol was the sword of war, despite the efforts of euphemists to redefine it as the scalpel of science.

Yet in defense of this necessarily nameless Solarian guard, it must be stated that he acted in strict accordance with the nature and training of his kind. All the pertinent regulations were imprinted on his awareness, and his decision was guided reflex. *By the book, he was correct.*

He saw the intruder in the private office of the Minister of Population, poking a tentacle into the computer file cabinet. It was after hours, the illumination had been set low, and no pass had been authorized. So the Solarian fired his laser stunner without challenge.

The intruder fell as the beam touched. It was a good shot; the Academy might not turn out many original thinkers, but it never loosed a sloppy shooter. The guard alerted his immediate superior by bodyphone, for of course he honored the chain-of-command requirements, and approached the suspect.

'A Dino!' the man remarked, employing a grossly vernacular term whose origin had been lost in Planet Outworld's antiquity.

Indeed, it was a Polarian, now heaped in a boneless mass about its spherical wheel, its tentacle as limp as a dead snake. Not dead, of course; spies were never killed, because of their interrogation value and because they often employed local hosts. It would not be right to kill the host for the actions of the transferee who possessed it. This creature of Sphere Polaris would recover in a few hours.

'Funny,' the guard remarked aloud. Despite the vulgarity he had used a moment before, he was not a Polaphobe; some of his best friends were alien creatures. This was, after all, the Imperial Planet, nexus of Segment Etamin, one of the ten major Empires of Galaxy Milky Way. In fact, without the constant flux of galactics in human or alien guise, he would have no job. 'Poles don't usually snoop. They call it uncircular.'

And this was true. Polarians, in the convenient informal analogy of the Cluster Tarot, equated with the Suit of Solid, symbolized by the Disk of Commerce and Culture. Circularity was the foundation of Polarian nature, and though to ignorant entities it sometimes resembled a runaround, it was also manifest that direct spying was foreign to Polarian concept. Something was very strange here.

The guard lifted the flaccid tentacle and played his recording beam over the little ball set in its end. 'Suspect in Minister's office,' he said tersely into his phone. 'Identity on record?'

Identification procedures were efficient on the Imperial Planet. Soon his superior's horrified voice came back. 'You bet it's on record, soldier! *That's the Minister of Research.*'

For an instant the Solarian guard saw his future laid out: unskilled manual labor, trimming the thornsuckers off the great vinetrees of the wilderness reservation, barehanded. Or maybe solitary duty aboard a farflung outpost planetoid, complete with pillmeals and femmecubes to satisfy his physical and emotional needs while his mind went slowly as berserk as the sanity shot permitted.

He had shot a Minister in his own office, a monumentally colossal blunder worthy of redlining in the annals of punishment. The Regulations Book would not protect him from the ravages of an inter-Spherical inquiry.

But then something clicked in the gray matter behind his frontlobe shock, a notion of almost whimsical desperation that abruptly fell into place. 'But he's in the *Population* office, not the Research office – without a pass, outside hours.'

There was a pause. 'It is not for Security personnel to

question the affairs of segment Ministers,' the officer said via the phone. 'He could readily have obtained clearance. He must be in that office ten times a day, consulting with his associates. He just forgot, this time.'

The threat to his future forced the issue. 'Sir, it *is* for us to question!' the Solarian insisted. 'According to the Book—'

A human sigh, one that implied volumes about dealing with Academy recuits in non-ivory-tower situations.

'You really want it by the book, soldier?'

Dry-mouthed, knowing his chances of salvaging even a vestige of respect were fading, the guard answered, 'Yes, sir.'

'So noted. You are the Entity on the Spot, per that Book. I decline responsibility for your action but I honor the Book. An investigation team will be with you immediately.'

'Thank you, sir.' It was like holding up one finger to stop an avalanche, pleading Book justification in defense against the coming charge of aggravated incompetence. He might well be shipped to the sunside mines of Inworld, a fate marginally preferable to full personality obliteration for involuntary hosting. *Nobody* shot a Minister with impunity! Not even if he stood upon a stack of Books. The Ministers had *written* the Book.

In just forty-three Solarian seconds the investigation team arrived: four entities from Executive. They had been selected by lot from the segment pool reserved for such occasions, and represented four Spheres: Nath, Canopus, Polaris, and Sol.

The guard made a formal if shaky salute to the four. 'I am the Entity on the Spot,' he said. *And how!* 'I stunned this Polarian, believing him to be an intruder. I proffer the Manual of Sentient Entity Protocol, Subsection Defense, on my behalf. I believe my action was technically justified.' He hoped no one would laugh out loud.

The Solarian officer made an elegant bow from the waist. 'I represent the interest of this Entity, who is native to my Sphere of Sol,' he said. The guard noted with mixed satisfaction and alarm that the man wore the insignia of a full colonel; a thoroughly experienced officer of Sol's military apparatus. This was good because his decision would carry

9

considerable force with the segment authorities, but bad because ranking officers were notoriously indifferent to the problems of enlisted men, especially when the image of the Sphere was involved. Still, the human advocacy was vital; at least a Solarian had the *capacity* to understand.

The Polarian glowed momentarily in salute, then buzzed his ball against the floor. 'I circle the Injured, who is of my Sphere of Polaris.'

The Nathian rippled its thousand miniature hooks in waves, resembling a windblown deep shag rug. A portable translation unit rendered its clicks into audible language. 'I pull for the situation, concerned with proper procedure.'

'I supervise,' the Canopian Master said in perfect Solarian. He resembled a monstrous insect, and he did not deign to salute. The Canopian Master species had evolved to command, and what it commanded was a humanoid species. In many respects Canopians were the true governing force of Segment Etamin. When it came to the efficient exercise of authority, this species was matchless. Even the often-unruly Solarians preferred to allocate their supervisory positions to the insectoids, knowing that the job would be done with precision and dispatch.

The formalities completed, Polaris lifted the stunned Minister by heaving him up with his trunk. 'My brother is unconscious but undamaged,' he announced, letting the Minister slump back to the floor.

'Then my client-entity can not be judged guilty of inflicting injury, merely of causing inconvenience,' the Solarian officer said. The guard relaxed slightly, his image of the sunside mines fading.

Nath swarmed over the body, blanketing it, his little hooks tapping everywhere. 'Require Kirlian readout,' it clicked.

'One might question the need for this step,' Polaris objected in the roundabout fashion of his kind. 'I recognize the Minister directly.'

'Yet he was out of place,' Sol pointed out. 'It is our duty as investigators to explore all potentially pertinent factors. A reading of his Kirlian aura could have bearing.'

10

'Agreed,' Canopus said, exerting his decision-making propensity. 'Recognition is not the issue; circumstance is. The Minister should have been aware he was in violation of regulations.' He produced a unit outlet and tuned it to the stunned Minister.

And exhibited surprise; an emotion uncommon to his species. 'This is not the aura of the Minister of Research.'

The guard looked up, hope flaring. 'An imposter?'

'But I am certain of his identity!' Polaris protested with uncircular vigor.

'Both true. This is a Kirlian transferee. An alien mind in the Minister's body. This aura is not in our records.'

'This is verging on the angular,' Polaris said. 'Our Minister would not lend his body to such use.'

'Not voluntarily,' Sol said.

'He has not been absent from these demesnes since the last routine Kirlian verification,' Polaris insisted. 'He was under no pressure to depress his aura, and in any event—'

'He remains with us,' Canopus said, studying the indicator closely with several facets of his eyes. 'I now perceive a second aura imprint, suppressed by the first. This second one matches his own.'

'He is an involuntary host?' Sol inquired challengingly. Such a thing was considered impossible.

'So it would seem. The Minister's aura is normal – one point two intensity, not in good health at the moment. The alien aura is more potent – twenty-seven. It has apparently overwhelmed that of the host. There are certain indications of strife between the two, augmenting the supposition that the hosting is not voluntary.'

'What is the identity of the alien aura?' Nath inquired.

'This is uncertain without computer analysis,' Canopus said. 'But it corresponds to the aural family typical of Sphere *, of Galaxy Andromeda.'

There was a brief silence as the implication sank in. The War of Energy had ended a thousand years before, but only because the Milky Way had achieved parity. If that parity had been upset, the Second War of Energy was upon them. It could mean the destruction of a galaxy. Without energy, a

11

galaxy became nothing, for energy was the very heart of matter.

'Well, verify it!' Sol cried in the thrusting manner of his kind. 'We've got ourselves a spy!'

'That might be uncircular,' Polaris said. 'If Andromeda can make hostage our Minister of Research, it may have done similar work elsewhere – perhaps in the most critical locations.'

'Hostage . . .' Sol mused. 'Involuntary hosting, without the prior demolition of the host-mind and aura. Apt term.'

'Pull-hook,' Nath agreed. 'And we cannot know how many other hostages are present. We cannot trust any entity of low aura anywhere. We may already be at war.'

'But if the highest levels of our government itself have been infiltrated, how can we save our segment – even our galaxy?' the guard asked. In this crisis, the distinctions of species and position were lost; all of them were galactics. 'We can kill *this* spy, but our own chain of command may be suspect.' Then he glanced quickly at the human officer. 'Present company excepted, sir.'

'*Not* excepted,' the officer said. 'You have made an excellent point, soldier.' There was a certain grimness about his mouth.

'We shall neither kill this entity nor ignore the implications,' Canopus said firmly. 'Our own Minister of Research is hostage. We can not execute him without due procedure. And to do this would be to advise Andromeda that we have discovered its plot. Obviously the infiltration is not yet complete, for the invading agents practice secrecy. This one must have been searching the records of Population for information on the strength of the auras of key personnel who can be taken over or neutralized. It is reasonable to assume that it requires a stronger aura to control an entity, as with normal hosting. This infiltration may be only beginning. We can therefore counter it if we can ascertain its full extent and master the technology to nullify it. Therefore we let this hostage go. The security guard shall be duly disciplined for his unwarranted attack on a Minister. He shall be removed to a far post for an extended tour, one no Minister would visit. I shall authorize and implement this myself, on the authority of the unanimous decision of this investigation team, with the concurrence and waiver of appeal by the Entity on the Spot. An innocuous report will be filed under the codename "March". I shall proffer the Executive's sincerest apologies to this wronged Minister for this blunder by one of our personnel. I doubt the Andromedan agent will take the matter further; he will not want any commotion that might expose him. Then, secretly, we shall indeed march.' He faced the guard, all facets seeming to bear on him momentarily. 'Do you concur, Solarian?'

The man bowed his head. 'I understand. My career is over – for the sake of my galaxy.'

'Yet if we prevail, and if any of we five entities survive,' Nath clicked, 'there will be recompense.'

'Such reward as you have not dreamed,' the Solarian officer agreed. He turned to Canopus. 'But how can we know who is loyal? We can't check the whole government! We are merely an *ad hoc* investigatory team with little authority.'

'It becomes necessary to preempt authority,' Nath said.

'But as my brother Solarian pointed out,' the human officer said, 'we ourselves are suspect. We have no basis—'

'It would be circular to verify ourselves,' Polaris suggested.

'Circular *and* direct,' Canopus agreed. 'We must ascertain that we five are not hostage.' His faceted eyes bore on all the others simultaneously. 'Amenable?'

Sol nodded. Polaris glowed. Nath rippled.

Canopus reset the unit.

'And after this,' Sol said, 'we shall trust no one without immediate aural verification. Especially not Ministers, though this does present a problem. They are nominally the heads of our segment government, the highest officers among us.'

'Nominally,' Canopus agreed, his inflection carrying significance that made the others reflect agreement in their separate fashions.

Sol looked at the hostage. 'What do we do with this one – at the moment?'

'We run it through an aural probe,' Canopus said. 'Thereby we glean relevant information about the mechanism of involuntary hosting. Then we take our information to the single organization we can trust to contain no hostages.'

Sol raised an eyebrow, a feat none of the other species could duplicate. 'Organization?'

'The Society of Hosts.'

The others, startled by the obvious, signified agreement.

'Lord God of Hosts, be with us yet,' the Solarian murmured, awed at the concept of this organization becoming the true government of the segment and perhaps of the entire Milky Way galaxy.

And the others completed the Litany of Hosts, taken from a poem written five centuries before transfer came to the author's planet: 'Recessional', by Rudyard Kipling. 'Lest we forget, lest we forget . . .'

Part One

Mistress of Tarot

1

Melody of Mintaka

occasion for preparatory briefing
—summon council governing sphere representatives linked thought transfer immediate—
COUNCIL INITIATED   PARTICIPATING * — / :: $^0_0$
—welcome ast, slash, quadpoint, doucire—
:: shall we dispense with the superfluities?   we have a galaxy to conquer ::
—you certainly bore into the subject, quadpoint—
:: your humor is flighty, as befits avian nature   what is the state of reduction? ::
—infiltration of all ten major segments of galaxy milky way has been accomplished   in each case concentration has been on war fleets and capital planets—
$^0_0$ ratios? $^0_0$
—400 agents per segment fleet, 100 agents per capital planet   total 5000 transfer agents in galaxy   all we can manage on present energy budget—
/also present limitation on kirlian resources/
—true   effort should suffice, as subject galaxy remains unaware of infiltration   no apparent reason to alter schedule of overt action—
seek concurrence for unrevised schedule
— / :: $^0_0$ CONCURRENCE $^0_0$ :: / —
:: no other business? ::
—none at present—
POWER
— / :: $^0_0$ CIVILIZATION $^0_0$ :: / —

Melody shuffled the deck by emitting dissonance at the mechanism. This could not be entirely random, but of course that was the point. While she controlled the arrangement of the cards, she was not supposed to be consciously aware of the details.

She touched the finished deck with the tip of one whip, activating it. Its music sprang up, setting her instruments to playing sympathetically.

It was the Queen of Energy that manifested – in an unfamiliar aspect. The Queen carried the familiar Wand, rendered as a scepter for this royal impersonation, that denoted her suit; the established symbols of the Tarot deck were older than the organized concept that was the deck. The Queen was naked, standing on a waveswept ledge, her appendages manacled to a huge stone. And she was Solarian – or more bluntly, human.

Now of course every card had a theoretic potential of 144 aspects. The Queen of Energy had faces showing 'Queens' of every sapient species in the Milky Way galaxy. But no physical deck contained all aspects of all faces; that would amount to 14,400 presentations in all, an unwieldy number. So the normal pack of the Cluster Tarot contained a representative sampling of each card. Melody had not been aware that a Solarian course had been included in this deck. Which only meant she had not been paying proper attention when she obtained it recently. She was getting old.

Well, this was her card for the day. She contemplated it, evoking the tapestry of tunes dictated by its impressed symbology. A human woman, wearing the rare-metal crown of royalty, with the luxuriant mane flowing from her head – Solarians were one of the species that had heads – and with the two great milk-mammaries of her kind. By human standards, a female on the verge of impregnation.

This was a notable concept in itself, well worth consideration. Solarians did not bud, they birthed; and the female was always the birther. She remained female for life, no matter how many times she birthed. Surely, she was chained!

In the distance of the scene was a ferocious sea monster, one of the subsapient creatures of Sphere Sol. It was obviously coming to devour the Queen, whose generous deposits of avoirdupois were surely delectable.

But what relevance did this have to her, Melody, an old Mintakan neuter entity without head or mammaries or fat? What was the Tarot trying to say to her?

Well, the five suits of the standard cluster deck represented five or more sapient species – those that had figured most prominently in the local formation of the galactic coalition, who had been the nucleus of this segment some 120 years before, at the time of the hero Flint of Outworld, Melody's ancestor. A thousand Solarian years, since those were pitifully brief. The Suit of Energy, symbolized by the sprouting, flaming Wand, was generally identified with the massed species of Galaxy Andromeda, because of their attempted theft of the binding energies of the Milky Way galaxy that had precipitated the first crisis of civilization. Yet no Andromedan species was represented in this card of Tarot. More locally, Sphere Canopus was a Scepter culture, but this card was not that, either. There *was* a humanoid species in that Sphere, but it was slave. The chains of the lady – indicative of slavery? Doubtful; normally this Queen was not chained. Rather she was arrogantly free, imperious, fiery. And this one was not human*oid*, but *human*, definitely Solarian, itself a pretty arrogant species, by no means slave. A chained Solarian was doubly significant, surely.

The Solarians were the reputed originators of the Tarot. Versions of the Tarot had been extant on their home planet for several Solarian centuries before the human colonization of space and formation of Sphere Sol. The Cluster deck itself was thought to be the creation of one of their males, the scholar called Companion Paul, or Sibling Paul, or Brother Paul. There was obscurity about his status, rooted in the human mode of reproduction. Some said there could be several offspring of a single human reproductive unit, called siblings, while others said humans sometimes called each other 'Brother' when in fact they were not closely related. Only the Solarians knew for sure! At any rate, the attribution of this deck to this Paul of Earth had to be a fond exaggeration; many of the significant aspects of that deck were unknown to Solarians at the time he had lived. The entire matter of the Energy War dated fifty Mintakan

19

years after Paul, for example – that was four hundred Solarian years – she really ought to get used to thinking in those trifling units, because they had become the standard for Segment Etamin, but the habits of an old neuter changed slowly – still, the nucleus of Tarot concept had certainly been Solarian, and the Temple of Tarot had spread rapidly from Sol to the other Spheres. Melody had suffered an apprenticeship at the Tarot Temple nearest her once, but had not been satisfied with their doctrine and had gone her own way for most of her life.

Her phone sounded. Melody activated it with a single clap of one foot, her strings vibrating dissonantly because of the irritation caused by the interruption of her morning meditation.

'Imperial Outworld of Segment Etamin summons Melody of Planet Counterpoint, Sphere Mintaka, for immediate presentation via Transfer,' the instrument played.

Melody emitted a musical snort and broke the connection. 'These practical jokers never give up,' she played. A female her age just had to be the subject of a certain amount of ridicule. Blat!

Then she remembered the card. A chained Solarian female – her key for the day. Could that relate to this call?

She considered the card again. A human woman, chained in the Andromedan suit. Who had chained that lady, and why? What could it have to do with herself, an entity of quite a different situation? The Tarot was always relevant, but at times she had a great deal of difficulty ascertaining that relevance.

Well, she would have to come at it the hard way, by going back to basics. She was a sapient entity of Sphere Mintaka, itself a unit of Segment Etamin of the Milky Way galaxy. Each Sphere was a number of parsecs in diameter, embracing a hundred or more inhabited worlds, the most advanced ones being near the center. Her own planet, Counterpoint, was in the midrange of a large Sphere; it possessed atomic science but not much more. It was a suburban world, where wealthy administrators liked to retire. Toward

20

the Fringe things became progressively more primitive, until a hundred parsecs from Star Mintaka the worlds were essentially rural. This was Spherical regression, that occurred in all Spheres, and could be abated only by the infusion of energy. But there was not enough energy; the Ethic of Energy had already spawned one intergalactic war and might some century spawn another.

So the Tarot Suit of Energy related to her general situation, though she herself associated with the Suit of Aura. Since every sapient entity in the universe was similarly affected by the availability of energy, this was unlikely to have individual meaning. It had to be more specific.

Very well. The manner in which energy affected civilization was primarily in transport and communications. There were three modes of travel between the stars. The cheapest was physical travel by spaceship. Fleets traveling at half-light speed had colonized the various Spheres long ago. But it took almost a full year – how many Sol-years? Oh, yes, eight – to cover a single parsec, and no single lifetime was long enough to traverse even the smallest Sphere. Ships were sufficient to colonize worlds, but not to build an interstellar civilization. For more direct communication, mattermission was used – instant transmission of the entity, whether person or thing. But this required a horrendous amount of energy, and though it had been much employed in the past, today it was limited largely to microscopic message capsules. So in practice, the really civilizing mode was transfer – the transmission of the Kirlian aura of a sapient (i.e. intelligent entity, as opposed to sentient or merely conscious entity) to the body of another sapient. The aura reflected the complete mental being, but required relatively little energy for transmission. Even so, there were crucial limitations, such as the availability of suitable hosts; the transfer across galactic distances did require significant energy.

So energy controlled civilization, and the Suit of Energy reflected that. Some even called that suit 'Civilization' but Melody considered that to be too narrow a view. Energy was more than civilization, and more than the quiescent Andromedan menace; it was a complex multi-relating phenomenon in its own right. And she still didn't know how it pertained to *her*, today.

In fact, no one knew the answer to the problem of Energy, and no one ever had – except perhaps the Ancients. The Ancients had spanned two galaxies in a unified, high-level culture. Yet they had passed from the scene three million years ago, and most of their works were defunct. They were identified with the Suit of Aura, because they had to have been a super-high Kirlian species, and they had evidently possessed Kirlian science beyond anything known to modern galactics. Melody had studied what little was known about the Ancients, fascinated by them, and she identified with them so strongly that she considered her own Significator, her particular card in the Cluster Tarot deck, to be the Queen of Aura. She would give anything to solve the riddle of the Ancients!

But her card of the day was not in the Suit of Aura, though it was a Queen. It seemed to have aimed for her but missed, although the Tarot never really missed. It had a will of its own that did not cater much to the foibles of its adherents. The Queen of Energy, a chained human lady – what *could* it mean? This was becoming a frustrating meditation!

She moved to her soniscope and listened to the great panoply of the stars. Each had its own faint tune within the magnificent symphony of the galaxy. Mintaka, home star of her Sphere, loud and bright and beautiful. Alnilam and Alnitac, twin brights. Rigel, blue-white beacon in the visual spectrum, hardly audible to her senses but still impressive. Red giant Betelgeuse. Oh, the marvel of her segment, her galaxy! And the foreign galaxy Andromeda, focus of Energy.

Suddenly it clicked into place. Suit of Energy – Andromeda – chained human lady – there *was* a connection! In the old myth-fabric of the Solarian originators of Tarot was the story of the female entity Andromeda, and it was relevant.

Andromeda was the child of Cepheus and Cassiopeia. Cassiopeia was a beautiful woman Solarian who, in the

22

manner of her species, tended to be arrogant and troublesome. She proclaimed that she was more lovely than the Nereids, golden-maned nymphs of the sea. This was not necessarily true, and the vanity of one obscure queen was hardly worthy of note, but the lord of the ocean, Poseidon, took umbrage. He sent a sea monster to ravage the coast of Cassiopeia's kingdom of Ethiopia. Oh, those Solarians! Their troublesome antics assumed the status of art at times. No Mintakan would have participated in such mischief.

Desperate to abate this menace from the sea, the Ethiopians consulted another intriguing artifact of Solarian culture: the Oracle. This was a fortune-telling entity; apparently no form of Tarot existed then. The Oracle informed them that only by sacrificing Andromeda to the monster could they achieve relief. Andromeda was even more beautiful than her mother, and did indeed rival the Nereids in appearance, which was perhaps why the monster desired her as a morsel. Melody found the motives of Solarian monsters to be as opaque as those of Solarian sapients, but it was not her task to revise the myth. So they chained this innocent, beautiful lady to a great rock by the edge of the ocean, to be consumed by the monster.

As it happened, the hero Perseus happened to pass by – coincidence was not a matter of much concern to mythmakers – and when he viewed this naked girl he was overcome by the urge to impregnate her. This too was typical of Solarian males in such circumstances: the very sight of the body of a young healthy woman caused chemical and physical reactions. Her mind or personality did not seem to matter. But Perseus could not simply impregnate and leave her, despite the convenience her situation offered. Chained as she was, she could not readily have resisted him, had she been so inclined, but her offspring would not have survived consumption by the monster, and therefore the reproduction would have been incomplete. In many other species the offspring formed immediately and became independent, but Solarians for some obscure reason suffered a delay in parturition after copulation. In this instance such delay would have been most inconvenient. So Perseus ac-

23

cepted the alternative course. He slew the monster and made Andromeda his formal mate.

There it was: Andromeda, the chained lady of the card, awaiting her fate. In moments the monster would be upon her. The hero Perseus was not visible in this picture, but presumably he was on his way. Andromeda did not at this moment know that her fate was to be impregnation rather than consumption. How would she have chosen, had she been given the choice in advance? Suppose things became confused, and the monster impregnated her before Perseus slew her? Or were the two actions merely aspects of the same theme? A most intriguing card!

But as this was her omen for the day did it mean that some such difficulty awaited Melody herself? She did not consider the Tarot to be precognitive; it merely revealed what was in the hidden mind of the querist, the one for whom the cards were read. But sometimes the net effect was predictive. She did not relish the implication here. Would she be faced with the choice between death or impregnation, figuratively?

The door sounded. She broke off her reverie with another chord of annoyance and opened it.

Outside stood Imperial troops headed by a Mintakan officer. 'One ignores the Eye of the Dragon at one's peril,' he played.

Melody's strings shook. That phone call had been genuine! The Dragon world of the segment had summoned her – and she had passed it off as a prank. Now she would pay the consequences.

In fact, she was about to be chained for the Dragon – of course, merely an aspect of the sea monster. The Tarot had tried to warn her. But she, mired in the complexities of its ramifications, had missed the obvious.

Was there also a Perseus on the way?

2

Yael of Dragon

*notice   transfer plus 200 level kirlian aura within
target galaxy*
—specific location?—
segment etamin   to imperial planet
—probably in order   agents there are on quest for
leading enemy auras to be nullified or converted—
this aura not handled by our agents
—possible enemy action, then   message the dash command of that segment to investigate—
POWER
—CIVILIZATION—

Melody emerged in alien form. At first she was alarmed
and disgusted. *This body has no music.* But soon she adjusted. She would not remain in Transfer long; only long
enough to find what the Imps wanted and tell them no. She
could stand it for that little time.

This host did have certain compensations. Its vision was
superior. In fact, she realized now that she had never before
experienced true vision, only a kind of sound-augmented
approximation. Touch was good, hearing fair. And it could
do something she had no prior experience with: smell.
Furthermore, it was young and bouncy, possessing quick
reflexes and more sheer muscular power than she had
imagined feasible. Why, it could even *jump.*

She was in an orientation cell – padded, silent, undis-
tinctive. Just as well, for she took several tumbles getting
adjusted to only two feet, and she preferred not doing this in
public. This body was bilaterally symmetrical, instead of
trilaterally, and it made a difference.

Set in one wall was a plate of highly reflective metal. Peering at it from an angle with her amazing twin focusing ball-shaped eyes she saw the image of part of the room. Now why would such a panel be so placed? She balanced herself on her stout legs – Solarians *had* to have superior balance, since in order to walk they had to hover on a single support while swinging the other about – and managed to get to the bright panel.

She saw the chained lady, lacking only the chains. The same flowing brown mane, the same huge mammaries, the same facial agony of sacrifice. Andromeda, alive!

No – it was herself. Her host-body, a Solarian female, in her natural state. Possessing all the stigmata of imminent impregnability. Since all human beings looked pretty much alike to her Mintakan mind, naturally she had taken it for the image fresh in her memory. But there did seem to be considerable resemblance.

Well, it should be possible to let the body do much of the work. She had been trying to make it operate with Mintakan reflexes; suppose she merely gave it orders and let the buried human reflexes perform?

'Across,' she murmured to herself, and was surprised to hear the host-voice speak in its own language, which she now understood. Animation of a host-body meant similar animation of the host-brain, so comprehension came readily. Transfer had solved the problem of interspecies communication. Now this body walked, smoothly, across the room.

A little practice of this sort would soon make perfect. But she didn't want it perfect yet, so she staged another fall. She knew the cushioned floor would protect her, and she had no doubt she was being monitored. When she had full control she would be removed for her interview with the Dragon, and she needed time for proper mental orientation first.

In another wall was a small computer terminal. Good; that suggested this confinement was at least partially voluntary. When she was ready, she could tell the computer to release her or to provide her with what she felt she needed. Such as human clothing, for she did know Solarians wore

26

clothing. It would be reasonable to dress herself, so as to avoid early-impregnation by Perseus – or whatever other human male happened by. She did not intend to *be* reasonable, just to *look* reasonable. A tantrum would be insufficient if not futile. She would handle this outrage in her own time, her own way. She would not remain chained to this body long.

She crossed to the terminal, experimented until she was able to manage the finger-finesse required, and pressed a digit to the access button. A peremptory note would have been better, but when in a Sol-host, do as the Solarians do. Finger, not sound. 'Bring me a good Cluster Tarot deck,' she said.

There was a pause. Would the machine deliver? If the Solarians were smart, they would have Tarot on the proscribed list. But this was not Sphere Sol, but Planet Outworld, where Tarot was not so well known. Few entities not conversant with the tool had any significant grasp of its potential. The average sapient thought it a mere game or harmless superstition – and the average Tarot adept was careful to cultivate this impression. It was the major protection afforded contemporary inter-Sphere magick – was that the proper rendering for this concept? Yes, with the *ck*: the fact that authoritative entities did not take it seriously, so felt no threat.

The wall-slot opened, and an object thunked down. Victory!

She reached in and picked it up. It was a sealed physical pack of cards, Solarian-style; she recognized it from her researches. She opened it and spread the cards in her two hands. It was a tri-channel, hundred-face collection; not merely a good deck, but one of the best, well illustrated with correctly aspected symbols. It would do. 'Appreciation, Machine,' she said.

'Noted,' the computer voice replied. That struck her as funny, for reasons she could not immediately define, and she laughed – and *that* struck her as funnier yet. What appalling sounds the human body made to express its mirth; what unholy quaking of flesh!

She sat at a table she drew out of the wall, already getting acclimatized to this body and habitat. Her Mintakan body, of course, was unable to sit. She laid the cards face-up in even rows of ten. There were thirty Major Arcana or Trumps, twenty Courts, and fifty Minor Arcana or Pips. The last group consisted of five suits: Energy, Gas, Liquid, Solid and Aura. The cards of each were numbered one through ten, with illustrations of their characteristic symbols: Wands, Swords, Cups, Disks, and Broken Atoms. Each card of the complete deck could be flexed into two alternate faces and the Ghost Trump had fifteen flexes plus a Table of Equivalencies enabling the reader to adapt the deck to Spheres not directly represented, such as her own Mintaka. Yes, excellent!

One face of the Queen of Energy was the same chained lady that had started this off. It was different in that this one was purely visual, rather than primarily sonic, but there was no question about the kinship. She picked it up and took it to the mirror, comparing her naked host-body to the figure on the card. The similarity was amazing. Had this host been specially selected to match? Or had the Tarot been aware of this host, and somehow – no, there was the route to insanity!

She returned slowly to the table. One thing was sure: The model for the picture was sexually appealing, so as to create the necessary urge in the mind of Perseus. That suggested that her present host was an extraordinary beauty – which just might be useful.

For perhaps an hour, Solarian time, Melody contemplated her hundred-face spread. She also flexed the Ghost through all fifteen alternates, dwelling about one minute on each. Apart from the necessary activity of her fingers, she did not move; in fact she had entered a light trance.

At last she gathered up the cards, shuffled them until her host-fingers were proficient at this, then cut the deck several times and turned up one card randomly.

It was a picture of another lovely young human female, with a long, light head-mane and slender firm body, nude. But this one was not chained. She half-kneeled on a green bank beside a pool, one foot resting forward *on*, not *in*, the water. She held two pitchers from which water poured; one into the pool, the other onto the ground, where it split into five blue rivulets. There were eight stars in the blue sky above her – seven white, one yellow – and a red bird perched in a tree.

'The Star,' she murmured, 'in one of the pre-Sphere renditions. Key of great hope – or great loss – its five rivulets flowing into the five suits, its smaller stars signifying the seven planets of ancient Solarian astrology, the large star sometimes called the Star of the Magi. Now why does this particular Trump manifest now?' Whatever its original meaning, the largest star actually reminded her of mighty Mintaka, center of the universe she had known so long ago as a bud. The nostalgia was suddenly so intense she had to close her human eyes and suffer its ravages without resistance. It was not merely that she was more than four hundred parsecs from it now, and in alien guise; time more than distance separated her from that stellar hope. What she had sought there had been lost in the distant youth of her lifetime, and never recovered, but even now the pain and shame could emerge from its capsule to haunt her. Her effort to shield herself from that agony had brought her to Tarot, but remarkable as that study had been, it could not make up for it. It had shown her the folly of her past, not the folly of her future.

She forced open her human eyes, staring at the card again. The Star-girl's hair flared from her head to the level of her knees, framing her body in a luxuriant cape. In fact, it was almost like an aura, that mark of distinction that made Melody herself remarkable. But what was the use of aura, when the essence of her life had been poured out like that of the two vases of this scene? Hope and loss – how well she understood!

She dealt another card. This was a semihuman female with two pouring cups, but in this case she had a fish's tail rather than legs, and she was pouring the liquid from one cup into the other. In the background was a section of the Milky Way galaxy, with recognizable constellations as seen

29

from System Sol. Naturally the Solarian deck was oriented to the Solarian view. This picture had strong points of similarity, notably the girl's full mammaries, but the symbolic meaning was quite different. 'Temperance,' Melody murmured.

She dealt one more. This was yet another young woman fully clothed and holding a large disk or coin, a unit of Solarian monetary exchange. 'Page of Solid, female,' Melody remarked.

She studied the three cards side by side, noting their parallels, which were impressive. Three healthy, sexually appealing young women. The Tarot was certainly trying to tell her something of importance, and this time she intended to continue her meditation until she comprehended it without undue distraction by her personal feelings. Again she moved into a trance.

Suddenly she snapped her fingers – an automatic Solarian gesture her Mintakan body could not have performed – in understanding. 'Girl, stand forward,' she said.

And inside her brain the host-girl presented herself as directed. 'Here,' the child-human whispered voicelessly, with associations of guilt and fear.

'I had supposed this body was vacant,' Melody said disapprovingly, also voicelessly – for this was a dialogue of two minds within a single brain, and Melody did not want the listening recorders of the Imperium to eavesdrop on this very private matter. She had never been in transfer before, but her mind remained her last reservoir of individuality, and she was a private person. To share a brain, to have every thought monitored even in the process of formulation . . .

'No – we are always present,' the girl said. 'We do not interfere, *can*not interfere, but we must live. We must not forget.'

'I fear I have not kept up with the times,' Melody said, making a mental twang of strings that translated into a figurative shake of the head. 'Transfer is now to live hosts?'

'Always. Was it ever otherwise?'

A woman out of touch with the present, transferred to the body of a girl out of touch with the past! 'Who are you?'

'I am Yael. I remained hidden, as instructed. How did you find me?'

A mental smile. 'The Tarot found you, Yael. It reveals what is hidden in the mind. In this case – another mind. Tell me about yourself.'

'We're not supposed to intrude—'

'So I gather. You are merely supposed to sit mute while an alien occupies your body. I understood slavery had been abolished in System Etamin.' A system was the next unit below the sphere, the planets associated with a single star. There was a major slave-culture within *Segment* Etamin, but not *System* Etamin – for what the distinction was worth.

'Slavery?' Emotion of confusion.

'You don't even know what the concept means? That's sophisticated servitude indeed! Even the slavemasters of Sphere Canopus have not taken it this far. By what right can any society require an individual to give up her own body? I should have thought the Polarians, with their adoration of the individual before society, would at least have made some roundabout objection.'

'Oh, you mean hosting,' Yael said. 'Nobody *made* me. I *wanted* to do it. I get good pay, and the Society of Hosts watches out for me, and I get adventure that I could never have myself, and—'

'Oh, I comprehend. It is a business.' The expression Melody used had tones of prostitution, a human vice much ridiculed in Sphere Mintaka, but only the literal meaning translated into human thought. 'Tell me about it – in your own concepts.'

Yael explained: She was the child of a poor farmer in the protected wilderness of Planet Outworld. Her parents had both been of subnormal intelligence, and had been allowed to beget offspring – limited to one – in return for voluntary commitment to the land. Few citizens wanted to reside in the vine forest or to preserve the ways of Outworld's Stone Age heritage, as this involved primitive hunting and planting, chewing of dinosaur hides, and much exposure to discomfort and danger. But this man and woman had so desired a family that they had undertaken this cruel life — and thrived on it.

But one day a wounded predator dinosaur had charged their hut and wiped them out. Only Yael had survived, because she had been gathering wild juiceberries at the time. Still a child, she had been taken in by another forest family — but it had not been a happy mergeance. When it became apparent that this low-aura, low-intelligence waif was about to mature into an astonishingly lovely woman, her adoptive father had made plans to supplement the family income by engaging her in concubinage to the highest-bidding local landowner. This would have been a life of inferiority and disillusion as her youthful beauty faded, terminating in the drudgery of servant-status. Yael had aspired to more than this; and she had the soul of an adventuress despite her circumstance.

'How did you get the notion of adventure?' Melody inquired, not unkindly. 'Wasn't mere survival among dinosaurs adventure enough?'

'Not after my natural folk died,' Yael said simply, and Melody knew immediate shame. But the girl continued, unaware of it. 'The dinosaurs weren't so bad, really, when you got to know them. They just figured the territory was *theirs*, since they were there first.'

'How did you select your name?' Melody asked, changing the subject.

'There are popular names here, after famous people in our history. Many boys are called Flint, after Outworld's first transferee, and many girls are Honeybloom, after his wife. When my family was lost, I could not keep the name they gave me, so I chose a new one. There was a poem they read to me as a child, and I always liked it, so I took the name of the ancient poetess who made it, Yael Dragon. It seemed to fit, because Etamin is the Eye of the Dragon in Solarian myth, and it was a dragon that—'

She broke off, and Melody realized that she was crying. As well she might. A dinosaur, a virtual living dragon, had destroyed her family; a cruel identification, but perhaps a necessary one.

'What is the poem?' Melody inquired, hoping again to take the girl's mind away from the tragedy.

'Actually, she didn't write it,' Yael said. 'It was *to* her, really. Does that make a difference?'

Melody thought again of her own uncapsulated past, the confusion and shifting of rationales. 'No. Not if she was responsible for it.'

'I never really understood it, but it does something to me. I – well, it goes like this.'

FOUR SWORDS

You are the Witch of Tarot
A woman not my wife
I may not say: Key Six.

In ways you resemble my daughter
Bright, sensitive, emotional, unstable
Perhaps I had to love you.

But in ways you resemble the minionette
Whose love means ruin
And so I have to leave you

Child and minion: aspects of myself
You cannot fit my script
And I dare not fit yours.

'Why that's a Tarot poem,' Melody said. 'The title means "truce" in the archaic framework of that day. Key Six means "The Lovers". And the four qualities in the second stanza are like the four archaic suits. Bright as a disk or coin—'

'As a penny,' Yael supplied. 'We still use metal money in the vine forest; it keeps better.'

'Yes,' Melody agreed, delving for more interpretations. 'Sensitive as a wand – the wand of a magician or musical conductor, and of course the second Tarot suit. Emotion refers to the Suit of Cups, the flow of water, or tears. And unstability – that's Swords, of course, that balance on the knife's edge, or the sword hanging by a thread. That refers back to the title, too, integrating the whole.'

'I never realized all that!' Yael exclaimed.

'Well, perhaps I exaggerate. It is too easy to interpret in terms of the familiar, and I see Tarot everywhere I go. Notice how the four triplets deal respectively with frustration, love, ruin, and conclusion – like the suits of Wands, Cups, Swords and Disks. And the poem stops just short of the thirteenth line. The thirteenth Key of the Tarot was traditionally nameless, or Death, which – but there I go again!'

'No, it's interesting. Do you know what the minionette is?'

'That would be a small, delicate, dainty woman, the diminutive of minion, which itself has special connotations of illicit charm.'

'I wonder who it was who made it for her?'

'I could analyze it more thoroughly, if you really—'

'No! I'd rather have the mystery. Then I can still dream that maybe it was meant for me, even though it was on another world over a thousand years ago. Is that crazy?'

'Poems are meant for the ages,' Melody assured her. 'And often they are not intended to be completely understood.'

And so the girl had sought the realm of interstellar adventure. But she had no personal brilliance or education, and her Kirlian aura was barely normal. Her soul would never range across the galaxy in transfer. Her dreams of being a great lady of space, visiting far planets, dazzling strange powerful men, and interacting with alien creatures were vain. Sheer foolishness, this wish to be rich and intelligent and cultured and bold and fascinating. (Melody matched those concepts with suits as she listened: rich as in Coins, bold as in Swords – she had to stop doing that!) But what a dream, to be a truly free woman!

'A dream we all share,' Melody murmured to herself. 'But so many of us are chained . . .'

So Yael had been realistic. There was only one way she could be a Lady of Space, and she took it. She had run away from home and made application to the Society of Hosts.

'The Society of Hosts,' Melody murmured. 'Whose symbol is the Temperance card of the Tarot, keyed into the Suit of Aura. Now the appearance of that card falls into place.'

'I don't know about that,' Yael replied uncertainly. 'But they do have a picture of a lady pouring two cups of water into each other – why, there it is!'

There it was, of course: the second card Melody had drawn from the deck and laid on the table. Yael did not recognize the significance, being unfamiliar with the Tarot deck and its related concepts. But Melody saw it: a soul being poured from one physical container into another. The starry background suggested galactic implications, as indeed there were. Transfer was the very essence of galactic civilization; without it modern society would collapse.

'Get on with your story,' Melody said.

'The Society accepted me,' Yael said. 'Just like that. I could hardly believe it. But now I understand. I don't have much of an aura or much of a mind, but my body is good, and that's what they need. Transferees don't care about the host-mind, and they can't use a high host-aura at all, but they like the best bodies. So I'm the perfect host! After twenty years of host service, I can retire with a good pension, if I want to. Meanwhile, I get adventure. But I'm only supposed to watch, not bother you.'

'There may not be much adventure,' Melody said. 'I'm of Mintaka, the Music Sphere, and I'm going home again first opportunity. I do not crave intrigue or excitement.'

'Oh,' Yael said, disappointed. 'You're such a nice entity even if you *are* an alien, and you have such a fine mind, even I can feel it. You're everything I wanted to be. I wish you'd stay.'

Melody found herself feeling flattered. 'You actually *want* to have your body controlled by an alien intellect?'

'It is the only way I can be what I can never be,' Yael said simply.

'But suppose a transferee abused your body? Damaged it?'

35

'The God of Hosts protects me.'

'The God of Hosts?' Melody inquired, amazed. 'You believe in that?'

'Of course. "Lord God of Hosts, be with us yet – lest we forget, lest we forget." That's the Society prayer. All hosts have to memorize it.'

Melody pondered. If a host forgot it would mean the loss of identity. It was the same for a transferee. Memory was all that distinguished one personality from another, when aura faded in an alien body.

Melody returned to the cards. 'The Star – that's your hope for glamor and adventure. To obtain it, you must suffer loss, the loss of your body. For twenty years. When you get it back, your prime will be gone. That's a terrible price.'

'It's no worse than what I would have had at home,' Yael pointed out.

Melody could not refute that. 'Well, I'll stay for a while,' she decided. 'I don't have much choice in the matter myself. But don't go away; I want you handy, just in case.

'I *can't* go away,' Yael said.

'You know what I mean. Don't play dumb. Don't hide in the woodwork. I don't like preempting your body, but I stop the music at preempting your *mind*.'

'You mean I can join in your adventure? Not just watch?' The girlish personality seemed incredulous.

'It's your adventure too,' Melody said. 'Now let's brace the Imperium.' She put away the cards, stood up, walked to the computer terminal, and pushed the contact button, her motions now sure and smooth. This wasn't a bad body at all, once she got acclimatized to it.

'I'm ready to deal with the authorities,' Melody announced out loud.

'Select clothing,' the computer voice said.

Melody played a sour note that came out as an unfeminine snort. '*You* dress us,' she said to Yael.

'In what style?'

'Any style you want. It's your body, and a good one.' Then she reconsidered, remembering the potential of the female body among Solarians. 'But cover the mammaries; I don't want to get impregnated right away.'

'The breasts are always covered. Why should there be any – any—?'

'You mean it doesn't happen automatically?'

'Only when a girl agrees, usually. There are laws—'

'Very well. Dress it up pretty.'

Yael was glad to oblige. Melody relaxed and let the girl use her own notions, ordering flimsy underclothing followed by more substantial overclothing. There was a two thousand Solarian year spread in human clothing fashions, and any dress within that range was currently acceptable. So Yael chose apparel approximating the style of her namesake, who had resided in pre-Spherical times on Planet Earth. She wore a white blouse with images of flowers printed on it, and a short black skirt that showed the lower half of her legs. Light slippers covered her feet. Her hair flowed free, behind and to the sides.

Melody really didn't understand the nuances of Solarian dress; Mintakans and most other sapients did not use clothing. But she was satisfied that this sufficed. As she kept reminding herself, it would not be for long.

3

Society of Hosts

COUNCIL INITIATED   PARTICIPATING * — / ${}^{0}_{0}$
—where is quadpoint?—
perhaps he swallowed a hard rock
AMUSEMENT
—some obstructions developing in selected segments
prior report of successful infiltration premature   three
segments appear to have become aware of our effort—
/bungling cannot be tolerated   which segments?/
—knyfh, etamin, weew—
${}_{0}^{0}$ detail? ${}_{0}^{0}$
(duocirc, your elements are misangled)
${}^{0}_{0}$?   sorry, recent recombination confuses ${}^{0}_{0}$
/if we are finished with the personal hygiene/
—etamin agent discovered and circumvented by locals
this indicates that natives are aware of our purpose and
are attempting to prevent our knowing *they* know   no
real problem as we have alerted our discovered agent, but
any spread of resistance would be awkward   knyfh is
sophisticated magnetic culture resembling ${}^{0}_{0}$ status there
uncertain   bears scrutiny lest they countertrap us at moment of action   weew may be a misreport   investigation
proceeding—
${}^{0}_{0}$ no adverse indications from lodo or bhyo?   These
also are formidable center-galaxy cultures ${}^{0}_{0}$
—no adverse indications   suggest delay of overt strike
until investigations completed   primarily knyfh—
concurrence?
— / ${}^{0}_{0}$ CONCURRENCE — / ${}^{0}_{0}$
POWER
— / ${}^{0}_{0}$ CIVILIZATION ${}^{0}_{0}$ / —

The door-panel slid open, and she stepped into a hall. A human man stood there. Sure enough, as Yael had reassured her, he did not leap to impregnate her, though he looked as though the notion had crossed his mind.

'Greetings, Mistress Melody,' he said. 'You have adapted very well. Do not be afraid; we shall take good care of you.'

The information was in her mind, but Melody hardly cared to delve through the layers of cultural meaning. She spoke silently to Yael: 'Why does he call me "mistress"? Why does he think I am afraid?'

'I don't know,' Yael admitted. 'Unmarried girls are Miss, and Mistress means a concubine—'

'He's going to impregnate us!' Melody cried, alarmed.

'He wouldn't dare. All we'd have to do is scream.'

So the Solarians did use sound for defense, just as Mintakans did. 'How would a mere scream stop him?'

'Other men would come—'

'Because *they* wanted to be first to do the impregnation?'

'To enforce the law. Alien transferees aren't supposed to be molested.'

'Oh. That makes sense. I was afraid—'

'But now I remember,' Yael interrupted. 'Mistress also means a rich lady, or maybe even a child, I think.'

'Or an alien lady?'

'Maybe.'

So the address confused the native too. Odd note. How had the Solarians achieved such galactic influence when their language suffered from such imprecision? But she knew the answer: A thousand years ago Sphere Knyfh had brought the secret of transfer to Sol instead of to one of the larger Spheres, for reasons that were opaque to those other Spheres, and this had given Sol a phenomenal start. But Sphere Sol had *not* been able to handle galactic matters effectively; thus the Fringe planet of Outworld, which possessed strong Polarian currents, had moved into prominence. Outworld's system of Etamin had taken over the segment without ever forming a sphere; perhaps that was one reason the Spheres were willing to accede to it. Outworld's interest was the segment, nothing else. If the segment fell apart, Outworld would be nothing.

The man guided her to a larger chamber set with plush chairs contoured for Solarian torsos. 'Sit down, my dear,' he said. 'The Colonel will arrive in a moment.'

Melody plumped down. The man looked away.

'Better close your legs,' Yael advised.

'Legs? Why? They're comfortable.'

'The dress – it spreads when you sit, so he can see up inside your thighs. That's not supposed to happen.'

'Why not?'

'Well, it – he – it just isn't—'

'Girl, you're dischordant!' Melody was aware that she was invoking another imprecision of the language; to her a musical chord was good and a dischord unpleasant, but the human 'discord' was unrelated. Well, she could not be held responsible for the inadequacies of human speech! 'What exactly are you trying to say?'

Yael was obviously embarrassed; Melody felt her reactions. 'When a man sees up a girl's legs, he gets all excited, unless he's a doctor. Same as when he sees into her blouse. Sex, you know.'

'Oh, that's right! Solarians are sexed entities,' Melody said, remembering. She had been acutely conscious of this all along, yet had overlooked it because she had been thinking in terms of mammaries. 'They cover themselves so carefully to avoid visual stimulation.' She pulled her legs together.

'Didn't you know?' Yael asked, surprised. 'You were so worried about impregnation—'

Melody was amazed. 'You mean sex is connected with impregnation?'

'Well of course!' Yael laughed with embarrassment. 'How else can—'

'Do you know, I never really made the connection?' Melody said. 'I knew the sight of mammaries caused the male to impregnate the female, but the concept of sexuality itself – I mean as an aspect of looking at the genital organs – well, Mintakans are basically neuter, and the genitals are

40

always exposed. We don't have sex play in that sense.'

Now Yael was amazed. 'Then how do you – make more Mintakans?'

'We bud them, of course. Sex has nothing to do with it, except as sex is affected *by* reproduction. And most buds are produced by paired males.' Then, as an afterthought: 'But if seeing up legs has the same effect as seeing mammaries, I'll certainly keep my legs covered. Why didn't you choose a longer skirt?'

'Well, a girl wants to have *some* sex appeal—'

'I don't understand that at all!'

'I don't understand Mintakan sex either!'

'But I *explained* it!' Obviously the girl's limitation of intellect was the problem here. 'Still, I should have grasped the pervasiveness of human sexuality from my Tarot studies. This shows how ignorant an entity can be, despite intensive study.'

'But aren't you female? Transfer can't change sex . . .'

'I am female *now*. However, if—'

'I'm getting confused again.'

The Colonel arrived: old, brisk, sauve, sure. 'So the little girl is with us at last,' he remarked, glancing down at Melody. 'Orderly, fetch some ice cream.'

'Little girl?' Yael inquired internally. She had no voice except when Melody expressly facilitated it. 'My body is twenty years old!'

'That's only two and a half Mintakan years,' Melody told her. 'I'm four times your age, chronologically.' Then she did a human double take. 'Ten Mintakan years – they forgot to make the translation!'

'You mean your years are longer than ours?' Yael inquired.

'Eight times as long, dear. I am referring to your standard Solarian years; I think there is another ratio for Outworld years.'

'There is. But we standardized on Sol, finally, because the Outworld year is thirty years long and it gets confusing.'

'Precisely. There has to be standardization. I'm an old neuter. Eighty Solarian years, two and a half Outworld

41

years. But here's the humor: *They think I'm a child of ten Earth years.*'

Yael began to laugh, and Melody joined her. Then it became overt. They laughed out loud.

'Are you all right?' the Colonel inquired, concerned.

'Where's my ice cream?' Melody demanded, stifling further laughter for the moment. 'I want my ice cream!'

'It's coming,' the Colonel said. 'Now I want you to understand several things, Melody. First, we are at war, but our own government doesn't know it yet. I am acting in a private capacity, and we cannot tell even our own segment Ministers. It's a big secret, you see. Do you understand that?'

'No,' Melody said honestly enough. How could the segment be at war without the Ministers knowing it? How could a Solarian officer – and not one of the highest ones, if she comprehended military rankings at all – keep secrets from his own superiors? It was nonsensical.

'Well, we'll return to that later,' the Colonel said. 'We never would have required the service of a person your age if we were not desperate. But we are doing all we can to protect your identity. Once the enemy gets at our Population files—' He shook his head. 'The point is, you have the highest Kirlian aura ever measured. Do you comprehend the significance of that?'

'My ice cream is coming,' Melody said promptly.

The officer rolled his human eyeballs expressively upward. 'Er, yes. Momentarily. Uh, Melody, the Society of Hosts forbids the exploitation of children, so they have no child-hosts. And it is essential that we work through the Society. That's why we had to transfer you to the body of a young woman. This body is larger and more, er, mature than you are accustomed to, quite apart from the change in species. When we get a dispensation through the Society, we'll retransfer you to a more appropriate host. I apologize for the uh, awkwardness.' His eyes strayed to her legs, which had fallen apart again.

Melody snapped them shut. 'I want to go home,' she said, screwing up her human face in its version of misery. She was beginning to enjoy this.

'I wish you'd stay,' Yael said wistfully. 'You're putting that officer through hoops! I'd never have the nerve.'

But the Colonel was talking again. 'We can't send you home yet, Melody. We are at war. Secretly. It is a crisis. Now first you'll have to join the Society of Hosts—'

Melody pouted. 'No.'

Yael objected. 'You *have* to join the Society! You're a transferee!'

'Where's my ice cream?' Melody demanded. And privately to Yael: 'That ice cream had better be good. Exactly what *is* it?'

The Colonel sighed, expelling wind through his mouth in a manner impossible to a Mintakan. He made a gesture with his hand, and the orderly entered, bearing a covered tray.

'It's fattening,' Yael said.

Melody worked that out rapidly. It seemed slenderness was a desirable physical quality, and what they fed children made the body grow. She didn't want to degrade her host's body.

'Here is your ice cream,' the Colonel said, forcing a smile.

Melody peered at it. It was a whitish mass of cold substance in a flat dish. Not at all like Mintakan food. 'No.'

'What?' the Colonel asked, startled.

'Eat it yourself,' Melody said.

The man's brow furrowed. 'You wish me to eat your ice cream?'

'You can't do that!' Yael protested. 'He's almost a *general*!'

'Yes,' Melody said aloud. Childhood had its privileges.

'Then will you cooperate?' the Colonel inquired wearily.

'I want to go home!'

The Colonel took the dish and began spooning the noxious substance into his mouth. 'Um, takes me back thirty years,' he remarked around melting cream. 'Now about the Society of Hosts—'

'They can have some ice cream too,' Melody said brightly. It should not require much more of this to convince them to send her right back to Mintaka!

43

The Colonel grimaced. He leaned over and touched a button. 'SOH rep to office,' he snapped.

'I think he just called your bluff,' Yael said nervously. 'He's just buzzed the Society of Hosts.'

Almost immediately a creature appeared in the doorway. 'Circularity,' it said. It resembled a large blob with a tapering trunk above and large ball below.

'A Polarian!' Melody exclaimed internally.

'I am Fltosm,' it said, buzzing its trunk-ball against its own hide.

'Hello, Flotsam,' Melody greeted it.

'Have some ice cream, comrade,' the Colonel said.

'If you will place a quantity on the floor . . .' the Polarian suggested, indicating with its speech-ball where the appropriate place for such a deposit would be.

The Colonel poured a little melted ice cream on the floor. The Polarian rolled over it several times. The cream adhered to its wheel and was drawn up inside its wheel-housing. 'Very good,' it said.

The Colonel turned to Melody. 'Now if you are satisfied . . .'

'I want to go home,' Melody repeated.

'You are very clever, Matriarch,' Fltosm said, glowing.

Melody grimaced. 'You solved the conversion!'

'Circularity.'

The Colonel looked around. 'What do you mean?'

'Never mind,' Melody said. 'What are the advantages to membership in the Society of Hosts?'

'It is essential to our war effort!' the Colonel exclaimed. 'We can't trust any other—'

'In a moment,' the Polarian interposed neatly. 'Matriarch, the home-body of the transferee must not be neglected. It must be occupied and exercised regularly, lest the synapses become detuned. Were an entity to remain in transfer for a period as long as a Sol-year without accommodation for its own body, that body would become unsalvageable, and the entity's aura would accelerate decay. The two are linked, always – aura and body – in fact they are one, mere aspects of the wheel of life. Separation is deleterious.'

'The wheel of life!' Melody repeated, thinking of the Tarot Trump titled the Wheel of Fortune. That was naturally the way a Polarian would think. 'Flotsam, you make unholy sense. The Society of Hosts take care of hosts – and of transferees too. But I'm not going to be in transfer long, so I am ill-behooved to join.'

'Circularity.'

The human officer puffed up. 'See here, are you *agreeing* with her?' he demanded of the Polarian. 'You know the vital importance to our galaxy of—'

'The interest of the individual is paramount,' Fltosm replied, vibrating its ball apologetically against the bulging expanse of its lower torso.

'But we *need* her!' the Colonel said. 'She has an aural intensity of two hundred twenty-three, the highest ever measured. With our own government infiltrated by hostages—'

Yael was amazed. 'Two hundred and twenty-three times normal? It's impossible!'

'The aura is possible,' Melody informed her. 'My cooperation may not be.' Then, aloud: 'Flotsam, I like your Polarian logic. Will you assist me in returning to my natural state?'

'With pleasure. It is merely a matter of—'

'Never!' the Colonel roared. 'We made a pact, the five of us, to save our galaxy. Do you want me to summon the Canopian? She stays here!'

So Sphere Canopus was involved in this, too. But not Segment Etamin's own government?

The Polarian was undaunted. 'This is not circular. Neither my culture nor the Society of Hosts permit involuntary transfer.'

'Well, *Andromeda* does!' the Colonel said. 'If we don't stop them, we'll *all* be hostages. Then where will your precious individual rights be? That's what this war is all about.'

Fltosm addressed Melody: 'I regret I cannot assist you without exchange of debt. In matters of interhuman protocol I cannot interfere.'

'I'm not human; I'm Mintakan,' Melody said. But the

45

Colonel's remarks about the galactic situation alarmed her. If another Energy War were really upon them, there was no security in Sphere Mintaka! 'I will exchange debt.'

'Watch it,' Yael advised. 'Debt is a mighty funny, mighty serious business with Poles. I don't understand it, really, but—'

'I am roughly familiar with the concept; it is in the Polarian aspect of Tarot,' Melody told her.

'In accordance with the Compromise Convention of System Etamin,' the Polarian said formally, 'I proffer a modified debt exchange, abatement inherent.'

'As an entity of vassal-Sphere Mintaka, I accept,' Melody said.

'You can't do this!' the Colonel shouted, stepping between them.

'You sure *can't*,' Yael agreed. 'We're under martial law here.'

'Shut up and watch,' Melody told her. 'Flotsam's one smart musician.'

'I hereby impress you, Entity Melody of Mintaka, into the Society of Hosts,' the Polarian continued. 'The Society is now your representative, and will require your return to your own physique within one Sol-day of now. You will perform the single service of exorcizing and interrogating one hostage-entity.'

'This is preposterous!' the Colonel said. 'No one can—'

'Agreed,' Melody said. 'Tell me how.'

'Necessary review,' Fltosm said. 'Originally transfer was to "empty" hosts, those bodies whose minds had vacated, and who were effectively dead, with no Kirlian aura associated. The true essence of personality lies in the aura, what some viewpoints call the soul. When the aura of one entity was transferred to the vacant body of another entity, that body became the living personality of the first entity. But the aura could not survive long away from its natural host, and faded at the rate of one normal intensity per Sol-day, approximately. Thus only high-Kirlian entities could transfer.'

'Hey, I didn't know this!' Yael murmured.

'More recent developments in the science of transfer have

resulted in voluntary hosting,' the Polarian continued. 'That is, the host is not vacant, but retains its aura, permitting the temporary occupancy of the more potent aura of a transferee. Because the host-aura is able to maintain its body compatibly, less energy is drawn from the visiting aura, and the fading of that visitor is thereby lessened. We have now enabled the transferee to survive in a foreign host as long as ten times the duration originally possible. In certain cases, tenure can be even longer, as with transfer between compatibile siblings of the same Sphere. You, Melody, now occupy the voluntary host of a young Solarian female native to this planet. You are not aware of her aura, as it is less than half of one percent the intensity of yours. But that aura is nevertheless promoting your welfare in transfer, and that aura is protected by the Society of Hosts.'

'See, I was supposed to stay hidden,' Yael said. 'If they find out I came out—'

'It is our secret,' Melody assured her.

'Now it seems the entities of Galaxy Andromeda have perfected a technique through which involuntary hosting is feasible,' Fltosm continued. 'They are able to transfer their high-Kirlian auras into lesser-Kirlian hosts without the prior consent of those hosts. And they have done so, taking over a number of our most sensitively located entities. We call them hostages: involuntary hosts. There is no way to discover a hostage except by aural verification, which requires the application of complex equipment. Thus we do not know which of our government officials are hostages, for we cannot require them to undertake aural verification without alerting them to our suspicion. It is an uncircular situation.'

'Agreed,' Melody said.

'I'll say!' Yael exclaimed. 'Can't test the spies without making it worse.'

'So we have initiated a quasi-legal program of hostage identification and research. This not under the direction of our governing Ministers, because we know that at least one of them is himself a hostage. But our program is essential to the welfare of our segment and our galaxy. If the Andromedans infiltrate and conquer us, our entire galaxy may

47

perish – literally. For they mean to draw away the binding energy of our atomic structure to facilitate the power required for their advancing civilization, and our very substance will disappear in the course of a few thousand years.'

Melody understood. She believed the Polarian, and knew now that it was no idle reason that chained her to this host. The survival of her galaxy was at stake. She would have to do what was required, however inconvenient it might be to her personal life.

'We operate through the Society of Hosts,' the Polarian went on, 'because they alone possess the aural expertise to assure the absence of hostages in their own ranks. This is why it is necessary for all our operatives to join the Society. Aural verification is an unquestioned requirement for entry. No suspicion attaches. The Society has undertaken research into hostaging, but has been unable to duplicate the Andromedan technology. Perhaps if a living hostage could be studied – but we dare not touch any that we know of on this planet, because that would give away our knowledge to the Andromedans and precipitate an immediate crisis that could cost us the war.'

The Colonel smiled approvingly. 'Not only are you sounding like a Solarian, now – you're talking like a military man.'

'At times thrust has its applications,' the Polarian agreed, glowing with distaste. 'But circularity will be required for the resolution.'

'Agreed,' the Colonel said. 'Sorry I butted in.'

'It is the nature of your kind,' Fltosm said generously. Then, to Melody: 'Society calculations indicate that a hostage can be reclaimed through our existent technology, provided the hostage is rendered unconscious and laid under siege by a completely superior aura of the same family. Perhaps a different aural family would succeed also; that is less certain. You understand how auras exist in related types, apart from intensity, some being compatible and others so diverse as to be incompatible?'

'Yes,' Melody said. 'This accounts for what was historically known as "instinctive" attraction or repulsion between

48

given entities. A parallel could be made to your Solarian or Polarian blood types.'

'Yes. But even with a reasonably close match, the margin of superiority would have to be at least four to one over the besieged aura. The technology of Andromeda has evidently abated this necessity, but we of the Milky Way must resort to comparatively crude force. Therefore—'

'I believe I understand you at last,' Melody said. 'You have located a hostage whose controlling aura is of my own aural type, too high for any other entity to overwhelm.'

'Precisely. It is a female hostage governed by an aura of fifty-two times normal intensity.'

'So you need an aura of two hundred and eight,' Melody finished. 'Not many exist.'

'This is true The highest available in Segment Etamin is one hundred fifty-nine, female – and she is of the wrong type. In fact, there are no female auras above one hundred and eighty in the galaxy – except for yours. You are thus indispensable. By the time the hostage's aura fades to under forty, enabling another agent to make the attempt (ignoring for the moment the complication of typing, which may after all be irrelevant), one hundred and twenty days will have passed – and we shall have lost a crucial advantage, perhaps even the war itself. The potential information this hostage possesses is incalculable, and the element of surprise is also vital. Because she happens to be in a situation in which the Andromedans are unlikely to suspect any attempt at counterhostaging, we may be able to conquer her without this knowledge.'

'So you will retransfer me into that body, whereupon I will be able to tap the secrets of Andromeda,' Melody said. 'This is the mission for which you originally summoned me, isn't it?'

'True.'

'But you cannot require any more of me than this one service. Within one day I'll be home – and Imperial Outworld won't bother me again, though the galaxy perish.'

'True. The welfare of the individual preempts that of

society in our Sphere, and the terms of the debt exchange must be honored.'

'Fair deal. Show me your hostage.'

'It is a Solarian officer aboard a Sphere Sol ship in space – the flagship of the Segment Etamin fleet. It will be necessary to mattermit you to a shuttlecraft, that is now completing its voyage to that fleet. After the mission, we will transfer you directly back to your Mintakan body.'

'Very pretty,' Melody remarked. 'Were I in a Polarian host, I could think of another manner to abate debt.'

Fltosm glowed. She had paid the Polarian the courtly compliment of suggesting it was a suitable partner for mating. Polarians, like Mintakans and in contrast to Solarians, arranged for mating on intellectual grounds. It was a system that made sense to the mature mind.

'I am jealous,' the Colonel said, smiling. And this was a lesser compliment, for he had seen up her host-legs and was reacting in the Solarian manner. But it reminded her: In this host, sex was not merely a mode of reproduction, but a tool of social influence. She must keep that in mind, in case she had need of it.

4

King of Aura

*you missed a council meeting, :: *
:: necessary omission   swallowed a hard rock   progress? ::
located focus of resistance in segment etamin   it is the society of hosts
:: that will require a special effort ::
I am sure dash will make it
:: with what result remains to be noted ::

The fleet was impressive. It was rather like a great city in deep space, or a miniature galaxy. A concentration of planetoids, a diffuse globe – no, a *cluster*, she decided, with the concentration in the center and thinning bands extending out. Beautiful.

It was of course an anachronism since such ships were limited to sublight speeds, so could not even traverse a single sphere, let alone a segment, in normal sapient lifetime. But the rationale was that it might one day be possible to transfer spaceships. At such time as that particular technological breakthrough occurred, the military reasoning went, the Age of Empire would come. So these ships were built and maintained and operated at phenomenal expense – in a parking orbit around Star Etamin. The other segments all had similar fleets. Similar follies, Melody thought. But the fleet *was* spectacular, at least in the shuttle's viewscreen.

The shuttle shot toward the center, decelerating with a vigor that caused respiratory discomfort to the host-body. Melody had been phased in to the travel-velocity of the shuttle, which itself was phasing in to the orbital velocity of the fleet; now there was a lot of inertia to counter. But

Melody insisted on sitting up so that she could watch the screen. There was also a port, but it was useless; the ships were not visible to her untrained naked eye. So she braced the sagging mammaries with one forearm, clenched her jaw to keep it from drawing down painfully, and stayed with the screen. She had never seen a space fleet before, and never expected to see another; this was interesting.

Beside her, a novice Solarian crew-member also watched. His head-hair was of reddish hue, and at the moment so were his eyes. Melody knew this was from the temporary stress of deceleration on the surface veins of the eyeballs; the normal color of the main part of the ball was white, even on brown or black-surfaced entities. But the contrast of red eyes and blue skin was momentarily striking. Though she probably looked much the same. Her host's skin, now that she thought about it, was a delicate blue. That was the native color of Outworld. *Green*, rather; Melody was not yet precise about color vision. It occurred to her, however, that this could be a handy coding system for species with a lot of skin surface, like the Solarians: a different color for each star.

'Isn't that – something!' the man gasped. Although he had been aboard the shuttle when she mattermitted on, he had not seen the fleet before.

'New to you, too?' Melody asked. This formal query when the answer was either known or irrelevant was one of the little Solarian nicities of interaction.

'Yes. I've never been to space before.' Like her, he spoke through clenched teeth, though his jawline still sagged somewhat.

'Neither have I.' Now they had a common framework and she was surprised to discover that it did make her feel more at ease. She paused for several shallow but difficult breaths, aware that his eyes were following the labored movements of her chest. This sidewise torque did his eyeballs no good; he should have clamped down his eyelids for added support. But it seemed the male liked to see even the suggestion of female points of distinction, despite the concealment of cloth and discomfort of gravity. 'Who are you?'

He hesitated. 'Call me March,' he said at last.

52

There was a suppressed stress on it that did not seem to be entirely due to the deceleration. Was that his real name? But he could not be another transfer agent; his aura was merely galactic norm. Normals could not detect the feel of neighboring auras, but high-Kirlians could. Maybe he had been drafted, and did not like being reminded of his happy past. Possibly he had been assigned to watch her, in case her own inexperience led to complications. Yet he had started the shuttle trip well before she had been summoned to Imperial Outworld. Could he have been a convict, released from the prison-colony planet of this system, now shunted to space service? No; he seemed too young, too innocent. She was inclined to trust him. To a reasonable extent. 'Yael,' she said.

'They messaged me . . . you were coming,' he said. His power of speech was fading; this deceleration was an awful strain. 'But they did not tell me' – a pause to catch up on breathing – 'how pretty you would be.'

'Hey, I like him!' Yael said.

'Then you answer him,' Melody replied to her. 'It's your body he admires. Mine would sicken him.' And she turned over control of the vocal apparatus.

'Thank you,' Yael said aloud. 'You're not bad yourself. Are you from Outworld?' As though a green man could be from anywhere else.

'The deepest backvines,' March admitted.

'Me too.' They exchanged smiles.

Then the stiffening deceleration forced them both to be silent.

Melody faded in and out, and time became expanded or condensed – she was not quite sure which. The view-screen showed them passing the layers of the cluster fleet like a comet swinging in to its star. First there were the small scouts, needleshaped because that made them harder to spot and hit as they moved about. It had nothing to do with atmospherics; they flew sidewise as readily as forward, orienting to keep their smallest cross section facing the enemy. They quested far beyond the main mass of the fleet, poking into whatever crannies of space they spied, like

53

curious insects, maneuvering unpredictably. How convenient the human-host imagery became; there were no insects on Melody's home planet.

Melody found her human tongue twitching around in her mouth, and her nostrils narrowing. She stopped it; she could not afford such reactions. The specialists of Imperial Outworld had insisted on providing her with a weapon of self-defense despite her protests. Now it was in her nose: two electrically neutral tubelike units whose mechanism could be invoked by the proper combination of air and pressure. She did not dare try to remove the units; they were of the self-destruct variety – or so the Colonel had assured her. But she had no intention of using them. So she quelled her reactions and returned her attention to the fleet.

The next layer consisted of the more disciplined system of attack craft – small, expendable ships which could move out fast and deliver a wallop. Like poisonous reptiles – another analogy lifted from the convenient mind of her host, who seemed to have a ready imagination for such things – they were brightly colored. Perhaps, however, that was merely enhancement by the screen, color-coding them to match the Spheres with which they were associated: Sol, Polaris, Canopus, Spica, Nath .. and even her own Mintaka? How beautiful it must look – if she could only be sure which one it was.

Of course many of these ships had not been constructed within the Spheres with which they were associated. It would have taken the Mintakan craft three thousand years to travel at half-light speed from Mintaka to Etamin – and that was longer than the segment had existed. Mattermission would have done it instantly, but was prohibitively expensive for an entire space ship. Transfer was instant and cheap, but of course it was not possible with inanimate objects. It was strictly an energy phenomenon: living energy in the form of Kirlian auras, dead energy in the form of magnetic power or 'strong' atomic force. Some theorists thought that the Ancients had been able to imbue physical objects with auras so they could transfer them cheaply to far parts, but few really believed that. Except, perhaps, the military entities who had conceived of these segment fleets all over the galaxy. Regardless, that technology did not exist today. So the ships had to be constructed right here in System Etamin, by transferred entities from other Spheres. Mind, not geography, was the guiding factor: a Mintakan ship was made by genuine Mintakans, though they used human or Polarian bodies. Any Mintakan spacefarer would be at home aboard it. Except someone planetbound like Melody, who had never even seen a Mintakan spaceship before.

Then she did a double take, surprising herself again by this human mannerism. It was a kind of backing up and second inspection with a sensation of mild amazement. 'That's Tarot!' she exclaimed.

'That's what?' Yael inquired, and March's head turned slightly. Each thought the remark had been directed at her/him, since Melody had spoken out loud.

'The Mintakan ship; it's shaped like the Broken Atom of the Tarot Suit of Aura. At least it looks that way on the screen.'

'It's to provide spin while gathering light-energy,' March explained. 'I was briefed about the fleet before I was exiled. The ships from Segment Knyfh are similar. An outer shell to collect the light, and an inner nucleus for the crew. The whole thing rotates just fast enough to provide proper gravity.'

'How ingenious!' Melody said. Then they both paused for breath again, and she wondered: What was this about his being exiled? But she was sure it would be inappropriate to inquire, and at the moment she was more intrigued by the shapes of the ships, now so clear in the screen.

Some were like great wide-bladed swords, others like monstrous coins, still others like wands or cups. 'To think it's been right there under my strings – I mean nose – all this time, all my life, and I never thought to look!' Melody exclaimed to Yael. 'All these ships of space – we are a Tarot-symbol segment!'

Yael was diplomatically silent. She knew little of Tarot, and less of symbolism, and hardly saw either the relevance or significance of such a connection. So what if a sword was used as the shape of a ship and the symbol on a card? What was wrong with that? So long as each design could collect the light, as March had explained, and spin up enough gravity...

And this in turn gave Melody further pause for thought. There was not only a substantial aura differential between them; there was an intellectual gulf. Yael was just below the human norm in intelligence, moderately below in education, and well below in intellectual experience. Melody was between 1·5 and 1·7 on the Mintakan intelligence scale, roughly analogous to the human scale, and possessed a Segment Doctorate in General Learning. And she had a full lifetime behind her. Yet she realized now that there were fundamental equivalencies between her mind and that of her innocent host. They were both female, despite the technical asexuality of Mintakans, and both were novices in this particular situation. Given that basic set of similarities, Melody was able to appreciate the human girl's view – and to grasp for the first time in her life what it meant to be intellectually handicapped. Yael genuinely could not appreciate the insights to be obtained from the observation of the parallelism of designs. But she didn't feel stultified, did not suffer directly; she was literally too stupid to know what she was missing. Yet she was in every sense a person, a conscious, feeling entity.

It was a lesson in perspective that Melody hoped never to forget in the few years remaining to her. For she knew most of the sapients in the galaxy were more like Yael than like Melody. Melody had existed in an ivory tower, and it was now being blasted apart by new experience, exactly as the applicable Trump of the Tarot suggested. She had never realized how specifically it could pertain to *her* – which was part of this very experience. The strike of the lightning bolt enabled her to understand the nature of that lightning bolt.

Now the shuttle's deceleration had eased off, and it was orienting on the hull of the mighty flagship, the *Ace of Swords*. The handle of the sword had seemed small from a distance, but it was a Solarian mile in diameter. This huge rotating mass resembled a veritable planetoid! The ship's magnetic tractor field took hold of the shuttle and guided it into the end of the handle, where there was no gravity right at the axis of rotation. In virtual free-fall the little craft settled into a huge airlock, and a metal covering slid over it. They had docked.

Gas flooded the compartment, and Melody was reminded of her Tarot yet again: Naturally there was gas, since war and all things military were associated with the Suit of Gas whose symbol was the Sword. Solarians as a species were identified with the same suit. Not for nothing was it said throughout the segment: 'Trouble, thy name is Sol.'

Pressure equalized. Melody unstrapped herself, discovering that she could stand, though gravity was minimal here. The port opened and she stepped carefully out, as March deferred to her in a reflex of Solarian etiquette that thrilled Yael. Half floating, Melody came to rest on the deck of the big ship. She found herself in a roughly hemispherical chamber formed by the inner curve of the hull and the dimly illuminated airlock panel above. 'So this is the *Ace of Swords*,' she murmured.

In a moment a door phased open and a space officer strode in. He was a handsome Solarian of middle age, the blazon of Imperial Outworld on his chest: a neat superimposition of the ancient letter symbols O and W, the straight lines of the latter segmenting the former into five subsections:

These stood for the five neighboring Spheres, each with a curved side and one or two straight sides. Curve as in curve of Sphere, straight as in communication between points. Curve as in Polarian circularity, line as in Solarian linearity. The fundamental elements of Outworld society, the mergeance of two Spheres to form System and Segment Etamin. The combination of thinking that had made this a galactic power. All vested in this simple symbol.

There was a chill of terror that half paralyzed the host-body. Melody realized that it stemmed from the host-mind. 'What is the *matter*, girl?' she demanded as the man approached.

'The magnet!' Yael screamed.

Now Melody saw something behind the man. It was a brilliantly colored globe that floated, yet it seemed quite solid. It was like a three-dimensional model of the Outworld emblem – a sphere with lines zig-zagging on it. 'I see it, but it doesn't look dangerous,' Melody said to Yael.

But the Solarian was upon them before Yael could explain. 'How pretty you are, Yael of the Dragon World,' he spoke, extending his hand as he glided to a stop. 'Welcome to the *Ace of Swords.*'

Of course they had not informed him of her real identity. The Society of Hosts protected the anonymity of those who wished it, and no one outside the Society could be completely trusted. So she used her host's identity as a cover, which delighted the real Yael. Here was adventure, in name as well as fact!

'Captain Boyd, I presume,' Melody murmured past half-lowered eyelashes. This sort of signal was not as good as a throbbing harmony, but in an amusical body she just had to make do. She took the proffered hand.

There was the electric thrill of intense auras interacting. This was the Captain, all right; he had the highest Kirlian rating in the fleet, 150, and that was much of the reason he *was* captain. With the hostage threat, the only real security of command was to have top officers with Kirlian auras too high to be taken over by the enemy technique. The Society of Hosts had circled delicately, as the Polarians would have put it, or pulled strings as the Solarians described it, to get this officer into place in this crucial location. This single ship was capable of destroying the civilization of a full planet – and of course the only civilized planet within range of this ship was that of Imperial Outworld.

Captain Boyd's aura was even higher than she had been informed. It was on the order of 175, the most potent she had encountered apart from her own, and it was first cousin to hers in type. She wasn't certain whether this was sloppy testing on the part of the Society of Hosts, or sloppy records, or variance in standards of notation between the Spheres. Probably the Colonel had simply misremembered it, being more concerned with the actual hostage than with the other personnel of the ship. A pleasant surprise, though!

'Dash,' the Captain said. 'Call me Dash . . . Yael.'

Melody made a little motion that accentuated her host's twin mammaries, and smiled. 'Dash.' Now that she knew that sexual interaction was possible apart from reproduction in this species, it was fun to see how well the equipment worked. So long as she never let it go too far. It was obvious that her body could never match the sheer physical power of the males of this species, so sexual appeal was also a potential equalizer.

Melody glanced at the hovering magnet that so upset Yael. 'Might I inquire about your companion?'

He smiled. 'Oh. Sorry. We tend to forget that planetaries aren't used to fleet ways. This is Slammer the Magnet, my bodyguard. Low Kirlian, low intelligence, but the most loyal friend an entity ever had. Say hello to the lady, Slammer.'

Slammer shot forward so quickly that Melody's reflexes were caught short. The ball slammed into her chest – and bounced away without impact. A grossly powerful magnetic field impinged painfully on her aura as contact was made.

Yael screamed, and part of that scream escaped the host-lips. They could have been crushed, host and transferee together, had that thing not reversed itself.

'Impressive, isn't it,' Dash remarked. 'You can see I'm quite safe with Slammer around. He's faster than a speeding bullet, more powerful than a locomotive – uh, that's a cute expression from deep in human past, but quite applicable here. One word from me, and the living cannonball clears the way. If an entity tried to draw a weapon in my presence – boom, no entity. But don't worry, Slammer is your friend too.' He turned his head to the hovering ball. 'Protect Yael. Understand?'

The magnet dipped in an obvious acquiescence. Melody made a mental note to learn a lot more about magnets, soon.

59

She didn't like being around a living cannonball, and now understood Yael's terror. This creature was dangerous!

The captain put his hand on the narrow section of her back and guided her gently forward. Again their auras overlapped delightfully. Instinctive attraction, Kirlian affinity – by any designation, it was a potent force.

'It's such a pleasure to encounter a genuine Kirlian,' Dash said, echoing her thoughts by no coincidence. If his 175 had such impact on her, what did her 223 have on him? 'Your beauty is more than physical; it surrounds you.'

'Naturally,' Melody agreed, making a little bounce to enhance the physical. In this fractional gravity, she bounced too high; only his hand on her kept her from rising to the ceiling. 'That is the nature of the aura.'

'Hey, he's on the make!' Yael warned.

'On make? Oh, I gather your thought now. He wishes to make an offspring, to impregnate this body. And we don't want that.'

'Actually, it might not be so bad,' Yael mused. 'I've never actually done it. My folks always kept me away from the boys, saving me for concubinage. But with a real space captain . . . I've had my antipreg shot, of course.'

So there was no risk of impregnation, regardless of sexual activity. That was good to know, but hard to adjust to, after Melody had so recently been forced to realize the close connection between the two, for Solarians.

Still, a good tool should not be used indiscriminately. 'Let's not rush it,' Melody said to Yael. 'I'm a bit curious about this phenomenon myself, but I haven't stayed female for eighty years for nothing. Actually it's the aura that dazzles him.'

But privately she wondered. She was aware that Solarians were thoroughly sexual creatures, with the males constantly stimulated by the visible attributes of the females. Her experience in a Solarian host, combined with the pervasive sexual aspects of the Solarian Tarot, made that abundantly clear. But even so, there were conventions, such as the compulsive wearing of clothing, that modified it, lest humans degenerate into perpetual sexual orgies. Captain Boyd was coming on very strongly, near the permissible limit of social convention as she understood it. After allowing for the impact of their extraordinary auras, was there still too much sexual push? If so, why?

March had emerged from the shuttle. He exchanged salutes with the Captain, who directed him to the personnel sergeant. Then Boyd showed Melody through another airlock into the main ship, and they took a slow slide toward the outer rim. Gravity increased as they progressed down the chute, until it was Solarian-norm. They debouched in a narrow hall many levels down; space was not wasted in space. This was not because there was no room, but because of the value of building materials. A larger ship required great quantities of precious substances, and more fuel in order to maneuver. So economy was the keynote. But still this was a very large, elegant, powerful vessel.

There were handholds along the walls and ceiling, reminding Melody that ships of space were not always operating with convenient gravity. *Up* could become *down*, and complete freefall would make perambulation awkward. So one had to be able to grab and pull.

They entered a fair-sized room, well furnished with bolted-down couches and tables – the officers' lounge. There was a quick round of introductions. Melody dutifully shook hands with each man and woman, mentally noting the names and aural intensity of each. They were all high-Kirlian entities – surprisingly high, in the fifty to one hundred range. Sphere Sol must have impressed every Kirlian available into service in the space fleet! Had the other Spheres done the same for their own ships?

'And here is your cabin – next to mine,' Dash said.

'Thank you. I will not be needing it, as I am returning to my home immediately after the completion of the mission,' Melody said briskly. 'If you will show me the subject and set up the equipment . . .' She avoided the term 'hostage'; surely the Captain knew her mission in detail, but the other officers would not.

'I assumed you would want to acclimatize,' Dash said. 'A young girl like you, first visit to the fleet . . .'

'He's on the make, all right,' Yael remarked. 'Why don't we go ahead and—'

But Melody still had the caution of age. 'Let's keep him guessing,' she told Yael. And to the Captain: 'I appreciate your solicitude. You can express it most conveniently by facilitating my mission.'

'You certainly are businesslike. That's good,' he commented ruefully. 'I would not have reported the, shall we say, subject, if I had not anticipated an efficient and circumspect response. This is a most important matter.'

'Yes,' Melody agreed as they proceeded down another hall. 'Do you have her under sedation?'

'No, of course not,' Dash said. 'We don't know how many subjects there are, but cannot safely assume this is the only one. If we showed that we were on to her, the others would act, perhaps killing her before we could interrogate her, and possibly going on to sabotage the ship. Since this is the command ship of the fleet, that would be problematical.'

'Yes, I understand,' she agreed.

'We would also lose whatever chance we had to crack this mystery, and that is far more important than either this ship or this whole fleet.' He paused. 'I'm going to introduce you to her as the daughter of an Imperial Minister, so she won't be suspicious. Our Ministers (no offense to Etamin!) are not necessarily overly bright, and they tend to meddle in things they hardly comprehend, and their children do the same. So your behavior will not seem peculiar to her. It will take us a while to get the equipment moved in and set up and tested, and we don't want to alert her. Don't get near enough for her to pick up your aura; if she recognized its strength she would take alarm.'

'I am not entirely ignorant of the requirements of the situation,' Melody reminded him primly, giving her bosom another twitch to abate any implied criticism. She had verified by her observation of the females aboard ship that her host's architecture was indeed superior to the norm.

'She's an officer in the medic corps,' Dash continued, giving that architecture a lingering glance. Whether as lowly as an exile crewman or as elevated as a seasoned captain,

62

they all *looked*. 'She is the officer in charge of atmospherics, among other things. A peculiarly vital spot. In time of crisis, she could sabotage this entire ship merely by making an "error" in the computer setting for the craft atmosphere. We hype our air a bit for action, you see, and damp it in periods of inertia.'

'You play a dangerous game, leaving her there,' Melody remarked.

'There are very high stakes.'

'How did you discover her?'

'My intense aura. Not quite in a league with yours, of course – but still, the highest in the fleet. I can tell a lot about a person merely by shaking hands with him. High-Kirlians have sensitivities that low-Kirlians hardly suspect, as you know.'

'Yes.' The normals thought that no Kirlian aura could be measured or typed except by the use of complex equipment. For *normals*, that was true.

'When I touched Tiala—'

'You are good at touching people,' Melody remarked.

'Quite. I'm not quite as aggressive as I seem. I allow myself the repute of a Casanova as a pretext to touch people long enough and intimately enough to analyze their Kirlian auras properly. I am assured, for example, that you have what may be the highest rating in our galaxy, though no prior information was given me about you. You must be well over two hundred! In Tiala's case—'

'How do you analyze male auras?'

'We have frequent physical fitness sessions, of course. We indulge in sports and unarmed combat. I happen to hold the ship championship in encumbered wrestling. It can take some time to overcome a man when your feet are bound.'

'I can imagine.' She could also imagine how difficult it would be to get away from this man, once he had hold – even if the magnet were not hovering close behind.

'In Tiala's case, I took her to bed – because I was suspicious. I made sure she had no inkling of my real interest in her. I am an excellent lover.'

'I believe it!' Yael said eagerly. But Melody kept silent.

'And I verified that there was a fundamental difference in her aura; it wasn't what it was supposed to be. For one thing, it was too strong, a good ten units above its official rating – or so I thought. But personal judgment is largely intuitive; only the machine can make a really precise read-out. So I photographed the aura secretly and sent the picture to Imperial Outworld for analysis. And it didn't match at all. So we knew an alien had made her hostage.'

'Very perceptive, Dash.' And ruthless. He had played sex with a girl to trap her aural secret. Did she think he loved her?

'Thank you. It is part of my job to protect my ship.'

And what else would he do – to protect his ship? 'It is important that I come to know the subject without arousing her suspicion,' Melody said. 'Perhaps I should play a game with her.'

'Well, I'm not sure the daughter of a Minister would—'

'Who can guess what the daughter of a Minister might do? I know some very good games. Tarot, for example. It—'

'Tarot!' Dash exclaimed. 'I happen to be a scholar of that discipline myself.'

Melody appraised him with renewed interest. 'Temple?'

'No. Free lance. I was never a Tarotist, just a casual student. But I dare say I know it as well as any.'

Marvelous, if true. Melody had spent most of her life in the study and practice of free-lance Tarot, and would quickly be able to determine his level of proficiency. But that could wait upon convenience. 'Really? What is your Significator?'

'King of Aura,' he said. 'Cluster deck, of course. Yours?'

'Queen – of Aura.'

'Oho! I should have known! High intelligence, strong will, intense aura. We are much alike.'

Very much alike. Melody could feel herself being drawn to this ruthless man, compelled by the commonality of qualities. She had never mated because she had never encountered an entity who was her equal, though a number had supposed they were. Or so she liked to tell herself. Perhaps the better, bitter truth was that after the Star of her hope and loss, so long ago, nothing in the universe could satisfy her. What weird chance had brought her to this handsome Solarian? Or was this Perseus, come to rescue the chained lady from the monster?

She decided to fend him off a bit longer, until she had opportunity to do a reading on this problem. There was still too much she did not know. 'Alike within a twenty percent tolerance,' she said. Since there were five Kings and five Queens in the Cluster deck, and these were the only cards normally used as Significators, for grown entities, the chances of matching suits were hardly remote. And entities in matching suits could be quite dissimilar in practice – as different as Solarian from Mintakan. She could not afford to attach undue importance to something which was really not a coincidence, but a reflection of their high auras.

'Do you think you can use Tarot to mask your purpose?' Dash inquired. 'It will require several hours, as I said, to set up. We've never done such a procedure aboard ship before. If she gets suspicious, the task may become impossible.'

'A necessary risk. I am a transferee myself; we shall thus have four auras interacting. This will be complex. I must have some clear notion of the personal situation, or failure is likely.'

Dash sighed. 'I see your point. Well, I shall introduce you and ask Tiala to take charge of you. Have you any medical training?'

'No.' Anything she knew would be Mintakan, at best inapplicable here, at worst dangerous.

'Too bad. Then we can't use that as a pretext for extended dialogue. Still, you are both attractive young women; perhaps that will be enough.'

They arrived at the life-support section. A female Solarian came forward to meet them. 'Sir?'

'Tiala of Oceana, this is Yael of Dragon, daughter of the Minister of Segment Coordination. She is touring this vessel.' He gave a slight human shrug, as though implying that he was humoring a spoiled child for political reasons.

Tiala smiled fetchingly; even Melody's nonhuman nature recognized the appeal of that expression. Dash would not have had to force himself very much to make love to this female, hostage or no. So Melody smiled back, trusting that her expression was as winning.

'I wonder if you could show our distinguished visitor around,' Dash continued. He used just the right tonal emphasis to suggest that he had better things to do himself than squire around such intruders. The hostage had no reason to be suspicious of what was in fact an order. 'I would be most grateful.' And the final, calculated hint: Humor this important nuisance, and perhaps I will make love to you again.

'If she doesn't mind waiting for the end of my watch,' Tiala said. 'Half an hour . . .'

'I don't mind,' Melody said. 'Unless my presence interferes with your job performance.'

Dash made a slight nod to Tiala.

Responsive to the directive, the hostage replied: 'No, I'm only keeping an eye on the dials. Actually, it's dull right now.'

'Very well,' Dash said, smiling again at Melody. Despite her awareness that it was a doubly insincere expression designed to deceive Tiala in the guise of deceiving the visitor, she found herself moved by it. That was something that didn't exist on Mintaka: a smile. It was like a complex harmony of camaraderie, very pleasant to receive. It was amazing how much could be conveyed on the purely visual level.

The Captain left, followed by his deadly magnet. Now Melody was alone with the hostage. She had to be very careful, for if the sapience that invested this nice-seeming girl were to realize what Melody knew, it would probably kill. The first intergalactic war had made plain that Andromedan agents were pitilessly efficient, virtually without conscience except for their absolute loyalty to their galaxy.

Melody turned to find Tiala's gaze upon her. Was the hostage assuming that Melody was to be the Captain's next mistress? Better abate that immediately, or there would never be cooperation! 'I'll be here only a few hours; I really don't understand space.'

Tiala relaxed. 'Understanding space is nothing compared to understanding *people*.'

'Yes, I'm sure that's true.' Melody sat down at the little table anchored to the desk. She misjudged the action slightly, and Yael took over suddenly to prevent her from cracking her hip against the rounded corner. All corners were rounded, in space; one never could anticipate when maneuvers would send entities into collision with objects. 'Do you play Tarot?' And Melody drew out a deck of cards.

'I have heard of the Temples,' Tiala said. 'But I really haven't had much interest in divination.'

'Oh, there is more to Tarot than divination,' Melody assured her brightly. 'The cards can be used for serious study, or for games. Look, let me show you. I fool with these all the time when I have nothing to do.' Absolutely true, yet in this context it might as well have been a lie. For it implied that Tarot was not a serious matter with her. Melody sifted through the cards a bit clumsily with her human fingers and brought out the classical face of one of the Trumps. 'For instance, what do you see?'

There was no hesitation. 'Communication.'

Melody concealed her startlement. She had never before encountered this particular interpretation. 'Now *I* see a lamp.'

Tiala's brow wrinkled. 'Are you sure?'

'This is the game. Each person sees a different thing. Then we try to reconcile them, and discover which has more validity. It's an intellectual exercise.'

'I don't see either one,' Yael remarked.

'It *is* something of a challenge,' Tiala said, becoming intrigued. 'To me, communications beams are quite obvious.'

Communications beams. Of course! On one of the major spheres of Galaxy Andromeda, /, lived a species who communicated by organically generated laser beams. Melody's own Kirlian ancestor had been an Andromedan transferee of that Sphere who had budded with the revered Flint of Outworld, both in Mintakan hosts, a thousand Solarian years before.

There were half a dozen light beams crisscrossing the face of this card. Because Melody thought and communicated in terms of music, not light, she had never interpreted the picture this way, but obviously there had been / influence in its

67

design, regardless of its supposed origin on pre-Sphere Earth. Here was a direct confirmation of the status of the hostage!

'I see that now,' Melody said even as these thoughts phased through her human brain. 'But look at my lamp: It is at the convergence of the beams, an enclosure with a star inside. In fact, it is from where the beams emanate. So is it not a more fundamental image?'

'But the beams *do not* emanate from it,' Tiala protested. 'They are emitted from other eyes; see, they diffuse right past your lamp.'

Other eyes. The light-emitting lenses: eyes of the slash entity. Yes. 'So they do. I must concede this round to you, then. But let's look again. I see . . . a three-headed dog.' The image did not come naturally to her as it was a Solarian canine, nonexistent in Sphere Mintaka. But she was long familiar with the roots of these cards; even in this restricted vision-style, she was not playing fair. She could draw a hundred images from this single face of this one card, while the hostage had never seen it before.

Tiala concentrated. 'Dog. Yes . . . there in the corner.' She had evidently made a quick delve into her host's memory to acquaint herself with the image. 'And I see . . . rolling disks.'

Again Melody was surprised. But spurred by necessity she searched . . . and spotted the figure in the opposite corner. And knew that it was another example of the Andromedan's special perceptual bias. The figure was actually of a coiled snake – but the / entities moved on great sharp rolling disks. 'Ah . . . I see them now. But they have nowhere to roll except out of the picture, while my dog is coming in toward the center.'

'That's right,' Tiala agreed. 'Yours is the more central image.' She studied the face of the card again. Now Melody was really curious. Would the Andromedan mind see the Solarian sperm cell? /s reproduced by exchanging mating-beams, eye-to-eye as it were. Melody was not clear on the details, but certainly no sperm cell was part of the process. Human entities might lock gazes as a preliminary to the physical interpenetration of copulation; /s might inter-

68

penetrate physically as a preliminary to visual copulation. Similar motive, different application.

'A man!' Tiala exclaimed. 'It is the figure of a human male man, carrying his light. See, there is his hand! And the dog is beside him.'

'You found it!' Melody said. 'You win! That is the figure of the Hermit. The one who walks alone. This is the card of the Hermit, in the ancient Thoth face of Solarian Tarot, said to date from a century pre-Sphere. A picture hidden behind a picture.'

'How clever. This *is* fun, though you evidently know more about it than I do. Perhaps you should handicap yourself. May we examine another card?'

'Why certainly. Choose any you wish from the deck. There are thirty Major Arcana or Important Secret cards, and—'

She was interrupted by a shudder that ran through the ship. Tiala jumped up to scan her dials. 'Hull punctured; atmospheric leakage,' she snapped into her bodyphone. 'Section sealed.'

Dash's voice came back. 'Pressure the section! There's crew in that region.'

Tiala's hands played over beam-controls, breaking the electronic synapses in a rapid pattern. This would come naturally to a /, Melody realized; she could do her job. 'Pressurized. But seal off that leak; we can't expend our gas indefinitely.'

The lights blinked and changed. Tiala relaxed. 'They got it sealed; the leak's stopped. I wonder what happened?'

'Felt like an explosion,' Melody said. 'Is the ship under attack?'

'No attack,' Dash's voice answered, reminding her that she could never be assured of real privacy aboard this ship. The whole vessel was geared for instant inter-communication. 'Detonation in the entry aperture. I suspect someone sabotaged equipment there.'

The entry aperture! That was where her shuttle rested – and its retransfer unit. This meant almost certain delay of her mission and return to Mintaka. But Melody could not express her alarm. Not in the presence of the hostage, not to the myriad ears of the ship. 'Maybe I'd better take that cabin after all,' she said. 'I'm only in the way at the moment.'

'Yes,' Dash agreed with ungracious readiness. 'I shall detail someone to guide you.'

5

Llume the Undulant

occasion for preparatory briefing

—is it necessary, ast?—

only by schedule, dash   investigations remain incon-clusive   there is nothing of new significance to report

—then let's fly over it this time   wait for something serious   not be bound by rote—

it is a time of great stress

—yes   at times I wish I were back on my £, hauling scentwood, carefree—

I had understood your species was airborne

—once, ast, once   with increasing brain, we lost our powers of flight   now our three wings are employed only for balance and communication   transport is provided by the £—

with victory we shall afford more technology for the home front

—yes   that is our dream   ironic that we the most civilized advanced cultures in the galactic cluster, should be confined to the resources of our ancestors in domestic cases, reserving all our technology for spherical matters   so readily could we extend that technology throughout an-dromeda, benefiting all our species, had we but the energy we were thwarted once, but not this time   milky way galaxy shall succumb, and its energy shall be ours—

I still have bad vibrations of another enemy agent like flint of outworld foiling us

—so do I, ast, so do I   segment etamin makes me nervous, though I know that prior interruption was a fluke   that is why I assigned one of our best operatives there—

In moments that entity arrived. It was a Polarian, a huge teardrop on a spherical wheel. Melody had assumed that the ship's complement was entirely human, since this was a Solarian vessel, but of course Polarians were integral to segment government and should be represented in at least token capacity here. There were probably other creatures scattered about, below the top officer level.

'I came to escort Yael of Dragon to her cabin,' the Polarian said, its ball vibrating against the wall. 'I am Llume the Undulant, Orderly of the Day.'

Once again Melody concealed her surprise. This was no Polarian manner, despite the form. 'I am Yael.'

Llume led the way down the hall, and Melody followed. She really had no choice. But she found herself wrinkling her nose again, conscious of the little tubes inside. She still did not intend to use the secret weapon, but what would she do in an emergency? She did, after all, want to live.

'I'm nervous,' Yael said. 'Isn't it fun!'

'You *like* being in possible danger?' Melody asked her. 'In a ship under fire in space?'

'Oh, yes! This is adventure! Of course it isn't really danger; it's just some accident in the hold. No enemy could get through those rings of attackships, especially when they're protected by your Tarot magic. But what fun pretending!'

Tarot magic? The girl hadn't grasped the distinction between symbolism and the supernatural. Well, not worth debating. 'I wish I had your attitude,' Melody told her. 'I have lived a settled life; I don't like danger or violence.'

'You're teasing me,' Yael said. 'A mind like yours – you're so much I could never be. It's like riding a supercoaster in the funpark. All I can do is hang on and enjoy it, knowing that no matter how scary it seems you really do know what you're doing. You have such terrific *competence—*'

'Untrue,' Melody said. 'I don't know how—'

'I can't even *imagine* the things you can do. Like that card-picture game. All I saw was the three-headed dog. But I could feel your smartness flowing through a hundred channels of my brain, making it work, making me feel like the genius you are . . .'

The awful thing was that in this girl's terms, this was true. What to Melody was routine thinking, based on a lifetime's study and experience, was genius to Yael. And the human girl could never do it on her own; it simply was not in her genetic makeup. She really *was*, in this respect, inferior.

'But one thing you have that I don't,' Melody said, trying to come up with a genuinely positive aspect of the situation. 'I'm not handsome, in my own form. I'm old, physically infirm, and even in my prime I was no beauty. I never believed it mattered. But now I comprehend what I was missing. You have a physical luster and emotional innocence that – that has *me* riding the supercoaster [quick flash-concept from the host-mind: tremendous velocity past painted frameworks, sensations of falling, sudden darkness, noise, screams of terrified pleasure, loss of equilibrium, glimpse of a handsome youth Sol male in the next capsule, idle fancies of romance, shocking intimacies, brief freefall like five-second love, abrupt triple gravity, struggle for breath, racing heartbeat] of your body. You are one of the most beautiful entities—'

Three men appeared in the hall. They carried blasters, antipersonnel projectors that could scorch living tissue without damaging the equipment of the ship. 'Hands up!' the leader bawled.

The Polarian rolled to a stop. 'I have no hands.'

The men ignored that. 'What are you doing here?'

'I am conducting our guest, the offspring of a Solarian Minister, to her compartment,' Llume said.

'Smartwheel dino,' the man muttered to his companions. Then to Llume: 'On what authority?'

'On Captain's directive.'

That made him pause. He looked at Melody. Quickly she lifted her two arms, having ascertained from the host-mind that this was a signal of capitulation that would prevent immediate attack. She felt the material of her blouse draw tight across her mammaries.

73

All three men looked at her chest. One pursed his lips and made a semimusical trill, a whistle.

'What's your name, hourglass?' the leader demanded.

An hourglass: a primitive device for keeping time, appearing as a symbol in the Tarot. Sand funneled through a narrow aperture at a controlled rate. A reference to the appearance of the host-body? Surely not a complimentary one!

'I am Yael of Dragon,' Melody said.

The man's tongue poked out of his mouth and traveled around the rim of lips, once. 'Must be all right,' he muttered.

'More than all right!' a companion agreed.

The leader shook his head as though clearing it of dust. 'Look, sorry about this; just following orders. We're supposed to clear the halls of personnel. You get on to your cabin.'

Melody lowered her arms. The men's eyes watched the fabric of her blouse relax and settle with the mammaries. 'Thank you,' she said.

'Maybe sometime we'll meet again,' the leader said.

'The hell, schnook!' Yael replied voicelessly.

'This is possible,' Melody agreed verbally. And to Yael: 'About supercoasters – did you see that entity's eyes?'

'He was really looking!' Yael agreed. ' 'Course you put your arms too far back, so you nearly busted the strap.'

Melody caught the image: Once Solarian females had used tight bands called 'bras' about their chests to make their mammaries stand up.

'Strange,' the Polarian murmured against the wall. 'Weaponed personnel are not normally permitted in the passages. We must move on. Please swim this way.'

'You are a transfer from Sphere Spica, then,' Melody said as she followed. 'Not a native Polarian.' Spica was a water world, represented in the Tarot by the Suit of Liquid, or Cups, while the Polarians identified with the Suit of Solid, or Disks. Much of the old Tarot had passed into segment idiom and many entities used the associations without knowing their origin – as she had already observed in the shapes of the ships of the fleet.

'Of course. I am an Undulant, as I said. I cannot swim on solid, so I utilize a solidbound host. You are also a transferee?'

'Yes.' Melody considered momentarily whether she could trust this entity, and decided not to risk it. Only the Captain knew her nature and mission here, and he had not been informed of her Mintakan identity. Solarians had a certain fetish for secrecy, but considering the nature of the Andromedan threat, secrecy seemed to be in order. When body and mind could be taken over and made hostage to an alien aura without warning or consent, no information in any mind was safe. There were only two reasonable defenses: an extremely high aura, such as the Captain's or her own, or fairly thorough mental ignorance of critical matters.

Llume halted abruptly. 'There is a magnet guarding the passage ahead,' the Polarian said.

Melody needed no further caution. 'Will it attack us?'

'Uncertain. Better to have its master admonish it, before we attempt to pass. The visibility of human milk-mounds will not distract *this* entity.'

Melody grimaced inwardly. *Everybody* seemed to notice Yael's mammaries.

The Polarian/Spican extended her tail to a stud high in the wall and depressed it. Melody remembered that the appendage was termed tail for the female and trunk for the male Polarian, and this was a female host. But Spicans had no fixed sex. There were rather three fixed forms whose role in reproduction depended purely on circumstance. In this regard there were strong similarities to the Mintakan system. Perhaps Llume had taken the female role most recently before transfer, so had come to a female host; on another occasion she might manifest as a male. Melody was sure the very notion of sex identity change would be deeply upsetting to Solarians, yet it was quite sensible. What rational entity would want to be confined all its life to *one* aspect of sexuality?

'*I* would!' Yael replied, embarrassed.

Which merely went to illustrate the limitations of form. The chained lady could not even conceive of freedom!

'I'm not chained!' Yael protested hotly. 'I *like* being a girl. Can't you understand that?'

'Llume to Captain,' Llume said, spinning her ball neatly against the stud.

'Captain occupied,' a voice responded after a moment. 'Alternate?'

'We are blocked by a magnet, master uncertain.'

'For that you must have the Captain. Ship is on curfew.'

'Please attempt to reach Captain, then. We are unable to honor curfew, owing to presence of magnet. I courier daughter of Minister; cannot risk harm to visitor.'

'Remain in place until contacted.'

They waited, but after several minutes there was no callback.

'Must be more trouble than we know,' Melody observed.

'It is unusual,' Llume agreed. 'May we converse?'

'I'd love to. I'd like to know more about Spica.'

'And I about the Music Sphere.'

Music Sphere – that could only mean Mintaka! How had Llume learned of this? Or was she guessing? 'But first,' Melody said, 'I'd like to know how these magnets function. They frighten me somewhat.'

'They are intended to,' Llume said. 'They evolved on a densely metallic world with very strong magnetic fields and fluxes. They moved by generating polar intensities, attracting themselves to metallic objects with great force, then shifting the pole in the manner of an electric engine.'

'Electromagnetic propulsion in a living body,' Melody said. 'This is new to me.'

'New to most entities who haven't been aboard military vessels,' Llume agreed. 'They were brought into space only in the past century or so, and Solarians have not been eager to spread information about them. Until recently they seemed to be merely a planetary anomaly; they could not survive on other worlds because there was insufficient metal and fuel.'

'Fuel?'

'Their mode of operation requires much power. They consume concentrated organic energy substances, such as petroleum and coal. They vaporize it or powder it, then

76

combust it, converting virtually all the heat into magnetic energy. The field of a well-fed magnet becomes intense.'

'I noticed,' Melody agreed. 'They would be associated with the Suit of Aura, no doubt. Which is an intriguing notion in its own right.'

'Finally, an intelligent Solarian realized that these magnets were ideally suited to habitation within metal spaceships,' Llume continued. 'The long clear passages, and the temptation of unlimited fuel—'

'Instant guard dogs,' Melody finished. 'Yes, I see it now. Not too intelligent and unable ever to leave the environment of the ship – this is guaranteed loyalty! All you have to do is feed your magnet.'

'Their nature is distressingly Solarian, despite their shape and mode,' Llume said. 'They are the ultimate thrust-creatures, objects of terror. They are largely invulnerable to conventional weapons even when directly struck, and they have such speed and power—'

'My sentiments exactly,' Melody said. She had learned much of what she needed to know about the magnets, but it was hardly comforting. If a magnet should get confused and attack her, what possible defense did she have? 'May we communicate privately?'

Llume placed her ball against Melody's human throat. It vibrated gently. 'This cannot be heard beyond your flesh,' the Polarian/Spican said, the words sounding like a voice in the brain. 'If you will subvocalize, it will be private, unless there is a spy-beam on us. I do not think that is the case.'

'Thank you,' Melody said, speaking almost as silently as she did to Yael. She was now aware of Llume's aura, a really strong one of about one hundred, very attractive. 'How did you identify my native Sphere?'

'Alien cultures are my avocation. There are typical nuances of expression and viewpoint. Yours conform to the pattern of Mintaka. But you conceal it very well. No one not trained as I have been would recognize this, and in some moments your reactions are so perfectly human that I marvel.'

Those moments would be when Yael's reactions came

through. This was a most observant Spican! 'That's a relief. You read my mannerisms, just as I read your lack of circularity.' Melody brought out the Hermit card from her deck, the same face Tiala had seen. 'What do you see here?'

Llume ran her ball over the card's surface. Polarians lacked sharply focused vision, as did Mintakans. The designs of these cards were in trace relief, however, so they could be read by tactile means. The Polarian ball was a very sensitive communication organ. 'This is a stylized Undulant swimming toward a star. I believe it is myself.'

The sperm cell: it was in fact a tiny swimming creature, in its element! That was what would naturally strike the attention of a true Spican first. 'Strange,' Melody said. 'I see communication.'

They were in physical contact; Melody was aware of the fluctuations in the other entity's aura. There was no significant deviation in response to this loaded remark.

'I suppose a star can be considered so,' Lume offered. 'It bears light that all may see.'

'I mean the beams.'

'The beams?' Still no ripple. Llume was genuinely perplexed. 'Do they form a significant pattern?'

One more test. 'It occurs to me that we may be related,' Melody said. 'Do you have any alien ancestors?'

'Yes. I have two. A thousand years ago, Flint of Outworld, a Solarian transferee to our home planet, raped a / agent of Andromeda. He had manifested as an Impact, she as an Undulant, and together with Sissix the Sibilant as catalyst they generated the infant Llana the Undulant. I descend from her. We are most interested in genealogy in Spican waters.'

'We also, in Mintakan fields,' Melody said. 'I descend from the same two aliens – manifesting as Mintakans. But my loyalty is to Sphere Mintaka.'

'And mine to Sphere Spica – and Galaxy Milky Way,' Llume said.

'Our auras are of the same family,' Melody said. 'Very close, the closest affinity I have ever encountered. We are as sisters.'

78

'Yes. Our aural linkage is much more intimate than our physical ancestry, though it is amazing that we *are* related.'

Melody chuckled. 'Illusion. In the thousand Sol years since Flint of Outworld thrust his favors so widely, there has been ample opportunity for every member of each of our Spheres to become related through him. A brief calculation will show that if we allow twenty-five years for an average generation, there would be forty generations in that period. If each female or equivalent produced two offspring, the descendants would now number approximately one trillion entities. Since the average Sphere supports about a hundred billion sapients—'

Now Llume laughed – an intriguing effect, in its silent vibration. 'And I supposed I was so special, possessing those illustrious historical ancestors! The remarkable ones are those who do *not* share this ancestry!'

'On the other hand, the nongenetic affinity of aura is quite significant,' Melody said. 'I have encountered no Mintaken aura as intense as yours, so closely allied to my own.'

'Perhaps we are guided in some fashion,' Llume said. 'I do not subscribe readily to coincidence.'

'Coincidence would have it that at certain stages like entities will meet, as well as unlike entities,' Melody said. 'This ship represents a deliberate concentration of extremely intense auras, and some will naturally be related.'

'For one who subscribes to Tarot, you are very practical,' Llume observed delicately.

'*Tarot* is practical,' Melody assured her.

'Apologies; no disparagement of religious views intended.'

Another miscue, but not worth correcting. 'Accepted. I believe I can accept you as a genuine Milky Way galaxy entity.'

'Of course! And I accept you. Why—'

'There are hostages among us.'

'Hostages?'

'Involuntary hosts, controlled by Andromedan auras. I am here to nullify them.'

Now Llume's aura veered wildly. 'Andromedans! Aboard this ship?'

79

'Yes. Tiala of Oceana is one; it has been verified. She is a / entity of Andromeda. There may be others. I suspect that is the source of this present commotion. Will you work with me?'

'I must ask the Captain first,' Llume said uncertainly. 'I never guessed – hostages!'

'By all means ask the Captain. But not over the ship's phone system.'

Llume laughed again at Melody's throat. 'Of course not! I am not quite that ignorant.' She looked down the hall at the magnet. Melody could tell she was looking by her attitude; her skin changed color and brightness slightly. Large objects were visible to Polarians, and of course this Spican intellect had Polarian-host talents. 'But assuming the Captain approved, how could I help? I don't know how to identify a hostage.'

'I would like to tell some fortunes,' Melody said.

Again the aura flexed. 'I do not comprehend Mintakan humor.'

'Of course not. No Spican would. Or Solarian. Or Polarian or Canopian or Nathian. But specially, no Andromedan.'

'No Andromedan,' Llume said, catching on. 'You can identify an Andromedan through the Tarot?'

'I believe so. With your cooperation. If you can tell a transferee by his home-Sphere mannerisms, you should have a good notion who our suspects are. If you can bring them to me without suspicion—'

'Now I understand! This is how you verified that Tiala was a hostage?'

'She was already known to be a hostage. I used the Tarot merely to distract her, but found it to be a better tool than I had imagined. As long as I'm confined to this ship, this is a worthwhile application of my skill.' For Melody now doubted she would get off this ship as rapidly as she had been promised. Not if it was infiltrated by a number of hostages.

'I agree. If there are many more hostages aboard, we must neutralize them promptly.'

'No. We must identify them — without their knowing it. Otherwise we place ourselves in peril.'

'But if we let them go—'

'An enemy known is an enemy neutralized — when the appropriate time comes.'

'Yes, you make sense. Probably that detonation in the hold was the work of a hostage.'

Melody wondered about that. No one on the ship besides herself and Captain Boyd had known her mission. How could a hostage have struck so rapidly and accurately?

'Captain to Llume,' the shipvoice said, startling Melody out of her reverie.

Llume's tail went up to answer. 'Awaiting.'

'All magnets have been advised not to molest our guest, Yael of Dragon. Pass without hindrance.'

'Understood, Captain, may I—'

But the connection had already been broken.

Llume made an elegant boneless shrug. 'I was about to inquire whether I could courier you for the duration; I could not have been more specific at this time. Yet he did not say negative.'

Melody laughed. 'That's right. I heard him fail to negate.'

They moved on down the hall, Melody walking, Llume rolling, neither using her natural mode of travel. The magnet hovered in place, ignoring them. But Melody's human flesh crawled as she passed it, and not merely because of Yael's terror. A living cannonball.

'I suspect the bomb was placed aboard the shuttle before it left Outworld,' Dash said. 'It was intended to destroy both the equipment – which it did – and the operative.'

'The operative,' Melody said, feeling cold. 'Me?'

'You. For this reason I feel it would be better for you to remain aboard this ship for the time being. Evidently someone on the Imperial Planet is aware of your mission, so you are not safe there. Until that entity is located and neutralized, you are safest here where your identity is unknown.'

'Yes ...' Melody agreed. She had already decided to remain for a while, but the notion that a direct attempt had been made on her life was appalling, and it unnerved her. But for an accident of timing, that bomb . . .

The Captain put his human arm around her shoulders. Suddenly she was crying in very human style against his shoulder. 'Oh, Dash – I'm *afraid*!'

'Perfectly normal reaction. But there is no need to be concerned – now. I have established very thoroughly that no attempt on your life originated *here*. I regret I had no chance to explain what I was doing, before, but of course I could not be *sure* until we had investigated. I regret that the equipment was destroyed, but that can be replaced in due course. All is well so long as *you* are well, and I shall ensure that you remain well.'

He addressed his magnet. 'Slammer, you will accompany Yael of Dragon until further notice, protecting her from any threat whatsoever. Understood?'

The magnet bobbed.

Oh, no! 'Captain, I'd really rather *not* have the magnet—'

'The magnet is your friend,' the Captain assured her. 'Pay attention.' He pointed to a metal chair anchored to the floor of Melody's cabin. 'I believe that object intends harm to Yael of—'

A blast of air rocked them back. The chair exploded. And Slammer hovered back where he had been, the heat of sudden motion dissipating from his shell.

Only Dash's strong arm around her had prevented Melody from being blown over by the impact of the magnet's motion. The chair was a flattened mass of partly melted metal. Yet it had been done so quickly that Melody had not even seen it happen.

The Captain gave her a final squeeze and let her go. 'No one will even *think* of harming you now,' he said. 'You are safe. Believe.'

Melody believed.

'I was always a sucker for fortunes,' the Chief of Coordinations said.

'You must understand, I make no claims for the supernatural,' Melody informed him, tapping the Cluster deck

82

lightly. She had combed out her hair so that it was long and loose, parted in the center and coursing down in brown streams just outside her eyes, in the fashion of the ancient human witches. Yael had been delighted, and had offered pointers on details.

'Well, as long as it doesn't take too long,' he said. 'I do have other business.'

Melody leaned forward carefully, holding the deck in both hands so that her arms pressed against the sides of her breasts, making them bulge out of the artfully low-cut décolletage. 'I wouldn't want to inconvenience you,' she murmured.

His eyes did a little male-animal dance upon her cleavage. 'Oh, no inconvenience. Take your time.'

'Do you know your Significator? The card that represents you?'

He glanced at her face momentarily, brow wrinkling. 'Is there a card named Hath?'

She smiled. 'I don't believe so. What is your planet of origin?'

'Conquest,' he said.

'Well, Hath of Conquest, let's look through these cards and see if any of the faces reflect your home. I am not familiar with it, so you will have to make the selection.' She showed him the first of the Major Arcana, numbered Zero in the deck. 'This we call the Fool, though he is not really foolish. It is just that his tremendous vision outreaches his footing.' The picture showed a young man about to step off a cliff. She flexed the face, bringing up an alternate. 'This is the same key, but in this aspect he is called the Nameless One. There are over a hundred versions of each card; I have only a representative sampling here.' She flexed it to the third face.

'No, wait,' Hath said. 'That second one; I believe that will do.'

'Oh?' She flexed it back. 'Why?'

'The arthropod. This typifies my world.'

'There are spiders on your world?'

'No. But related creatures, yes. We cultivate them; they are

83

our primary food. So arthropods are most important to us.'

'That makes sense,' Melody agreed. 'Very well. This is your Significator, and we shall use this facet of the deck. It is called the New Tarot, though it is not new any more. It was one of the decks created in honor of the so-called Aquarian Age of astrological Earth. It has been modified to fit the standard hundred card format, but otherwise it is reasonably authentic.'

She continued talking, careful to provide him a continuing view of her front so as to hold his attention, but her thoughts wandered. In fact, she had read of Planet Conquest, as it had a certain historical value. It had been the first human extra-Solar colony, the start of Sphere Sol.

A million Solarians had been moved by matter transmission at phenomenal energy expense to the system of Gienah, sixty-three light years distant from Sol, there to colonize a supposedly ideal virgin world. But the preliminary survey had overlooked a critical element of the planet's ecology, and it had very nearly wiped out the colony in the first year. The near-fiasco had been hushed up by the Solarian bureaucracy, but it was only a fraction of the disasters that beset the 'Fool' period of Earth's history. How aptly the Tarot reflected that situation! Yet, Melody reminded herself, the vision of Paul of Tarot also stemmed from that conflux . . .

Of course, such information was also available to the Andromedans. So if a spy or hostage wanted to claim origin on a planet of Sphere Sol, this would do. And a hostage entity would have no reason to pretend; it could draw from its host's mind. She would be wasting her time trying to trap it by means of misinformation. In fact, a person could have a great deal of misinformation about his home planet, since of course most people here in the fleet would be second- or third-generation émigrés whose ancestors had shipped at half-light speed from those planets. A man could call a planet 'home' as a matter of cultural pride, when he had never been there. This was another reason it was generally considered that the only sure way to identify a given entity was by aural analysis.

'Now these hundred cards are arranged in order,' Melody was saying meanwhile. She spread them in her hands, not forgetting to give her impressive bust another jiggle. 'First the Major Arcana, the important secrets, as it were, all thirty of them. Actually there are even more than that, but they don't all have separate cards. This one, the Ghost, has fifteen alternate keys. It really stands for all the missing secrets, whose number may well be infinite. So the full extent of the theoretical deck—'

'I don't really understand about such things,' Hath said. 'And I do have duties elsewhere. Would you mind doing the reading now?'

So her bosom would not hold him forever. Well, he had a typical human reaction. Few sapients were sincerely interested in Tarot; they only wanted a slice of their future handed to them conveniently. This would not be a good reading. The querist really had to understand the cards for that. But then, the reading was not her purpose. 'Please shuffle the cards now,' she told him, handing him the pack.

His eyebrows lifted. '*I* have to do the work?'

'You have to do the work. You may not be conscious of it, but as you shuffle the cards you are arranging them in an order that satisfies you. *You* determine their final order. I only lay them out and help interpret. There is nothing supernatural about it; the cards merely reflect your will.'

'I know you have to say that,' he said, his eyes straying at last from her décolletage to her legs, which she had disposed artistically to the side of the table. 'There are laws, aren't there? You can't claim anything about spiritual influences, but they're there all the same, right?' He shuffled the cards.

A born sucker; she had known the type in Sphere Mintaka. They wanted to believe in fantastic agencies, not in mundane reality. The truth was that modern space science had far more effect on most entities' lives than any possible spiritual agency.

'I only help you interpret the cards,' she insisted, knowing he would take this as confirmation of his conjecture. 'No spirits exist except as you have conjured them.'

He returned the deck. Melody dealt the first card of the

reading. It was the Five Serpents of the New Tarot, with the five snakes radiating out from the points of a five-pointed star. Too bad; these Minor Arcana were not complex enough to evoke the reactions she needed. What would she do if the whole layout turned out to be like this?

But she tried. 'What does this suggest to you, Hath?'

He hardly glanced at it. 'The patina of reproduction, of course.'

Melody forced her mouth to work. 'Of course.' Was he teasing her or was this a completely alien reaction?

She dealt another card; Unity, equivalent to The Lovers in the more conventional decks. It could be considered as representing the commencement of a new way, though of course it was far more complex than that.

'There is the first shoot entering the nutrient globe,' Hath said. 'Ready to fission in that egg into the five sexes that will consume the body of the female entity laid out as food, before emerging as shown in the prior card,' he said. He looked up. 'I'm surprised they are permitted to print such graphic material.'

'Sometimes they do have trouble with local censors,' Melody said somewhat feebly. For she had abruptly identified the applicable culture, the only one she knew of that had five sexes. Sphere * of Andromeda.

By the time she completed the reading, she was certain. Hath was another hostage. She gave him a nice 'fortune' and let him go. But her human heart was pounding.

Her first Tarot testing had been a success. But she was not precisely satisfied with its verdict. If a random sampling of personnel had so easily turned up another agent of Andromeda, *how many more were aboard this ship?*

Melody was tired, and so was her host. She had been awake and active for some time, and had experienced more new and unsettling things than ever before in her life. She had to relax.

'Let's take us a subsonic cleanse and estivation,' she told Yael.

'What?' Bewilderment.

86

'Oh – sorry, I forget. I mean a hot shower and sleep.'

'It must be some life, on Mintaka,' Yael remarked.

'It is some life *here*, girl!'

Yael laughed, pleased. 'It's my dream come true. I hope we're stuck here forever.'

Incurable lust for adventure! 'Very well. Why don't you strip us down and take us our shower, and I'll tag along for the ride.'

Incredulous thrill. 'You'll let *me* run the whole body? Even though I'm only the host?'

'The Lord God of Hosts is with you yet,' Melody agreed. Then, feeling the instant reaction: 'I'm *not* ridiculing your religion! It is possible to love and laugh at the same time, you know.' She was afraid that would not be enough, but Yael's mind brightened. Another advantage of lesser intelligence: it was easily satisfied. Melody's actual attitude toward Solarian religion was more complex and skeptical than the human girl could appreciate.

Yael took over the body, hesitantly at first, then with greater sureness. Melody had to school herself to let go, becoming completely limp in intent, so that it was possible. They/she began to shrug out of her blouse, letting the fabric tear down the front and back. As it was recyclable, it would be conveyed to the ship's clothing unit and merged with similar refuse. The oven would melt it down, and the centrifuge would spin out the dirt, and the jet-molds would squirt new clothes on order into the system. Little was wasted in space – apart from the fact that the whole space effort was a waste. Monstrous fleets that could never do battle . . .

Yael stopped, her bosom half-bared. 'The magnet!' she said.

Melody looked where the girl was gazing – the easiest of things to do, in the circumstance, since the eyes were under host-control. 'Slammer's all right; he's just hovering.'

'That's just it. He's *watching*.'

Now Melody laughed. 'Of course. He's protecting us. With those hostages around, that's just as well.'

'But he'll see – you know.'

Melody had to work this out before responding. Solarians wore clothes, lest the males be sexually stimulated by the sight of the female torso, and impregnate . . . but she hardly needed to rehearse that fact again. 'He's not human. He's a *magnet*. Breasts mean nothing to him – not even so fine a pair as yours.'

'How do we know?'

That stopped her. 'Well, it does seem unlikely. Anyway, he has no eyes.'

Yael was reassured. 'That's right! He *can't* see!' And she stripped away the rest of the blouse and skirt and stuffed them in the recycle chute.

Actually, Melody realized, the magnet *could* see. He merely used a different system. The human body's presence and density distorted its magnetic environment slightly, so that Slammer could locate it precisely. Clothing made little difference. Yael would be shocked if she realized that the magnet could probably perceive her most intimate internal functions.

'We'd better use the john,' Yael said, heading for the refuse cubicle. Then halted again. 'This is an *open* slot. And the magnet's right *here*.'

So the action of elimination possessed different scruples from the mere exposure of flesh! 'All creatures have natural functions,' Melody pointed out.

'That means it *understands*. It's *male*, and it's *watching*. Or *listening*. Or *something*.'

'That last covers the situation best,' Melody said. Odd that a function that both male and female Solarians practiced similarly should have greater social restrictions than one that involved sexual differentiation. Mintakans were not that way: they were quite open about intake and elimination. Sexuality seemed to extend well beyond the mechanisms of sex, here. She had no idea. 'We can tie a curtain to conceal the seat.'

'Yes!' That solved the problem. The Solarian girl was locked on vision; the curtain made no difference to Slammer, but relieved her problem of propriety.

After the toilet, the shower. This already had a curtain, to prevent the fine spray of water from splashing out wastefully. Slammer hovered close, but did not intrude within the shower itself. The magnet seemed to be satisfied to maintain a distance of about one human body-length. It hovered closer when potential enemies were about, hung farther away when things seemed secure, as now. He was an excellent bodyguard.

Something about that very proficiency bothered Melody, but she couldn't place her objection.

'I've checked six officers,' Melody said subvocally to Llume's ball. 'And all six are hostages. High-Kirlian Andromedans masquerading as loyal Segment Etamin entities.'

'I am dismayed, not surprised,' Llume replied. 'I had noted some possibilities, once put on alert. This why I brought these entities to you first. Is it time to take the matter to the Captain?'

'Maybe,' Melody agreed. 'But I don't know how he'll react. These are his trusted officers, after all. If he refuses to believe, it could be instant disaster, six against one. They'd kill him. I'd better play it pianissimo until I'm sure.'

'Yes.' The Spican, too, was uneasy. 'We swim through treacherous waters.'

But if they didn't swim, Melody thought, they would soon sink.

6

Chaining the Lady

action hour revised approaches
—we must delay it a little longer   segment knyfh
remains in doubt   we must improve our situation there—
  quadpoint will object
—droppings on quadpoint!   let him hammer out his
own tunnel   *I* coordinate this effort—

Melody had been finding so many hostages she was beginning to wonder if there was anyone aboard who was not a
hostage.

It was her off-shift, not that she really had shifts. Llume
was sleeping. Spicans might not sleep, but the Polarian host
did. Melody would normally be sleeping too, but now she
was awake and restless. Should she tell the Captain about
the hostages? When? How?

She garbed herself in reasonably nonprovocative attire
and poked her nose into the hall. No one was in sight. 'Slammer, let's take a walk,' she said. 'Lead the way—' She broke
off. Where did she want to go? She really had no desti-
nation.

'I wonder where March lives?' Yael remarked innocently.
'We haven't seen him since we left the shuttle, and so much
has happened . . . I hope he wasn't hurt in the explosion.'

'The crew's quarters!' Melody said with sudden inspiration. She might be able to make a quick survey for
hostages.

Slammer moved down the hall. Melody followed, pleased
to have the experiment work: the magnet could and would
take her where she wanted to go.

The officers' section of the ship seemed to be sealed off, a separate world, yet there was far more to this vessel of space than that. The whole sword-handle was almost a Solarian mile, 1/186,000 of a light-second, in diameter, and several miles long. Much of it was taken up with supplies and machinery and huge stores of emergency fuel, but even the residential levels were partitioned. Toward the end of the handle, away from the blade, was the crew ring, much larger than the officer ring. Crewmen did not even pass through the officer ring when on duty; they took light or heavy gravity bypasses. Melody regarded this as a form of discrimination. After all, March was just as much an individual entity as was Captain Dash.

Slammer brought her to an airlock. 'An airlock – here in the middle of the ship?' she asked, surprised. But she saw that the pressure gauge indicated no differential, so she waved one finger over the OPEN panel. The barrier slid aside, and she stepped through

A smart young man stepped up, saluting. 'Sir?'

'Oh, I'm not an officer,' Melody said. 'Just a wandering visitor.'

He looked at her again. 'With a magnet, sir?'

'Well, the Captain assigned – a courtesy gesture, so I wouldn't get into too much trouble.'

He politely let that stand unchallenged. 'And your business here?'

'I . . . thought I'd . . .' Would it get March in trouble if she gave his name? She decided not to risk it yet. 'I'd like to take a look at the crew's quarters, just from curiosity. I'm very new to space. Is this permitted?'

'Is this an official or unofficial visit, sir?'

'Unofficial. I have no authority, no rank. I'm just . . . I don't want to be any trouble . . .'

'Lagniappe?' he said.

'Lan of Yap? I'm afraid I don't understand . . .'

He smiled. 'Lagniappe. One word, not a place. It signifies – sir, you really *don't* understand?'

'I really *don't*. Have I given offense?'

His eyes traveled over her body, seeing what her demure clothing could not conceal. It was amazing the persistence

with which the Solarian male observed the Solarian female.
'Sir, there is no way you could give offense. If you will appoint me as your escort, and so advise the magnet, I shall be happy to explain and demonstrate' He smiled again. 'Lan of Yap – that's clever.'

'Slammer, I appoint this man as my escort through the crew's quarters of this ship,' Melody said to the magnet. Slammer nodded agreeably. Melody's initial fear of the magnet had rapidly faded. Cannonballs weren't dangerous unless someone activated the cannon.

The man spoke into the intercom. 'Replacement to Officer's Lock number Two,' he said crisply. 'Lagniappe.' Then, to Melody: 'It will only be a moment, sir. Please don this cover.' And he handed her a somewhat wrinkled brown jacket.

Perplexed, Melody put it on. The young man removed his hat, revealing bright yellow hair. 'Now if you will give me your name . . .'

'Yael,' she said. 'Yael of—'

'That suffices. I am . . . Gary. No more need be said.'

Another crewman arrived. 'Take over, Sam,' Gary said. 'I'm going Lan of Yap.'

The other smiled. 'Lan of Yap.' Then he peered at Melody, his eyes seeming to strike right through the jacket. 'With *her*? You lucky—'

Gary cut him off with a lifted hand. 'Carry on, E-Two.' Then he took Melody firmly by the arm. 'This way, Yael.'

As they walked down the passage, with Slammer floating sedately behind, Gary explained. 'Officers have to act like officers, because that's what they are. We enlisted men have more freedom to be ourselves. We fight, we cry, we laugh, we have wild parties, we goof off. So while the officers go slowly crazy we enlisted men get along pretty well. When an officer can't take any more of the gung-ho, he comes down here, off the record, and takes off his rank, and we let him in on some of the fun. We don't recognize him, we don't call him "sir", we just help him let go. It's like a night on the town. No one ever says a thing about it afterward; it just doesn't exist, as far as official ship's protocol is concerned. It's that little extra in his life, the lagniappe, the gift we give beyond the call of duty, no obligation . . . know what I mean?'

'Sounds like fun,' Melody agreed, though she was not entirely clear about the rationale.

'More than fun. Lagniappe is the way of space. You do a little something extra for your neighbor, and in turn he does it for you, because we all are here in space and there's nothing else but the ship. If we don't get along *here*, we don't get along at all.'

'What do you do, Gary, when you aren't . . . getting along?'

'I'm a foilman,' he said. 'When I'm not pulling guard duty. I put on my suit and get out there and clean the blade. It gets pitted and holed and dirty from space dust, you know, and—'

'You go outside the ship?' she asked, surprised.

'Sure; that's where the solar collection foils are. If we just let them go, next thing you know collection efficiency will be down ten percent, then twenty percent. We need that light-power to keep us energy self-sufficient.'

'Yes, of course. All the ships have solar collectors. I saw that as I came in on the shuttle. But Gary, the ship is turning, isn't it, and centrifugal force is more than one gravity at the outer shell. How do you stay *on*?'

'That's what makes it a challenge,' he said, inflating a little. 'I have magnetic soles on my boots, of course, and a safety line, but it's a bit like hanging by your toes. And I can't even do *that* on the sword-foil; it'd tear. So I have to use a support sling.'

'But if anything breaks—'

'I go swinging out into space,' he said. 'That's why I'm careful, very careful.' He guided her into a lounge. 'The job isn't bad, in fact I like it, but it takes a special kind of man. One who gets a bit paranoid about carelessness.'

Five crewmen looked up. Rather, three human crewmen looked, and one translucent jellylike Antarian quivered, and a jumper from Mirzam angled an antenna. Evidently there was quite a bit of physical travel between Spheres, for Mirzam was about eight hundred light-years from Etamin.

Maybe some entities had been mattermitted on a special mission, then left at Outworld to fend for themselves because of the enormous expense of the return trip. If the contingents representing other Spheres were staffed by Sphere-natives, this was another example of the tremendous waste of energy involved in the military – all for the sake of show. If all that energy were only used for more positive purposes – but probably that issue would never be settled. Waste, thy name is Empire, she thought.

'This is Yael,' Gary said. 'Lan of Yap.'

The others smiled in their separate fashions, enjoying the mispronunciation In turn they introduced themselves: 'Adam.' 'Joyce.' 'Manfred.' 'Slither.' 'Bounce.' Melody was glad to find an integrated crew, regardless of the waste. The officership was almost entirely Solarian, but it seemed any entity could join the crew. There would be plenty of Solarians and Polarians in the crews of other-Sphere ships, too, serving under other-Sphere officers. She was sure this was a deliberate policy, to prevent prejudices from arising between Spheres of the segment. Of course some adjustments had to be made, as the atmospheres of all planets were not interchangeable. She could detect a faint odor in the air here; presumably something had been added for the benefit of one of the other species. And the Mirzam entity seemed to have a mask of sorts covering part of its face, much as a Solarian would carry an oxygen inhaler in an oxygen-deficient atmosphere.

'Let's have a party,' Gary said.

There was a flurry of activity. Slither the Antarian cleared a table by englobing its surface in animate jelly. When the flesh withdrew, the table was spotless. The three Solarians fetched food and drink. Bounce of Mirzam remained to entertain the visitor. Melody felt a certain affinity to him, because she was an equivalently alien creature, and Sphere Mirzam bordered Sphere Mintaka. She was sorry she could not reveal her origin to him.

'We do not receive many Lans currently.' He spoke by vibrating one antenna against another, and his height varied as his legs extended hydraulically from their stout tube-

94

sockets. Mirzam was a jumping society, she knew; those three legs were made to deliver a lot of lift, and to absorb a lot of shock.

'Oh?' Melody inquired, accepting a squeeze-bottle of greenish liquid. In space, potable liquids were never poured; one never knew when a condition of null-gravity might occur. This drink had a sweet but strong flavor. 'I understood this was a regular exchange.'

'It used to be,' Gary said. 'But in the last two weeks no one has come except Skot, and the tabs have not been honored. Something funny going on. I have a message overdue from my buddy aboard the *Trey of Swords*. Usually Hath or somebody slips it in the chute during slack-time, but . . .'

So that was the nature of the exchange. Officers did little unofficial favors for crew, in return for a few hours' 'anonymous' relaxation that she suspected had something to do with intoxicants and amenable female Solarians. All off the record, of course. Getting along, in a fleet that never put in to planet.

And the hostages were fouling up the system. Because a hostage was not the same entity as the host. Hath of * had different priorities from Hath of Conquest. What was important to a member of a two-sexed species was not important to a member of a five-sexed species. So far no one but Melody knew the situation. And how would she make it known?

She was beginning to feel dizzy. 'The drink,' Yael said in answer to Melody's confusion. 'Alcoholic.' She giggled. 'Drink it slow, or you might wind up getting impregnated.'

Melody looked at the drink, startled. 'An intoxicant!' Yet why was she surprised? She had known from her host's memory that such things were common, and had reasoned that they applied to this lagniappe custom. She had merely failed to relate her intellectual comprehension to herself.

Suddenly a buzzer sounded in a rapid series of bursts and pauses. Gary looked up, dismayed. That's my call – emergency. It would have to come right *now*!'

'We shall see to your friend,' Bounce of Mirzam said,

95

jumping up. Literally. His feet left the deck. 'Like pogo sticks,' Yael commented, observing the way his three legs pistoned.

'No, I'll go with you,' Melody said quickly to Gary. She was glad for an excuse to stop taking the intoxicant, and she didn't want to have to explain to Slammer about a new escort; the magnet might get confused.

'Can't do,' Gary said. 'I've got to go hullside.' He started off down the hall.

Melody ran after him. 'I'd like to go hullside!'

He whirled on her, harried. 'You're crazy! – no offense, sir.'

But she stayed with him, and Slammer stayed with her. 'I won't get in the way!'

'I never should have gotten relieved from watch,' he muttered. 'Then I wouldn't have been on call.' He jumped into a chute, disappearing from view.

Melody hesitated, then followed him, sliding down through darkness. This crew chute was smaller and faster than the officer's access she had used before. Finally she leveled off in heavy gravity. She was, she judged, near the outer hull, her weight now about half again its normal amount. This was not a pleasant sensation; it dragged on her internal organs as well as her limbs, and her mammaries were uncomfortable. Although it was not as bad as the shuttle deceleration had been, she knew there was no immediate relief, and she had to stay on her feet.

Slammer arrived just after her. He did not seem discommoded. She wondered what the surface gravity was like on his home world. Maybe it made no difference to him.

Other crewmen were popping out of the chute. Gary was already stepping into his spacesuit. It opened like an ancient Solarian 'iron maiden' torture device; fortunately, it did not possess the internal spikes. As he entered it, it closed on him, locking automatically. Melody marched up to a similar suit that seemed to be her size and stepped in. She had a surge of claustrophobia as it closed, but fought it off. She *did* want to see the outside.

Air filled the suit. She found she could move her arms and

legs readily; the suit was so cleverly articulated that it presented no hindrance. It was not one of the invisible 'second skin' suits, but a rugged heavy-duty workman's job suitable for use in the special conditions of deep space.

Apparently Gary had forgotten her in his preoccupation with the emergency, and the others didn't realize she didn't belong. She knew she was taking a risk, but at least it was a release from the growing problem of the hostages. These people were *not* hostages; their auras were so low they were not even aware of her Kirlian nature. That was in itself valuable to know. As far as she could tell there had been no intrusion of hostages among the crew, unlike the heavily infiltrated officership. If she ever had to hide . . .

They crowded into a carriage on tracks set into the inner wall of the outer hull. She observed thick layering of foam-like material, evidently insulation. Heat loss could be a formidable problem in deep space, as would heat gain, if the ship moved into close orbit about a star.

Suddenly the vehicle was moving, accelerating to frightening velocity. The stanchions supporting the inner decks moved past at such a rapid rate they began to take on the appearance of the strings of a giant Mintakan harp plant, or the trunks of forest vines in Yael's memory of her home planet. How glad she was to be riding instead of running! Slammer followed behind, having no problem with the velocity.

Then the carriage climbed. At first this increased her weight, making her sagging flesh chafe against a suit built for a male torso, but soon it lightened as they came into the region of decreased gravity. Melody realized that they had passed the officers' section and were heading into the sword blade – the solar collector. The ship narrowed, forcing the ascent though they remained at the hull. If the job were near the axis, gravity would be mild. Thank the God of Hosts!

They coasted to a stop and jumped out. Now they ran down a short passage to a vast airlock. Melody felt dizzy and uncoordinated. Not the effect of the intoxicant, she decided, but the half-gravity of this region. This business of gravity constantly changing with elevation was intellectually

97

comprehensible, but took some getting used to in practice. The men, however, seemed to be used to it.

Slammer joined them. Now at last Gary noticed her. 'Yael!' he cried. 'You can't come out here!'

Melody shrugged. 'Why not?'

'Hurry it up,' another suited figure snapped. 'We're slow already. Crew B will pick up merits.'

There must be competitive interactions between crews, encouraging better performance. Good system, Melody thought.

Gary hesitated only momentarily. 'All right, Yael, stay tight on my tail. I don't have time now to take you back to your level. If anything happened to you . . .'

The lock closed. Pressure diminished, making her suit become rigid, although it was still flexible at the joints. Then the outer lock opened, swinging outward, and the huge dome that was one indentation of the tripartite sword-blade lay before them.

Dome? It should be a *valley*, thought Melody. But then she realized: Centrifugal gravity drew toward the outside, not the center. The lock opened from a bubble in the sword-handle; the entire ship was over her head. It just didn't seem that way from the inside.

The others went out, moving with peculiar dragging dance-like steps. Melody tried to follow – and found that the magnetic boots of the suit were holding her rooted to the deck.

'Go on *out*,' the man behind her said gruffly. 'Haven't you ever been on-hull before? We have to clear the lock.' He did a tap dance around her and was out.

Melody imitated his motions, and found that only the heel parts of her spaceboots were magnetic; the toe parts had no pull. Thus by pressing down on one toe she was able to draw the heel free without threatening her overall balance. Or so she thought. But suddenly it let go, causing her to lurch frighteningly. Fortunately her other foot held firm. She was grateful the pull was so strong; no danger of falling off accidentally.

Clumsily, she heeled-and-toed after the last man. She was

98

able to diminish the lurches by levering each heel up just so, not too much or too little. The man walked right around the curved lock until he was hanging from the top, then stepped out on the hull itself. Melody, still preoccupied with her walking, discovering how to lengthen her stride so as to make her heels pull up automatically behind, did not fully realize what was happening until she felt the blood impacting in her head. She was inverted!

Now she was hanging precariously from the huge hull. The half-gravity pull seemed like double-gravity; one slip and she would fall into the bottomless well of space! She was abruptly terrified.

But with an effort of will she reoriented. She was not *hanging*, she was *standing*, the great mass of the ship below her. Before her was now the valley of solar reflection. Yes, that was better!

'Here we are in a suit on the *Ace of Swords*,' Melody said to Yael. 'A suit of space and of Tarot.' But the host was too frightened of the vacuum overhead to respond to the pun.

The surface of the blade was mirror-bright, a concave reflector that focused the sun's rays on a suspended trough collector above it. From a distance the trough had been invisible, but now it loomed above like a guyed moon. At the moment it was dark, because this face of the sword was opposite the sun, but Melody knew that very soon that would change as the rotation of the ship brought this mirror sunside.

'It's in the trough,' Gary's voice said in her headphone. 'Meteorite severed one guy. See it listing there?' He pointed, and indeed Melody could see it: the trough bent to the side. 'We have to reconnect that wire before the next pass and tie it fast. We'll have maybe five minutes. If that focused energy hits us . . .'

Melody understood. The light of the nearby star was powerful, and focused it would be hundreds of times as strong, that was the point of this setup. A man in that region would be fried, his suit exploding from the heat.

'Here she comes!'

The sword accelerated, seeming almost to yank Melody

free of the deck. 'What?' she exclaimed involuntarily.

'The blades are geared to orient squarely on the sun,' Gary explained tersely. 'An even rate of turning would lose as much as fifty percent of the available energy due to imperfect angles of reception, missing the trough, and so on. So it clicks over the lean aspects more quickly. Uses up some energy, but gains much more. The whole blade's on a separate axle, of course. We could stop it turning entirely if we had to, without messing up ship's grav. But since the troughs are held in place by centrifugal force, that's not advisable ordinarily.'

'I had no idea there was such sophistication in space,' Melody said, genuinely impressed. Indeed, it was evident that her prior education had been scant. She had thought that the philosophical reaches of Tarot encompassed most of what was important. Next time the *Ace of Swords* appeared in a reading, she would react to it with a vastly changed perspective!

'A thousand years of experience,' he said nonchalantly. 'Look – sunrise.'

Mighty Etamin was rising rapidly over the valley horizon. The double star was too brilliant to look at directly, but she followed its progress by the moving shadows. It shoved its way almost directly overhead. Then the gearing slowed the rotation, causing Melody to fall abruptly to the side, and the star stood almost still.

Melody was intrigued. 'It used to be a fable, about making the sun stand still,' she murmured.

Gary spoke to the others. 'I'll jet out with the replacement cord as soon as the sun sets. Put the safety on me, and haul me in in a hurry if I run late. I'm too young to fry.'

Efficiently they attached jet-pack and safety line to him. Then as the star commenced its movement offstage, Gary took off. Like a shooting star he streaked into the half-dusk, trailing two lines, the jets augmenting the initial boost of centrifugal force. As he passed through the slanting beam of the vanishing star, the light refracted from portions of his suit in a splay of rainbow colors, a splendid effect.

'Superman,' Yael remarked.

Gary angled the jet at apogee just as the star set. He maneuvered for what seemed like an unconscionably long time before coming to rest. Melody realized that space jetting was more tricky than it looked, especially with the drag of lines changing the vectors. Several minutes passed before he got the old wires removed and the new ones threaded. Then the sword rotated again.

'The sun will catch him!' Melody cried, alarmed. And she jumped with both feet.

Suddenly she was falling through space – with no safety line. It had been a natural reaction, but a mistaken one. She screamed.

There was a clamor in her suitphone as the startled men exclaimed. 'The fool! Doesn't she *know* not to—' 'Get another line and jet!' 'No time; she'll be out of range before we can—' 'Look at that magnet!'

Melody looked as well as her slow spin in space enabled her to, though of course the remark had not been directed at her. Sure enough, Slammer had followed her into space, ever-loyal to its assignment. 'But you have no metal to interact with out here!' she exclaimed to it. 'You can't maneuver!'

Slammer of course did not answer. He could not even nod. He had become an aimless meteor.

The sun had not reappeared. Melody remembered that the blade was tripartite; that last adjustment had merely taken it another third of the way around. Gary had been in no danger. No question about it: She had reacted foolishly, and now was in trouble.

'I'll get her,' Gary said, sounding disgusted. Melody turned her head to face him – and her body turned the opposite way, confusing her. She was in freefall, unable to direct her progress. She found herself staring at the stars, some of which she knew were the other ships of the fleet. On the shuttle's screen they had looked large and close together, but here in the open, five thousand miles apart, they were nothings. Long stars were Swords or Wands; the others were uncertain. Her chance in intersecting one was about one in five thousand – after allowing for the three weeks it would take at her present velocity to get her there. She would not be bored, however, as she could anticipate suffocating within one day.

Somewhat sooner than that, Gary arrived, having jetted across to intercept her. He caught her by one arm and they gyrated crazily in space; then he enfolded her spacesuit in his arms and steadied them both with the jet. It was a tricky business, but he was expert. Almost immediately they stabilized.

'Save the magnet!' Melody cried.

'There's no time; the sun's coming back,' he said.

'No, we're in the shade of the ship,' she said. '*It* may be turning, but *we* aren't.' When he had been working on the trough, he had had in effect to race the rotation of the ship merely to keep up with it, but now they were flying straight out.

'But we have to get back to the lock. It will soon be in sun.'

Meanwhile, Slammer had passed them, going out. 'I don't care,' Melody cried. 'We have to save the magnet!'

Gary sighed. 'I'm a fool. I never could resist a plea from a pretty girl.' He timed their spin and actuated the jet. They accelerated after Slammer, gaining slowly.

Abruptly they stopped. 'Oh-oh,' Gary said. 'That's as far as the safety line goes.'

'Then give me the jet and let *me* bring it back!' Melody exclaimed.

Gary shook his head within the helmet and said, 'You are something else!' He was unaware how accurate that comment was. 'You really want to catch that thing?'

'Slammer is a living, sapient, loyal entity. He tried to help me. I can't let him die in space!'

'All right,' he said wearily. 'I'll put you on the line while *I* go after the magnet.' And he did so.

In due course he caught up with Slammer, put his arms around the sphere, and jetted back to Melody. Then she took the magnet while Gary grabbed her around the waist. They jetted as a mass back to the ship, following the spiraling safety line in.

They did have to land sunside, for the jet was now too low on fuel to permit them to stand off. They allowed the winding action of the ship as it turned under the line to reel them in. As they passed through the periphery of the sun-focus region, Melody felt the intense heat despite her suit. As they dropped lower, it abated, until at the deck the ambience was bright, not hot.

'Thank you, Gary,' she said as her feet took hold and Slammer assumed his own mobility. 'I will remember you.'

Gary merely grimaced.

The Captain was approachable. At his invitation Melody joined him for dinner in his quarters. The meal was not elaborate; they had the same tubed refreshments she had encountered before. But the atmosphere was different.

Captain Boyd did not mention her hullside episode, though he surely knew about it, and she was grateful for that. 'It is good to relax with a pretty girl,' he remarked.

Melody *was* pretty at the moment; she and Yael had taken great pains to perfect her appearance. But she passed off the compliment as inconsequential. 'For that, thank my host,' she said. 'In my natural form I would hardly appeal to you.'

'Untrue,' he said, squeezing liquid into a cup that strongly resembled a miniature Spican ship. That design was intentional; the knives were like Sword ships, the plates were Polarian Disks, and a large set of Canopian Wands were used to served the canned salad from an atom ship container. Naturally his interests in the fleet and Tarot would be reflected here! 'Your mind and aura appeal to me regardless of your form. More than you perhaps appreciate. I, too, am a transfer.'

Melody looked at him, startled. 'You?'

'Body is mere convenience. It is not in my records; very few entities know, and none aboard this ship. It is, in fact, a deep dark military secret. But I feel I can trust you.'

'No. Don't trust me. I am not your kind.'

He moved his closed human mouth about in an expressive

103

Solarian gesture. 'How can we know? They needed a high-Kirlian captain in a hurry, and a high-Kirlian anti-hostage agent. A similar situation brings us together. Perhaps we derive from the same Sphere.'

'Unlikely. Auras such as ours are seldom discovered proximately.' That was one of the problems of aura; no one knew the rules by which it manifested. They were not genetic, certainly, but then what *did* account for the wide variation? Regardless, she was not about to reveal her origin, though it was possible he already knew it. Llume would not have told him, but he surely had other sources of information, and he was not stupid. Not stupid at all. She suspected he was smarter than she was, though he underplayed that aspect. Besides, how could she be certain that they were not being overheard, even here? With so many hostages around, no words were entirely safe.

'True,' he said equably. 'I have no right to pry. Still, I feel a certain affinity.'

'It is the aura,' she said shortly. She still had not made up her mind whether to tell him about the six hostages, or even how to express it. The indecision irritated her.

'That too. I am in love with that aura; it is the most remarkable I ever expect to encounter.' He brought out a small box. 'You have adapted very well to your confinement aboard this ship, and I hope soon to have the clearance for your return to Outworld. But I must admit to a certain pleasure in your presence. You are an uncommonly attractive woman.'

'He's an uncommonly attractive *man*,' Yael murmured inside her, like an errant conscience. 'I'd like to take him and . . . would it really be wrong to . . .?' The remainder of the thought was inchoate but powerful: the urge to be sexually taken.

Melody was unable to debate it as she had the same urge. But she kept her voice controlled. 'Captain, what do you know of my mind?' she asked him.

'I have had reports of your expertise in Tarot,' he said. 'It becomes apparent that you are no dabbler. I am inclined to verify the extent of your commitment.'

'Do you want me to tell your fortune?' she inquired with a smile.

'Yes. But not with your mechanical deck. Use this.' And he opened the box and lifted out a cube.

'Watch it!' Yael warned. 'Might be a hypnocube.'

'I doubt I could be hypnotized by visual means,' Melody reassured her. 'My mind is sonically oriented. But thanks for the warning.' Aloud, she said: 'This is Tarot?'

'This is Tarot,' Dash agreed, smiling. 'Each face of it is a presentation, so you can do a full layout in one motion. You shuffle it by shaking it, so.' He shook it lightly. 'Then you set it down firmly, so.'

Melody stared. The sides of the cube had illuminated, each displaying a Tarot image. It was the Cluster deck, manifesting electronically.

The top of the cube showed the key called The Lovers. Dash reached out slowly and tapped the cube without moving it. The King of Aura replaced the prior card. He tapped it again, and now it was the Queen of Aura. He tapped a third time, and the three faces became superimposed, the King and Queen moving into the embrace of The Lovers.

Melody did not know whether to be more amazed at the capabilities of the cubic deck, the facility with which he managed it, or the message it contained. That last was an unspoken but quite specific proposition.

He leaned back, letting her decide. Melody picked up the cube, shook it, and contemplated the multiple faces that appeared, a different one on each side. It was possible to bring up all the faces of the deck in turn on any side, to superimpose them in combinations, or to form split-screen presentations for special types of readings. When cards were superimposed, the pictures merged to form a new scene. There was never confusion or obstruction. This was in fact a miniature, self-contained computer – and a dream deck.

'Do you like it?' Dash inquired with a straight face.

'It is the most beautiful thing I have ever seen,' she said sincerely. The fact that most of her life had been spent without vision as she knew it now was hardly relevant. The perfect Tarot!

'It is yours,' he said.

She did not answer. There was no answer she could make, no thanks she could proffer. No possible gift could have meant more to her, and there was no way she could refuse it. Her mental image of the Star-card returned, but this time it was fleeting, faded. Her greatest hope of the past had been weathered down, had lost its luster, become a matter of lesser concern. Now a brighter star was rising to preempt it.

She shook the cube once more, randomly (she thought), and set it down. One face lighted: the Two of Cups, in the ancient Thoth format. The picture showed a flower about whose stem two Solarian fish twined. From the flower poured twin currents of water that deflected off the heads of the fish to plunge into two great chalices, finally overflowing into a lake. And the written hieroglyphs spelled out the single word: LOVE.

It was her inner emotion, betrayed by the Tarot. She had been taken by surprise and overwhelmed.

Dash put out his hand. Unable to demur, she took it. Their auras interacted powerfully, more strongly than before, compellingly. She found it significant that he had not invoked this power before; he had let her wrestle with the cube and lose on her own. Slowly he lifted her to her feet and drew her body into his embrace.

Slammer shivered momentarily, then drew back to the far side of the room, having decided that no attack was being made on her.

'Wow!' Yael said. It was her maximum response to the situation, embodying virtually complete desire and abandon. Melody herself had no better comment.

Dash led her to the couch, sat her down, and gently removed her dress. Her full human mammaries were exposed to his male gaze and touch, but now she had no fear. Then her primary sexual characteristics were similarly exposed. His amazingly evocative hands slid over the contours of her body, amplified by his aura. Then he brought his lips down to kiss the human nipples.

The sensation became so strong that Melody gave in to a low sigh. Never before had she felt such exquisite physical and emotional stimulation. She reached up to enfold his head and press it to her bosom. Her heart was beating rapidly, and a pleasant warmth expanded in her chest. She wanted to give herself to him utterly, to be consumed by him, to merge, starting with those breasts. She wanted – impregnation.

'God of Hosts!' Yael whispered. 'I never knew it would be like *this*! I'm bursting!'

Dash paused momentarily to doff his own clothes. His host-body was a handsome figure of a man, lean and muscular and well proportioned. At its center, just at the bifurcation of the legs, projected a small limb: the copulatory organ of this species.

And she wanted that organ inside her body. It was pure Solarian-animal lust, whose true meaning she had never before properly understood in the Tarot. 'Thoth Eleven,' she whispered, visualizing the variant of the card that best symbolized her need. Girl astride lion, wide open: LUST.

Yet it could not be. For she was not a young Solarian female, but an old Mintakan neuter. She could not allow herself to bud – or in the present circumstance, to be impregnated. True, Yael had taken her contraceptive shot, but the *meaning* remained. For her, this *was* reproduction; the acts of love and lust and mergeance and creation could not be separated emotionally. If she did this thing, it would be real. Real in the only manner that mattered to her fundamental self-view.

She had to desist. Yet she simply lacked the will to deny the Captain's imperative, or her own. She was in this incarnation of a young woman, and he was a handsome man. He had given her a gift of incalculable value, and touched her with his aura and made her *live*. He had fairly won her.

The man came down on her, his phenomenal aura penetrating hers again, his flesh following.

Melody summoned her only remaining defense: her knowledge of what she was. 'Take over, Yael!' she cried, and blanked out.

7

Taming the Magnet

:: why has there been no scheduled council?::
dash suffers pangs of doubt
:: that birdbrain! we require more forceful leadership summon council::
but
:: do you wish to answer to the force of sphere quadpoint?::
council shall be summoned

Suddenly it opened into realization, that elusive objection she had to Slammer the magnet. He was an excellent bodyguard – but also a most effective jailer.

Slammer was the Captain's creature, not Melody's. The Captain was a fine man, and Yael was, as she put it, head over heels about him. (Heels over head better described the position actually assumed.) Only extreme discipline and awareness of her own nature prevented Melody from being the same. Sexual attraction was potent stuff, and she wasn't used to it. Perhaps it was already too late. And what would she do when she finally had to leave the ship? She knew Dash could not go with her. Love between the species was an exercise in futility.

Regardless, the magnet was not hers. Should things sour with Dash – and Melody's old neuter mind had to consider that possibility – she was in trouble. Love could turn suddenly to hate. Lovers had quarrels at times – this was in fact an aspect of their relationship – and sudden flares of anger. If Dash had such a flare, and Slammer took it literally—

She, Melody of Mintaka, could be abruptly defunct, along with her human host.

'Yael,' she said silently.

'You're worried about something,' Yael said wisely. 'It's heating up my nerves.'

'I think we should tame the magnet,' Melody said. 'Make friends with him, convert his loyalty to us.'

'But it must be loyal! You saved him from drifting into deep space!'

'He tried to save me, too, remember. In Polarian terms, we exchanged debt. But we have no evidence that magnets operate the same way. Do you have any idea how to proceed?'

'I tamed a dinosaur once,' Yael said. 'At least, I tried to. You can't ever *really* tame anything that big.'

'Slammer is every bit as dangerous as a dinosaur,' Melody told her. 'Maybe similar methods would work. What exactly did you do?' As usual, it was easier to ask for the information than to delve for it herself.

'I put out food for it. It was a needle-eater, of course; I wouldn't go near one of the meat-eaters.' Now there was a welling of emotion, as she was reminded of what the carnivorous dinosaur had cost her.

'It ate needles? Those ancient metal sewing slivers?'

Yael's humor returned. '*Vine* needles, silly! Tough, green things. But that's what they eat. Only this one was lame, and couldn't get enough because it couldn't jump. So I shinnied up a vine and cut down a lot of high tendrils. He'd come every day for more, but he never would let me get close to him.'

'Feeding,' Melody said. 'But our magnet is already well fed.' She considered. 'We don't want to take over feeding; it would make people suspicious. What else would Slammer be interested in?'

'Girls,' Yael said simply.

'Oh – are magnets sexed, too? I assumed the "he" was merely the convention.'

'They must be. How do they make little magnets?'

'Oh, there are lots of possibilities. Fission—' But she realized this concept would be difficult to explain, and might not be relevant. 'How *do* they?'

'Maybe we should ask Slammer,' Yael said.

'Slammer might not wish to discuss so private a subject,' Melody said. 'And how would he answer?'

Yael had no suggestion. Magnets were silent, except when they banged into something. They could hear and understand, but not talk.

'They're physical creatures,' Melody said at last. 'They must have needs. If not sexual, something else. Entertainment, perhaps. How do they relax?'

'They just hover,' Yael pointed out.

'On-duty, they hover. But off-duty?' Aloud, she said: 'Slammer, you never seem to rest. I am concerned for your welfare. Would you like some time off?'

The magnet bobbed agreeably. That meant he understood, but was otherwise noncommittal.

'I'm sure I'm safe, here in my cabin. Why don't you take a float around the ship for an hour?'

But the magnet waggled sidewise: no. He remained the perfect guardian – or guard.

'Suppose I walk with you, Slammer? Anywhere you want to go.'

The magnet was amenable. Perhaps he thought she was obliquely commanding it to take her somewhere, such as back to the crew quarters for another romp in space. Well, she would keep refining the directive.

They moved out into the hall. 'Where to?' Melody asked, stopping. 'This is *your* walk, remember.'

It took a while for the magnet to really understand or accept, but finally he set off slowly down the hall. Melody followed, and when Slammer saw that the correct proximity was being maintained, he speeded up. Soon she was running, and that brought her a new human phenomenon: breathlessness.

Abruptly the magnet halted. Melody drew up beside him. They were in a passage that turned at right angles a short distance ahead. It was a handsome section decorated with fiber paneling that showed the grain of its organic state. Unusual, in this ship; elsewhere there was little nonfunctional display. 'Where now, friend?'

Slammer jerked back and forth, then hovered expectantly.

'You want to go that way? Very well; we'll go.' And Melody walked on into the paneled section.

But the magnet did not follow, though she passed the body-length limit. Melody paused. '*Not* this way, Slammer? Sorry, I misunderstood.' She went back, passing the magnet, and started down the hall they had traversed.

The magnet still hovered in place. 'Not this way either? Slammer, I don't understand, and I really *do* want to. Is there a – a secret door here? Another route?'

The sidewise shake: no.

Melody brightened. 'You want to rest right here, where it is so pretty and peaceful!'

But again it was no. Slammer jerked forward, pointing out the way he wanted to go – but *didn't* go.

'Yael, do you understand this?' Melody asked.

'It's a mystery to me,' Yael answered. 'Maybe he doesn't like wood.'

Startled, Melody stared at the hall with new understanding. 'Wood! Not metal. This must be a solid wood section, not mere paneling.'

'Yes, it's pretty,' Yael agreed.

'Don't you see: the magnet *can't* go in here!' Melody said. 'Wood is nonmagnetic. The force of magnetism is very strong, but it fades rapidly with distance. The wood must extend so deeply that Slammer has no purchase.'

'Hey, like skidding on ice!' Yael exclaimed.

Melody fathomed her analogy: ice was cold, solidified water that had a greatly reduced surface friction. Entities that propelled themselves by means of frictive application against available surfaces – such as the Solarians aboard a spaceship – could suffer loss of efficiency on frozen water. In fact, they might become almost helpless, or even be injured by a fall. Skidding on ice – the inexplicable become explicable. 'Yes, the magnet is unable to propel himself through this region,' Melody agreed. 'Yet he wishes to go there.'

'Why doesn't he just *roll*?'

'There is a bend in the hall. He would be stalled, powerless, there, until some frictive entity carried him out.'

111

'Well, *we* could carry him.' Yael pointed out.

'So we could! Child, at times you are brilliant!'

'I'm not a child. Not after what I did with Captain Boyd.' Yael spoke with a certain rueful pride.

'I had no facetious intent about either your age or your intelligence. Sometimes the simplistic way is best.' Melody was unable to comment on the culmination with the Captain; she had blanked out. But from Yael's memory she gathered it had been quite a performance; the man *was* an excellent lover.

She approached the magnet. 'Slammer, I'll carry you, if you're not too heavy. May I put my arms around you?'

Slammer nodded. At last they understood each other!

Melody reached around him and drew him into her body. The magnet's surface was warm and he was vibrating. She had of course held Slammer before, but that had been out in space, and she had never actually touched his surface. Probably that space episode was the main reason he trusted her now. Magnets did not give their trust casually, she knew.

Slammer's powerful magnetic field phased through her aura, making her slightly dizzy. She had been right: The intensity of its field varied exponentially with distance, so that even a few feet brought it too low to be useful for propulsion. A magnet an inch away from metal could not be resisted; six feet away it was helpless. 'Now let go slowly, so I'll know if I can handle your weight.'

The magnet grew heavy. But when he was about half her host-body's weight, it leveled off. The host-body was young and strong; this burden could be handled

'We're on our way,' Melody said aloud, feeling the tingle of incipient adventure. It seemed she was acquiring the taste for this sort of thing! 'I hope it isn't far.'

She marched forward into the wooden hall. At the turn she swung about – and was baffled. For the passage immediately reversed to pick up on the other side. It had no likely purpose – except to inhibit the progress of magnets. 'But you know, Slammer,' she gasped – for she was tiring already – 'you could get through here if you had to. All you have to do is get up speed in the metal section, and cannonball right through this obstruction. You'd have enough impetus left over to roll the rest of the way, I should think.'

The magnet's field flexed momentarily. He understood. Like Yael back on her farm, he had been balked by appearance as much as by fact. And he had lacked the ingenuity to devise an alternative.

But Melody wondered *how* intelligent the magnet was. Slammer understood every word she said, and since it was a nonlinguistic creature, that suggested a very adaptable intellect. Limited by silence and by dependency on metal, the magnets seemed like animals; but granted the resources of the sapient creatures of the galaxy, why wouldn't they be comparable?

Yes, they could be smart enough. If a magnet slammed through the wooden barrier, his act would soon be known. So it would not do any such breaking without excellent reason. And how could anyone be sure the magnets were *not* linguistic? They could have their own magnetic language that no human had bothered to learn. Also, it would be the least intelligent magnets who would be lured into spaceship duty; the smart ones would stay clear. Unless they chose to come, and play dumb, until they knew enough to build and operate their own spaceships.

All speculation, probably without foundation. But she would keep working on it. She had to understand the magnets if she wanted to win them over.

They came to a second detour in the wooden hall. This one incorporated dips and rises in the floor, so that a magnet trying to roll through would be trapped. Melody's arms were hurting now, and she staggered along; she would have to exercise more to build up the human tissues. 'Next time, I'll *roll* you!' she gasped. The magnet could not roll himself up a slope, but she could push him.

Then the metal hall resumed, to her relief. As they came into it, Slammer's weight abated. Finally she loosened her grip, and he floated free. 'We made it!' Yael exclaimed, as if it had been a great adventure. 'But, oh, my arms!'

Now Slammer led the way with impetuous haste. He moved up a ramp, then up another. The passage branched, but the magnet seemed to know exactly where he was going. Melody had to run to keep up.

Abruptly Slammer stopped. Melody drew up, her chest heaving in a fashion she knew would have been an impregnation hazard in the presence of a male Solarian, and looked about.

They were in a storage chamber. Cartons of supplies marked in code were stacked in tall columns. They appeared to contain military hardware. This was deep within the ship, several levels above their starting point. The gravity had diminished slightly as they moved nearer the center. This made it good for storage, as the boxes could be stacked higher with less danger of breakage, were easier to move, and could be delivered to other parts of the ship readily by chute. So this was a well-protected spot, suitable for bombs, laser guns, and such. And isolated from magnets.

Now Slammer hovered nervously. When placid, he was unmoving; here he was doing little spins about a tight axis. What was bothering him? Surely he couldn't be afraid!

Then another magnet appeared. 'Oh-oh,' Yael said, suddenly worried. 'If magnet's can't get in here, how come—?'

Melody wondered the same. 'Slammer, are we in danger?'

But Slammer had already shot out to meet the strange magnet. The two banged together resoundingly, flew apart, and clanged together again. The sonics were deafening.

Melody covered her ears. Not since leaving Sphere Mintaka had she experienced clangor of this magnitude! But it hurt the less-sophisticated human auditory apparatus.

'They're fighting!' Yael cried. 'We'd better get out of here!'

At first Melody was inclined to agree. But several things nagged at her. If Slammer were protecting its human companion, it would not be politic to desert him. And if no magnet could cross the wooden barrier, what was the *other* magnet doing here? Slammer had evidently known where he was going, and expected to be met like this. But why would he go to all this trouble for a fight? What was so precious that he *had* to search it out and fight for it?

'That other magnet did not attack us,' Melody pointed

out. 'It's smaller, and not brightly painted. Not a warrior-type, I think. This is a magnet-magnet affair; we're probably safe.' She was hardly sure of that, but she also doubted her human body could get away fast enough to escape an aggressive magnet. 'And I want to see exactly what they're fighting *about*. It might be important.'

'And you say you don't like adventure!' Yael said admiringly. 'You've got nerves of steel!'

'All Mintakans *do*. Oh – you meant that figuratively! No, I'm extremely uncomfortable. But I honestly don't think we're in immediate danger. Slammer can protect us, and it would not have gone to this trouble to lead us *into* danger.'

So she poked around while the noise of the clashing magnets became even more intense. The ship must be sound-conditioned, otherwise the commotion would already have attracted attention, even from sleeping off-shift officers. The two globes were striking each other faster now, and with unerring accuracy, though they moved so swiftly they were only blurs. What a battle!

Suddenly Melody froze. She had peeked into an alcove in which some electronic equipment had been set up.

It was the retransfer unit, supposedly destroyed in the shuttle sabotage blast. She had been instructed in its use, back on Planet Outworld, because of the importance of her mission. There was no question about its identity; there was only one such unit in the fleet.

Captain Boyd had to have known the unit was safe. Why had he deceived her? Had he also salvaged the mattermitter?

Abruptly the noise stopped. Melody looked around nervously. Had one of the magnets destroyed the other?

Slammer shot into view. His colors were dulled, but he seemed to be in reasonable health. 'So you outbanged your opponent,' Melody said. 'Congratulations. What next?'

The magnet dodged toward the hall through which they had come.

'Time to go home, it seems,' Melody remarked. 'Didn't seem like much of a relaxation for you, though.'

They returned through the passages, Melody verifying her memory of the route. Now she had a special reason to know the way! The other magnet must have been assigned to guard the retransfer unit – it was certainly valuable enough to warrant that! – and somehow Slammer had known. And had shown her.

Why? Why should the magnet *care*? It didn't quite make sense. A Solarian or Mintakan might have done it because of her interest, in appreciation for what she had done in the hullside fiasco, but the magnets had evinced no signs of such sentiments.

Could Slammer have acted on the Captain's orders? But Dash could have told her directly. Why go through the charade of deceiving her?

Melody shook her head as they arrived back at her cabin. It was tempting to draw easy conclusions, but she was too old and experienced to do that. She lacked sufficient information.

But it certainly made for marvelous speculations!

Melody reassembled the manual Cluster Tarot deck thoughtfully. She did not use the elegant cubic deck Dash had given her; that was too precious to share with strangers, and there was always the risk of breaking the delicate mechanism. Suppose some dolt dropped it on the deck while shake-shuffling?

But the manual deck sufficed. She had just identified yet another hostage. That brought the total to nine – of nine tested.

Was the entire upper-officer cadre of this ship hostage, except for the high-Kirlian Captain himself? What a nest of subversion she had shuttled into! And back on Imperial Outworld *they didn't know*.

So many hostages! Could one of them have salvaged the retransfer unit, planted the sabotage bomb, and then made a false report to the Captain? That seemed likely. But that meant the retransfer unit was under the control of the hostages – hardly a reassuring situation!

Could the hostages know about her? No, for if they had

116

been aware of the threat she posed to them, they would have acted against her before this.

Slammer moved closer to her, now that she was alone. It was his way of asking for attention. That provided her with one reason she had not been bothered: she had a very able bodyguard!

Melody was becoming more adept at playing the game of twenty questions, as Yael described it. In moments she had identified the magnet's concern.

He needed to take another walk.

They used a different route, but ran into the same type of wooden barrier. She rolled Slammer through it with dispatch. She was getting a fair picture of the geography of the inner labyrinth of the ship, though that seemed to be regarded as a military secret.

As before, this was the off-shift for the majority of the officers, so there were few circulating. Also, she now realized, Slammer selected the route to avoid people. His mission, such as it was, was his own secret.

The other magnet was hovering at the far side of the wooden passage. 'Ouch!' Melody said, rendering the human equivalent of a chord of alarm. 'Must we go through this again?' But she decided not to interfere. If Slammer and the other magnet got their kicks by bashing each other . . .

But this time there was no banging. Instead, Slammer moved aside, and the smaller magnet came close. Melody concealed her alarm. 'What can I do for you, Slimmer?' she inquired brightly of the stranger.

A much smaller object circled the strange magnet, like a satellite around its primary. It hovered right before Melody.

Suddenly, like a splendid symphony of meaning, it burst upon her: a baby magnet! Slammer had had a tryst with his lady-friend, Slimmer, and now they had offspring. 'Hello, Beanball,' she said.

The mother-magnet withdrew. Slammer indicated the barrier.

'So you just wanted to see your bud,' Melody murmured. 'Well, I'm glad I was able to help, even if it was contrary to regulations. Here I thought you two were *fighting!*'

Yael laughed. 'Slimmer got banged up!'

Again, Melody had to delve for the interpretation. A Solarian bang or bash was an old-style party at which too-free leeway was fostered by consumption of mind-affecting substances. The kind of thing she might have been involved in, had the hullside emergency not interrupted it. Thus a female could get impregnated: banged up. With magnets, this banging was literal; it was their mode of copulation.

'Or maybe balled,' Yael added.

Balled: reference to the Solarian male's reproductive apparatus. 'Where do you pick up all this information?' Melody inquired teasingly.

'What information?'

The girl did not even know the derivation of her terms! Melody had been drawing on her own knowledge and Tarot insights to understand the Solarian situation. 'Never mind. We'd better go home.' Aloud she said: 'Come on, Slammer. We'll visit again when you want to. Goodbye, Beanball.'

But the little magnet hovered close. When Melody put her arms around Slammer to start him down the hall, Beanball remained in orbit about them.

'Now, wait,' Melody protested. 'Once we cross the barrier, you can't return to your mother, Beanball. You'd better stay here.'

The ball did not go. 'Slammer, can you explain—?'

Then she realized: The little magnet was too new to travel on his own power. He was controlled by the fields of his parents. He had gone to the father when the mother had departed, probably to resume her guard duty before some officer checked on it. The presence of the baby would be certain evidence of dereliction of duty. Slammer was better able to conceal and protect his offspring. So he had come, summoned by some magnetic communication, to assume his familial responsibility.

Melody sighed. 'Very well. I enabled this to occur; I must carry through.' Feeling a bit jealous, as she had never gotten to raise a bud of her own, she picked up Slammer and walked down the wooden hall.

Beanball hovered before them, held firmly by the large

magnet's field. Slammer could not move himself here, but he could still act strongly on any metal in the immediate vicinity.

At the barrier she set Slammer down and let him roll to the foot of the hollow. Beanball remained poised in air, not affected by the rotation of the larger form. Very precise magnetic control! At the far end of the barrier they resumed normal motion. Soon, unobserved, they were back at the cabin.

But Melody discovered her responsibilities had only begun. Beanball needed to be fed, and could neither forage for itself nor report to the refueling station for a handout. It was plain that the human officers did not know of the little magnet's existence – and should not be informed. Melody had seen no other little magnets; obviously the wood barriers were intended to segregate the sexes and prevent inconvenient trysts. Magnets were indisputably loyal to their masters, but their primary loyalty had to be to their own kind, especially their children. That was the nature of any sapient or near-sapient species. Culture could be fostered only by close parent-offspring ties. The magnets obviously had a culture of their own, and interpersonal ties – which the officers of this cluster fleet chose to ignore or suppress.

Melody did not believe in slavery. The situation of the magnets made her increasingly uncomfortable. She could not blame this on the hostages, for they were obviously carrying on a tradition that was well established in the fleet. Captain Boyd himself had his magnet, and the Captain did not object to the system.

Well, *she* objected! At such time as she acquired the power of decision, she would free the magnets and give them self-determination. But at the moment she hardly had control of her own life.

So she kept the secret, and helped provide for the baby. She visited the magnet dispensary and acted like a foolish girl, asking for a big chunk of coal as a souvenir. It was against policy, but a little heaving of her healthy bosom caused the man in charge to overlook policy. She took the chunk to her cabin, and watched Slammer pound a fragment

119

of it to dust. Beanball floated through this dust, guided by his father's field, and sucked it in through almost invisibly small vents.

Then Melody picked Beanball up and set him in the nest-box she and Yael had fashioned. Yael, of course, was thrilled with the whole thing, and proved to be quite helpful with the mundane details. She cleaned up the films of ash that formed in the nest, the magnet's waste product, and labored to locate usable metals for Beanball to ingest and grow on.

Melody appreciated these services. She tended to get bored with the routines of daily existence, and she had more philosophical matters on which to dwell – such as how much of the segment fleet was infiltrated by hostages?

Still, it was a novel development. She had set out to gain the loyalty of a magnet – and had become foster-mother to a little magnet. Some bearing *that* had on the situation!

8

Skot of Kade

COUNCIL INITIATED   PARTICIPATING $*/::{}^0_0$
:: where is dash?::
indisposed
:: require election of new leadership   the bird has been stalling::
there have been cautions   a resistance movement has been discovered in segment etamin   this could have caused much trouble   dash feels that premature action can negate the effort, as it did in the prior case
:: the prior case was under dash coordination! a thousand years were lost by that bungling   I put the issue: new leadership now::
concurrence?
SILENCE
:: (fools!)::

Llume the Undulant succeeded in bringing in another client. They were getting harder to fetch now, as the cooperative ones had been accounted for first.

This was a young, handsome officer, a mere 0-3 lieutenant, lowest in the command section of the ship. His aura was in the range of forty to fifty.

'I am Skot of Kade,' he said formally. 'Major Llume of Spica requested me to attend.'

Melody smiled and leaned forward enticingly. She had her most effective outfit on: a front curvature that fairly popped out the eyeballs of the average male Solarian, and a posterior tautness that made him pop further down. She'd have to be careful not to overdo these effects with so young a

121

man, lest it distort the reading. The cards were adept at reflecting emanations of lust.

Sure enough, Skot gawked and reddened slightly. 'Do you understand the nature of the Tarot?' Melody inquired, shrugging so that less cleavage showed.

'Some. I understand you've been doing readings on all the men. They've talked about it, some.'

'I'll *bet*!' Yael muttered. 'They talked about who could see farthest between two breasts.' But she seemed pleased. Female objection to male perception was never very deep.

'I hope they were satisfied with what they perceived,' Melody said aloud.

'Oh, yes!' Then he flushed a bit more. 'That is – they found it very interesting. The Tarot, I mean. Views, revelations ... uh ...'

'Of course. The Tarot is fascinating.' Melody could not resist flexing the muscles of one shoulder to make the mammary on that side twitch. She was playing a game – but the irony was that behind the cynical manipulation of the flesh, she rather liked this innocent-seeming young man. There were differences of personality among hostages. In fact, they were just about like other transferees, except for their alien-galaxy culture and their need to hide this. Were the two galaxies not at war, she would have been able to get along very well with them.

She reviewed the cards, then gave them to him to shuffle. Finally she laid them out, providing a facile spot analysis for each card that had nothing to do with her real observations. She was having trouble with Skot's responses; they were subtly wrong at key spots. Was she losing her touch?

As the reading concluded, she realized: she had been anticipating the response pattern of an Andromedan transfer from Spheres *, —, /, : :, or $^{0}_{0}$. Skot had not matched any of these. If some of the hostages were from unknown lesser Spheres, she would have extraordinary difficulty identifying them.

But she finally concluded that *this man was not a hostage.* In fact he was not even a transfer. He was exactly what he seemed to be: a young, friendly, naive Solarian male of high Kirlian aura.

He was perhaps the only nonhostage among the officers of the *Ace of Swords*. Apart from Llume and the Captain, of course.

'Skot – may I call you Skot? – will you come to my cabin for a moment?' Melody said, raising an eyebrow at him.

'Miss Dragon, I really can't—'

'Yael.'

'Miss Yael – it isn't – I mean—'

'Please. There is something important I want to show you.'

He swallowed. 'Oh. Uh, I'll wait here. You can bring it out.'

'Unlikely.' She took him by the arm and guided him from the lounge.

He balked at her cabin door. 'Miss Yael, you don't understand. I have a girl planetside—'

'Slammer, please escort this man inside my cabin.'

The magnet hesitated. This was a confusing directive, as Skot obviously was not attacking her and so did not need to be moved. And the secret of the baby magnet was inside.

The man became even more nervous. 'All *right*, miss. I'll talk to you inside. But it won't—'

As the door closed behind them, Melody's manner changed. 'We cannot be overheard here, Skot. Slammer has made certain. Here's why.' And she uncovered the nest and lifted out Beanball.

Skot gaped. 'A baby magnet!'

'Now you know I stand in violation of ship's regulations,' Melody said. 'I need some help in providing for this—'

'I cannot help you! The rules of the ship . . .'

'Will you turn me in?'

He gulped again. 'Miss, I'm sorry, but I have to. You know that.'

Melody let a strap slip artfully down one shoulder, baring a fair expanse of convex flesh. 'I'd be exceedingly grateful if you would not.'

123

His jaw firmed. 'I'm sorry. Had you really intended to keep this secret, you should not have shown me.'

He was quite right of course. But Slammer, recognizing the implied threat, moved, jamming the officer against the wall. 'Slammer – easy!' Melody cried.

Meanwhile, Yael had caught on to some of what was transpiring. 'What are you *doing*?' she demanded. 'You can't threaten him; he's an officer!'

Melody ignored the inner voice, though she found herself sickened at her own actions. She was not cut out for this!

She controlled her voice. 'Slammer will crush you if I suggest you mean me harm. He's not so stupid as not to know the harm your report could so. And if he got the notion you meant his baby harm . . .'

Sweat beaded Skot's forehead, but he did not relent. 'I am loyal to my ship. I must be honest. I must report. If you – if you do this, there will be an investigation, and the magnet will be discovered anyway.'

Maybe somewhere there were females who were natural conspirators, who actually liked this sort of thing. Melody knew she was not, and never would be that kind. She was doing this badly, hating it, disgusted with herself – still she had to proceed. 'True. Unless I hid the magnet and told them you had tried to rape me. I have reason to think that Captain Boyd would believe me.'

Skot closed his eyes, knowing enough of the ship's skuttlebutt to comprehend the probable rage of the Captain. But his voice did not waver. 'I must report. I will not be drawn into a conspiracy.'

The man was inflexible! The fear of death was on him but he would not yield a fraction of his honor. Feeling guilty, Melody switched back to sexual temptation. 'It is such a small thing I ask,' she said persuasively. 'A few lumps of coal, some bits of metal, a place under your bunk for the baby to hide. No one would know.' Now she shrugged the other strap down. The material peeled away from her front, suddenly exposing both mammaries in all their rondure.

Skot turned on her a look of disgust tinged with pity. 'No,' he whispered.

She dropped the burden. 'Slammer, let him go,' Melody said. 'He is a friend.'

The magnet withdrew so suddenly that the man stumbled forward. He caught his balance. 'You don't understand. I said—'

'I understand you are an honest man,' Melody said, drawing up her dress to cover her mammaries. She was not disappointed, in this case, that their appeal had failed. 'You will do what you believe is right, even though you die for it. You are loyal to your galaxy.'

He nodded, not trusting her. 'You will let me go?'

'Suppose I were to show you that your loyalty is misplaced?'

His eyes narrowed. 'You – you're an agent of Andromeda? You brought me here to try to convert me to—'

Now she could smile. 'I'm an agent of *Milky Way*. Were you aware of my aura?'

'It is very strong, the strongest I've encountered. But—'

'It is the most intense aura in Segment Etamin,' Melody told him without pride. 'Perhaps in the galaxy. Which is why I was drafted. I came here to overwhelm a hostage. Do you know what a hostage is?'

'No. A kind of transferee, I suppose.'

'An involuntary host. One who is controlled by an alien aura against his will, not under the auspices of the Society of Hosts. A normal person who is possessed by an Andromedan.'

'I thought that was impossible!'

'So did we all. But Andromeda has had a breakthrough. The hostage is aboard this ship. It can only be overwhelmed by an aura as strong as my own, coordinated with special retransfer apparatus.'

'I don't understand,' he said. 'Why are you breeding magnets, then? Why go out of your way to show it to me, then threaten me? This has nothing to do with your stated mission.'

'Because I had to be sure of you without giving away my real motive. In case you turned out to be . . . corruptible.'

Skot worked this out. 'If I had agreed to conceal the baby magnet, then—'

'I would have let you do it. And provided any other implied rewards. But not the hostage information.'

He waved one hand in negation. 'If I had agreed, then you would not have been exposed. But if I insisted on the truth, after proving myself, you could tell me all of it. So either way, you would still be safe – *if* you actually can justify breaking the rules.'

'Brace yourself,' Melody said. 'I'm sorry the test had to be so brutal, but I must admit I am not Solarian, so am not really interested in—' She flickered her eyes down toward her bosom. But she felt uncomfortable, because in this healthy young body she *was* interested in human love, as her experience with Dash had shown. Solarian romance was more a function of glands than of intellect. 'I had to know you were galactic and loyal. Because—'

'Well, I still have to report—'

'Because I have been using the Tarot readings to detect other hostages. Nine of your fellow officers are Andromedans.'

He stared at her. 'Impossible!'

'I know of only three who are loyal: you, Llume of Spica, and Captain Boyd. I still have three to test, but—'

'*All* the men you have tested – hostage? I just can't believe that!'

'You can verify it with Llume. I haven't told the Captain yet. I want to test the rest, and then give him a complete report.'

'You're telling me even my bunkmate Hath is—'

'Hath of Conquest was the first I verified. Work it out for yourself: What normal Solarian male speaks in terms of the serpent-patina of reproduction? That's typical of Sphere * of Andromeda!'

Skot considered. 'You know, you're right. He's changed, recently. I thought he was just out of sorts, but he does act a bit like an alien. Hardly noticeable, but I've known him for a long time.'

'Are you willing on the basis of this, to withhold your

report on the little magnet? At least until you are *sure*? I'm trying to win over the magnet loyalty to my side, which is the Milky Way side, in case there is a showdown.'

Skot shook his head in confusion. 'You place me in a very difficult position. I don't know where my loyalty lies. If what you have told me is true – but I'm not at all sure it *is* true.'

'Then just keep your mouth shut until you *are* sure – one way or another. On the one side is the mere abridgment of a nonsensical ship's regulation; on the other is serious peril to our entire galaxy. While you are in doubt, you have to weigh the consequences of each direction of error.'

He sighed. 'Yes.'

Melody smiled again. She knew she had acquired an inflexible ally who would be subverted by neither threat nor temptation. 'It is an immense comfort to know there is another loyalist among the officers,' she said frankly.

Beanball progressed rapidly. That was probably a survival trait among his kind. Melody didn't know what type of predators existed on the magnets' home world, but obviously early speed and power helped. The little ball learned to hover unsteadily, and could move about the edges of the cabin near the floor. It was instructive to watch him, sometimes he went too far into the center and lost control. Then he spun crazily and dropped nearly to the floor before regaining equilibrium. He appeared to operate more by repulsion than by attraction; otherwise he would have hovered near the ceiling. Of course attraction would have snapped him right into floor or wall, while repulsion kept him conveniently afloat at his natural limit.

Slammer hovered in place, seeming to give off fatherly emanations of pleasure.

Finally she got the last three officers interviewed. All were hostages. It was time to report to the Captain.

But first she had a council of war with Llume and Skot in her cabin, the only place where privacy was assured. Slammer might not care what electronic eavesdroppers were elsewhere, but he was well aware of the need for secrecy *here*, and could locate any telltale devices.

'Of twelve upper-level officers below the rank of captain, ten are hostages,' Melody summarized the situation. 'Tiala and nine males, all officers. There is no doubt in my mind; is there in yours?'

Llume buzzed her ball on the deck. 'None. My observations concur: all are hostage.'

Skot shook his head grimly. 'I have doubt, but not enough. I have to go along with your estimate.'

'Obviously they have concentrated on this ship,' Melody continued, 'because it commands the segment fleet. There simply can't be this number of hostages on other ships! They have chosen to remain concealed until receiving the signal to proceed overtly. That suggests that the hostaging is not complete. They would have struck already if they were sure of their power.' She paused, not liking this. 'Probably they infiltrated this ship first, but need to work on other ships of the fleet. When they are ready, they will kill Captain Boyd and the three of us, then use ship and fleet to intimidate Outworld itself and disrupt segment resistance. The key is right here, because the armed might of Etamin is here. So we must act – now, before they do. The captain's authority, backed by the magnets, should enable us to make a clean sweep of the ship. After that, we'll see about the fleet. But we have to convince the Captain without giving it away to the hostages prematurely.'

'I could conduct you to the Captain for an interview,' Skot said. 'That would be according to protocol.'

'But I'd like you both present, as witnesses,' Melody said. 'You are officers, while I am only a civilian visitor. I need your endorsement.'

'If we all go, the hostages might become aware,' Llume said. 'They surely know who they are, and that we are not of them.'

'Yes. In fact, we'd better not remain here in conference long,' Melody said. 'Suspicion means death.'

'I hesitate to suggest this,' Skot said, turning slightly red.

128

'But maybe a complaint— You are a beautiful woman, and someone might – that is–'

'Someone might make an advance?' Melody inquired, smiling.

'Understand, it would not be – well, you could complain to the Captain, with Llume as witness—'

'Brilliant!' Then Melody paused. 'But Slammer would—'

Skot frowned. 'I had forgotten that. Sorry.'

'Unless the female attacked the male,' Llume suggested.

'Yes, that would do,' Melody agreed. 'Skot turned me down before. I really was very pleased that he did so – no offense, Skot – but I understand rejected human women can become very angry. I might use the magnet to corner him, then—'

'And I would be witness on his behalf,' Llume said.

Skot looked doubtful. 'I'm not sure—'

'Oh come on, Solarian!' Melody said. 'One kiss won't hurt you that much. And it would certainly be a case for the Captain's attention, since I'm not of the ship's complement.'

'But you and the Captain . . .'

Just how much news had spread about the ship? Had that single episode forever defined her as the Captain's mistress? 'Yes, he would certainly want to know! Maybe we had better rehearse it,' Melody said mischievously. 'You are just entering the lounge here and I jump out at you—' She made a fine leap and planted a firm kiss on his open mouth. He had to put his arms around her lest she fall. 'And you try to push me away but I cling—'

'Unlimb that man!' Llume cried against the wall. 'You belong to the Captain!'

Just so. 'Uh, let's make a minor alteration in the dialogue,' Melody suggested, embarrassed.

'The Captain shall settle your hash!' Llume said.

Melody paused. 'That still does not quite—'

'This is a matter for the Captain's attention!'

'Beautiful!' Melody exclaimed, satisfied at last.

'Now, would you disengage,' Skot pleaded. 'Before I' – his arms tightened about her – 'before I forget . . .'

Melody disengaged quickly. There were unkind aspects to this game.

They lined up before Captain Boyd in his office: two in Solarian form, one in Polarian, and the magnet. 'Request privacy in this matter,' Llume said formally against the floor. 'Concerns protocol.'

Dash eyed Skot. The Lieutenant's uniform was in disarray, the Imperial Outworld blazon smudged, his hair mussed. 'So I see.' He waved a finger through the control field on his desk, and the door clamped shut. There were different kinds of doors on the ship; this was one of the swinging variety. 'We are securely private, now.'

Melody stepped forward. 'This is no complaint, Captain. It was a ruse to gain private audience without suspicion. We have a crucial report to make.'

'No complaint?' Dash inquired, brow lifted. 'Slammer?'

The magnet bobbed affirmatively. It hadn't occurred to Melody that Slammer was also a witness, but of course he was. Good. That was one report the Captain would trust.

Dash focused on Melody. 'This must be a serious matter.'

'I have ascertained that all your top officers except those present are Andromedan hostages,' Melody said, anticipating his incredulous amazement. He would take a lot of convincing!

'You are very clever,' Dash said. 'How would you like to marry me?'

Melody shook her head. 'Perhaps you did not understand—' She halted. 'What?'

Dash stood up and walked smoothly around the desk. He came to stand before her, ignoring the others. He put forth his hand to touch hers, and their auras overlapped. As always, there was the electric thrill. The sensation was so wonderful it made mental concentration difficult. 'I realize my aura does not match yours,' he said. 'But there are other things I offer. Travel about the galaxies, incarnation in a hundred unique forms. We can make love while winging through the warm mists of Zulchos, or swimming the nether-fen of Pemch. We can explore the tunnel library of Cluh, where every book is a complex of odors, sleep aboard the candy clouds of Hiaa. And we can read the Tarot in an Animation Temple – together.'

The thing was ludicrous, this proposal of permanent mating amidst the crisis of the ship. It was completely out of context. It was essential that immediate action be taken against the hostages, lest ship, fleet, segment, and galaxy be destroyed. Yet the force of the Captain's aura, mind, and personality were such that she had to consider his proposal seriously. She wanted to throw herself into his human arms, to marry him – never to be separated.

But in a moment her knowledge of herself reasserted itself. She was no young buxom Solarian girl, but an old Mintakan neuter. Like the girl of cinders of Yael's story-memory. She might dance with the prince – but at midnight she would revert to reality. *You cannot fit my script,* Melody thought sadly. *And I dare not fit yours.* Even though she desperately wanted to.

Dash had almost chained the lady – but failed because she was *not* a lady.

Perceiving her negation, Dash disengaged and returned to his desk. 'There is one you did not test,' he said, 'with your Tarot.'

Melody was the incredulous one, not he! She had not yet had a chance to tell him of her technique! 'You knew what I was doing?'

'I know Tarot. I must admit that you are more proficient in it than I, however. It has been a pleasure to watch you perform.'

'But if you knew – you must have known about the hostages yourself! Why didn't you tell me?'

Dash leaned back in his web-seat. 'Let me approach this obliquely. Let's assume the Andromedans wish to subvert a galaxy by transfer infiltration. They possess the technique of involuntary hosting. Unfortunately, it still requires a more intense aura to suppress that of the host-entity, and it is also possible to counter hostage infiltration by the use of really intense auras. Thus the program is vulnerable. What do you

131

suppose the Andromedans should do to safeguard their effort?'

It was Skot who answered. 'Eliminate the Milky Way galaxy's highest auras.'

Dash turned to him. 'But how should they do that? They don't even know the identities of those auras, and obviously lack the facilities to make a thorough search. Especially in the face of increasingly determined counter-espionage.'

Now Llume joined the game. 'They could set a trap. Bait it and wait for something to swim in.' She paused. 'But what would be bait for an aura?'

Suddenly Melody felt a cold premonition. A trap baited for high-aura entities . . .

'Very clever, Dash,' she said crisply, though there was horrible pain inside her. 'Or should I say, — of Andromeda?'

Skot jerked erect. '*What?*'

'The lady is remarkably perceptive,' Dash observed calmly. 'In addition to having the highest aura in two galaxies. I consider it a privilege to have captured her.'

Skot stared at him. 'You, Captain – hostage?'

The Captain nodded. 'Indeed, yes, Skot of Kade. I am Bird of Dash, or a Dash Boid, as you might render it. Bird, boid, boyd, however you wish, for we are winged in our natural state.' He turned to Melody, and now there did seem to be a birdlike quality to his quick motion. 'As you see, you are confined here, with my magnet, in my power. Your situation is hopeless. But Galaxy Andromeda is prepared to offer you most enticing terms, for we are great admirers of aura.'

Melody snorted. It was a gesture the human respiratory apparatus was good at. 'I doubt you can offer any enticing enough, bird.'

'To begin with, the lives of your two friends,' Dash murmured, glancing meaningfully at Skot and Llume. 'And of course your own.'

'At the price of our *galaxy*?' Melody demanded. She knew without asking that neither Skot nor Llume would capitulate to such a personal threat.

132

'You could actually salvage your galaxy,' Dash said. 'With your help, we could master the Milky Way with the expenditure of much less energy than presently projected. Since we propose to recoup that energy of conquest from the substance *of* the Milky Way, we would thus salvage a significant portion, perhaps ten percent of the total energy mass of the Milky Way. That is well worth your consideration, Melody of Mintaka.'

He knew her identity! What an effective trap this had been! The best efforts of the segment loyalists had only procured her aura for Andromeda. Yet she could not accept defeat. She knew she lacked the straight raw courage Skot had, but she had to resist somehow. 'If I yield to you,' she said, 'my galaxy may die. If I oppose you, my galaxy may live. We defeated Andromeda once before.'

'And you might defeat us again – were you free to oppose us. But this is not among your options.' Dash made a little winglike motion with his two hands, as of options flying away. 'You may join us, and salvage an amount equivalent to the entire segment of Etamin. In fact, I believe I can commit my galaxy to sparing that very segment in exchange for your voluntary services. Or you can suffer immediate destruction. I believe you are reasonable enough to select the lesser penalty – for yourself, your friends, *and* your segment.'

He stood up again, moving in quick spurts, his gaze flicking about, his posture almost strutting. 'And I hardly need to add, I would be extremely appreciative on the personal level. You are the finest Kirlian entity I have encountered, and you have a most remarkable mind considering your age and experience. I have prevailed upon the Dash Command of Andromeda to delay overt hostilities solely to enable me to obtain your cooperation. This is how important you are. My proposal of marriage between us is sincere. It can be arranged, with auras like ours.'

Again, Melody was horribly tempted. She would never again encounter an entity like Dash; she was certain of that. There were probably several higher male auras somewhere in the two galaxies, but he also had high intelligence and competence, and was not otherwise committed. She had waited all her life for a male like him. But if he were to learn her true age and status, he would find her a good deal less attractive. Only as Mintakans could they merge – and then, only once.

On that slender, almost irrelevant thread her decision was made. She knew that in her heart she had betrayed her galaxy, but circumstance rather than personal strength enforced her loyalty. 'No.'

Dash sighed. 'I do this with extreme regret, but you are too dangerous to set free. Slammer—'

'Sir!' Skot cried.

Melody glanced at him. A weapon had appeared in one hand – a Solarian laser pistol.

Dash shook his head. 'You cannot possess a genuine metallic weapon. There was no signal as you entered.'

'I entered parallel to the magnet; my weapon was masked by that.'

'Shrewd. But you cannot react faster than a magnet, and your weapon will not hurt Slammer.'

'True. But I can burn off your mouth before you can complete the order.'

What affected Melody most, even in this tense situation, was her realization that neither was bluffing. Dash really would order the magnet to kill, and Skot really would fire his weapon. Melody herself would not have had the nerve to do either, despite the stakes. As a conspirator, as a warrior, she was a washout; she understood what needed to be done, but lacked the gumption to *do* it. She felt weak, as though about to faint. This was not the first time she had reacted to news of a threat with foolish weakness, yet—

'Stand up!' Yael cried. 'If *you* fail, we're all dead!'

Shamed for the moment, Melody stiffened her spine, and fought off her faintness.

Dash would not be balked. 'In a moment the magnet will realize that you are threatening me. Then it will act anyway.'

'No. It is assigned to protect Yael of Dragon. I am not threatening her.'

But *Dash* was threatening her, Melody knew. How would Slammer react to that? Could she somehow . . .?

Dash nodded. 'It seems I underestimated you, Skot of Kade. You were reserved as our lone nonhostage, in case Etamin made a surprise verification of aural identities before we were ready to act. It appears that was our mistake.'

'I don't get it,' Yael said. 'Why doesn't the Captain just touch that button on his desk to call for help?'

The distraction of the question helped to firm Melody's wavering resolve. 'Because if he makes one move toward the desk, he'll be shot. All he can do is talk – and if he says the words "Slammer" he'll be shot anyway.'

'Then why doesn't Skot just shoot him now and be done with it?'

'Because then we'd all be locked in this office with a murder on our hands and ten angry hostages outside. We have to deal with Dash without overt violence – somehow.'

'I'm glad you know what you're doing,' Yael said.

Of course Melody had no idea what she was doing. She had formulated the rationale of the tactical situation only when challenged to do so. What a mess she had gotten them all into! A professional agent would have found some better, safer way to deal with the crisis. Melody could only watch.

'Stand well clear of that desk,' Skot said. 'Llume, roll to the desk and touch the door release. But first use the desk moniter to check the location of the hostages aboard this ship; they may already be waiting in ambush for us. We're going to eliminate every one of them – quickly.'

There, Melody realized, was a leader speaking. While she stood frozen in indecision and fear, Skot was acting with force and effect.

'Your effort is futile,' Dash said. 'Even if you killed every one of us, you could not affect the hostages in power on the other ships of the fleet. If you messaged Imperial Outworld, you would accomplish nothing; the very resistance movement that sent Melody here has been routed out. No nucleus of loyalists remains on the planet. We have nullified them and the Society of Hosts.'

Oh, *no*! Melody thought. The Colonel of Ice Cream and Flotsam of Polaris, betrayed by what they had tried to do for her, for their galaxy.

Llume moved toward the desk. 'Around the other side!' Skot cried, too late.

For as she passed between Skot and the Captain, Dash cried: 'Slammer – revert!'

Skot fired, but Dash was already diving for his desk. He collided with Llume, bouncing off her resilient Polarian torso. She remained between him and Skot, balking the shot. Slammer shoved forward, hesitating, since Llume had not actually attacked the Captain.

The magnet was back under the direct command of the Captain. Slammer had never comprehended the intricacies of transfer and hostaging; he took his orders from the apparent master. Melody's efforts to tame him had been well conceived, but vain.

'Yael of Dragon!' Dash screamed. 'Slammer k—'

Skot's beam lanced into his mouth. A front tooth exploded with the heat, ruining the handsome face, and the Captain fell.

Slammer flew across the room, too fast to avoid. During the episode of romance and fatherhood the magnet had seemed friendly, and Melody had lost her initial fear of him. Now, abruptly, she remembered exactly how dangerous he was. The magnet was no pet!

Dash had done it! He had tried to kill her!

Slammer passed between Skot and Melody and smashed into the wall. The metal bulged under the impact, and one side tore partially free of the door.

Melody stood paralyzed. Now she understood references in the Tarot about 'slow motion' effects in some species during the severe stress. Mintakans did not experience this, but the human host certainly did. To see, to comprehend, to be unable to react ...

Skot fired at the desk controls. Sparks splayed up as the beam cut through the delicate mechanism. Slammer hesitated again. Was it obliged to defend a *desk*?

'The magnet's confused!' Skot called. 'There are magnetic

136

effects of the short circuit on the desk, and it doesn't know what represents the most immediate threat. You girls get out while you can; I'll try to cover for you.'

Melody realized that they had already been saved by the magnet's confusion: Dash had been under attack by Skot, but had ordered Slammer to go after Melody. Slammer had thus split the difference between them, the compromise of imperatives, and so had hit neither and smashed instead into the wall. What awful power the thing possessed!

But the confusion would not last long. Had Dash been able to complete his order, naming the precise action, Slammer would have carried it through. Melody had been lucky – once. They had to flee. What that could gain she could not see, but so long as she were alive and free, there was a chance. Maybe she could hide in the crew section of the ship, smuggle out a warning to Etamin – no, that was no good – well, *something* . . .

Melody scrambled for the wall. Slammer jerked toward her, but Skot fired at the magnet, distracting it. A spot glowed white on the surface of the globe. Those lasers were only light, but what a lot of heat that thin beam packed! Then Dash groaned; he was not dead, but he was badly injured. Melody felt a kind of relief. Slammer moved over to his master.

Too bad the magnet had not been equipped to comprehend the truth! His real master had already been eliminated, supplanted by an inimical alien aura, possessed by a demon intellect. On the other hand, at least now Dash could not give Slammer a direct verbal order.

Melody put her fingers into the crack between the wall and door. She shook the door back and forth. Suddenly a catch gave way, and it swung open. She and Llume moved out.

There was no one in the hall. 'Come on, Skot!' Melody cried.

'I have to cover your retreat!' he called back. 'Move!'

Bold, suicidal, determined spacer! They moved. Melody feared that she would never see Skot of Kade again, but she had no choice.

9

God of Hosts

—so quadpoint tried to assume power!—

he received no concurrence

—I would have been satisfied if he had   then it would have been off my wings—

why did you miss the council meeting?

—ast, I was in pain of aura   I went to the shrine of our god aposiopesis and prayed for insight—

do you refer to an ancients' site?

—do you call them that?   aposiopesis means that ellipsis of communication that one is unable to present   so it is with the ancients   they have so much to inform us, yet they never quite convey it   that entity who comprehends the content of aposiopesis shall be exalted—

did you comprehend it?

—I?   you blaspheme!   I comprehended nothing—

then do you propose to yield power to quadpoint?

—there may come a time when power shifts from sphere dash to sphere quadpoint, but that occasion is not yet—

not as long as you control the major ancient sites, so that you are best able to worship aposiopesis

—you are perceptive, ast!—

yet we cannot withhold action hour much longer

—no, not much longer   but the dash command in segment etamin is about to secure for our use an aura capable of unlocking the key to aposiopesis   *then* shall true victory be ours!   surely that is worth a small delay of schedule—

Melody ran and Llume rolled down the hall. 'Where do we go?' Melody gasped. This human host was good for short bursts of power, but tired rapidly under sustained output.

'Where they least suspect,' Llume answered. 'Let me carry you; this host has greater velocity.'

Llume circled her tail about Melody's waist and lifted. The tail was amazingly supple and strong. They rolled down the hall at a horrifying rate. But this was good: They would soon be farther from the scene of action than the hostages would suspect. It was also painful: Melody's feet kept banging against the handholds set into the wall.

They were going toward the innership storage area, where the wooden barriers were. That would help – except that there was another magnet there. If *all* the magnets were put on the trail . . .

But Llume drew into a separate room on the near side of the barrier. She set Melody down. 'This is where metal for the magnets is kept,' Llume explained. 'They do not require it, except when injured or growing, so this area is safe. There is a chute to the main feeding area and from there are many channels to the outer ship. We can swim through—' She broke off as her ball lifted from the deck.

Melody heard it too: the keening of a magnet traveling at high speed. The labyrinth of narrow passages made it hard to tell how close it was, but it was coming nearer. The sound sent a chill into her.

'Slammer is looking for us,' Melody whispered. 'How I wish I had gotten him tamed!'

'I will divert him,' Llume said. 'You are the most important; there is no other aura like yours. Go to the crew section, seek a communications unit. Somewhere there must be loyalists who have not been caught, or they would not need this fleet to threaten the planet.'

'Yes,' Melody agreed. She could think of no better course.

'Swim well!' Llume whispered against Melody's hand. Then she was off down the hall, her ball touching the wall above the handholds to make a noise to attract the attention of the pursuit.

'Swim well!' Melody echoed, tears in her human eyes. There was something especially touching about the words, suggestive as they were of Llume's origin in the deep waters of her home planet of Sphere Spica. That powerful aura, such a perfect match for Melody's own – why did this savagery have to be? They both knew the sacrifice Llume had made; her chances of survival were slender.

But if somehow they both survived, there would be a debt between them. When one entity saved the life of another . . .

Melody could not dawdle, however poignant her thoughts. To delay was to die. She went to the chute, then hesitated. This course was too simple, too obvious, and she had just thought of a better alternative. Across the wooden barrier, not far away, was the transfer unit. If she could get to it, she might transfer herself to an Outworld host without the hostages knowing, locate some powerful loyalist via a Tarot reading, and give warning directly.

But that could be a very dangerous alternative. In a room like this she could hide, at least for a while, and dodge. The magnet might be fast, but its mass prevented instant maneuvering, however it might appear at close range. Too many turns at speed, and it would tire; she had observed that in Beanball. All things, from civilizations down to amoebas, were subject to the limitations of energy. But in the halls, straightaways, she would be visible and vulnerable.

Unless there were a way to confuse the magnet. To make it look for her in the wrong place. *Not* by sacrificing more friends – apart from the fact she was out of friends, having permitted two to throw away their lives for her! – but by some mechanical means . . .

She looked at the cartons of metal. For the magnets, to build their bones. It had to be highly magnetizable stuff. The magnets perceived people by their auras; a low-aura person was little more than furniture. And they obviously could not discern aural families, for then Slammer would have known the significance of the change in the Captain. (And why hadn't Melody herself realized what an actual strength of 175 meant, in a person listed at 150? The magnets were no stupider than she!) There must be a magnetic component to an aura, a trace overlap that the creatures could detect, that remained stable even when an alien aura of greater intensity took over.

Sometimes magnetism could be transferred by proximity,

a little like sympathetic vibrations in music, or companion analogies in Tarot. This metal . . .

She tore into the nearest carton with her inadequate human hands. It was filled with slender metal rods. She drew one out. It was imprintable material, all right; she could feel the partial channelization of her aura in its vicinity. Ideal for her purpose!

She held the rod by its ends and concentrated. More of her aura passed through it, aligning the molecular structure. It was not much, for an aura was a very diffuse thing, even one as intense as hers. But even the barest smell of her aura might deceive the magnet. It was certainly worth the try.

She set the rod down and took out another. As she held it and concentrated, she explored other facets of the problem. Because the magnets oriented on an aspect of aura, and aura did not extend far from the host, the creatures would not be able to perceive her from very far away. In fact, beyond a certain distance, she should be able to see the magnets far better than they could perceive her.

The trouble was, the halls were metal – and narrow. A magnet could shoot the full length, and if Melody were anywhere in that hall, there was no way she could escape detection and destruction. Perhaps they had been designed with just this sort of thing in mind. The magnets could cruise up and down with such velocity that she was bound to be caught. So her long-distance vision would not help her much, unless she happened to be at an intersection and could get far enough out of the magnet's path before it passed. Even then, it was a deadly gamble, for the thing might turn into the new passage. Or two magnets might approach, one in each passage.

But her charged rods might give her the chance she needed. The magnet could be confused.

Her life depended on it. 'Lord God of Hosts,' she breathed, 'be with us yet.'

'Is it safe to come out now?' Yael inquired.

Melody jumped. 'I forgot all about you, child! Did you enjoy the action?'

'No,' Yael admitted. 'When the shooting started, and I

141

saw that it was all-the-way real, I was so scared I just . . . hid. I never thought adventure would be like this.'

'I was *afraid* it would be like this,' Melody said. 'I really didn't have much time to get scared – but I'm terrified now.'

'That's *my* terror you feel!'

Oh? That was possible, Melody realized. 'Unfortunately, there is more coming. We may not survive.'

'I thought I liked adventure,' Yael said. 'But when I saw what a heel that captain really was, and that magnet—'

Heel: a Solarian portion of anatomy, back of the foot or of the shoe covering that foot. That portion whose weight would fall on whatever was below. Implication: The man's whole personality resembled the crushing force of such stepping-on, and an attitude heedless of the sensitivities of others. One who used and deceived others without regret.

'The Captain's not a heel,' Melody said. 'He is fascinated by your body and my aura, but he is the dedicated agent of a hostile power. His personal interest conflicts with his duty. He tried to bring them into alignment, and failed, so now the stronger loyalty governs.'

'Heel,' Yael repeated firmly, though her mood had changed.

'To do otherwise would make him a traitor to his galaxy.'

'Heel,' Yael said again. 'Not him, now. *You.*'

Melody almost dropped the rod. '*ME?*'

'*You* don't love him. You analyze him without caring. You made him make love to *me* thinking it was *you.* You took his gift of the Tarot cube, but you didn't give anything back. You wouldn't go with him when he asked you. You let Skot and Llume sacrifice themselves. You wouldn't even save our segment—'

Yael halted. She was crying, and the tears coursed down Melody's cheeks. Where was the truth?

Melody *had* had been sorely tempted by Dash's offer; but a combination of factors had balked her acceptance. Not least among them was the horror of accepting reprieve for her segment at the price of the rest of her galaxy. She thought she had done right, but she wasn't *sure.* And how could she expect Yael to comprehend the complex weighing of values that was involved? Sometimes a principle, such as the greatest good for the greatest number, required the painful sacrifice of purely personal considerations.

She took a new rod. It resembled a wand, as in the Tarot Suit of Energy. That suit suggested life and work, while the Ten of Wands signified oppression. But this was not the tenth rod; she was dissembling. This was the fifth rod, and it signified competition and strife. How fitting!

'Oh, *damn* your Tarot!' Yael cried. 'Don't you have any feelings for *yourself*?'

And suddenly, surprising herself, Melody told her: 'My personal feelings died in Sphere Mintaka when I was your age. Now I am an old neuter. I cannot love an alien male; it would destroy me.'

Yael was silent.

'We don't have sexes in Mintaka. We reproduce by budding; any two entities joining to form the new shoot. Our sexual identity is only a convention, a convenience in dealing with other Spheres whose creatures don't comprehend our changeability. As young entities we are neuter; as mature ones we are female until we first bud. Thereafter we are male, to one degree or another. I – lost my prospective mate, and chose never to give up my status for a lesser entity. So I am, in your terms, an old maid. Or as we put it in my culture, I have nine feet.'

'I don't see how—'

'Don't you understand, girl? Your female nature is protected for the duration of your life; you will always be as you are now, only older. If I mated now, not only would I be false to my lost love – *I would become a male*.'

'God of Hosts!' Yael cried, appalled. 'I can't believe that . . . but I feel its truth in your mind. You can't—'

'I can't *love*,' Melody finished simply. Temporarily numbed by her confession, she took up the sixth rod.

Now Yael was contrite. 'I'm sorry. I—'

'You didn't know. I should not have told you. I know the concept disgusts you.'

'I mean about the – the heel business. I'm frightened and mixed up and I didn't really mean it. I really like March

143

better than the Captain, even if he weren't Andromedan, and—'

March – the crewman they had met on the shuttle coming in. Low Kirlian, low rank, an exile of some sort new to space, pretty much an average Solarian. Of such stuff was a girl like Yael's ambition fashioned. Where was he now?

Yet Yael had not responded to the sex-change matter. That was answer enough. The concept *did* disgust her.

Armed with the six rods, Melody moved out. She headed directly for the nearest barrier. Since chance would probably determine her interception by the magnet, her best strategy was to minimize her exposure.

But just in case: She set the first rod at the entrance to the storeroom. 'Ace of Wands . . . the beginning,' she murmured to Yael. 'If Slammer passes this way, it may think I'm in this room.'

She walked rapidly down the hall, trying to keep her progress silent. Her shoes insisted on clattering. She stopped, drew them off, and tucked them into the crook of her left arm along with the five remaining rods. Now she could move quietly.

She turned a corner – and almost ran into Hath of Conquest, the first Solarian officer she had interviewed via Tarot, and found to be Hath of *.

Melody tried to bluff, hoping the man had not yet learned about the events in the Captain's office. She was still wearing her provocative clothing, fortunately. She made a little forward bow, exposing her cleavage. 'Good day, sir.'

Hath hesitated. Then his hand shot out to grasp her arm. 'Yael of Aura, come with me.'

He knew! Melody had one arm taken with the rods and shoes, the other captive to his strong hand. She felt helpless. She tilted back her head to look at his face . . .

And remembered the weapon the Imperial Outworld authorities had given her. Two tubes set within her nostrils, positioned so as not to interfere with normal breathing. She had forgotten them entirely during the fracas at the Captain's office. Some presence of mind *she* had under pressure!

144

All she had to do was wrinkle her nose and snort a gust of air, activating the mechanism . . .

No! Beneath the alien presence was the real Hath, the involuntary host. She could not bring herself to destroy that captive, and she could not kill the Andromedan without also killing the Solarian. Maybe that was what had blocked off her memory when the Captain exposed his Sphere — identity – though by now he might be dead anyway. Or Skot might be dead. Or both. All the skills and knowledge that had so impressed her. The *real* Captain might be the entity she could love, if she ever could allow it.

No, that was untrue. It was the Andromedan Dash that fascinated her, forbidden as that was. He knew Tarot and he had a charisma that the mere Solarian entity could never match; she was perversely certain of that. And it was Dash of Andromeda who had professed his love for her. Why should he have done that, had it not been true? Could she be certain that he had intended to order her death? Maybe he had been about to order Slammer to 'keep Yael from leaving'. She knew now that she never could have hurt him, though her galaxy hang in the balance.

Yael's charge against her had been false. Far better had it been true, for Melody had been on the verge of betraying her galaxy for purely personal reasons. Only her Mintakan nature had prevented it. No credit to her, for her loyalty!

But now she was captive, or virtually so. She had been so preoccupied by the threat of the magnet that she had forgotten the threat of the hostages themselves.

Her thoughts had moved explosively; it had been only a moment. 'Yael . . . do you know how to fight?'

'Are you kidding?' Yael replied tremulously. '*All* backvine farmers can fight. And their kids too. Or they don't grow up alive.'

'Then take over.' And Melody let slide control.

'Gee, thanks!' Yael said sarcastically. 'You sure called my bluff. But I remember when a man grabbed me like this once, and I—'

Yael's head dropped down, then rammed forward into Hath's stomach. The air whooshed out of the man, and he fell back, gasping, letting go of the arm. Yael stiffened that hand and sliced it into the side of his throat. He slumped against the wall, trying to grab her around the waist. Her dress began to tear. Yael shifted her weight so as to bring up her knee.

'No!' Melody cried, fathoming the girl's intent and diving in to thwart it. 'You'll kill him!' For the knee would have smashed into the man's face and perhaps split his head against the metal wall.

'Near killed that other man,' Yael said. 'That was one time I didn't get punished, 'cause they were saving me for—'

Melody took over and ran down the hall. She still held her rods and shoes. 'You certainly do know how to fight! But we won't catch another hostage by surprise.'

'We won't need to. There's the wooden tunnel.'

They had made it! Slammer could not follow. Her nose-weapon would deactivate the magnet guard (maybe) and she would transfer to Imperial Outworld before the hostages knew she was gone. Then Segment Etamin could act.

She paused. How could they act? Most of the offensive might of the segment was right here in this fleet. Andromeda had evidently concentrated here, knowing that the ships could dominate the worlds of the segment. Probably the same thing was going on in every segment of the galaxy. Control the fleets, and through them the Imperial worlds, and through those the vassal-Spheres – what an efficient way to maximize the effect of comparatively few hostages! Once the fleets were captive, the planets hardly mattered. In fact, they could be virtually ignored. The Andromedan technicians would set up their energy-robbing mechanisms and start draining the galaxy, and the planets would simply disintegrate along with their suns. Or whatever it was that happened. Melody was no energy expert, but did know that life in the galaxy would be wiped out long before significant deterioration of matter occurred.

The real battle was right here. If she gave up this ship, she might as well give up the galaxy.

She turned about. 'Hey!' Yael protested.

'I can't transfer out,' Melody said. 'It would leave you helpless before the hostages.'

'I never thought of that! This isn't mattermission; I can't go with you! I'm stuck here on this ship.'

'That's right. We have to make our fight right here.'

'But we *can't*! We'll just get killed!'

'You fought pretty well a moment ago.'

'That's not the same. When a man grabs me, I know what to do, one way or another. But in a long-range campaign I'd be helpless.'

Probably an accurate assessment. But Melody put the best face on it. 'Not if we work together. We'll capture the hostages one by one – and transfer *them* out. Then we'll have the real officers back again. The more we do, the more help we'll have, until we can recapture the ship.'

'Yes! Let's go drag Hath to the transfer unit and—'

'I think it would be better to start with the Captain,' Melody said. 'After we do it once, the other hostages will know what we're up to. If we begin at the top, he can order the others to the unit before they catch on.'

'Besides which,' Yael said in that wise way of hers, 'you're worried about the Captain. You don't want him hurt.'

'I will do what is necessary!' Melody snapped.

They turned a corner – and there at the far end of the hall hovered a magnet.

A thrill of terror ran through Melody, and she was sure it wasn't all her host's emotion. She set the second rod in the intersection and hurried on down the right-angle passage.

'All hands!' the ship's wall speakers blared suddenly. 'Be on alert for Solarian female Yael of Dragon. She is an aural agent who attacked the Captain. She is dangerous; do not attempt to capture her physically. Merely advise her locations; the magnets will rendezvous.'

'Oh-oh,' Yael said. 'We're in trouble already. I'm terrified.'

'So what else is new?' Melody inquired in the girl's own vernacular. What use to continue passing the burden of fear

147

back and forth? They had to keep functioning regardless – or die. 'But my fear for my galaxy is greater than my fear for myself, so I'm blocking out as much of the emotion as I can.' She moved on ... and was surprised to discover that her fear diminished. Did her rationale actually make sense?

And they met another hostage.

Acting on inspiration, she threw one of her shoes at him. The man ducked, thinking it a more formidable weapon, and tumbled to the floor. But as he fell, he bawled: 'Subject spotted in inner passage, coordinates—'

Yael got to him before he finished the numerical designation. This time she swung a rod. It cracked into his head, rendering him silent.

'For someone afraid of action,' Melody remarked, 'you do very well.'

'I *like* action,' Yael replied. 'I just hate danger. Hand-to-hand I understand, but lasers and things like that are awful. And I'd sure rather fight a man than a magnet.'

'Agreed.' Confidence was being restored.

Suddenly they heard the high keening of a magnet's swift progress. Apparently the partial coordinates had given it enough of a clue as to where they were.

The thing came around the bend. It wasn't moving with the blinding velocity of which it was capable; it was questing, not attacking. But Melody was trapped in the hall, and could not outspeed it. The moment it came within range ...

Melody threw a rod at the magnet: rod against sphere. The metal stick clattered on the deck and spun to a stop.

'What's the third wand stand for?' Yael asked nervously. They both knew that if the ruse failed, they were done for, but the immediate horror of incipient death had been blocked out, leaving the minor distractions.

'Enterprise,' Melody said. 'Strength. Cooperation.'

The magnet came close. It was not Slammer; its painted decorations differed. Melody wondered fleetingly whether the creatures objected to the indignity of such designs, as though they were mere beach balls. Probably they simply didn't take notice.

Suddenly the magnet shot foward, then backward, over

the rod. It had evidently expected something larger. Now it hovered above the rod in confusion.

'It works!' Yael cried jubilantly, and there was a sensation associated with this trifling victory wholly out of proportion to the reality. For their situation remained desperate.

'For the moment,' Melody said, relieved. 'But it won't last long. Let's get moving.'

They moved. They had escaped a magnet – once. The luck might be short-lived – like them.

Melody started down the last passage to the Captain's office. She had distributed two more rods strategically along the way, and had only one left.

Another magnet appeared.

It was cruising toward her at a fast clip. She started to backtrack, but she was exhausted from running and her bare feet were sore.

She hurled the last rod with all her strength. It clattered far down toward the magnet, but this time the creature paused only momentarily, then continued on. It had figured out the nature of this ruse. No hope of escaping it now.

Melody tilted back her head, squeezed her nose, and snorted. Would her secret weapon work?

Two beams speared out. One was pale yellow, the other pale blue. They converged about two body-lengths ahead of her.

She pushed at her nose with her fingers. The beams veered. Their point of convergence shot forward.

The oncoming magnet intercepted that point. The beam-light flashed purple, not green, on its surface. There was a strange crackle and sizzle.

The magnet exploded. Its fragments ricocheted off the walls.

Melody hunched down as shrapnel flew past her. One jagged piece of metal struck her leg. She fell forward, clutching her torn flesh as blood welled out. It hurt terribly.

Suddenly she had become much more clearly aware of the specific meaning of danger. Her host's red blood dripping on the deck spoke with a force that matched all the rest of this adventure. This was the beginning of dying!

149

She had slain the magnet. But most of its remains lay jagged and smoking in the hall ahead. Her bare feet and injury made approach to the Captain's office hazardous at the moment. And what could she do, even if she did get there? She had to crawl back toward her own cabin where she might be able to bandage herself.

Yet what a weapon she had been given! Skot's laser had heated only one part of the surface of a magnet; this twin-beam had blasted it apart!

'Lord God of Hosts,' she moaned. 'Be with us yet . . .'

She reached up to grasp the handholds of the wall, drawing herself erect. Hitherto these holds had been a nuisance; now they were essential! She was able to move along with fair dispatch by holding and hopping, but her wounded leg hurt with every motion and dripped more bright red blood on the floor. She was leaving a trail . . . of her own life-stuff.

'I'm not doing well by your body,' she told Yael apologetically. 'Or by my mission. I don't know how we're going to save the galaxy now.'

'I don't know either,' Yael admitted. 'Oh, it *hurts*!'

She was referring more to the leg than the galactic defeat, but Melody didn't choose to quarrel. 'Do you think we might find some way to blow up the ship? That might alert the authorities.'

'We don't have the strength to even figure out *how*,' Yael said. 'We're losing blood, getting faint . . .'

It was true. Only an iron will kept Melody moving; iron that was already melting. She knew that her intense aura had a kind of healing property that enabled this body to continue functioning; Yael alone would have collapsed already. 'Just a little time,' Melody said. 'Get to cabin, bandage, rest . . . then we can think, plan—'

She collapsed.

Melody was unconscious only a moment. The human body adapted to strife. When its systems malfunctioned, it became horizontal. Then more of the depleted blood supply reached the brain, improving its performance. A fail-safe mechanism. Intriguing; Mintakans lacked this faculty, as they did not possess blood.

150

'God of Hosts,' Yael said. She was praying.

Melody lay and listened, suffering a private revelation. The girl *believed*. She really did honor the God of Hosts, and believed in its beneficence, contrary to all reason. Yael thought the god would intervene to save her. No – that the god would safeguard her interests, intervening if that were required, letting her perish if that were best. And if she died, that god would take her into its bosom of hosts and recompense her for all her pain and doubt. It was an altogether naive and charming belief.

'And save Melody too,' Yael concluded.

That simple, sincere addendum struck Melody like the impact of a magnet. Despite everything, Yael had blessed Melody with her good will. Yael *cared*. Even as she lay dying.

'I wish I had your faith,' Melody said.

'You have it. You call it Tarot.'

A second impact, as hard as the first. Melody's god was Tarot! Why had she never realized that? She prayed to her Tarot every day, calling it meditation.

'Yes. I worship the God of Tarot,' Melody said. 'Do you resent that?'

'Why should I? It's the same God.'

The same God. Melody could not deny it.

She gathered her strength and drew them up. 'God is with us,' Melody said. 'I have to believe that.'

After that the journey to the cabin was easier. The bleeding had slowed, and Melody's consciousness remained clear. The door opened at her touch and slid into its frame. Now she realized that it was merely a convenience door and not airtight. When the atmospheric composition of the ship was changed, the air of the regular cabins changed with it, but the Captain's office could be isolated. The moment the hostages gave up their present strategy of pursuit with the magnets, they could trap her with certainty by putting knockout vapor into the air system. They could protect themselves by donning masks. The odds were more against her than she had thought! But if she could mend herself and get to the Captain's office and get Dash to the transfer unit . . .

There was the keening of another magnet traveling toward them at high speed.

Melody leaped into the cabin, hoping to seal it behind her before the magnet arrived. The metal would not hold the thing back long, but maybe she could catch it with her nose-beams as it burst through.

But her bad leg gave way, and she suffered a stab of pain that brought her to the floor halfway through the portal. She rolled and drew her legs up, her dress falling up in a fashion that would have invited impregnation in the presence of a male. She tried to get one hand on the panel as her feet cleared it, but could not.

The magnet shot into the room. It passed directly over her, stopped, and hovered in the center of the room. It was Slammer, and she knew why he hesitated: He had been deceived too many times by the rods she had scattered about. This time he wanted to be sure of his quarry before crushing it.

Slammer moved. But not as fast as before. Melody shoved her legs, propelling her body across the floor – and the magnet missed her. He was tired, after all his searching; he was running low on fuel and had to conserve!

Melody tried to orient her nose, but could not do it while lying on the floor, half on her side. Slammer was coming over her, ready to crush her between his body and the floor, where his magnetism was strongest. She reached up and flung her arms about him, dragging him down with her weight so that he could not get momentum for a strike. She weighed twice as much as the magnet and he was heated from his own exertions. Maybe she had a chance—

Slammer jerked back, but she clung, her fingernails scratching across his surface. Parts of the creature were rough, where his eating and breathing vents were; that gave her purchase. Her feet dragged along the deck, but she retained her hold.

Now the magnet was desperate. He shook back and forth violently, and puffs of burning hot air escaped from his vents. But still she hung on, knowing it was her only chance.

Her face was against his metal, assisting her grip. But she could not get her nose focused on him.

Slammer dragged her to the wall and started banging her hands. Sudden pain shot up her arms; her fingers were being crushed! Then they turned, and it was her shoulder and head getting smashed. Little white sparks flew up inside her eyes; she was getting knocked out. But her albatross-weight was wearing the magnet down; his motions were slowing, and it was descending to the floor. Soon she would have him ...

Slammer made a final effort. He jammed toward the wall, crushing her arm, then spun and pulled violently away. Melody threw her legs up to enclose him, but the blood from her reopened wound leaked out over his surface, and her hand slipped. Suddenly the magnet squirted free, leaving her to collapse.

She had almost beaten him. Almost. Now, her hands, arms, leg, and head hurting, she could only lie where she was. She lacked the strength to go after the creature.

Slammer paused across the room, recharging his power. The struggle had weakened him, but not quite enough. Blood was smeared on his surface, the four scrape-marks of her last despairing handhold forming a fingerpainting. One other scrape-mark curved below, like the scythe-blade of the Grim Reaper in the Death-card of the Tarot.

There was a stirring in the corner. The lid to the nest lifted, and little Beanball emerged. He started toward her.

Oh, no! 'Beanball, stay out of this!' Melody screamed, trying to pull herself to her feet, but failing. The little magnet did not comprehend many human words yet, but should get the gist. If he came to her now, he could be crushed accidentally as she was struck. Or at least he would perceive her demise: a horrible thing for any youngling. Melody loved Beanball in her fashion, and knew that love was returned. 'Get back in your nest! Close the lid!'

But Beanball continued, arriving just as Slammer stabilized. Melody had learned to read the reactions of magnets to some extent; Slammer was about to strike again. He would launch himself from across the room, so that she had no chance to stop him, and this time he would not miss the mark. 'God of Hosts!' she repeated, staring at the friend who had become Death.

Slammer moved – and so did Beanball, leaping forward in an amazing burst of vitality. The two met, the massive and the tiny – and it was the massive that bounced away.

Melody, resigned to death, stared. What had happened?

Yael comprehended first. 'Beanball's defending us!'

Because Melody/Yael was the primary parent the little magnet had known. They had brought him coal and metal, and talked to him and been moved by his little successes. They had cherished him. Slammer had been there too, but more aloof, so was not the primary loyalty. As Slammer honored the Captain, so Beanball honored Melody. It was the magnet way. She was a surrogate mother. And so when the crisis of choice came, Beanball had to protect her – even against his father. Obvious – in retrospect. She had tamed the wrong magnet!

Slammer had rebounded. No physical force from the tiny magnet could have accounted for that. It had to be a conscious decision on Slammer's part. Given the conflict between his orders and the welfare of his son, he had chosen the stronger loyalty.

For Slammer was no longer attacking. He hovered quiescently. He could easily have gotten around Beanball, or thrown him out of the way with one magnetic twitch. But he could not change the little magnet's devotion – and perhaps did not want to, knowing it was justified. Perhaps, despite the ferocity of Slammer's actions, his ultimate loyalty had been based on an extremely narrow margin of decision – and now the lead in favor of the Captain had reversed.

'Are you with us, Slammer?' Melody asked, petting Beanball, hardly daring to believe her fortune.

Slammer nodded. No indecision for him, once the balance changed!

'Then you know that those who sought to kill me are false.'

Hesitation. Slammer's decision had been based on a personal level, not a philosophic one.

'The Captain and the other officers are hostages,' Melody explained. 'Captives of alien auras. Haven't you noticed the changes in their imprints?'

Now the magnet nodded affirmatively. The change had not had significance for him before.

'Enemies have taken over their bodies. We must capture them and send away those enemies. Then your real masters will return. Do you understand?'

Slammer nodded again, more positively.

Melody drew herself upright, feeling good despite her bruises. 'Then tell all the other magnets of this ship. You can do that, can't you?' He nodded. 'We must govern this ship until the real masters return.'

And Slammer was gone. Victory was theirs, for the magnets represented the ultimate disciplinary power aboard the ship. Whoever had their loyalty, had control.

The God of Hosts had answered.

Part Two

Mistress of Space

10

Lot of *

notice: trouble in segment etamin
—details?—
discovery and capture of dash command by enemy
—(chagrin!) who is backup command there?—
slash, then quadpoint
—conceal the news we cannot risk action yet—
council will not favor further delay without explanation
—we must gain advantage galaxy-wide! the situation in segment knyfh is not yet secure, and knyfh is more vital to our thrust than etamin action in etamin now will prejudice that more serious encounter perhaps the backup command in etamin can still salvage the aura we require this has more importance than may be apparent—
under protest, I yield
—appreciation, ast you always were an understanding entity I suppose the fact that your kind has five sexes makes you especially diplomatic—
to call our situation five sexes is not quite correct
—regrets I was trying to—
actually, I regard this as an aspect of the lot of ast
—yes, I am aware of that convention it is a good one, used in many spheres—

Compliments on a masterstroke of strategy, the Captain's note read. Dash was unable to speak because of the mess Skot's laser had made of his mouth. He was missing two front teeth, part of his lower lip, and a section of his tongue; at the moment he was not handsome. *We thought the magnets were incorruptible.*

'They are,' Melody said. 'They remain loyal to their

galaxy.' She kept her voice firm, not wanting him to know what the sight of his grotesque injury did to her. 'Please step into the transfer unit.'

Without objection, Dash of Andromeda entered the box. He made no plea, no threat; he took his defeat in stride. She was proud of him for that – and dared not show him that, either. She limped over and threw the switch. Her shrapnel wound needed proper attention, and she had a headache and bruises all over her body from the fight with Slammer, but the present task was more important. She could not relax until the flagship was free of hostages.

The indicator on the machine swung down from 176 to 151, and the dominating aural family shifted. The alien aura had gone.

'I hope your new host is in good condition, Dash,' Melody murmured. The Andromedan had not been sent home, of course; this little unit lacked the power for interstellar projection, let alone intergalactic. Melody had oriented it on a backward colony planet circling close to Etamin. She had ascertained from Yael's mind that there was a prison colony there that operated very hot mines, where presumably a number of desperate entities lost their auras. The Andromedans would not be able to do much in that situation, but would be well cared for until more permanent arrangements could be made.

Now Skot of Kade stepped forward to assist the man out, while Melody fought again to control her emotions. She had done it; she had sent Dash away! She would probably never encounter him again, and that hurt, despite the chance it had given her galaxy. Had love passed her by a second time?

The Captain seemed dazed. 'Sir,' Skot said. 'You are free now. How do you feel?'

But the Captain slumped, unconscious; Skot barely stopped him from hitting the deck.

'We'd better get a doctor,' Skot said. 'Something's wrong.'

'No,' Melody said firmly. 'Transfer is harmless to the host. It's probably just the sudden release, and the shock of his physical injury. The only available doctors are in the lower ship, and we can't afford to advertise to the crew what has happened here. We can't even notify Imperial Outworld, because the hostages there could intercept the message and cause trouble for us. As far as Outworld is concerned, this ship is and always was completely loyal – and as far as Andromeda is concerned, it remains secretly hostage.'

'More hostages?' Llume inquired. Skot had survived by keeping his laser trained on Captain Dash, thus slowing the organization of the pursuit of Melody, until Melody's victory had relieved him. But Llume's unscathed escape seemed like an act of the God of Hosts; it had surprised and gratified Melody. She liked Llume, and was glad that the magnets had not been assigned to kill her.

'Bound to be more hostages, in this ship and in the fleet. We can't possibly run every crewman through this machine. We'll just have to let them function as they are. So long as they don't know the situation in the officers' section, they probably won't be any trouble. It is a necessary and I think reasonable gamble.'

They ran the other hostages through the unit. 'That may become a lively prison,' Melody remarked. 'But I don't think they'll be able to get word to their home galaxy in time to change anything here, and they won't dare risk contacting the hostages of Outworld for fear of exposing them.'

At last Tiala, the original hostage, came up. 'No,' Melody said. 'You can't go quite yet. You were the bait that brought me here – and I compliment you on your performance. Because of you, the whole resistance program of Outworld was betrayed. Yet there was substance in your lure: we need the information that is in your mind.'

'No,' Tiala said, backing off. 'I don't know anything.'

'My dear, I cannot afford to trust you,' Melody said. Her recent experiences had made her a good deal more cynical. 'The survival of my galaxy may depend on what I can glean from your mind.'

'Please . . . I will tell you everything I can,' Tiala pleaded. 'Only don't destroy me! Let me go with the others.'

'My dear, I am not going to destroy you. I am merely going to make you temporarily hostage, until I have what I

161

require. Then I will return to my present host, and send you after your friends.'

'Don't you understand?' Tiala cried. 'Hostaging damages the host-mind! Look at your Captain and his officers! They can't function. It will take months for them to recover, and some may die.'

Melody looked around dismayed. '*Months?*'

'When an aura is forced on an unprepared host it is like rape. Even when the transferee departs, that host is—'

'Months! How can they run this ship?'

'They *can't*,' Tiala said. 'You'll have to let them rest and give them rehabilitation treatments until their faculties are restored. If you try to push them, you'll only hurt them worse. And me ... you don't have hostaging equipment. If you overwhelm my aura, it will be much worse. I may never recover.'

Melody considered. Tiala's aura, like Llume's, was very much like her own, and that created a natural affinity. She did not want to hurt the Andromedan. 'I am not certain I can believe you.'

'Put me under torture! Compulsion drugs! Anything. But don't destroy my aura!'

Melody was forced to take the girl seriously. As a hostage, she ought to know the effects of hostaging. The Andromedan effort had been more brutal than Melody had chosen to believe, but since these aliens were planning to destroy the entire galaxy, why should they care about the welfare of their hostage hosts? No need to save the mind of a creature who would shortly perish anyway.

'What is the secret of hostaging?' Melody asked.

'I do not know. We were told none of it so that we could never betray it. Even our allied Spheres don't know the secret.'

'What Sphere *does* know it?'

'Sphere Dash. They discovered an Ancient site that they call Aposiopesis, one they had missed before, and there it was. There are many very good sites on their Imperial planet, but they are very hard to penetrate safely. Perhaps Planet Dash was an Ancients' military base or governing capital. So Dash has the secret, and the Council cooperates, because' – Tiala shrugged – 'Andromeda needs the energy.'

'Sphere Dash,' Melody repeated thoughtfully. 'It seems I sent the wrong aura away.'

Tiala smiled. 'Yes. He is the only one who might know. He really is a captain 07 in Andromeda; had he succeeded here, he would have become an admiral.'

'A dashing captain,' Melody murmured with a brief smile. She could have been an admiral's mate . . .

'And I,' Tiala continued. 'I would have jumped rank to 06. Now I will settle gladly for my health.'

'Very well. Answer my questions honestly, and I will leave you that.'

'Then I would be traitor to my galaxy, and my Sphere of /.'

Melody glanced at her with annoyance. Did this alien think she could renege? 'It seems you must choose between health and loyalty.'

'We have a convention in my Sphere,' Tiala said, and Melody was reminded that Andromeda was not organized into segments. Apparently they did not operate as efficiently as Milky Way species, so could not amalgamate into segments. If they had concentrated on efficient use of energy, instead of theft of it, they would have been better off. Was the entire Andromedan galaxy philosophically defective, that they could not perceive this basic truth?

But now she had, through her drift of thought, missed what Tiala was saying. 'Would you restate that, please?' Melody asked.

'It *is* complex to outsiders,' Tiala said, mistaking the reason for Melody's request. 'It is a compromise between opposing loyalties, with honor. One must perform a certain degree of service, set by circumstance. This is known as the Lot of *.'

'I had understood your own Sphere was slash.'

'My Sphere *is* slash. But Andromeda has been effectively unified along Spherical lines for a thousand Solarian years, ever since the First War. We have to a considerable extent merged cultural conventions, at least on Imperial worlds.

163

Sphere Slash has honored the Lot of * for many centuries.'

Melody nodded. 'As we of Mintaka honor Polarian circularity and exchange of debt. I will consider your convention, if I can comprehend its specific mechanism.'

'In this situation, I would agree to answer a number of questions to the best of my ability. You would free me thereafter.'

'I am not certain I stand to benefit. How would I be assured of accuracy?'

'Put me in the transfer unit. The fluctuations in my aura will reveal my state. Under the Lot, I am obliged to give responsive answers without deceit, drawing on what I know of your needs. You would get better information than you would in crude plumbing of my aura.'

That was possible. Melody found it easier to put a question to Yael than to delve for the answer directly; and Yael was a cooperative, voluntary host. The host always had the best command of its faculties. Now Melody was tired and uncomfortable, and the hostage would not be voluntary. It would not be a pleasant chore. 'How many questions?'

'Determined by chance?'

Melody considered again. She didn't want to hurt the girl if she didn't have to, despite her certainty that Tiala had hurt her own host. Why undertake this difficult, perhaps risky procedure, if she had a ready alternative? And time was of the essence; she did not know how much time they had before the other hostages in the fleet caught on to what was happening and attacked. 'I agree.'

Melody brought out her Tarot cube, another poignant reminder of Dash. 'This deck presents Trumps numbered from zero to twenty-nine, and five sets of suit cards numbered from one to fourteen, in effect. Is this a fair range of numbers?'

Tiala nodded. 'It is fair. But the dealer controls the presentation.'

Melody shook the cube and set it down. The face manifesting on the top surface was the Moon, symbol of hidden things. The Tarot was always responsive! 'Select a number from one to a hundred,' Melody told Tiala.

'Sixty-four.'

'So Sphere Slash has an octal numeric system,' Melody remarked. 'Skot, key this deck to present the sixty-fourth card in the present order.'

Skot, not conversant with the nuances of Tarot cube operation, did it the hard way. He touched the surface sixty-three times, watching a new face appear each time, until the sixty-fourth face appeared. It was the Three of Energy, with flaming, sprouting torches crossing each other.

'Three questions,' Melody said. 'Agreed?'

Tiala nodded. 'You have a certain flair.'

'How many hostages are present in the Segment Etamin fleet?'

Tiala concentrated, her brow furrowing prettily. 'I can't give the exact figure. It is a massive effort; Etamin isn't considered a major target, not like Knyfh or Lodo or Weew with their sophisticated center-galaxy organization and technology. But Planet Outworld was the origin of the aura that balked us the first time, so ...' She considered a moment more. 'There are about a hundred ships in this fleet, and I think about four agents were placed on each ship, concentrating on the key vessels. About four hundred total – that's as close as I can make it.'

Four hundred hostages! Melody had eliminated only the eleven in the officers' section of this ship! The whole fleet might well be hostage ...

But still, there was some comfort in it. With an average of four hostages per ship, the concentration had to be on the officers. The flagship had a greater number, as it was the most important, but still it was unlikely that much effort had been expended on the crew quarters. And the Andromedans' overall perspective was of interest, also; they were most concerned with the center-galaxy segments like Knyfh and Lodo, and not with the Fringe segments like Qaval and Thousandstar – and Etamin. It put her own effort into perspective, such as it was. Tiala had provided a more than responsive answer.

If the Andromedan effort of a thousand years earlier had been organized like this, the hero Flint of Outworld had foiled it by pure luck! How could a Stone Age barbarian have halted the ongoing program of a major galaxy? But by the same token, how could an old female neuter isolated in an officerless ship in space even hope to . . .?

I wish I had known you, Flint! she thought. For, in addition to his other capabilities, he was supposed to have had a Kirlian intensity of over two hundred, the only other such rating in this galaxy before her own. High-Kirlian entities were doomed to be lonely.

But she had to get on to the second question. 'What is the specific locale of the secret of involuntary transfer hosting?'

'I'm not sure. But I *think* it is Planet £ of Sphere Dash. It is a hotbed of Ancient sites, good ones, regarded as shrines to Aposiopesis. Certainly it is *somewhere* in that Sphere, and that is where they've set their closest guard, though it is not one of the advanced Dash worlds. It is said to be quite primitive, actually, though the Dash have occupied it for millennia. Now they have a fleet like this one hovering near it.'

Planet £ of Sphere Dash in Andromeda. If only the Milky Way could transfer an agent there, undetected. Obviously no frontal approach could succeed.

Melody shook her human head. The task was virtually impossible – but it would have to be attempted. She hardly envied the entity assigned to it!

Now for the third question. Too bad the Tarot had not granted her fifteen questions, but it must have had its reason. Three of Energy – meaning, in the old fashion, strength, virtue, communication, and cooperation. Three of Wands. How did that apply to this situation? She was cooperating with Tiala to gain information for her galaxy that would strengthen it, but there seemed to be little virtue in it without stretching the implications.

Virtue – the missing element. Was that the hint? Should the third question relate to that?

Tiala looked at her expectantly. The aural indication showed increasing stress. Something was preying on her; she was afraid of that third question. That meant there was something vital, something Melody should not miss. What *was* it?

She couldn't stall; that was not fair play. She had to make her move – right or wrong. Virtue or vice. Maybe . . .

'What have I overlooked?' Melody asked.

The aural indicator went wild. 'How can I know what—?' Tiala demanded, terrified.

Hot on the trail! 'That is a nonresponsive remark. You know something I should know. There was no restriction on the type of question I could ask. You are aware of something vital to my interest. Tell me that thing.' It could be that this would amount to two questions: the nature of the subject, and the specific information; she would just have to hope Tiala wouldn't think of this.

'I – *can't*!' Tiala cried.

Melody frowned, not liking this but knowing she had to do it. She knew Skot was squirming; she was putting pressure on Tiala as she had put pressure on him, once. 'You *can*. Only the manner of the telling is in doubt.'

But Tiala only shook her head.

'You are aware that this constitutes reneging?' Melody demanded, forcing a fierceness she did not feel. Why did there have to be so much brutality to adventure? 'You know the alternative.'

The girl nodded mutely. Tears were on her cheeks. *Oh, my sister of aura, why must this be? What sense is there in it?* But Melody steeled herself. How could she afford to be moved by affinity or pity in the face of the savagery of Andromeda's thrust into the Milky Way?

She glanced first at Llume, then at Skot. 'It seems I must after all make siege against the aura of Tiala of Slash. Opinions?'

'There is *something* she knows,' Skot said reluctantly. 'If you're sure it's safe for you . . .'

'We all do what is necessary,' Llume said with unusual grimness for her. As an even closer sister of aura, she was highly sensitive to the implications.

Melody's course was clear. Yet she was uneasy. If the Tarot were guiding her to this, why hadn't it offered a face of the Suit of Aura? This was surely a matter of transfer, covered by that suit. Instead the Tarot had shown her

Energy, the Andromedan suit. She was about to chain another lady – and this one really *was* Andromedan. Why should the auspices be dubious?

More correctly, why should she *think* they were dubious? The card had to be exactly right for what the Tarot had to say. The focus was on Andromeda, not on aura; aura was merely the means to the information. Melody would have her answer, though she might not like it.

She set the machine for the process of overwhelming. Tiala did not move or protest. Why should this entity of Slash refuse to tell what she knew when it would immediately be extracted from her mind anyway, at far greater cost? She had only to give one answer via the Lot of *, and she would be released, with her galaxy no worse off than it would be via the aural overwhelming technique. For Tiala to balk *now* did not seem to make sense; she well knew Melody was not bluffing about her ability to get the information. Melody was the one entity in this galaxy capable of accomplishing this.

Melody realized that she had a Tarot-type riddle to deal with. Like the pun for dilettantes: What has five suits but exposes everything ? The Cluster Tarot deck, of course. The symbols and meanings were present; she had only to interpret them properly. What pattern fit this seeming irrationality? What was there *about* this Lot of *?

It had to be that the unknown question related in some way *to* this Lot of *, so that the revelation would somehow nullify it. Was this another trap? Yet what type of trap could it be, that a lie would not have fostered better than this balk? Tiala obviously did not *want* to have her aura overwhelmed; her readings showed her terror of it. Why this suicidal course?

Then, from somewhere beneath full consciousness, Melody began to get a notion. She could not quite bring it to the surface, but it was appalling. In fact, it was a thing she very much preferred not to know.

Melody reset the machine and activated it. Tiala slumped.

'You sent her away?' Llume inquired, surprised.

'Yes. We have other business to attend to.'

'But she had not answered the question!' Skot said.

'She answered in her fashion.' Melody pondered momentarily. 'Now I must transfer myself to Imperial Outworld to give warning.'

'What?' Yael said, astounded.

Melody looked at Skot. 'You will have to run the ship. You and Llume.'

'I can't run this ship!' Skot protested.

'Well, *I* certainly can't!' Melody retorted. 'I know nothing of the operations of either ship or fleet. And Llume ...' Again she paused. She liked Llume a great deal, but ... 'Why don't *you* transfer to Outworld, Skot? We girls can take care of the crew until help comes.'

Yael was screaming voicelessly. 'You know Outworld is a death trap! You can't send him there!'

'Yes, that might be better,' Skot agreed. 'There is something about this I don't understand, but—'

The ship shook.

Llume put her ball to the deck. 'That resembles a meteor impact!'

'Odds are against it,' Skot said. 'Meteors strike the ship all the time, but it is extremely rare for one to be big enough to be felt like that. I think someone's firing on us!'

'The hostages!' Melody said. 'They have taken over another ship and attacked us! We have no officer in the control room to keep track.'

'We'd better check it out right now,' Skot said. 'My report to Outworld would be no good if you got blown out of space.'

'Come on, Slammer,' Melody said. 'We have business.'

Llume's assessment had been close, and so had Skot's. The command room's view-globe showed the glowing hulk of a Polarian Disk ship. It had been blown up, and shrapnel fragments were spreading through space. One of them had struck the *Ace of Swords*, but caused only slight damage.

'The hostages must have tried to take over that ship, and been balked the hard way,' Melody said. 'It could have happened here.'

The message-input was alive. Calls were on tap from

several other ships of the fleet. 'This is the flagship,' Skot said. 'The nerve-center of the fleet. The other ship captains need directives.'

'But our captain is nonfunctional,' Llume pointed out.

'If this fleet loses its central organization, it will be a setup for hostage takeover,' Skot said. 'If we don't handle it, a hostage ship *will*.'

'In fact,' Llume said, 'this ship was slated to handle it – as a hostage-command.'

'Yes,' Melody agreed, seeing it. Dash of Andromeda, the highest aura of the hostage force, operating in the name of Imperial Outworld, had in fact been forwarding the interests of Galaxy Andromeda. But for her freak of luck in converting the magnets, Dash would now be in control. 'We have to conceal what happened – not only from the legitimate officers of the fleet, but from the hostages – until we have identified and nullified those four hundred Andromedans.'

'But if the legitimate officers don't catch on to our state here, the hostages will,' Skot pointed out. 'Either way, disaster.'

Melody walked around the room. She had discovered that muscular exertion facilitated the operation of the human brain, apparently by pumping more fresh blood-fluid into it. '*I* can't bluff either group. I'm no space entity or military entity, just a visiting non-Solarian civilian. Skot . . .'

He shook his head. 'I'm only 03. I was never privy to command decisions, and never a hostage. I'd flub it, both counts.'

Melody faced Llume. 'But you're 04, and you have associated with all the officers, and substituted for most of them at one time or another. You know their jobs about as well as they do. And you helped me run down the hostages; you know where they're from, how they react. You could bluff other hostages – for a while; at least until we have a better idea of where we stand.'

Llume glanced at the Polarian hulk in the globe again. Her Polarian host-state had to affect her reaction. 'Yes . . . I could . . . for a while.'

'Then you handle communications. Tell them Captain Boyd is occupied with pressing internal problems – the hostages will know why you can't mention it on the fleet net – so you are handling coordinations. Keep the ships reassured; don't let anyone panic. Meanwhile, Skot and I will try to get one of the *real* officers into operative condition. I know it is not good for the health of an ex-hostage, but this is an overriding emergency. With luck, in a couple of hours we'll have Boyd or someone else able to put up at least the semblance of competency. We must keep up appearances.'

Llume glowed briefly, knowing that was a futile hope. The officers would hardly be ready that soon. But she had the grace not to say so. 'I will try to coordinate,' she agreed. 'The secret must be kept.'

'Come on, Slammer,' Melody said. 'We have to revive your master.' And she led Skot of Kade away too.

But she didn't go to the infirmary. She went back to the transfer unit and set it for her own aura.

'I don't understand,' Skot said. 'If you go to Outworld now, the fleet – I thought we had agreed that I—'

'Not to Outworld. The hostages have taken over the key positions there. I never intended to ship you there, either.'

'But this unit won't reach farther—' He paused. 'You're not going after the Andromedans we sent to the sunside mines!'

She shuddered. 'No – they'd crucify me, literally!' She took his hand. 'Skot of Kade, I need your opinion. My aura is supposed to be able, with the aid of special equipment, to overwhelm a hostage of one-quarter my own intensity. Do you think this is possible at a short distance as well as in close proximity?'

'I'm no transfer expert. But I don't see why not. Transfer is essentially a long-distance mechanism, and the Andromedans did it all the way from their galaxy, a million light years away. But what relevance—'

'You see, I wouldn't want to make a hostage of one of our own people, and damage her as the Andromedans did. But I wouldn't have such scruples about an already existent hostage. That host has already been hurt, and the Andromedan deserves no better.'

Skot gaped. 'Yael, you're not thinking of—'

'I am Melody of Mintaka. No need to conceal it anymore. Skot, someone has to identify and deal with the hostages on the other ships. We can't let those ships fall into enemy hands.'

'If I transfer to Outworld, maybe I can—'

'No! That would only give us away. I need you here. I'm going to transfer to some of the other ships, but I don't want anyone else to know. My host, the real Yael of Dragon, will conceal my absence, but you will have to help her, because she knows no more about space than I do. If she makes a slip, your ingenuity will be needed.'

Skot shook his head. 'Llume's the only one who might catch on, and we don't need to worry about—'

Melody put her hand on his arm, turning him about to face her. 'I don't want Llume to know. It could only distract her at a very inopportune time.'

Skot looked down. 'Oh. Yes. Of course.' Then he looked into her eyes and she knew she had a conquest if she wanted it. 'Just how dangerous *is* this mission?'

'No worse than my mission on *this* ship.'

'Thanks for the reassurance,' he said wryly. 'You're limping, bruised, and bloodshot, lucky to be alive. You look like a worn-out witch. And you say—'

Melody reached up to kiss him. 'The physical violence has not affected my aura. This is the only transfer unit in the Fleet, so I will have to return in another host. Will you recognize me as a lovely Polarian?'

He had to smile. 'No problem,' he said, letting her go after a slight hesitation. 'I'll know your aura. But we'll need a code word when you come in by shuttle. I can handle that part of it; ship-to-shuttle is on a different beam, not part of the fleet net, and Llume won't even know about it.'

'Lot of *,' Melody said, smiling.

He nodded. 'Lot of * it is. If I don't get that word, I'll treat anything that comes in as a hostile craft. So you make sure you—'

'Don't worry! I've seen how you shoot!'

Melody reviewed the transfer unit procedure with him, and they oriented on the nearest ship – another giant Disk of Polaris. Then she entered the unit.

'Oh, one thing,' Skot said before he activated the mechanism. 'Is your host a nice person?'

'You'll find out!' Melody said, laughing merrily.

11

Mating the Impact

the other members of the council are becoming restive
—I am aware of it   they lack the patience or perspective—
their position is comprehensible, dash we have a thoroughly worked-out plan of action, well implemented   it requires only overt action at this stage, before too many individuals of the subject galaxy become aware of the hostages among them   already our delay seems to be causing regression in segment etamin
—you are very practical, *   I suppose an explanation is in order—
it would be appreciated
—when I prayed to aposiopesis, I was granted a revelation, a small share of the nature of ultimate reality   it is this: we are very like our sister galaxy—
that hardly seems relevant
—it is relevant, ast   our leading spheres are very like theirs   our / resembles their sword cultures, that the temple of tarot calls the suit of gas, of transformation   both cultures employ laser weapons and have the thrust mentality
—

but our slashes roll, while their sword cultures such as the solarians employ frictive propulsion
—rolling is frictive too   but physique is of little significance   it is the basic nature that matters   our slashes cut enemies to pieces with their knife edges and lasers, and their solarian swords do the same   it was that similarity of nature that caused the archcriminal flint of etamin to pervert our highest-kirlian agent, thereby blunting our first effort   he was of sol, she of slash   had we anticipated that

174

affinity of types we should have modified our policy and prevailed then—

perhaps so   yet the other cultures do not

—but they *do*, ast!   our dash resembles their wands, even to the physical aspects of deriving from flying creatures, even to the social aspect of utilizing a companion-species beneficially, though I deem our £ superior to their huma- noids   our ast resemble their disks, quadpoint is like their cups with only the medium of rock exchanged for that of water   our duocirc are like their auras being magnetically based—

naturally all species fall into certain broad functional classifications   this has long been known

—the resemblances are too strong, too fundamental to be coincidence!   they are in fact our brother species   if we destroy them, how may we answer to aposiopesis?   shall we not ourselves be destroyed?—

yet our advancing civilization depends on this

—that depends on how we define civilization   progress based on the destruction of a kindred culture—

I think it necessary for you to vacate your leadership the council will not accept your views

—we must cease this attack against our neighbor   we must seek accommodation instead   together the galaxies can comprehend aposiopesis   is this not clear?—

I regret it is not

She stepped guardedly out of the unit. If the hostages were alert, she could find herself in immediate difficulties.

Surprisingly, she was in a human body. And the ship seemed to be identical to the one she had just left.

'Melody!' a voice cried. 'Or is it – Yael?'

Melody did a doubletake. 'Oh, no! It didn't work!'

'You didn't go?' Skot asked, looking relieved.

'Let me see. It doesn't have to mean a malfunction. There has to be a suitable host at the other end. In this case, a female. If there were none aboard the ship, I should ... bounce.'

'Oh. Yes, of course. That tells us something.'

'It does. If you have any communication with the *Polaris*, insist on talking with a female. You will know whether she's a hostage or not.'

'Maybe we can check them all out that way.'

'No use. With almost four hundred hostages remaining in the fleet we know a good many ships are suspect, and we don't want to alert them by checking. And it occurs to me there could be a number of female hostages whose auras are over one quarter intensity of mine, so I would not overwhelm them anyway. I have to get to those ships and eliminate the hostages directly. Otherwise the hostage ships won't hesitate to blast the loyal ships out of space. That may have happened in one case already.'

He nodded gravely.

They reoriented on a Cup of Spica, the *Four of Cups*. Skot activated the unit again. And Melody . . .

Found herself in a battle for her life.

It had not occurred to her that her potential host might resist. The transfer to Yael of Dragon had been so simple, but there was a deadly difference between a voluntary and an involuntary host. And that helped explain why the Andromedans destroyed the minds of their hosts: They *had* to, because the hosts resisted as long as they were able.

She was in the body of a Spican Impact, a fin-propelled creature of the deep sea. Spicans were neuter or triplesexed, depending on one's viewpoint. There were three fixed physical types, but the sexual role of each was determined by the manner in which a trio came together. Any two could interact without sexual excitation, but the arrival of the third sex acted as a catalyst, and there was immediate and explosive mergeance. More correctly, *im*plosive mergeance.

Melody, as a basically neuter Mintakan, could occupy any Spican host. But the hostage she happened to orient on possessed a female Andromedan aura. So this had to be considered a female form.

But it was a spitfire! It tried to push her out – but of course there was nowhere to go, and its aural intensity was less than a quarter her own. It had prior possession of the host, however, which gave it considerable initial leverage. The battle seemed to be about even.

: : Who? : : the alien female demanded, ramming again.

No concealment necessary or possible, here! 'Melody of Mintaka – Galaxy Milky Way.' She let her aura flow around the thrusts, seeking the living heart of the host. This was aura against aura, but in certain respects it resembled a physical battle.

: : Chisel of quadpoint : : the alien said : : Galaxy Andromeda. Now get *out* of my *host*! : : The emphasis was contributed by two more ferocious shocks.

The alien mode of communication was intriguing, distinct from all Milky Way modes Melody knew of. But she had no chance to cogitate on that at the moment. 'Sorry, Chisel. You took a host against her will. You must now suffer the same conquest.' And Melody flowed again, enveloping and nullifying the thrusts.

The Impact body spun erratically in the water as now one mind, now the other activated its mechanisms.

Gradually Melody's superior aura asserted itself. In a pure Kirlian contest, no entity of this galaxy could match her – and probably none of Andromeda either. She was *the* Kirlian entity, and now she appreciated the translation of her aura into raw power. She infiltrated, permeating Chisel's lesser aura, nullifying it, reaching ever deeper into the essence of the Spican host.

Breakthrough! Melody found herself within the memory of the Andromedan. For a moment she experienced the state of : : consciousness. She was a quadpoint, moving through the warm deep layers of lithospheric rock. This was the habitable zone of the planet. Far above were layers of frozen ammonia, surmounted by turbulent frigid gases. Sometimes a quake opened a fissure and let in some of that awful gas, a reminder of the hell that was the surface. At other times boiling lava welled up from the nether depths – the opposite hell. It took an alert, resourceful entity to avoid both hazards long enough to reproduce itself. Yet it was these intrusions of gas that provided the pockets necessary for breath, and the hardened lava was the food of subsequent generations. Without both hazards, life within this planet would soon die out. Ironic.

Melody didn't like this. She was invading another entity's intimate privacy, committing a kind of rape. Against an unknown enemy, she could do it, but this was becoming a known, understood entity – one who had feelings and comprehensible motives. It hurt to hurt her.

Through the rock, searching for sustenance. It was a pleasure to strike forward with the tongs, spearing into the hard vein, dislodging it, sifting out the nutrient element, imbibing it through the tong-orifice, heaving the refuse sand back to block the passage. To fail to plug the tunnel behind would be a severe breach of manner and potential hazard: open passages were apt conduits for descending surface gas.

Another block of rock came loose, leaving the : : imprint of her chisels: a neat extraction. This was a good vein! But in a way it was also bad, because she would fill herself faster, and have to report to the Imperial Annex for her next tour of duty. There were rumblings of excitement shaking the Galaxy of Andromeda (the name-concept differed from Melody's, of course, but the identity was clear), but that meant difficult duty, probably transfer duty, for one of her aura. Transfer meant danger, and the occupation of strange, unpleasant hostile bodies. But she really had no choice. Duty to one's galaxy . . .

Melody clamped down. The victory was hers. Yet it was too bad, this suppression of sapient, feeling sentience. A rock-boring entity, with pronged multiple-function extensions that speared into solid stone, powdered it, tossed it, and also were walking feet. An intriguing lifestyle, comprehensible. There were probably similar species in the Milky Way galaxy.

Then Melody made contact with the host entity, the Spican Impact, who was in a sorry state. The aural overwhelming involved in hostaging had severely damaged her psyche, and the Andromedan had driven her mercilessly, the suppression had been severe, much harsher than it needed to be. Chisel of quadpoint had taken care to preserve only the technical life of the host aura, so that the advantage of a living host would not be lost. Health had been superfluous. When the alien departed, only the shell of the Impact would remain.

This was what had happened to the hostages aboard the flagship. It was not merely that the hosts had fought; they had been deliberately brutalized into schizophrenia for the convenience of the invaders. The Lady Andromeda was a harsh mistress! Without question she *needed* to be chained!

Melody swam about, getting the feel of her new body as she explored the host and hostage minds for information. Apparently there were five hostages aboard this ship; the other four were male, three Sibilants, one Undulant. They had not yet taken over the ship, but at the signal from the command ship they would kill the Spican captain and his loyal officers and assume control.

This was, as Yael would have put it, a gold mine! The Andromedan code signal for action hour was 'Six of Scepters'. A Tarot code! Scepter was another term for Wand, a more royal-sounding variant. The Suit of Energy was associated with Galaxy Andromeda, the greatest energy thieves in the universe. And the Six of Energy signified victory, victory for Andromeda – in a simple code few if any Milky Wayan space officers would comprehend.

She now had the information she would have gotten from Tiala – or *did* she? There was no hint here of the thing she suspected. But of course Chisel of : : had no need to know the details of the larger plan; she was concerned only with her ship. So Melody's suspicion could still be valid. She hoped not.

Now she had a job. She had to eliminate four more hostages, advise the Spican captain of the situation, and return to the *Ace of Swords*. Then go out again – and again. She had no hope of neutralizing every hostage in the fleet, but she had to build a nucleus of secure ships for the moment the 'Six of Scepters' was invoked. With luck they would be able to postpone that order indefinitely, since it probably was supposed to come through Dash. But it might be a generalized signal from Andromeda itself, unstoppable. Then it would be—

She tried to shake her human head, and of course it didn't work, as she wasn't human any more. So she played a complex chord of mixed emotions – and that didn't work either. Her change of host and the battle with an alien aura had unsettled her, evoking inopportune responses. Her Impact body merely expanded momentarily, causing her to jerk toward the surface of the sea – only there was no surface.

The ship was a huge cup, the hollow of it oriented on the near star, Etamin, reflecting its rays of light into a focal point for collection and conversion to ship's power. Power, as always, was crucial. Every ship of space had two prime requirements, and the first was power. The Swords of Sol slashed against sunlight, the Disks of Polaris intercepted it, the Cups of Spica dipped it. Small ships could operate on stored power, but they reported often to their host ships for recharging. The big vessels had to have a continuing influx of energy, and only the stars could provide that. Thus the big fleets were always parked near stars, their orbits eliminating the need for drivepower and their shapes serving as solar collectors. They might resemble the five suits of the Tarot, but this was no mere fancy; these were efficient shapes for prolonged action in space. Any interstellar ship that did not possess substantial light-collection apparatus was suspect; it could not support living entities directly.

The other requirement for spaceships was gravity. No better mechanisms had been discovered for controlled artificial gravity than centrifugal force. So every major ship had to spin, which meant that it had to have an axis of rotation and be symmetrical; an off-balance ship could not spin effectively. While there was no need for streamlining in space, the requirements of symmetry and light collection produced ships that were fairly simple in outline, and smooth.

Gravity was less of an immediate factor in the water-medium of this ship, since the liquid was all-supporting. But gravity was still necessary to avoid the chore of pressurizing the entire ship, and to provide orientation. There had to be an 'up' and a 'down' or swimming became awkward. Spicans also required the continuing exercise of adjusting to changing pressure; of rising by expanding the tissues, and sinking by contracting them. If these abilities atrophied by too-long immersion in constant pressure, the space-going individuals would be unable to return to their home seas. Solarians faced a similar necessity of gravity, for their muscles atrophied if not constantly exerted. Gravity was not a matter of mere comfort, but of survival.

Melody came to a colored marker suspended in the water. Her host-mind gave warning; this was the boundary of the Sibilant zone. Unlike Solarians, Spicans had to be segregated by sex. Any two sexes could associate, but never all three, unless mating were intended, and even then, never in groups.

Melody had excellent reason not to mate! She shied away from the marker. However, this posed a problem: She was an Impact, and the other hostages were Sibilants and an Undulant. She *had* to get into the other zones – and that meant the risk of mating. For once the three sexes met mating was not voluntary. Three together meant immediate mergeance and parturition – and a shift of sexual identity for Melody. Of course in one sense it would not matter, while she was in a Spican host, for this same Impact could accommodate a male or a female mind. But it would become impossible to return to her human female host. And Melody dreaded to think what forced participation in Spican reproduction would do to her if she were trapped into it in the masculine role. She might forfeit her sanity. For she could not turn the function over to her host-mind; the host Spican was borderline insane now, and Chisel of : : would not readily yield control once she recovered it.

Well, she would have to manage. Maybe she could report directly to the Captain. She fished for information in the host/hostage minds. He was Llono the Undulant, an experienced, competent spacer and a high-Kirlian, which was why he had not been taken hostage. The few higher-aura entities in the Andromedan invasion squad had been reserved for more important positions. Good. Melody would be able to relate to him. She thought of the Captain as male, though this was meaningless in the Spican scheme. He had procreated before, therefore he was male by Mintakan

181

definition, even though his next mating might make him a mother. In Sphere Mintaka there was no mother-father distinction, anyway.

She swam for the command chamber, which was around the side of the cup. She used one of the reserved corridors, so that no non-Impacts would be encountered. The water was not in the center section of the cup, but in what Solarians thought of as the rim and sides. The center was of course hollow, to focus and collect the light energy. So she had to follow a broadly circular route. Fortunately her host, who was Datok the Impact, was off shift now, and free to circulate. When on shift, Datok was Chief of Gunnery, in charge of the huge water bombs that were the primary offensive armament of the ship. Melody was not certain how this weapon operated in space, but she didn't want any squirted at the flagship.

She came to the Undulant markers. No help for it; she had to enter this zone in order to reach the Captain. She dared not used the ship's communications system as the Communications Officer was a hostage. The Captain was a practical sort; he would not be easy to convince without direct evidence – and that would be impossible to provide without a transfer unit. She would have to convince him of *her* identity, then have him message the *Ace of Swords* under the code phrase 'Lot of *' and get confirmation from Skot—

No, that message would go through Llume, as it was not a short-range shuttle beam, but Llume did not know the code. That would distort the response, and leave the Spican Captain unconvinced. No message!

Then how could she convince him? She would simply have to tell him the truth, and hope he was smart enough and objective enough to verify it in his own fashion. If she failed . . .

'I'm only an old neuter,' she told herself. 'I *hate* adventure!'

Then she swam on through the dread Undulant zone toward the command pool.

She was in luck. Captain Llono the Undulant ran an 'open' pond, and was freely accessible to his officers. His alarm net informed him of Melody's approach, and by the time she arrived he had cleared the pool of other entities.

'Salutation, Datok the Impact,' he said. 'What brings you swimming here in such haste, unannounced?' This was, of course, a serious breach of form; an entity could get abruptly merged that way. But the Captain was taking it in stride, in his nonstriding fashion.

'Sir, I must communicate with you privately,' Melody said. 'Complete privacy.' Like him, she spoke sonically, using a vibrating mechanism inside her body. Sound was very efficient in water. Too efficient; their exchange would be audible far away.

'My office is secure,' Llono said, swimming gracefully toward it. His general outline was similar to that of Melody's host, but he lacked flippers; he moved by flexing his flattened, sinuous torso. An Undulant in motion was an elegant thing, justly praised in Spican lore.

'Sir – I fear it is not,' Melody called hastily, thinking of the hostage Communications Officer who would surely have the office bugged.

The Captain paused. Her remark about his office was insulting, but again he flowed with the wave, taking no offense. Llono was known for his extreme diplomacy. 'Then we shall converse in the garden.'

Melody plunged into her host-memory again. It really had been so much more convenient to have the Yael-host answer her questions; this constant spot-research was fatiguing. The garden was the single concession Llono made to his personal creature comfort. He was a career space entity, satisfied to live the rest of his life in this ship. But he missed the pretty vegetative life of his home seas. So he cultivated a garden. This was considered an anomaly, but not a serious one. He allowed officers and crew to swim through it on special occasions, and this contributed greatly to the morale of the ship. It was obvious that he believed Melody was angling for just such a swim, so he obliged. In the general stress engendered by the unexplained destruction of a neighboring spaceship, he was conscious of the needs of his crew. Melody found herself liking him.

They entered the garden. Pastel-colored streamers floated vertically, anchored by organic weights and floats. They formed arches and passages, and they spread a flavor in the water that was delightful. This was a miniature Spican paradise!

There were unlikely to be any mechanical listening devices here; the plants didn't like electrical things, and they also tended to damp out sounds. They glowed faintly, their hues indicating their types. Some, she realized, were actually animals, with intricate filaments combing the water for sustenance, and long vinetails descending to the bottom. The plants needed some light, but the animals could get by without it. The ship's main food supply was a special lake containing hardy, edible species of such animals, together with masses of plankton. But the Captain's garden was more natural, seeded with sea-insects as well. Now Melody heard the gentle chirruping the animal-flowers made to attract those insects. Oh, this was lovely!

The Captain halted. 'Your message, Datok?' Gently spoken, but it had better be good!

'I am not Datok,' Melody said. 'I am a high-Kirlian transfer agent from Sphere Mintaka. If you touch me, you will feel the strength of my aura.'

This was another social gaffe, with homosexual overtones, as Spicans did not touch each other apart from mating. But the Captain's broad-mindedness rose to the occasion again. He undulated toward her, until he touched – barely. Melody felt his aura now: about 110. Very high, for such a position; had the segment had more warning of this crisis, he would have been conscripted for transfer duty.

He evinced surprise. 'I did not know auras of that magnitude existed! It must be double mine!'

'Correct, Captain. Mine is the strongest aura recorded in Segment Etamin. I have taken over the body and mind of Datok in order to implement a mission for our galaxy. We are at war, again – with Galaxy Andromeda.' Quickly she explained the nature of the hostage threat, and her counter to it.

'This is most serious business,' Captain Llono said. 'I

184

must accept your statement of the threat of hostaging, for you are obviously not Datok, and there has been no opportunity for any substitution of physical entities. But I have no certainty that you are not yourself Andromedan.'

That made Melody pause. 'Captain, you are astute! I had feared you would not accept my thesis. You are right; I must prove myself to you. But how may I do this?'

'I am inclined to believe you. You would not have informed me of this Andromedan plot if you were yourself such an agent. Still, I am disinclined to take action without verification; your mind might operate more deviously than mine.'

'Yes.' Melody remembered how she had assumed that Captain Dash Boyd of the *Ace of Swords* was loyal. Assumptions were treacherous. 'I could relate to you certain obscure facets of Mintakan culture—'

'I am not conversant with Sphere Mintaka, except with respect to space armament.'

'I don't know anything about armament, Captain. I was a mere old maid, unversed in military—'

'Interesting you should mention your mating status. In this lies the proof.'

'Captain, I don't understand.' But she had a cold premonition.

'When a Spican trio merges in the act of reproduction, the flesh and nervous systems overlap. The thoughts of each become known to the others, enhancing the unity. Generally these are notions of copulative appreciation – but a question of identity would also be clarified.'

Beautiful! No deceit among lovers. But – 'Captain ... I can't do it.'

'Does the notion of merging with me repulse you?' Llono inquired sardonically. Obviously it was her galactic loyalty he was questioning; interpersonal attraction had little to do with Spican mating. Her refusal threw her whole statement into doubt.

'Captain, such mergeance would very likely destroy me,' she said. 'I would be unable to return to my human host.'

'Why would you *want* to?'

'I—' She stopped, unable to explain because she did not understand it herself. If she became male, she could transfer to male hosts, and eliminate some of the male hostages that seemed to be in the majority. Why not? 'I'm an old female neuter,' she said, aware that this concept, virtually a crutch to her thinking, was not particularly clear to a non-Mintakan. 'I can't change *now*.' Ridiculous but true. She saw suddenly that this was another reason that she had never budded; she had become accustomed to her status, and didn't care to change it. Such shifts of sex were all right for young entities, who could adopt to the new set of relationships, but she was far from young, and had grown much accustomed to her present status. She simply could not *feel* herself as male.

'I regret the necessity,' Llono said. 'But the matter you have raised is too vital to the welfare of our galaxy. I must insist.' He made a short piercing call.

Another entity appeared. It was a Sibilant, jetting rapidly toward them in answer to the Captain's summons. The third sex.

For a moment Melody froze in place. She knew Llono was correct; the matter had to be decided, and this was the way to do it. She could not preserve her sex at the price of her galaxy. She played an internal chord of leavetaking from her human host, Yael of Dragon. Melody had come to love that girlchild, in her fashion. And there was another hidden motive surfacing in this instant of truth. How would Yael function by herself, bereft of transfer aura?

Then she recognized, via the host/hostage minds, the approaching Spican. It was Zysax the Sibilant, ship Communications officer – and a hostage.

Melody's flippers churned the water as she stroked rapidly away, almost getting snagged on one of the plants. Now she was really in trouble! The hostage would quickly catch on – and convince the captain that Melody, not Zysax, was the enemy. Even now Zysax and Llono were coming together, comparing notes . . .

'What the discordance am I made of?' Melody demanded of herself. 'The hostage is the very one I *want* in this trio!'

She turned and stroked even more vigorously back toward the pair. Zysax did not see her; he was preoccupied by what the Captain was telling him. Llono saw her, but stayed put.

Melody gave a final heave of her flippers and launched into the pair. The force of the collision shoved her flesh right through theirs.

Suddenly they were in the throes of mergence. 'What have I done?' Melody asked herself in the despairing ecstasy of union, knowing that she had *had* to do it, whatever the personal consequence.

You have proven your identity, Melody of Mintaka, Llono answered along her/their nerves. *And you, Zysax — are hostage to a : : of Andromeda.*

: : *I am betrayed!* : : the alien entity cried.

Melody sympathized, for her own reasons.

They climaxed in literal explosion. The three entities flew apart, and a mass of merged flesh was torn from the bodies of Llono and Zysax. The Sibilant was now the parent of a little Sibilant, and Llono was the sire.

Zysax and her baby slid out of sight beyond the veil of plants, driven by the force of the reproductive schism. It was important that there be an immediate separation after mergence, so that a trio would not be trapped into another cycle of mating. The Captain swam back, his body reorganizing after the loss of a sizable segment of flesh. Spicans were not solid in the manner of Solarians or Mintakans; their flesh was frothy and malleable, and the deletion of a chunk meant only a temporary inconvenience.

'Now I possess data,' Llono said. 'I shall promptly dispatch the remaining hostages, and send you back to your ship. In fact, I believe I will volunteer for transfer service myself; my aura is higher than that of most hostages.'

'We can use you right now,' Melody said, surprised and grateful for his gesture. 'But the work is dangerous,'

'I am aware of that. However, it would be more dangerous to allow hostages to take control of a ship in this fleet whose weapons bear on my own ship.'

'Irrefutable logic,' Melody agreed.

'Doubtless. I got it from your mind.'

They swam back to the Captain's office, where he gave orders concerning the disposition of the hostages, and made new assignments to fill the vacated positions, including his own. 'I would have been killed soon by the hostages,' he explained. 'It is fitting that I employ the life I have recovered in an attempt to save the lives of my companion captains.'

Then they swam into a shuttlecraft for the trip to the *Ace of Swords*. The craft was of course filled with water, and was very heavy, so acceleration was slow. As the water cushioned even that thrust, Melody was hardly aware of their motion. Llono piloted it expertly, allowing Melody her thoughts. They were not happy ones.

'You seem despondent, my recent mate,' Llono observed.

'It's not a matter of galactic importance,' Melody said. 'I simply haven't gotten used to the notion of being male.'

'Why should you *have* to?'

'I had thought you understood. When Mintakan buds—'

'I understand the convention. But this does not apply.'

'You of all entities should certainly be aware that—'

'Do you *feel* male?'

'No,' she admitted uncertainly.

'Then you have not changed. It is only your self-image that modifies, since your Mintakan body has not participated.'

'But we merged! There was offspring!'

'True, we merged. But you were neither Parent nor Sire.'

Melody's flippers wiggled. 'I was the *catalyst*!' she exclaimed, realizing. 'I caused it to happen – without giving of myself. *I have not budded!*'

'I had supposed you understood,' Llono said. 'That was a clever maneuver, retreating and returning, so as to assume the catalytic role. Had you not done so, you would have become the sire, and I the parent, a decidedly less convenient arrangement for us. I would not have been free to transfer, had I borne the child.'

'I remain female . . .' Melody said, and somehow it seemed the most wonderful thing possible.

12

Drone of Scepters

COUNCIL INITIATED   PARTICIPATING $* - / :: {}^0_0$
issue of new leadership
—if this must be, I propose slash—
:: slash betrayed us to the enemy in the prior war!
quadpoint will assume leadership   concurrence ? : :
SILENCE
slash proposed for leadership   concurrence?
CONCURRENCE
/grant me a period to orient my lasers and sharpen my
blades   there will be another council soon/
POWER
$- / {}^0_0$ CIVILIZATION ${}^0_0 / -$
:: (fools!) ::

There were a series of minor problems, such as identifying
themselves to Skot of Kade and getting their water-borne
bodies into the transfer unit without suffering damage. Skot
was being ably assisted by Yael, who seemed to be enjoying
her tour as a self-determined adventuress. The two of them
and Slammer got the transfer unit set up at the edge of the
temporary pool in the hold, and helped first Llono and then
Melody flop into the unit. Gravity was so slight that the
maneuvers were not as hard as anticipated. In fact their
main concern was preventing the water from vaporizing
every time the air pressure was reduced by their travels.

Llono went to another Spican ship whose captain he knew
personally; he expected to have all the Cups washed in due
course.

Melody tried for another Polarian Disk, expecting to
bounce again. But this time she got through – and found

herself in the body of the hostage Polarian captain. This was a marvelous break. She was able without fuss to arrest the three other hostages her memory identified, and to explain things to the ranking Polarian, whom she installed as new captain. The Andromedans here were all from Sphere *, of interest to Melody because of the Lot of *, but she did not try to comprehend the nuances of their five sexes. In their natural state they were serpentine entities that twisted into complex convolutions, every knot having significance; perhaps this made it easier for them to occupy the tailed Polarians. Melody was beginning to recognize certain broad families of Andromedans corresponding to those of the Milky Way. Some were foot walkers, some borers, some fliers, some swimmers. As with families of auras, they fell naturally into functional categories.

She returned to the flagship to discover that Llono the Undulant had already completed his first mission and gone out again. That was one efficient entity! Their nucleus of 'safe' ships was now four. Given enough time and luck, the whole Fleet might be redeemed bloodlessly! Skot and Yael were working so well together that Melody began to wonder whether her return to her human host would be welcome.

She had freed the *Ace of Swords*, the *Four of Cups*, and the *Three of Disks*. Time to try a Canopian Wand, or Scepter. The particular term did not matter in Tarot; it was the concept that counted.

Skot activated the unit – and Melody bounced right back. 'All right ... try another Wand,' she said, vibrating her Polarian-host ball against the floor. This was a nice body! 'I want to be sure of at least one of each kind of ship.'

But the second Wand bounced also, and the third. 'Either they're all loyal,' she said, 'or they have no moderate-Kirlian female hostages.' She considered a moment. 'Let's try a straight transfer instead of a hostage takeover; they just might have a vacant female host. Canopians are smart about things like that.' So Skot adjusted the setting and tried it again.

This time she found herself in a humanoid host. For a

190

moment she was confused; then she remembered that the Canopian insectoid Masters used humanoid slaves. Naturally any hosts they reserved would be of this type!

She explored her new mind. No . . . this was *not* a prepared host. This was $fe of Y ⋏ jr. Y ⋏ jr was, or had once been, a warrior planet/tribe, with fierce people and primitive customs. $fe was a Slave, but she was fiercely loyal to her Master. The ferocity of independence in her genetic makeup had converted nicely to the ferocity of dependence. Her Master's fall from power had created such stress in her that her aura had vacated.

Melody rechecked that, dubious. It was true: $fe's Master was her life, and evil to his person was evil to her soul. The concept of his loss of power was literally unthinkable to her. So here she sat in a state of collapse – and because she was merely a slave, and not even an important one, no one had even noticed her demise.

Melody held her position while she worked out more of her current situation. $fe of Y ⋏ jr was body-Slave to Drone. Drone? Melody had to plumb a welter of concepts here. Canopian Masters were known by combinations of letters and numbers, such as A ::: 5, F ::: 3. They were essentially neuter, or neutered females, like the worker-bees of Sphere Sol. This explained why Melody had bounced on her previous attempts. She was also a neuter female, but the direction differed. She had proceeded from neuter to female, while Canopians went from female to neuter, becoming essentially male in their final evolution. She could not identify with that! The slave, in contrast, was a full female humanoid like Yael of Dragon, capable of reproduction, but virginal. Much better associations, there!

But this Drone Master – ah, here it was! Every initially female Canopian entity possessed the potential to become a full female if properly fed; a queen. But queens never went to space. They mated with full males, or drones, the only truly masculine Masters. A drone, in the insectoid hierarchy, was parallel to a queen, but since only one drone could mate with a queen, the others became expendable. So they went to space – as captains of ships. Because they were not stunted neuters, they did not fit the mechanistic classification system; but since only one was aboard each ship, he needed no private designation. He was simply the Drone, the Captain – the ultimate authority. For reference between ships of the Canopian continent, this was the Drone of the *Deuce of Scepters*.

Melody looked up. Across the chamber from her stood the Drone. He was huge, much larger than ordinary Masters, and beautiful. Bright bands of color traversed his abdomen, and his wings were irridescent. His six limbs were stout and strong, his mandibles powerful, like monstrous pincers. There must have been a time in the evolution of the species when the drone was the warrior-king, the fiercest fighter of the tribe, protecting the queen and minions. But most compelling were his eyes: two great multi-faceted crystals that reflected the light of the room like little mirrors. Hundreds of miniature images, like the massed thought of his great mind . . .

There was a film of dust on the fur of his feet. $fe reacted with horror. She had to clean away that dust instantly! It profaned the Drone! She got up and started toward him.

'Desist,' the Drone said immediately. Even the formidable timbre of his voice sent a shiver through the host's nervous system. This was $fe's god!

$fe would have been frozen in her tracks by that directive, but Melody was no slave, and her response to the warning was not swift enough. Her forward arm touched a shimmering curtain that crossed the room between them – and the searing pain caused her to fall back, exclaiming in agony.

The surface of her arm was turning red. She had been burned by a sheet laser; there would be blisters and sloughing of skin.

She paused to consider the situation, while the savage pain subsided slowly. The Captain had discovered the hostages prematurely, and they had made him prisoner by using the discipline box on him. This was a pain-generating unit that could be set to cause steady pain on a scale of one through ten, or to cause variable pain as the prisoner tried to resist it. The box picked up the myriad indicators of the functioning body and adjusted its output accordingly. It was a most sophisticated device; no entity could resist it. The Drone could not even *think* consciously of escaping.

The Drone-Captain was in a sheet-laser cell, so that he could not even accidentally escape the box. Its effect faded rapidly with distance, so it had to be kept close to the subject. It was not tuned to Melody's host, so she could have approached and turned it off, but a double laser barrier curtain separated her from it.

She paced around her scintillating cell. The Drone surely knew how to deactivate the box, but even if she were free, he could not *tell* her, because that would be an escape-thought. He could warn her against danger to herself, because that did not relate to his escape, but that was all.

So they were helpless. Melody's host simply did not know enough to get around the barriers, and the Drone could not tell her. What a trap!

'Regret,' the Drone said.

There was no need to clarify his meaning. Melody's host-system thrilled to her Master's expression of concern. She had taken injury on his behalf, and he had taken note. Instead of chastising her for her negligence, he had issued a word of consolation. She would gladly have taken a thousand similar injuries, for similar reward.

But Melody was not §fe. Perhaps if she could communicate this to the Drone . . .

'Canopian,' she said clearly.

The reflections from his facets shifted as the Drone looked her way. It was not necessary for him to turn his head at all, since several facets covered her regardless of the way he was facing, so this was a signal of special attention. A Slave did not address her Master in this manner!

'Please approach the curtain,' Melody continued.

Again the shifting of reflections, his only indication of surprise. Now he was definitely aware of a change in his Slave. The Drone walked slowly to the barrier, stopping just beyond it.

Melody moved up to the limit on her side. They could not touch each other, but they could approach to within the thickness of a molecule, if they were careful. Melody put one hand forward with extreme care.

The Drone did likewise with a forward appendage. As their extremities came close together, the two auras began to interact. The laser curtain had no effect on an aura, of course. The Kirlian intensity of the Canopian was extremely strong – about 140 – which explained why he had not been taken hostage. By showing him her own aura, Melody had documented her status; the aura capable of making *her* hostage did not exist.

After a moment, the Drone withdrew. Melody knew he had felt her aura, and so he was now aware that she was a transferee. The fact that he did not speak suggested that he knew their speech was being recorded.

But he might think she was an Andromedan spy! No, for if the Andromedans had an aura like hers available, they would not have wasted it on a mere Slave; they would have taken over the Drone himself, instead of imprisoning him. So his logic should tell him that she was not one of the enemy.

The Drone now knew her nature, and knew what to tell her to do – but still could not show or tell her directly. So maybe she had gained nothing – but she felt she had made progress. She returned to the table and sat down. Her arm was still hurting from the burn, and she hated to waste valuable time, but all she could do now was wait and try to figure out the necessary course of action.

After a time, a Canopian Master entered the room. He (she/it) was a Solarian-sapient-sized black insectoid, perhaps half the mass of the Drone and not nearly as handsome. A hostage, obviously.

'So your little Slave has revived,' the hostage remarked callously. 'Good. We can use her. Slave, come out.' It touched a control on a portable instrument, causing one curtain to fade out.

Melody hesitated, and it was well she did, for she discovered that $fe would not have obeyed the hostage's directive. She could have given herself away that readily! She remained where she was.

'Drone, tell her to obey me,' the hostage snapped. The snapping was literal: its mandibles clicked.

'Do,' the Drone said.

Now Melody stood and crossed the room to stand before the hostage. She was tempted to attack it, but still didn't know enough to free the Drone, so attack was pointless. Better to wait for a better opportunity, unless the hostage discovered her powerful aura and forced the issue.

'Go to the Master's galley and fetch food,' the hostage said melodiously. Canopians had excellent linguistic ability, and always spoke well. 'Feed the Drone.'

Melody drew on her host's information and made her way down the corridor to the galley. This was a routine chore; she not only cleaned her Master, she fed him and carried away his wastes. With no personal distractions he was able to devote his full attention to his position as captain. Even from the uncomprehended fragments in the uneducated Slave mind, Melody perceived the massive capacity of the Drone. He had, by any definition, a first-rate intellectual competency.

Slaves operated the galley. 'Hey, $fe,' the server said. She recognized him as Øto of Ath. 'What's going on up front? The Masters have been acting strange.'

'This ship has been taken over by Galaxy Andromeda, Øto,' Melody said.

He laughed, not equipped to believe the truth. "Here's your order; go throw burl at Andromeda."

Melody carried the canister, pondering. Burl – a plant cultivated on several worlds of Sphere Canopus. The berries were solid, and could be thrown. They were also squeezed for their juice, which was made into food for the Masters. To throw burl, thus, would be an insulting waste. It was, of course, safe to insult Andromeda, though it was apparent to Melody (if not to $fe) that the identity stood in lieu of a more proximate if unnameable enemy. The humanoids of the / intonation *obeyed*, but did not necessarily *like*, their insectoid Masters.

Interesting double-culture, this. Melody had reviewed Sphere Canopus as part of segment geography, way back in her bud stage, and of course there were references to it in the Cluster Tarot. Canopus was represented by the Suit of Wands (called Scepters by Canopians) and was one of the first and stoutest allies of Sphere Sol. The suit of Energy stood for many things, as did all the suits; any suggestion that there was any affinity between Canopus and Andromeda would have been fiercely denied by both parties. Flint of Outworld had visited Sphere Canopus in the host of a Slave. But there were many spheres in the segment, and many segments in the galaxy, and many galaxies in the cluster, and it simply was not possible to know or remember the details of all the species in them all. In addition, Melody's personal aversion to sapient slavery had put a certain intellectual distance between her and this one. Now she wished she had choked off her own prejudice enough to give her a sufficient understanding of this culture. She did not have to *like* what she was finding here, but Canopus *was* a vital ally, and Şfe's devotion to her Master was genuine. In fact, it was so thorough it had to indicate that there were some redeeming features in the culture.

She entered the Drone's room. 'You have one unit,' the arrogant hostage said. That was a measure of Canopian time equivalent to about a quarter of a Solarian hour. Feeding and grooming the Drone normally required three units, so this would force her to hurry. Possibly they were keeping him alive because they might need him as a figurehead in dealing with nonhostage ships, at least until the overt takeover occurred. The Slaves would obey the Drone without question, but might balk at running a Droneless ship; the familiar symbol of authority was important. The captain could be forced to perform to a certain extent with the discipline box. So they kept him at least minimally healthy.

The hostage phased out the laser curtain so Melody could pass, then restored it behind her. Now she was in with the Drone, but still didn't know how to free him. This box-laser combination was a simple yet excruciatingly effective prison.

She opened the warm canister of burl-juice and set it under the Drone's proboscis. He dipped his imbibing tube into it and slowly drew the liquid in. Meanwhile, Melody picked up the set of brushes that were on the floor beside him, and brushed out the fur of his abdomen and legs. The wings needed attention too, but it was impossible to treat them in a hurry; she would only tear the gossamer membranes. Such a beautiful figure of an entity, this super-Master; how it hurt her $fe-mind to groom him so hastily.

He knew how to be freed – if only he could tell her. Yet how would he do that, with the pain-box monitoring his reactions?

'Time,' the hostage said coldly.

So soon! She had hardly started. But she dared not dally; the hostage would act ruthlessly. She set aside the brush, picked up the empty canister – and found it half-full.

Strange. The Drone always consumed a full ration; it was necessary for his health. He had typical Canopian Master nerve; his predicament would not have affected his appetite or performance. He was not sick. He must have slowed his consumption deliberately, an internal matter that would not activate the discipline box. Perhaps he was trying to commit suicide by starving himself – no, the box would stop *that*, too. So something else . . .

The hostage-insect touched the control, phasing out the curtain. And suddenly Melody caught on.

She hurled the canister at the hostage. It struck it on the head, the juice spraying over it. It stumbled back, cursing in some Andromedan language. The blow alone would not have hurt it much, but the sticky juice coated its faceted eyes and filmy wings and distracted it.

Melody ran toward the shelf on which the discipline box sat. The curtain here had not been phased out; the hostages were too canny for that. She took a breath, closed her humanoid eyes tightly, and launched herself at the box.

The laser caught her in a ring of fire that singed off her hair and clothing. The agony was momentarily unbearable, but her flying inertia carried her into the wall. Her hand struck the box, caught it, held it though her legs remained in the curtain of agony and were being inevitably cooked. She gritted her teeth and grabbed the setting-knob, twisting it violently.

Immediately she realized it was the wrong knob, the wrong direction. The Drone stood stiffly, shuddering; she was inflicting nine- or ten-level pain on him, up near the fatal range! Quickly she turned it down to zero, then found the personal tuner and wrenched it around. He was free!

The Drone moved so quickly he seemed a magnificent blur, or maybe it was her burned eyes fading. He shot over to the hostage, picked it up in his two front legs and stove its head in with one crunch of his deadly mandible pincers. Then he took the laser-control and turned it off.

In another moment the Drone was back with Melody. He lifted the box from her flaccid fingers and twiddled with it. At that moment another hostage entered the room, but it froze as the Drone found his setting on the box. Stiffened by pain, the hostage could offer no resistance as the Drone calmly moved over and crunched *its* head.

Melody, satisfied the situation was under control, fainted.

She woke in pain. Another Slave was tending to her. But as soon as her eyes opened, the Drone came over. '$fe of Y ⋏ jr, I am in your debt,' he said.

There was something strange about his intonation. In a moment it came to her: he had omitted the baton sinister! Not the $fe of Slave-status, but $fe of free-status. There was no finer reward for a Canopian humanoid.

But of course she was neither slave nor humanoid in her home-Sphere. 'I am Melody of Mintaka,' she said with difficulty, for her lips were burned. It was hard to look at him, because part of her eyelids was also gone and her eyeballs were drying. 'Please return me to my ship – the *Ace of Swords* – so I can transfer to another body.'

'Immediately, alien ally,' the Drone said. 'This host of yours is finished; we preserve animation at this moment only by application of strong drugs. You acted with extraordinary courage. How may I repay my debt to you?'

Courage? *Her?* She had acted before she had a chance to consider the personal consequence, and once she was in it there had been nothing to do but carry through. But evidently debt was not merely a Polarian or Mintakan concept. 'Just use your ship well on behalf of our galaxy – and be kind to your next body-Slave.'

'Agreed,' the Drone said, not bothering to quibble with her implication that he had not treated his prior Slave properly. $fe had loved him; he had obviously treated her well. But Melody was already fading out; she knew this body was dying. Little of the skin remained, and the legs might as well have been amputated.

She woke in her Yael body. The Canopian shuttle had brought her home, and Skot had retransferred her. She must have given the code signal somewhere along the way. 'What happened?' Skot demanded to know.

'Bit of trouble. Let's get on with the job.'

13

Ship of Knyfh

/I wish the support of quadpoint in this crisis/
: : only proceed to action hour   you will have support : :
/and if there are complications of the nature — feared?/
: : then quadpoint will resolve them : :

Melody transferred next to a ship of Segment Knyfh. She
had no idea what she would encounter there – which was
why she selected it. She now had a rough working knowledge
of the Swords of Sol, the Cups of Spica, the Disks of Polaris,
and the Scepters of Canopus, but the Atoms of Knyfh were
a complete mystery to her, despite the fact that her own
Sphere Mintaka used a roughly similar type of ship. She
didn't understand her own Sphere's ships either. A mystery
in the power of the enemy was not good; she had to know
its capabilities.

The Knyfh vessel was indeed like a giant atom, an almost
perfect replica of the symbol for the Suit of Aura in the
Cluster Tarot deck. Two spheres spun in close magnetic
orbit about a common center, like a proton and a neutron.
Farther out there were a number of rapidly orbiting spots,
moving so fast they were virtual rings or globes: the electrons.
These were the light-gathering units, but they also seemed
to serve admirably as a kind of defensive shield. What
would happen to any solid object that attempted to penetrate that glittering barrier?

Segment Knyfh was generally considered to be more
advanced than Segment Etamin. A thousand years before,
an emissary from the then Sphere Knyfh had brought the
gift of transfer to the then Sphere Sol, initiating the explosive
expansion of Sol's empire of influence. However, there had

never been a close association between the two. Segment representatives met from time to time to determine galactic policy, but news of these contacts was not generally published widely in Sphere Mintaka. So the nature of the other great segments of the Milky Way galaxy was almost as mysterious to Melody as those of Andromeda. She knew the names of the ten major segments, and that was about all.

'Freng, Qaval, Etamin,' she thought to herself in a kind of supportive litany. 'Knyfh, Lodo, Weew, Bhyo, Faj, Novagleam, and Thousandstar.' In her youth she had dreamed of what life must be like in Thousandstar, most distant of the segments, and popular literature had many fanciful stories about such places. But genuine information was scant.

So now she went to this representative of the token contingent of the allied segment, and found herself in the incredible body of a sophisticated relative of the magnets. This was no physical ball, but a miniature of the ship, with a compact nucleus of five spheres and a scintillating outer energy shell that *rolled* across the deck. The magnets Melody had known were bound to the metal passages of a ship, but these atom-hosts used magnetism mainly internally. They could levitate in the vicinity of metal, but could also travel elsewhere, much as Polarians did, utilizing the principle of the wheel. Most – virtually all – of the mass was in the nucleus, so that there was plenty of leverage to control the orientation and motion of the shell.

It was a very nice body, though it was not precisely a body at all by her prior definitions. But she could not concern herself about that; she had to deal with the Andromedan entity that had made it hostage. And it was a savage one: Bluefield of 0_0. Not the blue of a field of Solarian flowers or of a mournful Mintakan tune, but the hue of an intense magnetic field. Had this entity possessed an aura to match her electrical power, Melody would never have been able to transfer to it. Bluefield fought in the fashion she knew best, sending jolt after jolt of magnetic energy through host and aura, disrupting both by associated currents. Melody was very nearly dislodged before she learned to parry the ferocious

201

onslaught. As she had nowhere to go, loss of her hold would have meant extinction; contrary to spiritualistic folklore, no aura could exist in the absence of some type of host.

But again her overwhelming superiority of aura saved her. She simply had more intensity than any other entity could cope with. She closed in on the Andromedan sentience, tightening her hold. 'Yield, Bluefield – so I won't have to destroy you.'

To her surprise, Bluefield yielded. Suddenly Melody was in her mind. The $^0_0$ entities were of the broad class of magnetic sapients, structurally between the solid magnets like Slammer, and the atomic Knyfhs. They had two charged spheres in orbit about each other, but no outer energy shells, and could move anywhere by 'walking' the spheres. They were unique (in Melody's limited experience) in that their sapience was housed in two physically unconnected units; a single unit could not function intelligently. The magnetic interactions between the parts not only made motion possible, it made *thought* possible!

Melody's Mintakan brain was tripartite, each section dominating a type of music: string, percussion, wind. The Solarian brain was bipartite, resulting in confusing dichotomies. This $^0_0$ mind reflected the split brain of the Andromedan creature, but it was not very much like the human brain. The two parts could separate and reunite with other parts, forming new entities. There were actually four sexes, which could unite in six distinct combinations. The complete entity was therefore technically neuter, or bisexual. Melody, a changeable neuter, had been able to enter this hostage; a truly sexed entity would have been balked.

The Sphere Knyfh host was also technically neuter. Any Knyfh could mate with any other, their mergence of nucleus and electron orbit resulting in prompt fissioning into two new compromise entities. Thus in both species, population was stable; new entities could be produced only from the parts of the old ones.

Melody paused. There was something strange about this. Population could shrink, from the demise of individuals, but if population could not grow . . .

202

How had either Knyfh or $^0_0$ ever gotten started? There *had* to be a way to create *new* individuals, to increase the size of the total population. Otherwise the colonization of a sphere or segment would have been impossible. A planet might have several billion sapient inhabitants; a sphere required trillions. Where did they come from?

Melody probed ... and her amazement grew. Neither Knyfh nor $^0_0$ *knew* the source of their populations. Mergence and fission proceeded indefinitely; prior combinations were impossible to trace down. Their populations *did* expand, but there was no known origin of individual entities. They were just there, and seemed always to have been there, logic to the contrary.

Knyfh and $^0_0$ logic did not struggle with this concept. It was not a logic Melody could readily understand, but it seemed to serve well the needs of the species who used it.

At the moment, she had another concern: to rid the ship of hostages. There were nine of them, all with high auras. She had overwhelmed the one with the lowest Kirlian intensity. This ship was the *Ace of Atoms*; Andromeda had regarded it as a critically important target!

Bluefield was liaison officer to the Knyfh crew. On this ship, like all so far, none of the crew was hostage. The most efficient use of Andromedan power was in making the leaders hostage; the crew merely followed orders. It simplified recovery of the ships; eliminate the hostages and all was well. The crew would never know the difference.

Melody performed the routine duties required of her host, drawing on the hostage-mind. There were always snarls to be untangled, substitutions of all entities, special situations. Melody could not leave her post without suspicion until her shift expired, which meant delay, but she managed to use the time to fill in her gaps of knowledge. She hovered at the communications console, making her decisions known by coded fluctuations of her electron shell, and learned.

This ship's armament was magnetic. Since metal was much used in all ships of the fleet, especially alloys of iron, all were subject to magnetism. The fields generated here were so strong they could operate at intership distance, alternately attracting and repulsing the enemy with such force that his ship could be damaged or even broken apart. At greater distances, the enemy's control instruments could be sabotaged magnetically. These magnetic weapons lacked the almost infinite range of the Solarian lasers, but in near proximity, the Knyfh attack would be devastating. Melody knew she would not want the flagship to be in range of a hostage-controlled Atom.

At least she had time to plan her local campaign. She picked out each name from the hostage mind. The Captain was free. He had an aura of 160, too high to take over by an available $^0_0$ entity, and was probably the highest loyalist of the entire fleet. But the Transfer Officer was hostage to a $^0_0$ with an aura of 135, and—

Transfer Officer? Melody focused on that. Sure enough, *this ship had a transfer unit aboard!* Melody had assumed that the unit on the *Ace of Swords* was the only one in the fleet, but of course this Atom was a representative of another segment, a more sophisticated one. The presence of the unit made this ship doubly vital. The Andromedans could use it to take over more entities. No . . . her host-mind informed her that it was not the proper type. To modify it for hostaging would be to put that secret in the field, something that could not be risked. This was inflexible policy; the secret never left Andromeda. In fact, it never left Sphere —, and hardly left Planet £ of that Sphere. Bluefield's information confirmed Tiala's; the / hostage had not lied under the Lot of *. Melody found that vaguely gratifying. And the policy itself was wise, in terms of Andromedan interest. Had Melody been able to capture a modified unit, Galaxy Milky Way would have had equalization of technology at a single stroke.

Still, that unmodified unit was important. It was probably heavily guarded as it was potentially a key mechanism of communication. Put a low-Kirlian voluntary host at each end, and the ships of Segment Etamin and Segment Knyfh could coordinate operations closely. Spot a hostage ship, and if it escaped Knyfh's magnetism, Sol's laser could beam it down. The Andromedans thought the loyal members of

204

the fleet had no communications that could not be monitored by strategically positioned hostages – but here it was!

Should she go first to the loyal Captain, or tackle the hostages one by one herself? Obviously the first. It would be almost impossible to nullify eight more hostages without attracting unfortunate attention. The Captain could handle it most expeditiously. That approach had worked twice before, and as Yael would have put it in her cute Solarian idiom, one did not change a winning game.

But she could not just roll into the Captain's office. On this ship there was protocol to be followed. This was essential in *any* encounter here, since any two Knyfhs possessed the capacity to mate. Such mating would change the identity of each, and that would be awkward in a military situation. In fact, mating – or as the Knyfhs put it, *exchanging* – was forbidden during this tour. The Captain especially was protected from temptation.

'Request permission for private audience with Captain,' Melody signaled formally into the officer's circuit. Her present body possessed none of the senses of the Segment Etamin hosts she had previously used; everything was magnetic. But she was becoming accustomed to differing modes of operation, and hardly noticed.

'Hold,' the network responded. Presumably the Captain was preoccupied at the moment. Melody returned to her routine.

Soon a Knyfh appeared. 'Request dialogue,' it signaled.

Melody oriented on it. The magnetic imprint resembled that of the Captain, but the aura differed. She had become highly attuned to aural nuances, for this was her primary tool for identifying hostages. This entity had a powerful aura; too powerful. It had to be a hostage!

'You are not Bluefield,' the hostage signaled. 'Therefore you must be—'

Melody attacked. She could not afford to have her identity betrayed to the hostages yet! She hurled herself at the globe of the other entity.

Unfortunately, she had not had occasion to study the art of Knyfh personal combat. Her attack was a clumsy thrust that the other entity easily avoided. Melody rolled past and received in return a disorganizing jolt of current. Her prior aura versus aura battles had seemed equivalent to physical encounters, since they were all on a single level, but now that she was in a *real* physical encounter, she discovered there was no real parallel at all. In aura versus aura she had a tremendous advantage; here she was merely even – or less than even. That dimmed her confidence considerably.

$^0_0$ So you are a segment counterhostage $^0_0$ the other signaled, lapsing into his native mode of expression. $^0_0$ Your fiendishly strong aura will not avail you now. Do you wish to exchange identities before I destroy you? $^0_0$

'No,' Melody replied. She recognized the other entity now: it was Greenaura of $^0_0$, the Transfer Officer hostage. And she knew the Andromedan was bluffing, at least in part; he would not kill her until he knew more about her. The existence of counterhostages would be a terrible threat to the hostage effort, and Greenaura would have to get at Melody's mind to discover the full ramifications. For all Greenaura knew, she was one of hundreds.

On the other hand, she could afford to dispatch the Andromedan any way she could manage. So the terms of the combat were not so disadvantageous.

Greenaura rolled toward her. His electron shield scintillated with flexible power; he was a fine figure of a Knyfh, in optimum health, and an experienced soldier. The military mind might be rigid to the point of obtusity in general matters, but in combat on this level he was an expert. Melody knew she did not have a chance against him. But she had no chance to escape.

Here she was, vacillating wildly in her estimations, one moment expecting to win, the next moment knowing she would lose. And the Drone had thought she had courage!

Their shields interacted. Controlled current touched her stunningly; Melody's strength was drawn off. She had let herself be vulnerable to a ploy no native would have fallen for. It was like allowing her Mintakan strings to be cut, or her Solarian throat to be looped without opposition. Her shield was now soft, permeable, laying her nucleus open to

206

penetration; she could be fissioned – which, in the absence of prior mergence, meant destruction.

'Help me, Knyfh host!' she cried inwardly, reaching past the quiescent hostage within her to the original Knyfh mind.

And the stunted, suppressed, half-insane Knyfh mind sprang out, knowing only one cause: her galaxy needed help. This mind was Gnejh, a low-Kirlian tigress; on a purely magnetic level, a deadly foe.

Greenaura sent a spear of current through Melody's shield, brushing her nucleus. The sensation was awful; she felt as if her nucleus was being sundered. $^0_0$ You will identify yourself, now $^0_0$ the Andromedan signaled. He knew the pain he was inflicting, and he would torture her until she broke under the strain.

Melody was silent. She felt the host-entity gathering, waiting, building up a nuclear charge. There was something horrible about it, like poison dripping from the jaws of a half-crushed reptile.

Greenaura's spear came again – and the host struck. *Jaws slicing through, twisting, severing, KILL, KILL*. The spearhead was cut off, trapped inside Melody's shield. *DIE, DIE!*

Greenaura screamed, $^0_0$ $^0_0$ $^0_0$ $^0_0$ $^0_0$, a single spasm of current, the sheer agony of amputation – and the Knyfh touched his shield and drew off twice the charge Melody had lost. The predator had poked the supposedly helpless body of his prey, and been caught by the counterstroke. Now the advantage had been reversed.

Gnejh of Knyfh, insane but victorious, went for the kill. Melody let her. The host launched a devastating bolt through Greenaura's weakened shield . . .

And it aborted! Bluefield of $^0_0$, the Andromedan Melody had displaced, had flung herself into the charge and thwarted it as it passed between the two shields. Bluefield herself was destroyed by that interception, but she had accomplished her aim. Melody and her mad host were helpless again.

Greenaura, weakened, still had more strength than Melody did. He rolled into contact, the currents of his shield battering at hers. When that shell collapsed, Melody's host would die. Slowly, surely, her last reserves waned, as they were drawn off to augment the thrust of the Andromedan's shell. *The broken electron orbit*, Melody thought. *So like the Tarot symbol for Aura, of plasmic matter.* Was this a fitting end for her?

She suffered a terrible shock. Energy buffeted her shield, hurling her across the room. She had—

No! *Greenaura* had fissioned! Her enemy was no more. And abruptly Melody knew why: The hostage Knyfh that Greenaura had suppressed had chosen this moment of distraction to strike, just as Gnejh had struck before. The Knyfh had fissioned, destroying himself and his captor.

Melody rolled slowly around the room, gathering in some of the ambient energy released by the explosion of her rival, regaining her strength. She was half dazed by the violence of the battle; these Knyfhs and $^0_0$s were savage warriors, giving no quarter! She didn't want any more encounters like that!

No wonder Segment Knyfh was regarded by the Andromedans as a major galactic target. Not only were they technologically sophisticated, they were resolute opponents. A Mintakan might yield when he saw that the issue was hopeless; a Knyfh would fight harder. Which perhaps explained why Mintaka was now a satellite sphere, while Knyfh was a segment.

Two hostages down, seven to go. Did the other hostages know about her? Probably not, because Greenaura had not been certain of her nature until the encounter – and the hostages had to hide themselves from the legitimate officers. Greenaura had investigated privately – and now would make no report. However, soon Greenaura's demise would become known . . .

'Private audience with the Captain; urgent,' Melody signaled into the network again. Then, as an afterthought: 'Matter of crew discipline.' That would justify her request, gaining the Captain's prompt attention, while reassuring the other hostages. Crew discipline was not a matter to worry about; it was the Captain's concern.

Sure enough: 'Audience granted,' the net responded. 'Immediate.'

This meant that Melody was immediately freed from her

duties in order to visit the Captain. She hurled herself through the energy network of the ship, maneuvering around magnetic stops as though solving a giant maze. This ship seemed to have no solid walls, but a magnetic baffle was every bit as effective, as she knew from her experience with Slammer on the flagship.

She came into the Captain's presence. He dispensed with protocol, moving in to touch his shell to hers to facilitate private dialogue. 'What an aura!' his surface current exclaimed.

'Sir, I am Melody of Sphere Mintaka, Segment Etamin,' she pulsed. 'I come to inform you that your ship has been infiltrated by Andromedans of Sphere 0_0. They—'

'I am aware of the 0_0 intrusion,' Captain Mnuhl of Knyfh replied tersely.

'You are . . . *aware?*'

'I have reserved taking any action until I knew more of their strategy,' he explained. 'I do not know how many other hostages exist in your fleet, or when they intend to strike. To eliminate the nine Andromedans aboard my ship without that knowledge is futile.'

'There are about four hundred in the fleet,' Melody said. 'We have eliminated perhaps thirty. They wait for the signal "Six of Scepters" from their hostage-captain on the *Ace of Swords* – a signal that will never come, because we have dealt with that command-entity.'

'I note you have tapped the minds of the hostages themselves,' Mnuhl signaled. 'This I was unable to do.'

'It requires a four-to-one aural superiority, and adaptation of a transfer unit to orient on hostage-hosts,' she explained. 'Even then, it is by no means certain, as the hostages resist strongly. I can show you how to set your transfer unit.'

'What of my original officers? I do not wish to do them harm.'

'The harm has already been done. The Andromedans destroy the minds of their involuntary hosts. Do you wish to speak with Gnejh, my host, to verify this?'

'I do.'

Melody allowed her host-mind to communicate with the

209

Captain. After a moment he drew back. 'You are correct, Melody of Etamin. Her personality will no longer integrate with our society, and to permit her to fission reproductively would be merely to spread the malaise.'

'Yes,' Melody agreed regretfully. 'Andromeda is no gentle maiden. She must be chained.' Then she gave a pulse of innovation. 'Reproductive fissioning . . . would that destroy the hostages?'

'Not if the host-minds are defunct. It probably would only spread the hostages.'

'Not worth the risk,' Melody agreed.

'So I shall act,' Mnuhl pulsed with decision. He moved over to the net input and ran a current through it. 'They are now gone.'

'Already?'

'The applicable code current will fission any entity of our species,' he signaled. 'I made arrangements when I identified the hostages. The matter could not be left to chance.'

Again, Melody experienced an internal flux of horror. These military entities, of whatever Sphere, operated with a savage efficiency that dispensed with sapient lives as though they were unimportant. She could never be that way!

'Let me show you what is necessary,' she signaled. 'Then you can transfer me to another hostage ship.'

'Agreed. My technicians will—'

He was interrupted by an incoming message. It was only three symbols, but their import chilled Melody to her nucleus.

SIX OF SCEPTERS

Some hostage had caught on, and given the action signal. Now all the hostages would proceed openly to take over their ships. The battle was on.

14

Heart of Spica

/action hour   message all field commands: strike as suitable for individual situations/

The human host was in pain. Yael and Skot sat at a table in the control room, watching Llume the Undulant operate the fleet communications net. The magnets were hovering idly.

'Melody!' Yael cried internally, gladly. 'How did you—?'

'Segment Knyfh has transfer units aboard their Atoms,' Melody explained. 'What is going on here?'

'Llume – she – the pain-box . . .'

Now Melody recognized the sensation. It was a low setting on a Canopian discipline-unit, the device that inflicted pain in the entity to which it was oriented. She had had recent experience with this aboard the *Deuce of Scepters*, but hadn't known any of these deadly boxes were on board the *Ace of Swords*.

'Llume put you and Skot on the boxes? Why?'

'She came to talk with you, and found us with the transfer unit. She asked me questions I couldn't answer, and felt my aura and knew you were gone. I tried to hide it—' Yael started crying.

'Dear, you could not hide your lack of a two hundred-plus aura from one possessed of a one hundred-plus aura, once she was suspicious. It was just bad luck she checked, not your fault.'

'She went away, but then she came back with the pain-boxes. We didn't know what they were until – Skot tried to fight the one fixed on him, but—'

'You can't fight one of those discipline-boxes. The Canopian Masters who make them are expert at handling

211

humanoid slaves. Once the unit is oriented on a specific person, even his thought of trying to get away from the box triggers—' She broke off as the wave of pain swept through her host. 'Yes, precisely,' she finished as it subsided. 'It is turned to your bodily reactions, tensions, so just don't think about—' The pain started rising again. '*Anything*,' she finished hurriedly.

'Skot wouldn't answer her questions—'

'He wouldn't.'

'So she turned up the – Melody, I just don't understand! Why would a close friend do that?'

Melody had forgotten that Yael had not had the same insights she had; in fact, Melody had not really believed it until now. Better to get the painful truth out, though: 'Because Llume is another Andromedan agent. A most sophisticated one. That was what Tiala would not tell me in the Lot of *.'

Yael was confused. 'I knew there was something funny there, but you didn't – *why* didn't you take over her mind, if you thought that?'

'Because making certain of that fact would have killed me – and maybe you. Tiala knew that I should be told about Llume . . . but she also knew that Llume would kill me the moment I learned. Tiala must have known about the discipline-boxes, and that Llume would use them. Llume could not act against me directly because of the magnet, but Slammer doesn't understand the discipline-box. He would not have known what was going on, and I would not have been able to tell him. So Tiala would have violated the Lot of * by answering accurately, because an answer that destroys the querent is not valid, by the definition of that code. Tiala had integrity.'

Yael mulled that over, not fully comprehending it. 'But if you had taken over Tiala's mind . . .'

'That would have been outside the Lot of *. She would no longer be bound to tell me anything responsively, or to protect me, once the Lot had been invalidated. So she had to submit in silence, lest she betray her honor or her galaxy.'

'Then why didn't you—'

'Because Llume would have acted against me the moment I overwhelmed Tiala's aura. Only by remaining ignorant could I save myself – if what I suspected was true. I didn't *want* it to be true . . . but it seems it was.'

'Your mind is so complex! Why didn't she use the box on you anyway; and why did you let her keep working? You could have told Slammer to bash her! By now she must've told the whole fleet how you got rid of the hostages here!'

'Worse than that. She broadcast the "Six of Sceptres" – the Andromedan signal for the overt takeover. Now, all over the fleet, ships are running up the Andromedan flag, figuratively. The battle is on – and we aren't ready for it.'

'But—'

Melody realized she hadn't yet answered Yael's question. 'She had no reason to act against me, as long as I didn't know what she was. And I – needed a hostage to reassure the other hostages of the fleet that things were under control despite the setback at the *Ace of Swords*. So we – tacitly – agreed to let each other alone. For a while.'

Yael was amazed. 'I don't understand that at all!'

'Well, I'm not sure I understand it either. It seemed the expedient thing to do at the time, since I wasn't *sure*, and couldn't afford to *be* sure. Her aura is so much like mine, I just couldn't believe she was Andromedan, though of course aura is no respector of galaxies, and one of my own ancestors was a / of Andromeda. I was pretty foolish.'

'And now we're trapped,' Yael said bitterly. 'Just when we thought we were winning. Llume used the box on me, and I – oh, I told her everything I knew. The pain—'

'I understand. I saw to it that you didn't really know much. It was lucky that I *wasn't* here, or she would have had it all.'

'But she's watching for you now!' Yael said with sudden new alarm. 'The moment you come back in a shuttle to retransfer, she'll—' She stopped. 'But you transferred back! She doesn't know—'

'Precisely. So we may have a certain subtle advantage. I knew something was wrong when that "Six of Sceptres" signal was broadcast, so I didn't take any chances.' Melody

213

sighed. 'But I am still helpless; I can't fight the box either.'

Then Melody lifted her hand casually and set it on Skot's hand on the table. She could do this without any reaction from the box because she had no intention of attacking Llume or turning off the device. She just wanted to put Skot's mind somewhat at ease.

Skot looked up, startled at the contact. He felt the intense aura and looked at her, wide-eyed. Melody nodded slowly.

'Why didn't you catch Llume the first time, with the Tarot cards, the way you did the others?' Yael persisted. 'And why did she *help* you catch the others?'

'Because she is a very special agent,' Melody said. 'She doesn't work with the others. In fact, probably only Dash and Tiala knew she *was* a hostage. She was their backup. It was her job to protect her secret until the time came for her to act. She was extremely well trained, so that she really thought like the entity she represented – a Spican transferee. Any little slips she might have made would be covered by the confusion between her Spican/Polarian identities. She is an expert in cultural nuances, and knows more about them than I do. She well knew what I was doing with the cards. There was no way I could expose her. All her actions were consistent with her role; where a true Spican would have helped me, *Llume* helped me – even against other hostages. Of course Dash knew what I was doing all along, and *he* was expert in Tarot, too. They were just letting me play my game, keeping myself busy, while Dash tried to convert me to his cause.' She sighed again. 'It was a beautiful setup, and it came closer to success than I like to admit. Had I not happened to be an old Mintakan neuter . . .'

She looked at Llume sadly. 'It was a most sophisticated operation, ruthless yet effective. All the other hostages of this ship were not worth as much to Andromeda as Llume, which was why Dash accepted defeat and exile without betraying her. He put his duty first.'

'I liked Llume,' Yael said. 'Is that wrong?'

'I liked her myself,' Melody said. 'Very much. I suppose that was the main reason I didn't want to believe what I suspected. We are undone by our foolish foibles.'

The ship's large viewglobe showed a holographic image of the fleet with image enhancement to make the picture clear. Bright motes shone: little swords, cups, wands, disks, and atoms representing the ships of the segment. The flagship was marked in red in the very center, surrounded by the other Sphere command ships. Farther out, but still in the nucleus, were Sphere contingents, grouped like protons. Then, beyond the battleship the rings of smaller ships began. These were not so readily identifiable by shape; they depended on thrust instead of spin for their internal gravity, and did not collect light. A Polarian scout looked much like a Solarian scout, both being needleships.

'This is Llume of /,' Llume announced to the fleet. 'I am in charge of the flagship, *Ace of Swords*, having assumed command in the absence of the scheduled command, Bird of dash of Andromeda, who was lost in the course of ship take-over. I received the Action Hour notice and issued the "Six of Scepters" alarm; I now coordinate this mission. Hostages have now had time to assume command of their ships as programmed. Vessels will now cluster about me, that we may know our strength. Any ship that approaches without demonstrating its Andromedan nature will be fired on by my lasers. I repeat: I am of Sphere slash, and Sphere slash now coordinates the entire galactic project.'

'Very bold bluff,' Melody remarked to Yael. 'The lasers have the longest range in the fleet. As this ship has the most powerful laser cannon of all the Swords, it can act against any other ship before that ship can bring its own weapons to bear. And she reminded us that she is a slash entity; the slash are natural laser-users, so they really know how to handle such armament. So unfriendly ships will probably keep their disance.'

'Then it's no bluff,' Yael said.

'But neither the Andromedans nor the Milky Wayans know that Llume is operating the ship alone. She has no drive technician, no laser cannoneer. So she can neither maneuver nor fire – not while she's operating the communications net. Any ship could come and blast her out of space. So it's merely a nice ploy, and she has a lot of nerve.'

215

'You still like her, don't you,' Yael observed.

'The Andromedans are entities like us. The do have their redeeming qualities. Llume may be my enemy, but she is still a lot like me.'

'*You* never betrayed your friends!'

'I fear I have betrayed my entire galaxy by misjudging Llume,' Melody replied sadly. 'The hints were there, so obvious in retrospect, but I refused to pay attention because I liked her too much. I did not take proper steps to nullify her. And this is the result.'

Yael was silent.

Llume rolled away from the console and came to the captives. 'I will turn the pain to zero intensity,' she said, 'if the two of you will give me your pledges as Solarians to cooperate with me. The boxes will remain set to your frequencies but will not affect you unless you attempt to renege.'

She oriented first on Skot, placing her tail before him on the table. 'You will operate the laser cannon controls, firing only on my order.'

Skot stared at her with obvious hostility. 'No.'

Llume's ball moved to Melody. 'You will handle maneuvers, moving the ship on my order or in emergency defense of this vessel. It is more complex than you can readily handle, Yael of Dragon, but I will give you specific directions.'

Melody watched the Polarian ball. If it came much closer, Llume would pick up the strength of her aura and realize that Melody was back. As long as she thought Melody was somewhere else in the fleet, Llume would be uncertain. So the secret had to be protected; small as it was, it was all Galaxy Milky Way had.

'Yes,' Melody said.

Skot jerked up – then froze as the pain caught him. He couldn't even call her traitor, but he didn't need to.

The ball traveled back to Skot. 'Yael has agreed. She is not as strong-willed as you, and she doesn't like pain – but her direction is sensible. Will you now join her? I will not require you to do anything actually harmful to your allied ships; it will be a matter of firing warning shots.'

Skot's only answer was to stiffen in agony.

'Then I set your box on two, while you consider,' Llume said.

Meanwhile, Melody's pain had ceased. The boxes stimulated the pain nerves of the body, doing no actual physical harm. They were superlative control devices. 'Please,' Melody said. 'Set his level down again.'

Llume paused. 'Since you cooperate, I honor your request. I return his setting to one.' And Skot relaxed somewhat.

Llume led the way to the maneuvers console, and gave Melody a quick general rundown. Melody paid close attention, while standing as far from Llume as she could without arousing suspicion, so that no chance contact could give away her aura. If she ever got free of the box, she wanted to know how to operate this ship.

A warner sounded at the communications console. Llume returned to it. 'A capsule is approaching,' she observed. 'It could be Captain Llono of Spica, in which case I would welcome him though I should have to confine him. I have a certain fondness for Spica; my host there was very nice. She was voluntary, having no knowledge of my true mission; the same is true of my Polarian host. I do not believe in damaging hosts, despite Andromedan policy.'

'Perhaps you should join the Society of Hosts,' Melody remarked.

'You have picked up certain mannerisms of your prior transferee,' Llume said. 'That remark is typical of her.'

Melody had forgotten that Llume was a specialist in alien cultures. She had nearly given herself away! 'I liked her,' Melody said.

'So did I. She was a resourceful, intelligent entity with a fine lovely aura,' Llume said. 'It is with extreme regret I find myself opposing her. If she survives this war, I hope to be her friend again.' She studied the viewglobe. 'I wish this host had better vision; I cannot be sure of the precise origin of that approaching shuttle. But in any event, I cannot take the chance that it is innocent. It could contain a radiation

217

bomb.' She rolled over to the short-range radio. 'Identify yourself, shuttle. Andromedan or Milky Way?'

There was no response.

'Identify yourself,' Llume repeated. 'Otherwise I must destroy you.'

Captain Llono must have been en route in the shuttle when the 'Six of Scepters' announcement was broadcast, so didn't know of the change in situation. This challenge from Llume probably confused him; it was on the wrong beam. So he was bluffing it out in silence while he tried to contact Skot on the other beam. Only Skot was no longer on duty in that capacity. Possibly Llono had caught on from these hints that something was wrong. Melody didn't know whether to say something, and decided with regret to stay out of it lest she give herself away. She could not be certain that Llume's conjecture about the radiation bomb was not correct.

Llume rolled over the laser control console, oriented one cannon to verbal directive, focused on the shuttle, and fired.

Oh, Llono! Melody cried internally. Why hadn't she spoken? Better that he be captured than wiped out!

A mote flicked out in the viewglobe.

'No explosion,' Lume observed. 'Then it was not a bomb. Perhaps merely debris from the sundered Polarian craft.' But she did not sound convinced.

The irony was, Llume had acted entirely reasonably, by the standards of war. She had challenged the approaching craft, informed it of the consequence of unrecognized approach, and only then destroyed it. Had she not done so, all the fleet would have known she was bluffing. How could Melody blame her for that?

She glanced across at Skot. He was writhing in agony. Obviously *he* had tried to do something!

There was a period of silence, as if in mourning for the lost craft that might have been a bomb, and the inadequacies of those who might have allowed a brave entity to die needlessly. Melody rehearsed script after script in her mind that might have saved her friend, knowing it was pointless. She

218

was guilty of the slaughter of a sapient entity, not in self-defense but in stupidity.

The fleet net came alive abruptly. 'I am Mnuhl of Segment Knyfh,' a voice announced. It was a human voice, an automatic translation from the magnetic charges that were Knyfh communication. The net was geared to handle the full range of languages and modes of the fleet components. All messages were transmitted in common code, to be translated upon reception to whatever mode was applicable. 'In the seeming absence of leadership in Segment Etamin, in the interest of Galaxy Milky Way, I am assuming temporary command of the loyalist forces of this fleet. I base this assumption on information obtained from Melody of Etamin, a special segment agent who helped me free my vessel of hostages. Loyalist ships will close in on my ship, the *Ace of Atoms*, after identifying themselves to me. It will be necessary for each vessel to acquiesce to search by my personnel to verify absence of hostages.'

Llume glowed. 'This is Llume of Andromeda,' she said into the net. 'The loss of your vessel is a blow to the cause of Andromeda, but I deal with you as *pro tem* Admiral of Segment Forces. Will you permit hostage ships to clear your vicinity without harassment, in return for a similar truce on our part?'

Melody could not help being fascinated by the military nicities. To indulge in a random melee would be wasteful and pointless, with ships firing on their own allies from confusion and ignorance. Therefore the two commanders negotiated politely to defer hostilities. Could she have saved Captain Llono the same way?

'Mnuhl here,' the Knyfh Captain responded. 'I compliment you on your offer, and acquiesce.'

'Truce established,' Llume said. 'One private question: Does Melody remain with you?'

'I do not feel free to divulge that information.'

'Was she aboard the shuttle that just approached my ship?'

'I must decline to answer.'

Melody nodded to herself. Captain Mnuhl was giving away nothing; he knew the importance of keeping the hostages in doubt about Melody's location. Every hostage captain would be afraid that a high-Kirlian counterhostage was aboard his ship. That fear would multiply her effectiveness many times. Too bad she wasn't able to make that threat genuine!

'Thank you, Captain.' Llume terminated the private exchange and returned to general information: 'This is Hostage Command: do not fire on loyalist ships as they maneuver. Truce is in force. Andromedans will orient on the *Ace of Swords*; loyalists on the *Ace of Atoms*.'

Llume shut off the net. Then she sank into a glowing heap. It was, Melody realized, the Polarian way of expressing complete grief.

Skot looked up. 'Andromedan, are you ill?' he inquired. His tone was not friendly, but the query was relevant. If Llume became incapacitated, Skot and Melody would be left under the control of the discipline-boxes, unable to free themselves – with the Andromedan fleet closing about them. If Llume did not maintain communications, the hostages would become suspicious and blast the *Ace of Swords* out of space.

Llume drew herself more or less erect. 'It is an illness of the soul,' she said. 'I fear I have slain my sister.'

'What is she talking about?' Yael asked. 'She didn't kill—'

'Let's wait and see,' Melody said to her. 'If what I suspect is true . . .'

'You are killing our galaxy,' Skot said coldly. 'Why should one Spican matter to you?'

'Captain Llono!' Yael exclaimed, just catching on. 'In the shuttle! Poor Spican Undulant!'

'I thought it was a trap, a bomb,' Llume said. 'That is what an Andromedan would have done, testing the defenses. But it didn't detonate under the laser. The Knyfh tried to conceal it, but I could tell Melody had left his ship.'

'She thinks *you* were in that shuttle!' Yael cried. Skot, torn by mixed reactions, did not speak.

'She was more like me than any I have known,' Llume

220

continued, slumping again. 'Such an aura! The Dash Command of Andromeda put out a directive to save that aura at any price short of capitulation, I had even more reason to preserve her from harm. Instead, in an inexcusable lapse of logic, I betrayed the affinity of aura.'

'But she *didn't* kill you!' Yael said to Melody.

'Wait,' Melody told her. 'This just may be—'

Llume righted herself and returned to the communications console. 'This is Llume of slash,' she said into the net. 'I hereby resign my commission and become captive to the ranking remaining loyalist officer of this ship, Skot of Etamin. Please allow the *Ace of Swords* to join the loyalist cluster.'

Then she rolled across to Skot and turned off his discipline-box. 'You are now in command. Orient the box on me.'

Skot, amazed, took the box. 'You are betraying your kind?'

'No. I announced my captivity. The next in command will now assume coordination.'

Sure enough, the net was already active. 'I am Hammer of Quadpoint, Andromeda. I assume command. Gather around my ship, the *Ten of Disks*. Truce holds.'

Skot deactivated Melody's box. 'Shall I tell her?'

'Let me.' Melody crossed to Llume and put her hand against the Polarian hide, letting her aura manifest. 'Thank you for showing me your heart, sister,' she said.

'I have been in transfer too long. I have become a true Spican Undulant.' Then Llume glowed with realization. 'Melody! I brought you back! I chose you over my galaxy — and now I have you back!'

'Yes,' Melody agreed, remembering the sacrifice of poor Captain Llono. Then she put her human arms about Llume, and cried human tears.

15

Sword of Sol

report: complications manifest
/as dash thought!   specifics?/
*strong resistance in segments freng, qaval, knyfh,
etamin, weew   progress in lodo, bhyo, faʒ, novagleam,
thousandstar*
/so it is by no means a clean beam!   it may be a difficult
war   dash was right to be cautious   we lack the reserves
for extended campaign   we were not sufficiently prepared
   action hour was premature/
do you wish to turn over leadership to quadpoint?
/yes, that seems best now   only that force of approach
can bring this to a proper conclusion, now that we are
inextricably committed   we must prevail or suffer extinction ourselves, for the enemy will soon achieve parity of
technology as it did before/

Melody had to experiment for a while with the Communications console before she got the hang of it. Skot assumed the navigation and gunnery duties. They needed
more officers, but Melody didn't want to force Llume to
assume any of these tasks, though it was possible the discipline-box could make her perform. Could the magnets be
made to understand any of the necessary chores of spaceship
operation? She would have to explore that possibility when
she had a chance. But first she had to establish private communications with Captain Mnuhl of Knyfh. The fleet net
would not do for battle strategy!
The net was a diffuse magnetic field that encompassed the
entire fleet. No ship-to-ship privacy had been necessary
before the hostage intrusion, so little provision for it had

been made. The only alternate mode of communication available was laser radio, used at short range to contact the shuttles. But that had to be aligned in laser style, which meant any ship contacted was simultaneously vulnerable to an attack-beam, and the other ships would hardly sit still for that right now! What else was there?

The transfer unit! Now she could try her notion. 'Skot, we need some low-Kirlian hosts. I want to use paired transfer units to handle conversations with Captain Mnuhl, so no enemy can intercept them.'

'We have several former hostages in the hold,' Skot said dubiously. 'Those entities you and Lono brought back.'

'Ideal! If we can get word to Mnuhl privately, so he can set up similarly without the Andromedans knowing . . .'

'I can try to transfer to his ship,' Skot said dubiously.

A Polarian rolled into the room. Melody and Skot looked up, amazed. It was not Llume.

'You will remain absolutely still,' the Polarian said against the wall. 'I possess magnetic weaponry. Identify yourselves.'

Had another hostage developed? Melody saw no weapon, but didn't want to risk it. She could put her hand on one of the discipline-boxes in a moment. 'I am Melody of Mintaka.'

'Skot of Kade.'

'Llume of Slash, Andromeda.'

Suddenly Slammer launched himself at the Polarian. 'No!' Melody cried, too late.

But as the magnet came near the intruder, he lost power, and dropped helplessly to the floor. 'I am Mnuhl of Knyfh,' the Polarian said.

Melody's relief was so great and sudden she found herself laughing weakly. Of course! Mnuhl had thought of the same thing she had, and had already acted on it, taking over the available Polarian host. Had Llume not given herself up, Mnuhl would have contrived to overcome her.

'Come, feel my aura,' Melody said. 'I may look strange in my human host, but I am she whom you met aboard the *Ace of Atoms*.'

He did not approach. 'In what guise?'

Melody realized that Mnuhl, too, had thought she was dead. He had come over to verify the situation personally. 'In the guise of Gnejh, the mad one.'

Now he approached. 'Then you are not chained!' he said as their auras confirmed each other. 'I was concerned.'

'How did you stop the magnet?'

'We have long experience with lesser creatures of our type,' Mnuhl said. 'It is not damaged; I merely depleted its power temporarily.'

Indeed, Slammer was now recovering.

'We are very short of officers,' Melody said. 'Our crew-Solarians won't do for command posts as they are untrained. So am I. Will you be able to help us?'

'We are drawing replacements for our own losses from Segment Knyfh via transfer,' Mnuhl replied. 'But we are very short of hosts. Will some of your Solarians serve?'

Melody hadn't thought of that. 'Knyfh officers in Solarian hosts! I will verify in a moment.' She activated the crew-circuit. Her experience aboard Mnuhl's ship had facilitated her competence here. 'Require six volunteers for alien host duty,' she said. 'Security of ship depends on it. *Volunteers*, not assignments.'

'Sergeant Jones of Personnel here, sir,' a male Solarian voice replied. That 'sir' startled her, as it always did. She was also surprised by the immediate and routine answer, and had to remind herself that as far as the crew was concerned, nothing unusual had happened. They didn't know about the savage battle in the officers' section, or the loss of all but one of their regular officers – or even about the Andromedan threat. In a way, she envied them! 'Will there be a performance bonus?'

Melody looked at Skot for advice. She was not familiar with this sort of thing. Skot nodded affirmatively. 'Any reasonable requirement will be met,' Melody said crisply. 'Use your discretion, Sergeant.'

'Six volunteers on the way,' Jones said.

Just like that! Melody hardly trusted the 'volunteer' status, suspecting coercive assignment, but she would make

224

sure before she used them. 'We expect to have six suitable hosts,' she told Captain Mnuhl. 'Does it matter which sex they are?'

'Immaterial. We are sexless in your sense, and can utilize whatever is offered.'

That had to be true, for the Polarian host he was now using was female.

'Then we shall be ready shortly,' she said.

'Excellent. Bring your ship into proximity so that we can use laser radio in case of emergency. Inform us when you're ready.' He rolled away, going back to the transfer unit. Skot followed.

Melody decided to take a chance. 'Llume, I propose to use you as you used my host. I shall set the discipline-box on you and ask you to guide this ship toward the *Ace of Atoms*. Do you object?'

'No,' Llume said. She went to the propulsion console while Melody tuned the box. The ship began to move.

Melody watched the viewglobe. Already the fleet was fissioning into two clusters. About twice as many were moving toward the Andromedan nucleus as toward the Milky Way nucleus. How were they going to overcome a fleet that was twice their number? Her efforts had only been token; perhaps half a dozen additional ships salvaged.

The truce held. By the time the *Ace of Swords* joined the loyalist nucleus, Melody had six human volunteers, and had verified that they were indeed voluntary. The promise of bonus and special privileges had made them eager, and they were quite curious about the ship's maneuvering and what was going on in officer country. They were also motivated by a genuine patriotism for their sphere, segment, and galaxy, once they understood the nature of the threat. They were, in short, good men.

Captain Mnuhl transferred six Knyfh officers into these willing hosts, and suddenly there was a sufficient and highly competent complement. They introduced themselves formally and moved efficiently to the key stations. It was evident from the outset that they were expert. Melody had no further concern about the technical operation of the ship, although she was a bit awed by the evidence that aliens had such a thorough working knowledge of the Solarian ship. They could not have drawn the information from the minds of their human hosts, because the humans knew next to nothing of these jobs. The Andromedans were quite right to view Segment Knyfh as their greatest obstacle to victory!

Her concern about the coming space battle was another matter. The ratio was holding: two hostage ships to each loyal one. Those four hundred hostages had really done their job. Soon the final tally was in: sixty-six hostage, thirty-three loyal. The hundredth ship had been blown up in the preliminary action.

The original cluster fleet: one hundred ships – like the one hundred cards of the Cluster Tarot deck. Probably only a partial coincidence. Had there been Trump ships along with the Suit ships – but that would have been stretching it too far! This ostentatious display of useless power, this show of segment unity that was the fleet, now it threatened the very existence of Imperial Outworld. What irony that this vanity of space was now to be used exactly for what it had been designed: destruction.

Two to one; how were they going to prevail against that force?

There was a Solarian game in Yael's mind, an ancient system of shaped pieces on a checkered board, called chess. Here there were five types of pieces disposed to protect their King, each with its unique mode of operation. In the game of chess, position and strategy were more important than the individual value of the pieces; was that also true in space?

The net spoke: 'Hammer of quadpoint.'

'I have expected your call, Hammer,' Mnuhl replied.

'We appear to have a decisive advantage. Your ships are outnumbered and underpersonnelled. No help can come to you in time to reverse this. We cannot allow you to return under arms to your segment capital. We shall proceed there ourselves, to place Outworld under siege and force capitulation of the segment government. We can accomplish this with half our present force. Indeed, we can accomplish it with a single ship. You therefore can gain nothing by forcing an engagement. We do not wish to destroy good ships unnecessarily, or to indulge in pointless hostilities. We therefore proffer you amicable terms in exchange for your surrender. The demolition of this section of the galaxy will not proceed immediately; you will be permitted to retire for the duration of your lives in planetary comfort, unmolested.'

'We must consult,' Mnuhl replied.

'I await your return call. Truce.'

Truce. Melody was reminded of Yael's poem, 'Four Swords'. But that had signified dissolution of whatever relationship had existed between the parties, a refusal to fit scripts. Now there was fleet truce between the grotesquely animated Swords and Atoms and Disks and Cups and Scepters. She wondered briefly how the ships of the fleet were numbered, as there were some twenty-seven Disks spread across three Spheres, Polaris, Nath, and Sador. There had to be some duplications. That broke down the analogy some more, and was perhaps a hopeful sign.

The Polarian host rolled in again. 'You are the ranking Kirlian among us,' Mnuhl said to Melody. 'Do you wish to assume fleet command?'

Melody was amazed. '*I?* Captain, I know nothing of command and less of space tactics!'

'The chain of command has little to do with space tactics. I myself am not even of your segment. I acted because I believed I was the only entity in a position to act, but I can not retain command here more than briefly. My first priority is to ascertain the appropriate admiral and invest that entity with authority over the loyal fleet. I would not have presumed to meddle in the affairs of an alien segment even to this extent were it not for the preemptive need of our galaxy.'

'But I haven't the least idea how to direct a fleet or to conduct a battle. I'd walk into the first simple tactical trap the hostages set. I have already made many mistakes, and survived only by chance.'

Mnuhl's Polarian voice resembled that of a patient instructor. Melody fancied she could hear the firmly remonstrative chords behind the frontal tune, though the Knyfh's voice was actually filtered through his Polarian ball. 'The years of direct commandorial supervision of battle are long over. What is required is a figure of unquestionable authority, who will designate deputies to handle the technical details.'

Melody began to understand. 'Details – such as the conduct of the battle!'

'Correct. As admiral, you would maintain liaison with the enemy admiral, clarifying the rules of the situation, negotiating specific complications. The present truce is the result of the procedure developed in prior commands.'

It really was a functional system. Millennia of interspecies contacts had perfected such conventions on an intergalactic scale. Andromeda honored the same general set of rules. This brought a certain order out of what would otherwise be chaos. 'Then – I could appoint *you* to handle the battle,' she said.

'Correct. It would not be presumptuous of me to act as your delegate. I have met you; I know you. There is no Kirlian entity to match you in my segment, and certainly not within this fleet. You are the natural commander, for you alone are unquestionably loyal; you alone cannot be rendered hostage. I urge you to assume the position of admiral – for the good of our galaxy.'

It was hard to decline a plea like that! Still, Melody hesitated. 'Captain, I am not young and strong and bold, regardless of the way this host appears.' But suddenly she was conscious of the fact that the host was bruised and disheveled, with a bandage on the leg. 'I am old, very near the termination of my natural life span. My judgment may be suspect. What will you do if I decline?'

'I will retain command, as I cannot be sure of the identity of other captains of this fleet. Given time I could locate one suitable, but the enemy will not permit us that time.'

Would the Drone of the *Deuce of Scepters* be suitable? Melody kept that thought in abeyance for now. 'I mean, what would you do about Hammer of : :'s offer?'

'I see no alternatives except to yield or fight. Since by

228

conventional wisdom our situation is untenable, we must yield.'

This, from the representative of a leading segment of the galaxy! Would the Drone see it the same way? 'We *can't* yield! It could mean the end of our galaxy! We have no idea how things are turning out in the other segments; we may be the only—'

'I have had reports via my incoming transfer officers. Segments Qaval and Weew are holding, while Segments Bhyo and Thousandstar are in deep—'

'I don't want to hear it!' Melody screamed. '*We* can't give up!' Was it that she could not bear to hear of the fall of wonderful Thousandstar, her budding fancy?

'The result may be the same if we fight. It would be best to reduce the destruction, trusting the Andromedans to grant us longer life than we should have otherwise. An entity like Hammer of : : would not have been granted high status among his kind had he not honor. If I command, I must do what seems reasonable to me. Perhaps your wisdom is other than conventional.'

'You bet your sweet notes it is!' But Melody still hesitated. She knew herself to be incompetent to run a ship, let alone a fleet, but she could not stand by and watch her galaxy go under. She had already faced that sort of compromise, and her reaction had not changed. 'I'd rather gamble and lose,' she said, 'than lose without gambling. I will assume command.'

'I will support you completely, though I may not privately agree with all your policies,' Mnuhl replied gravely. She could almost see his handsome face smiling – which was strange, because of course he had no face, either in this host or in his natural state. He did, however, have a handsome aura.

'Are you competent to handle the battle, despite your objection to it?' she asked him.

'I am competent to handle a conventional battle. But we shall surely lose it. Unless you have some innovative strategy.'

'Yes. Very well; let's reply to Admiral Hammer.'

Mnuhl transferred back to his own ship, and activated the net. 'I regret the delay of consultation,' he said.

'Quite all right,' Hammer of : : replied with almost Solarian gruffness. 'What is your decision?'

'I have yielded command of the loyalist forces to Melody of Etamin, who will answer you.'

Even through the computer mockup, the startled reaction was apparent. 'Melody of Mintaka survives?'

'I survive,' Melody said. 'As ranking Kirlian entity, I have assumed command of the Etamin fleet. I decline to accept your offer of amicable terms in exchange for surrender. Instead I offer you similar terms for *your* surrender.'

There was a snort of incredulous mirth – from Skot of Kade. It was exactly the sort of answer he would have made.

Hammer was too sophisticated to react emotionally. 'Your response is noted; your offer is declined. This terminates our state of truce, subject to the standard period of grace. Do you agree to abide by the Intergalactic Conventions of Warfare?'

'I must consult,' Melody said. She turned off the net and spoke to Skot. 'What's this?'

'An assemblage of practical conventions,' he replied. 'Individual ships are allowed to surrender when disabled beyond combat capability; equitable treatment for prisoners without unreasonable terms for release; sharing of hospital facilities in neutral zones; surrendered captains permitted to retain their commands on their own recognizance as noncombatants; no attacks made on fleet command ships – that sort of thing.'

'The ancient code of chivalry!' Melody exclaimed. 'You have it all worked out so neatly, like a polite game.'

'Courtesy and accommodation are inherent in military space,' he agreed.

'Discordance!' Melody swore. 'That's not courtesy; that's pusillanimity! The admirals don't fire at each other, the ships quit when they get nicked. Certainly it cuts losses, but it also rules out unorthodox methods. We *can't* win that way!'

Skot smiled wolfishly. 'That's right!'

Melody wondered whether Mnuhl would concur. She would soon find out! She reactivated the net. 'Hammer, I decline to honor the Intergalactic Conventions of Warfare. Anything goes.'

The hostage seemed unperturbed. She wished she could see his face, though she didn't even know what type of host he occupied; it might have no face. 'As you prefer. Your ships shall be destroyed without quarter until such time as you yourself yield the remainder of your fleet.'

'Uh, wait,' Melody said. This Andromedan was one tough negotiator! She did not want to condemn all the loyal entities of her fleet to violent extinction. 'Will you consider an alternate mode of settlement?'

'Identify it.'

'Single combat of champions.' That was straight out of the legends of Thousandstar! 'One ship from each fleet.'

There was a pause. Good. At least Hammer's mind was not a complete calculator! 'Melody of Mintaka, your mind intrigues me. However, I must point out that a one-to-one ratio would not reflect the relative strengths of our fleets. I would consider a contest of two of our champions against one of yours.'

'The :: is right,' Melody muttered. 'The contest has to reflect the fleets. I suppose that's better than having dozens of ships and thousands of lives destroyed, though. If one of ours can't take two of theirs, how can thirty-three of ours expect to take sixty-six of theirs?'

'Except we're all sunk if our one ship loses,' Yael said. 'And if *they* lose, how do we know they'll honor it? They're playing by the rules only because they're winning.'

'There is that,' Melody agreed. 'They talk of Intergalactic Conventions, but look at the way they took over their ships! Precious little honor in *that*! Any way we look at it, we're in serious trouble.'

'Maybe one at a time . . .' Yael said.

'That's it!' Aloud, Melody said: 'Hammer, suppose we pit one of our ships against two of yours – in turn? If yours wins either match—'

'I personally am inclined to agree,' Hammer said. 'I am

231

extremely curious about the merits of individual types of fighting ships, as these are similar to ours of Andromeda. But I am constrained to point out two things: First, I do not believe I have authority to surrender a superior fleet, in the event your single ship had the fortune to prevail twice; my next-in-command might well have me deposed for treason to my galaxy. Second, individual combat does not necessarily reflect group-combat potential; the ship that wins singly might lose in a mass-action. I therefore must qualify this matter. I will send ships singly against yours in a line match, but will not permit my fleet to be bound by the result. The victor of each contest will meet the next ship from the other side. After a ship has won twice, it may retire from the field if it chooses, since limitations of fuel and ammunition prevent indefinite continuation. Each encounter will affect the strength of the fleets, however, and this might lead to renegotiation of terms after several actions. Should the first twenty victories be yours, your position would be considerably strengthened both on the field and in negotiations. But chance still gives us an advantage commensurate with our total force.'

'A remarkably cogent analysis,' Melody agreed. This entity was no dummy, unfortunately! 'I shall honor the prior truce until the individual encounters desist.'

Privately, she discussed the matter with Skot. 'Are you able to select a champion? I don't know how the types of ships rate against each other.'

'*No* one knows how they rate against each other,' Skot replied. 'Similar types exist in many segments. When one type demonstrates superiority, refinements are made in the others to counter it. There has been very little inter-Sphere conflict in the past few centuries. This would seem to be a unique opportunity to test the merits of design in the field, and the Andromedans are probably just as curious about it as we are. I would guess, however, that the competence of individual captains and crews is the decisive factor.'

'I wonder if a natural captain should do better than a hostage captain.'

He shrugged. 'That, too, remains to be tested.'

The totals were not encouraging. There were six Solarian Swords including the flagship in the loyalist fleet, while the hostages had fourteen. Melody had seven Canopian Scepters to the hostages' thirteen; the enemy also had two Wands of Mirzam and two Rods of Bellatrix. She had five Spican Cups to fourteen of the enemy's, buttressed by three Chalices from Antares. There were ten loyalist Polarian Disks and nine Andromedan but three of the five Nath Disks were hostage, and both Coins of Sador. She fared best with the Atoms of Knyfh, having three of the four, but both Mintakan Atoms were hostage, a special indignity. No matter what type of ship was deemed best, she had no advantage.

'Let's start with a Scepter,' she decided.

'The Canopians are certainly excellent craftscreatures,' Skot said. 'They have inflexible will and responsive crews.'

'Because their crews are Slaves, accustomed for millennia to taking orders from insectoid Masters,' Melody said. But she remembered the Drone of the *Deuce of Scepters* and relented. 'We'll send out the *Deuce*.'

She contacted the Drone on the net. 'Yes,' he said, as if it were the only possible choice for such a mission.

The Scepter moved out of the fleet cluster, into the vacant space between the two forces. It was a rod with a ball on one end, like a cross between the handle of a Sword and the body of a small Disk. It traveled sidewise, maintaining its orientation to the sun. There was something so graceful, so elegant about that smooth progress that Melody hummed a chord of admiration, as well as her human vocal apparatus permitted. 'Now if only it can fight!' she murmured fervently.

From the hostage fleet floated a Cup. It, too, maintained its attitude, the deep indentation toward the sun. It, too, was pretty as it spun. And surely it, too, could fight.

Suddenly her idea about the matching of champions seemed ludicrous. 'I have to come up with something better than this!' Melody muttered. 'Something. Anything!'

But her eyes remained on the globe. This horrible encounter was so important!

Melody had a general notion of the propulsion and weapons systems of segment spaceships, but that was all.

She knew that most ships used mixed chemical and electric or 'ion' drive, not atomic. Strict inter-Sphere conventions regulated the discharge of contaminants into navigable space, and radioactive substances were inevitably associated with atomics. Even the Atom ships were not atomic, ironically. So these ships were both 'clean', depending on chemical drive for emergency maneuvers, and on electric for steady acceleration.

Several needle scouts and satellite ships were accompanying each champion, but they hardly showed in the globe at this range. No fleet ship operated alone; the skilled use of extensible eyes and expendable defenses was crucial. The scouts zoomed close to the enemy, pinpointing its position and enabling the mother ship to home in its weaponry. A ship without its scouts was virtually blind. The very globe she peered into was a function of the *Ace of Sword*'s own satellites. But one tended to forget about the needles and shuttles, and to see the whole thing in terms of the single central ship.

'Skot,' Melody said. 'My comprehension is imperfect. Will you stand by me and explain the match?' What she really wanted was the reassurance of his presence; she was afraid she had bargained the loyalist fleet into deeper trouble than before.

'Yes, Admiral,' Skot said. That startled her, but of course, though Llume had turned over the ship to him, Melody herself had assumed command of the entire fleet, so now ranked him.

'I need to understand the capacities and limitations of each type of ship. I don't know whether I can come up with a winning strategy, but ignorance certainly won't get me there.'

He did not comment. She watched the arena. The two ships moved together steadily, but not on a direct course; each followed a kind of curve. 'Like two gunslingers walking down the street,' Yael said.

'Why don't they fire?' Melody inquired aloud.

'The range is too great,' Skot explained. 'Each employs a form of missile, and accuracy decreases with distance. Also, even an accurate shot from too far out could be avoided or intercepted by a needle. They must come close enough to strike without giving the other ship opportunity to man-euver clear. Wasted shots are trouble; each one represents a sizable investment of material and/or energy.'

'You make it very clear,' Melody said. And inwardly, to Yael: 'It *is* like two gunslingers! They need to save their ammunition for when it counts.'

'Space opera,' Yael agreed.

Then almost simultaneously, the two ships jerked in space, or at least they seemed to shiver in the viewglobe, which probably exaggerated the effect. 'They both fired,' Skot said. 'But neither will score. They're still five thousand miles apart.'

Melody translated the figure into Mintakan units. 'Why, that's the diameter of a small planet!'

Skot smiled. 'You get acclimatized to spatial distances. It is close, in terms of space. Normally ships within the fleet are separated by that amount, so they don't get in each other's way. To hit a target one mile thick from that dis-tance requires an accuracy of one part in five thousand, which is about all a physical projectile from a moving ship is good for. Even when the missile travels at a hundred thou-sand miles per hour, it takes about three minutes to cover the distance. The target ship knows about the shot in a frac-tion of a second, so—'

'So it has three minutes to dodge,' Melody finished. 'Yes, I understand, now. Five thousand miles is the fringe of the action range. Why did they fire so early, then?'

'Well, it is very hard to track a missile, and some of them have homing devices. So it is better to destroy the missile in flight; but it takes a lot of concentration. While the target ship is preoccupied with that, the attacking ship is coming closer, improving its chances for the next shot. So the first shot is not really wasted; it may facilitate the effective fol-lowup.'

'So they keep coming closer, until one scores on the other.'

'Approximately. The difference in weapons complicates this, though.'

'I thought you said they both fired missiles.'

'The Canopian Scepter uses proximity-explosive missiles, yes; a near-miss can shake the target and perhaps disable it. But the Spican Cup uses water bombs, otherwise known as nebula envelopment. The bomb explodes into a cloud of liquid that surrounds the target ship, cutting off its light-input, fouling its broadcast mechanism, interfering with its control over its satellites and corroding its hull. A direct hit normally doesn't kill the crew, but it leaves the ship helpless.'

'How clever,' Melody said with a shudder. 'The Wand strikes physically, and the Cup pours water. We cannot escape the Tarot relevance.'

'I assumed the Tarot was patterned after the cluster fleet,' Skot said.

Typical ignorance! He knew a tremendous amount about space tactics and armament, and nothing about Tarot.

Now the two ships were quite close together, within a thousand miles. Melody knew that was approaching pointblank range for accuracy, and cut missile-avoidance time to thirty-six seconds or less. Was that enough, for a mile-thick ship? One or the other had to go!

The Cup squirted again. Immediately the Scepter used its chemical propulsion to jump aside. 'It'll never make it!' Skot cried. 'It'll have to maintain five or six gravities to clear its own diameter in that time – and it takes more than that to escape a cloud.'

Melody was too tense to ask for further explanation. She watched as the seconds passed.

There was a puff as the vapour-cloud formed, sooner than she expected. But it was not at the Scepter. 'Premature formation!' Skot exclaimed. 'What a break; some Cupper will be hung for that—'

Then the Cup exploded. A sudden new cloud developed, as its life-water puffed into vapor in the vacuum of space. The ship was through; none of the Spicans within it could have survived.

'What happened!' Melody demanded. 'The Drone didn't even fire!'

'I see it now,' Skot said, awed. 'Very sharp tactics! The

236

Scepter waited for the Cup to fire, then homed one of its needle scouts in on the missile. That set it off early. The Scepter accelerated to conceal its true defense, and to cover the recoil of its own firing. So the Cup didn't catch on, and stood still for a direct missile hit. Beautiful!'

'Yet those are home galaxy entities, the great majority of them nonhostage crew,' Melody said, shuddering again. 'All horribly dead of decompression.'

'That's war,' he said. 'They knew the risk when they signed on. We face the same risk.'

But the victory was scant comfort to Melody, who was thinking again of Captain Llono and their sudden mating. A whole shipful of unique triple-sexed Spicans, gone!

'There comes the second ship,' Skot said. 'A Polarian Disk.'

No time for grief! The victorious Scepter now had to face a fresh enemy. 'What's the weapon of the Disk?'

'Polarians think in terms of circularity. All ships must spin at the rate of one revolution every five and a half Solarian minutes in order to maintain gravity at the comfortable level in the officers' section. Slower for the Disks, of course, as they have larger diameters, but the principle's the same. If that spin is changed—'

'All hell breaks loose!' Melody finished. 'How ingenious!'

'Circular,' Skot corrected her with a smile.

Melody looked around. The six human-hosted Knyfh officers were at the consoles, looking as competent as ever. She had little idea what they were doing, but she felt reassured. She returned to the globe. 'But how can one ship change the spin of another?'

'Several ways. Generally, by anchoring a missile to the hull. A missile on a long line can exert considerable torque. Several can wreak havoc. The gravity changes make things fly about, and the crew gets sick, the instruments malfunction . . .'

'I can imagine. Trust Polaris to think of something like that.'

The two ships came together. The Scepter, having expended two missiles in the first encounter, was far more cautious this time. 'They have only six missiles,' Skot explained.

'I told you!' Yael exclaimed. 'A six-shooter!'

Melody closed her eyes. 'I've doomed my friend the Drone of *Deuce* to destruction, then. Even if he wins every match, when he runs out of missiles—'

'Can't ever tell. Canopians are pretty sharp, and they have nerves like tungsten. Maybe the other ship will run out of ammunition too, and it'll be a standoff.'

A standoff. Was there a possibility there for stopping the hostage fleet? Get them all to use up their ammunition uselessly? *How?*

Melody liked this situation less as she came to know it better. Yet the alternative was to throw all her ships into the fray against twice their number. To replace single slaughter by mass slaughter.

The Disk fired. The Scepter maintained course, not even firing back. 'He's trying to intercept the anchor,' Skot said. 'I don't think that stunt will work again, though.'

The Disk fired again. Now the Scepter jetted – but not evenly. Instead of moving out of the way, it began to turn end over end. 'Something's wrong!' Melody cried.

'Drive malfunction,' Skot agreed. 'That's unusual in a Canopian ship; they're finicky about details. But those chemical boosters are tricky when they're hot. Only one side came on.'

The Scepter shook. It was only a token, magnified by the imaging mechanism of the globe, but it loomed like a planet-quake to Melody's nervous eyes.

'He's anchored!' Skot cried as if feeling the shock of contact himself. 'And he never even fired back!'

The Scepter shook again.

'Second anchor,' Skot said gloomily. 'That's the end.'

The Canopian ship twisted in space, tugged by two missiles on strings. The Disk moved in close. 'But the ship has not been destroyed,' Melody said hopefully.

'They'll set hull-borers on him, or inject poisonous gas,' Skot said. 'A ship anchored is a ship vulnerable. The Scepter will yield in a moment; pointless to stretch out the agony.'

238

Then the Disk exploded.

Melody and Skot both gaped. 'What happened?' Melody demanded to know, staring at the fragments of ship spreading outward.

Skot shook his head. 'Sabotage, maybe. I can't figure—'

Something clicked in Melody's mind. Sabotage . . .

A Knyfh looked up from his console. 'The anchors fastened on opposite sides of the Scepter,' he said. 'Their vectors canceled out. A very pretty maneuver on the part of the Canopian.'

'That single jet!' Skot exclaimed. 'That was deliberate! To twist the ship so that the anchor misplaced. It seemed like a malfunction . . .'

'So the Drone won with a single missile this time.' Melody said wonderingly. 'But he's playing it extremely close!'

'He has to. With three missiles left, and the entire fleet of Andromeda before him . . .'

But now the hostage fleet's sole Knyfh Atom came out of the enemy cluster. Melody sighed. 'Poor Drone . . . I have sentenced him to death.'

'We have the right to recall him; he has fought two battles,' Skot pointed out.

Melody activated the net. '*Deuce of Scepters*, you have completed your assignment. Retire from the field.'

'Message declined,' the Drone replied.

Skot stretched his mouth in a way that certain Solarians had to express mixed surprise and respect. 'He's staying in the lists! That must be some entity!'

'He is that,' Melody agreed. 'I suppose technically this is mutiny, but I'd hesitate to call it that. I have a personal interest in his welfare, and I suppose he feels he owes me something. We'll just have to let him perform. He certainly has done well so far.'

The Atom and the Scepter drew close together. This time the Scepter fired first.

'He doesn't dare get within magnetic range,' Skot explained.

'True,' a Knyfh officer agreed. The involvement of a Knyfh ship seemed to have excited their interest. The Knyfh contingent had the best record for loyalty in this fleet – another testimony to the formidability of the segment.

The Atom narrowed the distance, unaffected. Its repulsive magnetic force makes the missiles shy away,' Skot said. 'You have to get very close to score with a physical missile on an Atom – and then you're in its power if you miss.'

The Scepter fired again, without effect. 'Only one chance left,' Skot said. 'If the Scepter can loose a missile just as the Atom starts its pull-phase – there!'

The ships drew together more quickly. Then suddenly they reversed. There was an explosion. 'The Atom out-timed him,' Skot said sadly. 'The missile didn't make it before the field reversed. Now Knyfh will shake Canopus apart.'

Sure enough, the two ships drew together, then apart, then together again. 'But the Atom is shaking itself as badly as its opponent,' Melody said.

'The Atom is constructed to take it,' Skot said. 'That nucleus and shell system, cushioned by magnetism – you could just about throw it against the wall and it would bounce.'

'Like Slammer,' Melody said gloomily and the magnet bobbed behind her, thinking she was addressing it.

'Tougher than Slammer. You can hardly hurt a Knyfh by concussion.'

Melody remembered how readily Captain Mnuhl had stopped Slammer, just as a Solarian with a club might handle an Earth-planet canine. If the hostages had been no more successful with the main fleet of Segment Knyfh than they had been with this small contingent, the loyalists would have a three-to-one advantage, and that segment would be secure. Perhaps it would then send out more aid to the other segments, and the Milky Way would be saved. So she was not disappointed to witness the power of the Atom, but, oh, why did it have to be demonstrated on the *Deuce of Scepters*?

No miracle strategy saved the Drone this time. He was finished. Finally the Atom hurled the Scepter away. It turned end over end, obviously dead. Andromeda had won this one. 'Poor Drone,' Melody said again, feeling the tears in her eyes. 'I wish . . .'

'Let the Sword of Sol avenge him,' Skot suggested. 'The *Four* is with us; that's a bold ship . . .'

'*Four of Swords* to the lists,' Melody said into the net. And privately to Skot: 'I hope you're right. If I had any better way to stave off Andromeda . . .'

The *Four of Swords* moved out immediately, as if it had been expecting the call. Melody couldn't help experiencing a particular quickening of interest. She was aboard the *Ace of Swords*; just how good a ship *was* this type?

Sword and Atom moved toward each other. 'Why don't any of these ships maneuver more?'

'It wastes energy and fouls up their spin,' Skot said. 'It's hard to turn a spinning ship in space; precession sets in and fouls it up. Better to orient on the target and knock it out fast, and only dodge when you have to.'

Melody again visualized the two gunslingers of Yael's imagination walking toward each other. Dodging bullets was hardly worthwhile; better to shoot fastest and best. Yet she felt somehow disappointed. The contest seemed to lack flair.

The Atom exploded, startling her. 'The Sword didn't even strike, did it?'

'Lasers don't make recoil,' Skot said. 'It was firing as soon as it got within the five-second range; and it scored before the Atom could get hold of it. A laser strike in the right place can fission an Atom.'

Melody smiled but Skot wasn't joking. He spoke with deep pride. Then she looked again at the fragmented ship of Knyfh, and shuddered. No joke at all! Captain Mnuhl was aboard an Atom. If Swords took Atoms so easily – the enemy fleet had over twice as many Swords as the loyalists did.

Now a Scepter came out from the Andromedan mass. Melody bit her human lip nervously. She had already seen what a Scepter could do! Somehow she had to stop this destructive exhibition. Thousands of sapient lives were being lost, and for what purpose? Why had Galaxy Andromeda ever set out to take what it had no right to – the binding energy of the Milky Way! Andromeda was surely wrong, and there had to be some way to stop it, to chain the lady and make her behave. Even these ships she used had been pirated from the Milky Way's own fleets, taken hostage . . .

That was it! She had assumed that the counterhostage effort had to be completed before the battle began. But the enemy was actually more vulnerable now than it had been before. With proper strategy, she could destroy its fleet without the loss of any more of her own ships.

'I have to go see Captain Mnuhl,' she said, rising. 'You keep an eye on things here; don't let on to the net that I'm gone.'

Skot nodded. She hurried to the transfer unit, and a Knyfh officer activated it. She landed in the same host she had had before, and in a moment met with Mnuhl.

'I declined to honor the Galactic Convention,' she reminded him. 'Does that mean there are no rules to break?'

'Anything, as you Etamins put it, goes,' Mnuhl agreed. 'However, while the individual contests are in progress, we are under an understood truce.'

'Yes, of course,' she signaled. 'But when that truce ends . . .'

'Only the practical laws of physics prevail,' Mnuhl said. 'No, I must qualify that. I would not condone treachery—'

'Nothing like that! Here is what I have in mind.' And while she kept one perceptor current attuned to the Knyfh equivalent of the viewglobe, tracking the single combat of champions, she described her plan.

'That is legitimate,' Mnuhl agreed at last. 'I shall implement it the moment truce abates. I compliment you on an innovative strategy.'

'It is a desperation strategy,' Melody said. 'I can't stand to see—'

The Scepter exploded. The sudden burst of magnetism made her shield blanch.

'One of its own missiles detonated before it fired,' Mnuhl remarked. 'Exceedingly apt laser accuracy at that range.'

'The Sword of Sol strikes again!' Melody said, pleased in spite of her horror. She was slowly getting acclimatized to this sudden, massive killing. 'That's four to one, our favor. Do you think our management is better than theirs?'

'It may be,' Mnuhl pulsed. 'A hostage probably is not as efficient or motivated as a natural entity or volunteer transferee. This could throw judgment off, make close decisions harder, gunnery less accurate, encourage errors under stress. I would not wish to take an examination in marksmanship with a hostile or insane host dephasing my surface.'

'So maybe that two-to-one ship advantage of theirs is not so much as they think,' Melody returned. 'I'd better get back to my ship.' She rolled to the transfer unit, and in a moment was back in Yael. She hurried to the control room.

'We won the last,' Skot announced. 'But now they're sending out another Sword.' He licked his lips. 'Sword against Sword!'

'You seem to enjoy the prospect.'

He looked embarrassed. 'At least this is fair play. If our handling is better, this will show it.'

'I suppose it will,' Melody agreed. 'Skot, please get in touch with the crew's quarters and get some more volunteers. They'd better have Kirlians of at least two. Make sure they understand that this will be dangerous, uncomfortable work – but extremely important.'

He looked curiously at her and left after a last glance at the viewglobe. Melody knew he wanted to watch this particular match but her other project was more pressing. She could have set it up herself, but if Hammer of : : called her on the net while she was away he might catch on that she was up to something.

The two Swords approached each other, and again she watched compulsively. While she hated this destruction and loss of sapient life and the emotions it roused in her, she was nevertheless fascinated by the competitive aspect. All sapient species were highly competitive, she thought; that was how they got to be sapient. Every Spherical species lusted for death and glory, however much individuals disguised it with the veneer of civilization. If even an old neuter like herself felt the urges, what of the young males?

The hostage Sword fired first. Melody had learned to in-

243

terpret the flash on the globe. It would not be a direct glimpse, for that would mean the laser had struck her own ship; but there was always some trace leakage and refraction that the instruments could pick up and amplify. Lasers were designed to diffuse with distance, so that those that missed their targets were not a menace to other ships of their own fleets. Missiles were also detonated or defused automatically after a certain number of minutes, for the same reason.

The hostage bolt missed. Now the *Four of Swords* fired – and scored. There was a bright splay of light as the globe amplified the reflecting beam. But though struck, the hostage was not dead. The trouble with lasers, she realized, was that unless they struck a vulnerable section, they didn't do much damage. It took several scores to put away an opponent, and in that time the enemy might reverse the advantage by a good or lucky shot of his own.

So there really was no inherently superior weapon, she concluded. The lasers had speed and range, being impossible to avoid or intercept, but no punch. The missiles had plenty of punch, but could be dodged or triggered prematurely. The magnetic fields were fast and could not be avoided but their range was short. So it all came out even, with a good sharp ship of any type able to overcome a sloppy one of any other type. Chance was a considerable factor. Ideally, ships should fight in sets, with a Sword to snipe long distance and an Atom to handle any enemy ship that tried to move in close, and – but that led right back go the present mixed-composition fleet.

The two Swords were very close now, within a thousand miles of each other. Both were firing and scoring, but neither was disabled. In moments one of them would die, though both had been built in the shipyards of Sphere Sol and were crewed primarily by Solarians. Whoever won, Solarians would die. Friend was killing friend.

Suddenly her sickness of it all overcame her. 'Call it off!' she cried aloud. 'I can't stand this ritual slaughter!'

But Skot was away on his assignment, the Knyfh officer had other jobs, and the net was off. She was talking to herself. Her hand went out to activate the net – and she saw the hostage ship explode. Its air gouted out. Though the hull remained almost intact, the ship was dead.

Then the same thing happened to the *Four of Swords*.

Both had been destroyed ... seconds before she had been able to call a halt. 'Damn my indecision!' she cried, gritting her teeth. Her host's leg started hurting again, and she felt very tired.

Now she activated the net. 'Melody of Mintaka here,' she said. 'Terminate the contests of champions. Abate truce.'

The sixty-six–thirty-three ratio of hostage to loyal ships had shifted to sixty-one–thirty-one; an improvement, but still highly disadvantageous. Would the Andromedan command have gone along with the one-to-one battles much longer?

'Truce terminated,' Hammer of :: said. 'Intergalactic Conventions not in force.'

Skot hurried up. 'I have the volunteers. What's this about terminating the truce?'

'We are about to get down to the real combat,' she told him. 'In fact, let's give our project a code name, so we don't have to risk enemy interception of the details. Call it ... call it the Lan of Yap.'

Skot looked at her strangely. 'I don't even know what the program *is*.'

'That's all right. Transfer over to the *Ace of Atoms* and tell Captain Mnuhl to implement the Lan of Yap. He'll understand.'

Skot hesitated then departed again. But Melody's eyes were still fixed on the two drifting, leaking hulks, the Swords of Sol. She shook her head. What a waste!

16

Lan of Yap

progress report
:: proceed ::
the following segments have fallen: lodo, bhyo, faȝ, novagleam   progress in freng and thousandstar   continued resistance in qaval, etamin, knyfh and weew
:: knyfh and weew I comprehend   they are center galaxy cultures, sophisticated   lodo is a surprise   I thought it would be another center of resistance, and perhaps bhyo too   instead we encounter trouble in the lesser regions!
what is there about qaval and etamin? ::
they are centers of the cult of tarotism, said to have originated in etamin prior to the first war   their spheres orient on tarot symbolism, and the name of qaval derives from qabalah
:: does this cult study transfer science? ::
not as such   but it makes use of animation
:: that relates   prepare reserves ::
POWER
:: CIVILIZATION ::

'That's some strategy!' Skot said as he returned. 'Mnuhl gave me the details.'

'I thought he would,' Melody said. 'Now let's review. Each Knyfh ship has a long-range transfer unit aboard, but three of the four Atoms stayed loyal, and the fourth was destroyed in single combat. So the chances are they can't do it back to us.'

'They would have removed the transfer unit to another ship before risking it in single combat,' Skot pointed out. 'Mnuhl says it would have to be on one of the two Mintakan vessels, as Knyfh transfer units do not operate outside an Atom-type ship. Something about the magnetic fields—'

'May my Sphere be sundered by a sour note!' Melody swore. 'I'd like to get into one of those ships and find out what happened.'

'Mintakan Atoms are pretty much like other ships of the fleet,' Skot said mildly. 'They even have a few magnets. Some spheres won't touch magnets, but Mintaka feels they go well with the type of ship. So probably their capture by the hostages was just the luck of the draw. And since the secret of hostaging remains in Galaxy Andromeda, we shouldn't have much to fear from that particular unit.'

Melody touched his hand. 'You are more generous to my Sphere than I am.' She returned to business. 'Now we have four transfer units, and your volunteers should be arriving soon. Best to have Solarians for the Swords and Spicans for the Cups.'

'Yes. And if I may suggest, we should first initiate distractive action, so that the enemy will not be aware of our real thrust.'

'Yes, of course! What do you have in mind?'

'A conventional long-range bombardment. If we reset our ships' missiles for fixed-range detonation, they will explode among the ships of the hostage fleet. It is highly unlikely that any will score, but it would resemble an attack.'

'Good enough,' Melody agreed, though she was concerned about the waste of irreplaceable munitions. 'We can time our Lan of Yap effort to coincide with the arrival of the first missiles.' She glanced across the room, her eyes attracted by the arrival of four crew members. 'Do they understand this will be hazardous?'

'They do,' Skot said.

'I shall make sure,' Melody said. She beckoned them over. Two were female Solarians, but of course she had known that crews were of mixed sexes. Single-sex confinements were unhealthy for a double-sexed species, especially for prolonged tours in space.

'You are about to become transfer agents, which is what I already am,' Melody said. 'You will transfer to available voluntary hosts aboard the enemy ships. You will acquaint the members of these crews with the fact that their ships are controlled by enemy officers. You will incite mutiny, which will really be a restoration of management to the proper authorities. If you are unable to take over a ship, you will sabotage it so that it is unable to fight. I estimate your chances of surviving this mission are less than fifty percent. However if this tactic does not work, the chances of the *Ace of Swords* surviving are also less than fifty percent. You may now withdraw from this assignment if you so choose.'

She looked at each, but no one withdrew.

'We know the fleet is in bad trouble; Officer Skot briefed us,' one of the men said. 'That's why we're here.'

Suddenly Melody recognized him. 'Gary!' He was the man who had taken her out to fix the light-collector trough, hullside.

'I qualify,' he said defensively. 'My Kirlian aura is two point five.'

'Yes, of course.' She could not exclude him simply because she knew him. 'Do you realize what happens to you if the hostages discover what you're up to?'

'The same thing that happens to our whole galaxy if the Andromedans win,' he replied evenly.

Melody nodded. 'If you do manage to take over your ship, try to conceal that fact from the hostage command. When you hear the code phrase "Lan of Yap" on the fleet net, identify—'

Gary snorted with laughter. 'Lan of Yap!' Then he was contrite. 'Sorry, sir.'

Melody smiled. 'Don't be. I picked a code name that no hostage would understand, and that every crewman would appreciate. I am aware of its original meaning.'

'Yes, sir,' Gary said, trying to keep his face straight.

'When you hear that phrase, if you are in control of your ship, identify yourself on the net and fire on any neighbor-ship that has not similarly identified itself. Then try to disengage from that fleet. Do you understand?'

'Yes. We do not want our recovered ships firing on each other.'

'Hit and run,' one of the women said.

Melody smiled. 'If you rejoin our fleet, we will have you transferred back to your own bodies.'

She turned back to Skot. 'Take them to the transfer unit and send them through in rapid order on my signal. Good luck!'

The volunteers marched out. Melody shook her head. 'I am probably sending them to their deaths,' she said. 'But we can be sure the crews of the hostage ships are loyal, and if they'll just believe the truth, they'll act. An average of four hostage officers on each ship can't stop a crew of a thousand! If we can take over or nullify even ten hostage ships without Admiral Hammer knowing it, it may tip the scales in our favor.'

'I know,' Yael said. 'I sure hope it works. I wish I could go myself.'

There was a delay while she organized the details with Captain Mnuhl and made sure the other ships had their volunteers ready. A contingent of Lan of Yap transferees were to make a special effort to recover the two Mintakan vessels. Shuttles carried volunteers from all the Spheres to the four ships with transfer units, so that there were enough to send at least one agent to each hostage ship.

'Bombardment commenced,' Mnuhl announced on the net. The hostages would overhear this, but it didn't matter since it was only a distraction. It didn't even matter if Admiral Hammer fired back, so long as he didn't know what was going on. Maybe he was laughing over-confidently at this seemingly ludicrous ploy. But his thinly spread hostage officers would hardly be paying much attention to what was going on in the depths of the crew quarters . . .

The missiles started exploding. But there was no apparent damage, and the enemy did not return fire. Admiral Hammer was biding his time, refusing to be shaken or to waste ammunition.

More time passed. Under Mnuhl's directions, the loyalist fleet shifted about, getting into battle formation, but not approaching the enemy. Admiral Hammer must really be wondering!

How was Gary doing? The girls? The other Sphere volunteers? Were they getting through to the crews of the hostage ships? How would it show? Captain Mnuhl was giving them ten minutes: not much time to infiltrate and take over a ship.

There was one positive sign: All of the volunteers had been transferred successfully. That meant they had found willing hosts. Surely the crews were aware that something was going on; they should be ready to listen.

'Do you really think it'll work?' Yael asked worriedly.

'You know I'm afraid it won't,' Melody told her. 'You can feel the courses of doubt washing all through our nervous system.'

'Yes. But Gary is pretty competent and Skot—'

'Skot! He's not going out there!'

'Yes, he is,' Yael said. 'I got to know him while you were buzzing around the fleet. He's a man of action.'

Melody spoke into the ship's circuit. 'Skot of Kade report.'

'Admiral, he has transferred,' a voice replied.

'Then who in the orchestra is talking now?'

'Bnalm of Knyfh, sir. It was necessary to have an officer take over in the Solarian's stead.'

'I *told* you,' Yael put in.

Melody closed her eyes. 'Oh, Skot, you just *had* to get in on the action!' she muttered, pained. 'But I needed you *here*.'

Llume approached. 'Skot knew that a high-Kirlian entity would have a better chance of getting through than a low one, and his officer's expertise would enable him to operate the ship more effectively. I would like to go also.'

'Llume, you know you're a prisoner of war! Even if I could trust you aboard an Andromedan ship, it would be unethical—'

'I am a Slash,' Llume said.

'Precisely. An Andromedan—' Melody paused. 'Oh. You mean you honor the Lot of *?'

'I could readily disable a hostage ship.'

'No,' Melody said firmly. 'You will not turn traitor to your galaxy on my account.'

Llume retreated. Melody tried to analyze the strong

250

emotion she felt, but was interrupted by Captain Mnuhl's announcement on the net. 'Lan of Yap.'

Tensely, Melody watched the viewglobe. Nothing happened. But of course it would take a moment for the agents to react, assuming they had completed their takeovers. To orient on the other ships, to make their announcements ...

The net erupted. '*Trey of Swords* – Milky Way.' '*Fourteen of Cups* – Milky Way.' Then a jumble of voices.

Suddenly there was firing in the hostage fleet. It seemed to have turned on itself, with ships battling each other at point-blank range.

'Phenomenal success!' Mnuhl's exultant voice came over the net. Melody had supposed Knyfhs lacked emotions, but of course she was wrong about that too. 'Three ... four ... six ships blasted! Seven!'

'Like a chain of fireworks!' Yael exclaimed. 'There's another – and another!'

'It *worked*!' Melody said unbelievingly. 'It actually worked!'

'I must admit I had reservations,' Mnuhl said. She could barely distinguish his voice amid the melee of communications, but the proximity of his ship gave him an advantage. 'I anticipated perhaps two ships inactive. But now we have ten inactive! Hammer was caught completely offguard!'

'He was deceived by the nonmilitary mind,' Melody murmured, still hardly believing it herself. Yet the evidence was before her. Hard-hitting Hammer had never thought of resubversion.

'Analysis,' Mnuhl said. 'Initial optimism exaggerated. Ten enemy ships destroyed, but this does not indicate that a similar number have been retaken. Some may have fired upon two or more neighbors. Projected losses to enemy, all factors; sixteen vessels.'

'They lost five before,' Melody said. 'That brings them down to forty-five, against our thirty-one. We're gaining on them.'

'Yes, certainly,' Mnuhl agreed. 'It was a tactical masterstroke. But we remain at a disadvantage. We have merely

251

culled their most vulnerable units, and they still outnumber us.'

Now a separation took place in the enemy fleet. 'Our retakes are drawing apart, as directed,' Melody said. 'Six ships.'

'An apparent loss of ninety percent of our transfer agents,' Mnuhl reminded her. 'Considering the success, a favorable ratio.'

A favorable ratio! Was Skot of Kade among the statistics of acceptable loss? Gary? The two young women? The other gallant Knyfhs and Polarians and Canopians and Spicans?

'Recoveries are being pursued,' Mnuhl reported.

'Can we help them?'

'Only by closing upon the enemy fleet.'

'Do it, then. They took a terrible risk for us; we can do the same for them.' Then, conscious that the enemy could overhear this dialogue she stopped talking on the net.

Llume rolled near again. 'You can help them only by distraction,' she said. 'They will be subject to the fire of the enemy for some time.'

'No, we can surround our six ships and protect them,' Melody said. 'The hostages won't be able to—' But then she realized what the problem was. It took a lot of energy to accelerate, and a lot to decelerate a huge spaceship. The six fleeing ships had a head start, but the pursuing hostage fleet would be in phase with them. The loyalist fleet, approaching from the opposite direction, could pass right through both the six and the forty-five without having any protective effect.

The *Ace of Swords* began to move, the chemical acceleration pressing Melody sidewise. She suffered vertigo; now she could not decide which way was down. Her command seat held her in place, however.

Llume had no problem; she merely tilted on her wheel to match the new vector and stayed in place.

'Well, at least we have six more ships,' Melody said. 'Counting those recoveries, we shall have thirty-seven to their forty-five. That's not such a bad ratio.'

'Not such a *good* ratio either,' Llume warned her. 'By this time Admiral Hammer will have rounded up some captive transferees and will know everything they know. He will rout out any others remaining in his fleet and try to use them against you. If he retains a transfer unit—'

'Sour grapes,' Yael said. 'You thought of a good tactic, so everyone says it doesn't count.'

Sour grapes: another Solarianism. Melody traced down the imagery. Grapes were succulent fruits of Sphere Sol that developed on vines. When ripe, they were sweet, suitable for consumption. A carnivore was said to have desired some grapes, but found them to be out of reach. A *carnivore*? Such a creature consumed flesh, not *fruit*. There must be a confusion.

The other Polarian host appeared. It was Captain Mnuhl. 'There will soon be battle,' he said. 'Ships will be lost, and we may become unable to remain in contact. I think it wise to employ the Knyfh cluster-charge. This is a generalized magnetic field similar to the net that poses no threat to individual ships, but will tend to draw derelicts in to a common center. This will facilitate rescue of personnel in the absence of Intergalactic Convention.'

'By all means,' Melody said. 'We shall want to save any entities we can, from any ships – ours *or* theirs. The great majority of entities are ours, and there is information we'll want from any hostages we might capture.'

He made a glow of agreement and departed.

The two fleets accelerated toward each other, the six repossessed ships between. Melody was pleased to note that one of the six was Mintakan. Had they recovered the missing transfer unit, or had it been destroyed? She wished she could be sure it was not operating in the remaining enemy Atom. Llume had made a good point there.

In the globe it seemed as if the six ships would be crushed between the converging masses of the two main fleets, but she knew that they were mere dust motes in the hugeness of space. With an average separation between ships of five thousand miles, there would be no collisions. What seemed like masses in the globe were actually diffuse clouds in space.

What she could see in her globe, the Andromedans could see in theirs. When the *Ace of Swords* got close enough to fire on the enemy, the enemy Swords would be close enough to fire on the *Ace*. Suddenly she had a queasy feeling; she felt incompetent to handle it. She wanted to turn command of the ship over to Skot for the action, and of course could not, and not merely because he was gone. The hero-fool! She envied him.

'Coming into range of enemy vessels, sir,' a Knyfh officer said. '*Seven of Cups*, followed by *Ten of Disks*.'

What should she *do*? She had no experience at this sort of thing! Was that why Captain Mnuhl had made his last personal check, to see how she was taking the prospect of coming under fire herself? He should have stayed a little longer, and he would have seen her dissolve!

'Fire as appropriate.' Llume murmured against Melody's arm. 'No need to give specifics to an experienced space officer.'

Bless her! 'Fire as appropriate!' Melody said loudly. A weight lifted from her, and she felt better. Part of it was physical, because of decreased acceleration, but the rest was internal. She had not shown her indecision, except to Llume, who had not given her away.

'Something about those ships,' Yael said. 'The *Ten of Disks* . . .'

Ships were firing all about them. In the globe a Sword exploded; was it friend or enemy? A Cup sprang a leak. A Wand went dead – maybe. A terrible carnage, and how was it possible to know who was benefiting?

The *Seven of Cups* loomed close. Melody saw the Knyfh laser cannoneer orienting on it, centering it on his crosshairs screen. She knew he would not miss.

'The *Ten of Disks*!' she exclaimed, Yael's comment registering at last. '*That's Admiral Hammer's ship!*'

Llume straightened up. 'So it is! I should have realized. That is a preemptive target.'

'Don't I know it!' Melody said. Then, to the Knyfhs: 'Orient on the *Ten of Disks*. Blast it out of space. Ignore the Cup.'

The excellent Knyfh officers responded immediately, making no argument. The *Seven of Cups* drifted away from the cross-hair focus as the ship reoriented, and the *Ten of Disks* drifted in.

The view in the globe faded out. 'Hey!' Melody exclaimed in annoyance. 'This instrument's malfunctioning!'

'We have been enveloped by a cloud from the *Seven of Cups*,' a Knyfh reported. 'Visual interference, corrosion of lenses proceeding.'

She had made them ignore the cup, just when they had been about to blast it! *Why* had she interfered?

The view resumed. 'Only caught the fringe of it,' Melody said, relieved.

'The corrosion proceeds,' the Knyfh said tersely. 'Repair crew: replace external lenses. Verify other damage.'

Now the blips in the globe were fogging. The cloud projected by the Cups was large and diffuse, able to envelope a ship traveling rapidly, and its final effect was momentary. But once the corrosive agent coated the external appurtenances, it kept acting after the ship had shot clear of the cloud. A Sword whose lenses were fogged lost its offensive punch, and one whose communications and perceptions were fouled would have trouble avoiding other attacks.

'Solar vanes coated, bearing fouled,' the Knyfh reported, reading his indications. 'Reduce power draw.'

Immediately the internal illumination dimmed, as the systems cut power. It was not wise to draw on the reserves unnecessarily.

There was a wrench that would have knocked Melody from her chair had she not been hanging on. Her stomach writhed within the cavity of her torso.

'We have been secured by a contra-rotation anchor,' the Knyfh reported. 'Repair crews: preemptive mission – disengage anchor.'

Melody knew the ship was in trouble. Blinded and muzzled by the Cup cloud (result of her folly!), and now hooked by an anchor from the enemy flagship, this Sword was helpless unless the repair crews could free it quickly. Already she felt the vertigo of a shift in gravity.

There was another wrench. 'Second anchor attached,' the Knyfh announced, showing no emotion.

'Can the same crew take off both anchors?' Melody asked.

The officer was silent.

Llume had wrapped her tail around Melody's bolted-down chair. Now she unwound so that she could speak. 'The repair crew is gone,' she explained gently. 'They were on the hull when the second anchor struck—'

'Oh, no!' Melody cried. 'Knocked into space by the impact!'

'It will not be possible to free the ship of the anchors now,' Llume continued. 'I wish to have your release.'

'Release?' Melody was having trouble thinking clearly.

'Your forgiveness. Expiation. For the wrong I have done you. Before we die.'

'We aren't going to die!' Melody snapped. 'If you really want to help, come with me.' And she pushed herself from the chair.

'Admiral, what is your intent?' an impassive Knyfh officer inquired.

'I intend to round up a crew and free this ship of anchors!'

'That is not feasible,' the Knyfh said. 'It is necessary to abandon ship.'

Melody halted, maintaining her balance precariously in the face of the shifting gravity. 'Abandon ship! Ridiculous!' The music of challenge and irritation rang in her mind. There were times when the lack of her Mintakan body severely hindered her expression. A couple of strikes on the ship, no real damage done and they were all ready to quit! 'You had better have most chordant reason.'

'Our ship is disabled, therefore vulnerable to further enemy attack,' the Knyfh said with the same infuriating calm. Melody couldn't even be sure it was the same one she had talked to before; behind the varied faces of the human hosts, they were half a dozen faceless competencies. 'A missile or beam can hole the hull momentarily, and our handicapped repair systems may not be able to act in time. The corrosive acid itself may penetrate the hull, causing loss of atmosphere. The probability of loss of life-support prior to successful de-anchoring and necessary repairs is sixty percent according to established tables of risk.

'This ship has lifecraft capable of removing the entire crew promptly, so that another ship can pick them up. The probability of salvaging ninety percent of personnel prior to loss of life-support is eighty percent. Our chances are therefore approximately twice as good if we abandon ship. Therefore, according to the galactic manual, we must signal derelict status and vacate. No enemy will fire on us in this circumstance.'

A completely reasonable lecture – from the military view.

'But then we could still repair—' Melody started. The Knyfh's frozen expression showed her that was useless. To signal disablement falsely would violate the military code of honor, and these veteran officers would not do it. Strange (though perhaps only to her nonmilitary view) how very similar the military minds were to each other, despite gross difference in physical format. A magnetic entity shaped like a model atom had treated her to the exact line of reasoning a Solarian or Mintakan officer would have! Yet she could not blame these officers; in fact, she knew that in this instance they were right and she was wrong. Had she only kept her mouth shut and let them blast the Cup first, the *Ace of Swords* might not be in this predicament. 'We aren't derelict until we signal?' she inquired instead.

'Not officially. It would be wise to signal promptly, so that we will not be fired upon again.'

'*Don't* signal,' she said. 'We'll repair ship instead.'

'Admiral, the manual—'

Melody blew out an obscene note. But again, it didn't work, in this host. 'All *right*! Explain the situation to the crew, and evacuate all who want to go. But don't signal. I'm going to stay here and repair this ship alone if I have to, and use it to finish the battle.'

'You're absolutely crazy!' Yael said admiringly.

'This is not feasible,' the Knyfh insisted. 'Do you desire a detailed analysis?'

'No! I'm sure reason is all on your side. But we aren't fighting a reasonable battle, *we're defending our galaxy*. If we lose here, we lose our segment, and if we lose that—'

'That may be. But your proposal is likely to accelerate that loss.'

'I'm still Admiral!' she screamed. 'You handle your job, transfer back to your segment, and leave me alone!' And she proceeded out of the control room, angling to counter the slant of the deck. Hardly a gallant exit!

Llume followed. 'I join you, if I may.'

When friends deserted, support by the enemy was welcome! 'You may.'

But Llume halted. 'It is necessary to bring the discipline-box. Once I pass out of its range . . .'

'That box became inoperative when ship's power was cut,' Melody said. 'Didn't you notice?'

'You should not take the risk.'

'If you want your freedom, get a lifeboat,' Melody snapped. 'I can't use you unless you're with me all the way.' And she moved on, Slammer following.

'You have the courage of a fool,' Llume said, spinning her wheel in her haste to catch up.

'That is a compliment to a Tarot fanatic.'

They entered one of the long stem-to-stern access-halls. Motion was awkward because the anchors were still slowing the ship's rotation. The decline was jerky, as first one strand went taut, then the other, then both together. This threw them against the walls, bashing into the metal handholds. The passage was in the inner section of the ship, positioned to facilitate efficient transport by reducing gravity – and gravity itself was diminishing erratically.

'Like a crazy house!' Yael said, enjoying it.

Crazy house; but Melody did not need to delve for the underlying concept. Any species capable of enjoying disorientation like this *was* crazy!

Slammer shot off down a side passage. 'That's not the route!' Melody called. But it was soon out of sight in the dusk. The reduced power made a twilight zone of the entire ship, giving the passages an eerie quality.

'Slammer probably needs stoking,' Yael said.

Good guess. Melody had snatched bites to eat along the

way, hardly consciously; the crew stewards, like the Slaves of Sphere Canopus, were very obliging. But she hadn't thought about the magnets. 'We'll wait a few minutes,' she said aloud. 'Slammer will return.'

'He can readily locate us,' Llume pointed out. 'The loss of the ship's power has no effect on magnets.'

Melody nodded. She was tired and hurting again, but she didn't have to manufacture pretexts to rest! 'I'm not thinking straight. Of course you're right. We'll go on.'

'Permit me,' Llume said, twining her tail around Melody's torso. For a moment Melody resisted; if Llume were going to do her harm, the absence of the magnet would make this the ideal time. But then she felt the aura, so very like her own. The most compatible sister-aura she had ever encountered. How could she distrust an aura like that?

She yielded. The Polarian form, adapted to balance, was much better suited to this mode of travel than the Solarian form. Llume picked Melody up and accelerated down the hall. The added weight restored the wheel's traction against the deck.

Then Melody heard the whine of a rapidly traveling magnet. She looked back, and there was Slammer, gaining on them. He had a satellite: Beanball. 'Of course!' Melody exclaimed, relieved. 'We couldn't leave the baby alone in that cabin!'

The group continued on down the length of the ship – and almost collided with a group of crewmen who emerged suddenly from a side passage.

'Sirs, the evacuation route is this way,' one said, saluting.

'We know,' Melody said. 'We are going to remove the anchors.'

The crewmen did a doubletake. 'Sir ... weren't you ... ah, informally ... hullside with Gary's team?'

'You were on that job?' Melody asked as Llume set her down.

'No, sir. It's just that word gets around. But we have met.'

'March!' Yael exclaimed joyfully. 'The man we traveled with in the shuttle!'

So it was! 'Of course, March,' Melody said, as if she had

never been in doubt. 'We can use you now, if you care to volunteer. But if you do, you will miss the lifecraft out, so don't do it unless—'

'Sir, I understand,' the man said. 'I shall remain with this ship.' He turned to his companions. 'Get the hell on to the boats!'

The others moved on wordlessly. 'Sir,' March said. 'I don't know much about hullside work, but you'll need three more.'

'We'll make do with whatever we have,' Melody said.

'I mean, to carry the laser torch. It weighs two hundred pounds. The foot-magnets won't hold.'

Melody visualized a two-hundred-pound weight hanging from the hull, and remembered her jaunt into space. She shivered. The man was right; it would take a proper crew. 'We'll just have to see,' she said.

The lights failed. The hall became absolutely dark, for this was no planetary surface with diffused light. But in a moment Llume glowed, illuminating her own way. She depended more on sound than sight anyway.

They took the chute down to the hull, but now it was a giddy ride through the impenetrable dark. Melody felt as if she was floating upward. She had increasing doubts that what she was doing was wise. If they turned about right now, they could still catch a lifeboat . . .

And maybe give the segment to the Andromedans.

'Of course you're right,' Yael said. 'We can't do that.'

'You mean that was *your* thought, about turning back?' Melody asked.

'I guess so. It's funny. I always liked adventure, and you didn't. But when it comes to the crunch, you plunge in while I waver.'

'I have a more galactic view.'

'You have more damn *courage*!'

'Me? I'm just an old—'

'An old Mintakan neuter liar!'

'No, really; I'm terrified. But my life is mainly behind me, so I don't have much to lose, and when something has to be done—'

'That's what I mean,' Yael said. 'Being scared simply doesn't stop you. You keep saying how old you are, but I'll bet you were the same when you were young.'

When she was young . . . She had been a conceited fool, a real one, not a symbolic Tarot fool. The Tarot fool had substantial redeeming qualities, while young Melody, in contrast, had thrown away her life. She had paid with eight subsequent Mintakan years of isolation. Only here in the human host had she really come alive. But how could she explain that?

'You don't need to,' Yael said.

'I have no choice,' Melody said, reverting to the first subject. 'If I had a way to save the galaxy without risk to myself, I'd take it.'

'Big concession!'

Melody realized she was no longer moving. She extended her feet and found the floor beneath the chute exit. They had reached the suiting room.

In a moment a brightening glow announced the arrival of Llume. Dim as this illumination was, Melody found it enough; her human eyes had adjusted, and she could now see most of the room.

Two more men arrived down another chute. 'Didn't you get the word?' March demanded. 'Evacuation. Now.'

'We got the word,' one said. 'We're staying with the *Ace*.'

There was no further conversation, but Melody felt an overflowing of pride. This quiet patriotism in the face of threat – these men knew they were likely to die, but they weren't fazed. '*There* is true courage,' Melody told Yael. 'You and I are ignorant—'

'Babes in the woods.'

'Yes. We don't know the risks. But March and his companions understand completely – and they are taking this risk. What finer recommendation of character can there be than that?'

The group suited. Llume's spacesuit was a special one with a flexible tail assembly and a magnetic wheel; it must have been manufactured in Sphere Polaris. They all trundled out the laser torch. This was a barrel on a tripod,

261

ungainly, evidently intended for interior work. It looked heavy, but the reduced gravity had cut its weight in half.

'How do we know where the anchors are?' Melody asked.

'Doesn't matter,' March said. 'If we can *see* them, we can *cut* them, with this. If the corrosion doesn't get our suits first.'

Corrosion ... suits. Ouch! But if they were careful to touch the hull with nothing but their armored feet ...

They advanced to the nearest lock. It had to be operated manually, because of the power failure – and it was stuck. 'The corrosion,' March said. 'It has sealed the outer lock. We'll have to knock it loose.'

Melody and Llume stood back as far as they could in the compartment while the three human males put their shoulders to the lock door.

The door would not budge. The human form was not well adapted to this sort of action in low gravity, and was as likely to damage itself as to break open the metal.

'Try repressuring,' March said. 'Fifteen pounds per square inch should force it open.'

The pressure system could be operated manually. Like most hull equipment, it was fail-safe. Their suits lightened as the air built up but even at twenty PSI the door did not budge. The corrosion was really effective – as the Knyfh officer probably could have explained, had she given him the chance.

'The magnet,' Yael said.

Yes! 'Slammer can do it,' Melody said aloud. 'Just give it room.'

They moved aside, and with one joyful bash Slammer hurled open the lock.

The release of pressure was explosive. Melody, Llume, and the men hung on to the rails, and the big and little magnets used their strong attraction to resist the outward thrust.

Suddenly, the bulky laser torch, forgotten, was caught by the wind and thrust out into space. And not one of them had thought to bring along a jet-pack or safety line, for none of them were experienced in this line of work.

17

Service of Termination

*progress report   three more segments have fallen:
freng, weew, thousandstar*
:: excellent!   that leaves three::
*qaval is near collapse   knyfh and etamin are continuing
stout resistance*
:: I have knocked into this situation   the essence of
enemy action lies with knyfh   a knyfh contingent in
etamin is responsible for the extraordinary opposition
there   eliminate knyfh, and etamin will fall immediately
send the reserve force to knyfh::
but if that fails, we shall be without
:: it shall not fail   the bold strike is what prevails   that
is what dash did not understand::
POWER
:: CIVILIZATION ::

Chagrined, they stared after the laser torch. 'We had only
two in service,' March said. 'The other was lost when the
primary repair crew went out.'

There was something a bit noble about his despair, and
Melody wished she could kiss him. Or maybe that was
Yael's urge; it was getting harder to tell them apart. There
was a lot to recommend these sturdy, thrust-culture Solarians, yet Melody was not moved to any more serious attach-
ment. None of them had that power of aura that Dash had
or the affinity of aura that Llume had. Too bad Dash had
been an enemy, and Llume another female incarnation.

'Well, I liked March from the start,' Yael said. 'He's from
backwoods Outworld, like me, and he's the first spaceman
we met.'

As though those were sufficient recommendations! Melody gave a mental shrug; to each her own values.

But now they had a problem. They had lost their torch; and apparently there was no other way to remove the monstrous anchors from the hull. Magnetic, so they could not be pried off, the anchors were designed to hold the weight of an entire ship! The huge cables were impervious steel, uncuttable by normal means.

The group stood on the hull, hanging by their footmagnets from the planetlike mass of the ship. A film of corrosion covered the metal, like mold, weakening the strength of the footholds. The ship was, indeed, a moldering corpse.

Melody looked along the length of the great vessel, down the handle to the flaring blade of the sword. The light-collecting troughs were still in place, but she knew that soon they would collapse as the decreased rotation became insufficient to keep the guy-wires taut. Then there would be no further energy input, even if it were possible to fix the corroded mechanism and wash off the fogged surfaces. One little brush with a Spican cloud . . . doom. It seemed very final, out here.

She looked into space and saw the lights of the lifecraft, already in space, moving across the mighty starry field of the Milky Way galaxy. They were signaling to other ships for a pickup.

Marooned on a derelict. No doubt the battle still raged, but with the naked eye nothing was visible; they might have been alone in the universe. Was this the ultimate reality of the supposedly exciting engagement of fleets, the War of Two Galaxies?

At last her gaze fell on the two magnets. They were touching the surface, despite the corrosion. Of course! Their normal mode of repulsion would send them shooting into space, here; Slammer had surely learned that. Had he rolled across the hull when he was out here before? He must have, and she had not been paying attention. The magnet species was remarkably well adapted to space. She would have to clean off the corrosion once they went back inside, though. No sense having it eating into the magnets.

They walked to the nearest anchor, scarcely a quarter mile around the hull. It was a block of metal, three feet thick and twenty across, with its chain rising at an angle. Its field was so powerful that Slammer and Beanball could not approach it; the current would have overcome them.

Too bad! But for the overwhelming field, Slammer might have attacked the anchor-cable and perhaps frayed and severed it. No chance of that now!

They tramped silently back into the airlock and climbed carefully in. No one except the magnets had touched the corroded surfaces with anything but footwear (or Llume's wheelwear) – but what did it matter? Death was only a matter of time.

'You and Llume can still transfer out,' Yael said.

'Where would that leave *you*?' Melody retorted. 'And the men?'

'There are worse ways to die than alone with three men,' Yael said. 'I guess if I'd been able to choose it, this is the way I'd go.'

Melody considered that, and decided she couldn't find much fault with it. But she did not feel free to admit that. 'The others know we're here. When they see the ship remains derelict, they'll send a boat back.'

'First they have to get picked up themselves,' Yael pointed out. 'And we might get blasted or holed before they get here.'

All this time, rotation had been slowing. Now gravity was hardly an eighth normal, and fading rapidly. Melody started to strip out of her suit, but hesitated, realizing she would have no footing without the magnetic shoes. The air, under shipwide pressure, seemed good; each level of the ship was sealed to prevent pressure rising inordinately near the hull. But with the access-chutes open and power off, there was a draft as the air settled. And more than air was required for life support! Still, no sense using up the suit prematurely. She doffed it.

'Men,' Melody said aloud as their helmets came off. 'It appears we are going to die, perhaps quite soon.' She was not certain in her mind that this was so, but the odds seemed to favor it, so she was playing it safe, ironic as that was. 'I am an old Mintakan in transfer to this fine young Solarian host. The host-entity has volunteered to entertain you as you may wish during the final moments. There is a transfer unit in this ship. I shall, if you choose, use it to transfer my identity to some other host in the fleet. Possibly I can arrange for your rescue. But I think you should not gamble on my success to the extent of turning down my host's offer. Are you amenable?'

And privately she thought that if she had had perspective like this in youth, she never would have thrown away her adult life.

The three men exchanged glances in the light of Llume's glow. 'Sir,' March said after a moment. 'This is generous of you – and your host. You are surely aware that you have the aspect of a remarkably attractive woman, despite your present dishabille. Physically *and* mentally. But I have lived in a civilized manner, with the interests of my world and my species paramount, and I prefer to die that way. I would not touch you or your host unless it were your honest preference, with the prospect of life ahead of you – and I doubt that is the case.'

'That's all you know,' Yael muttered. 'Who cares about Kirlian aura – that's a *man*.'

'I suggest we hold a Service of Termination,' March continued. 'Then see how we feel.'

A Service of Termination. This was a segment convention, so Melody understood the concept directly. It was a means by which entities of different Spheres could together comport themselves for approaching demise without the rancor of contrasting philosophies or customs. It was contrived to have no objectionable elements, yet to provide strong support for all participating entities. And it did not have to wait for the certainty of death; any reasonable likelihood sufficed.

'I agree,' Melody said. She knew she should transfer out,

because of the value of her aura to the segment, but this was a matter of personal integrity. These people were here because of her; she could not desert them. Not before the service. She glanced at Llume.

'I also agree,' Llume said. 'This convention is known to Sphere /.'

March stiffened. 'The Polarian is of *Andromeda*?'

'Andromedan – Spican – Polarian,' Melody said. 'She is a transferee of the enemy, but she renounced her galaxy in favor of ours. In this situation we may not discriminate against her.'

Again, the men exchanged glances. 'Agreed,' March said tersely.

They gathered in a circle, facing out. March flanked Melody on her left, and another man was on her right. Then Llume, and the third man.

'One moment,' Melody said. 'Slammer. The magnet is entitled too. He's a sapient entity.'

No one protested. Slammer and Beanball moved to March's left, completing the circle. The humans kneeled; Llume settled, and the magnets dropped near the deck.

For several minutes all remained in silent meditation. Melody tried to compose her thoughts, but they were a jumble of uncertainties. What decisions could she have made to avoid this present doom? Had there ever been any hope, or was the Andromedan onslaught prevailing galaxywide? Surely Segment Knyfh was holding out, and the other center-galaxy cultures. Maybe Captain Mnuhl was winning the battle at this moment! But how could she be *sure*? Regardless of the condition of this ship the service might be in order – for the termination of the Milky Way galaxy.

Then she spoke aloud. 'I yield my floor to my host. Yael of Dragon.' And she released the body to its natural mind.

'Everybody here stayed to save the ship,' Yael said. 'To save the galaxy. Even if it didn't work, I think that's great, and I love you all.'

After a moment, the man on Melody's right spoke. 'I

always admired the Society of Hosts, and I thought about being a host myself. Now I admire it more. I hereby proffer my membership, for what it's worth now, and I hope the God of Hosts will accept my spirit.'

He didn't know that the hostages on Planet Outworld had infiltrated the Society of Hosts and nullified it. Still, did that make any real difference? The Society had sent Melody herself out here, and she had done her best to honor its original aims.

Then Llume: 'Let this struggle be resolved without loss of a galaxy, though it take a thousand years. Let my people of / redeem themselves as truly civilized entities, not as exploiters.'

The other man did not speak, but hummed a tune. He had inexpert control, but it was recognizable as a folk song common to Solarians. After a moment Melody picked it up, drawing the tune from Yael's memory, using her inherent Mintakan musical ability to fill out her host's voice. She had been without music for this whole adventure, and suddenly she missed it terribly. To die in music; that was her real wish.

Llume joined in, her ball vibrating against the deck in such a way as to make the sound seem to rise from the entire deck in descant, adding a dimension. Her body glowed in time to the beat, adding visual appeal. Now the two remaining men added their voices, and though they also were untrained, the imperfections seemed to cancel out, leaving the whole more perfect than it might have been.

Yet there was more, a special tonal quality that Melody did not at first recognize. In her own Mintakan body she could have identified it instantly, but the human ears were far less precise. She searched it out while she sang – and suddenly placed it. The magnet! Slammer was vibrating in such a manner as to produce a sustained sound, varying in pitch in time to the musical beat. And Beanball contributed a high pitch.

The magnets were singing too.

The harmony swelled, becoming much more than it had been, more than the mere total of the contributing voices. It expanded into a transcendent experience that suffused air, body, and spirit. It was almost like home, after all!

At last it faded. Melody opened her eyes, unaware of when she had closed them, and saw a ring of spheres around the kneeling group. The other magnets of the ship had come, attracted by the sound. How could she have forgotten them? They were all living, feeling creatures, doomed to die with the ship. Magnets could not travel well on lifeboats; there was not enough metal, and the necessary coal-crushing was too hard on the light hulls. They all belonged in this Service of Termination. But she made no immediate sign, letting it proceed.

Now the song was over, and it was Slammer's turn. Of course he could not speak – not in human voice – but the magnet was entitled to its space. It vibrated.

Llume spoke. 'I translate the message of the magnet,' she said, as though this revelation of magnet speech were routine. 'He is aware of the crisis, and wishes to help. The magnets do not wish to perish. They can make this ship operate to a certain extent, but they lack direction.'

Nice gesture, Melody thought. But the human crew could make this ship operate, too – if it were operable. About all they could do was close off a section and enhance life-support mechanisms there, so as to extend life and comfort. The magnets had even poorer comprehension of such realities than Melody herself had had. That made their offer useless.

It was March's turn. 'In this my last day, perhaps, I want the truth to be known. I was a guard at the Ministerial Palace of Imperial Outworld. I shot a Minister by accident, but he turned out to be an agent from Sphere * of Andromeda, the first hostage we discovered. I was exiled so that the hostages on Outworld would not know they had been discovered. But we were already too late, for the hostages had taken over the fleet. So it was for nothing. Had we known . . .' He faltered, then continued. 'It is pointless, but I did not want to die under an alias.'

There at last was the answer to the riddle of this man! He had, in his fashion, been responsible for bringing Melody here. He had done what he could to preserve the Milky Way galaxy, and now feared, as she did, that it had not been enough.

'This time I speak for myself,' Melody said in her turn, suddenly appreciating how well the Service of Termination served to ease its participants. 'March's sacrifice was not wasted. Because of the discovery he made, the segment's highest Kirlian aura was summoned, drafted against her preference to fight for her galaxy. I am that entity, and though the effort may have failed, we believe we came close to repelling the Andromedan takeover. It was worth the effort, and now it is an honorable demise. I thank you all for showing me the nobility that exists in your several species. I was near death anyway; this is a better termination than I would otherwise have had.' And why not accept it, remaining here, instead of going out again in transfer to witness the humiliation of her galaxy?

Their statements complete, they paused for another period of meditation. Then, slowly, guided by a common impulse, they turned inward. Those in Solarian form reached out their arms to touch their neighbors. The men on either side of Slammer touched his surface with their fingers, and it was the same with Llume.

'God of Hosts, be with us yet,' Melody said with feeling. Slowly, in the course of this adventure, she had come to believe in this concept.

'Lest we forget, lest we forget,' the others responded sincerely. *Lest we forget our galaxy!*

Now Melody projected her aura along the channels provided by the touching bodies. It merged with Llume's aura, and with Slammer's magnetism, and as the song had done, it expanded in circuit. The trifling auras of the three Solarian males were magnified beyond anything they could ever have experienced. Like an invisible flame it rose, like the glow of sunrise on a planet, transformed into ethereal radiance, health, joy.

This is *nirvana!* Melody thought, and felt the agreement of the group. The failings of her body and of her mind faded, replaced by exhilaration, by perfect health and beingness. Nirvana -- the final unity of all sentience, in which self did not exist because self had become the universe. It was not bliss so much as fulfillment, that fulfillment that sexual congress only hinted at. It transcended male–female mergence, because it was the mergence of life itself. *We are all siblings*, she thought, and felt the concurrence of the service.

For a moment that was eternal it remained, this holy unity, this fragmentary vision of identity; then the glow subsided. Melody opened her eyes again, feeling her body and mind healed, and saw the face of the man across from her shining wet. Then she became aware of her own face, soaked with tears.

Their hands dropped. The service was over.

Melody felt clean.

Then she stood and turned to face the waiting ring of magnets. 'I think there is little we can do,' she said. 'But we have to try. To what extent are you capable of making this ship function?' She felt no particular emotion; she was satisfied to allow her life to end, now. But as a matter of consistency, it was necessary to explore all available avenues.

Beside her, Slammer hummed. Llume translated: 'We can activate magnetically controlled systems and manual systems. These include life-support and weaponry.'

'Let's go back to the control room and see what we can do,' Melody said, putting a positive face on what she knew remained disaster. They were all doomed, and had accepted that doom. She herself might escape it, but for what purpose, if the galaxy had fallen? Only by saving this ship, it somehow seemed, could she save the galaxy.

Now there was some light from lens-vents in the hull; the slow turn of the ship had brought this side sunside. But even though rotation was greatly reduced, they would be darkside again in due course. And there would be no lenses in the interior levels.

So first they needed light – reliable light. The power remaining in storage had to be conserved for emergency life-support, or they would perish as the quality of air in the ship deteriorated and the temperature changed. Unable to rotate the vessel, they could not get the solar collection system functioning properly; there would be no power renewal. But there were so few breathing entities aboard now that the reserves could be made to last for a long time. A worse problem might be the interior weather caused by the uneven heating and cooling of the hull. Hot air was already beginning to push through to the cold side, making vague howling noises in the distance. A true poltergeist – a noisy ghost. The ship was a haunted tomb.

'There are lamps at the hobby shop,' Llume said. 'Antique fossil-fuel devices for novelty parties, cumbersome and inefficient, but self-contained.'

'Excellent,' Melody said. 'Will you fetch some for us?'

Llume's glow disappeared down the hall. Melody watched it fade with mixed emotions. She liked the Andromedan, but still could not afford to trust her completely. If this dead ship should *not* be the end for them, would they be enemies again?

'We'd better get some emergency supplies, too,' March said. 'Food, water.'

'Yes,' Melody agreed. It was amazing how the acceptance of death had stimulated them to handle the little details of life! 'I'll wait here.'

They departed, using oddly gliding steps. Melody was alone with the magnets, who simply hovered in place. She started for a sanitary cubicle; tension and exertion had a certain effect on the Solarian body. But with her first brisk step she sailed into the air so forcefully she banged her head on the ceiling. Without her foot-magnets she'd have to watch her step, literally! She rubbed her hurting human head as she bounded-glided the rest of the way to the cubicle and used it.

Too late she realized that, in the absence of power, the refuse could not be pumped up to the reclamation unit. Well, no help for it. The functions of life continued unremittingly while life endured.

The men returned with packaged supplies, forming a pile on the deck. Llume rolled back with a contraption of metal and transparent glass.

'I recognize that!' Yael exclaimed. 'It's an old-fashioned kerosene mantle lamp! My folks used them all the time.'

Melody gave her rein, and Yael removed what she termed the 'chimney' – a glass tube open at both ends – turned up the 'wick' – a fiber tube whose top end was barely visible as it projected from the body of the lamp – struck a 'match' – a tiny stick of wood with a dab of frictive flammable substance on one end – and touched it to the fuel-soaked wick. When it ignited the whole way round, she turned it to a low circle and replaced the chimney above it. The whole thing was so incredibly complex that Melody wondered how the primitive Solarians had ever managed after the sun subsided.

Yael turned up the flame, slowly – 'so as not to crack the glass,' she explained – and abruptly the suspended mantle – an inverted cup of webbing – glowed with a pure white light. The transformation was miraculous; from a flickering yellowish flame had issued a steady, strong, beautiful illumination.

'That's lovely!' Melody said appreciatively. 'This is a Tarot analogy. Solid circular shape like a Disk, liquid fuel, using air to make flame, and from it emanates a brilliant aura. The light seems a thing entirely apart, yet it is dependent on the crude material body.'

But she would have to meditate on the significance of these things another time. Gravity was still declining, and she wanted to get to the control room while she still had weight enough to walk. If she had to, she could use the net to summon help. Now that the ship really was a derelict, why not say so?

But if a rescue craft came, and lifted off the flesh entities, what of the magnets? Could Melody accept her rescue, knowing she was leaving these loyal allies to slow death?

The men fashioned packs and bags, and the group started the trek toward the officers' section.

Motion was easy, too easy. They took increasingly long strides despite their loads. When they ascended the ramp to the next inside level, their weight diminished further.

In the heart of the darkest interior, the lamp flickered and

273

puffed out, its flame expiring in a desperate lunge. 'Out of fuel?' Melody asked, chagrined.

'Out of air,' March said in the dark beside her.

'But we have air!'

'Gravity's gotten too low. Fire needs circulation, to bring in new oxygen. The hot air expands and rises out of the way. But without gravity, there's nowhere to rise, so it just stays there – and stifles the flame.'

'Yes, of course,' Melody said. Elementary physics! 'We shall have trouble breathing, too.'

'Not if we keep moving. The force of our exhalations circulates the air; convection doesn't have much to do with it. If we can rig a forced-draft for the lamp, it'll burn.'

'Better just use the battery-flash,' one of the others said. 'We have three, and they're good for several hours. But then we'll be at the control room, and can turn on what lights we need.'

Melody took one flash and March another, and they continued. They had stepped forward several thousand years in basic technology, perhaps, but were not better off. The gravity was so slight it was difficult to get friction with the deck; now they had to use the handholds to hurl themselves forward.

When they were about halfway to the control room, the ship shuddered violently, as though suffering its final death agony. Gravity ceased altogether. The anchors had completed their grisly work.

Suddenly the passage was filled with floating junk, jostled loose by the terminal convulsion. Theoretically, everything in the ship was secured, but in practice the steady gravity had permitted considerable laxity. Tools, articles of clothing, books, fixtures – all were drifting in the wan beam of Melody's flashlight.

'We're in trouble,' March said.

'We can shove this stuff aside; it won't hurt us,' Melody said, though the eerie drifting alarmed her.

'The solids, yes. The liquids, no.' And he pointed with his beam.

Now she saw it: a spreading python of liquid emerging

274

from an open cabin. It was sanitary refuse that had not reached the recycling unit because of the power cutoff. Now it was diffusing into the air, closing off the passage. 'I'm not unduly finicky,' Melody said, 'but let's see if we can find an alternate route.'

They took a side passage, but that, too, was clouding up. 'Soon we'll be breathing vaporized urine,' Melody muttered to Yael. 'Unhealthy prospect.'

'Ugh,' Yael agreed.

'I think we'd better get back into our suits and plow through,' March said.

Quickly they unboxed the suits and donned them. The magnetic shoes helped now, making the footing secure. Then they tramped through the sordid mists to the control room.

The ship was in a shambles. The loss of gravity had caused the fail-safe mechanisms to lock and the controls did not respond. The magnets were willing to help, but had to be given precise directives to enable them to override the fail-safes and establish workable partial systems.

Melody, Llume, and the men hardly knew what to do themselves. Poring over the instruction manuals, they gradually got portions of the ship functioning again, including the main computer. Then it became easier.

The laser cannon were partially operative, but the drive mechanism was beyond repair. The *Ace of Swords* might be able to fire, but it could neither pursue nor avoid an enemy ship. They had only confirmed what the Knyfh officers had known all along: the ship was a derelict.

18

Fleet of Ghosts

report: segment qaval has fallen   segment knyfh is in final stage

: : then conquest is complete! : :

not yet   resistance continues in segment etamin

: : oh, yes   but that will fall when knyfh support is lost : :

this is uncertain   resistance seems to be native

: : etamin!   why so much trouble with that insignificant region?   we did not anticipate trouble there! : :

dash did

: : dash was a supercautious coward!   why did he fear etamin? : :

because it was the segment of flint of outworld, who foiled us before

: : flint of outworld is long dead!   no such fluke can occur again   all the rest of the milky way galaxy has fallen! : :

the dash command of etamin has been recalled   he feels otherwise

: : the one who was discovered and nullified?   who yielded his command to slash and finally to quadpoint, who is about to complete this conquest?   the opinion of this creature is irrelevant   he shall be assigned to degrading duty   *why* does he feel otherwise? : :

he says there is another like flint of outworld who coordinates the resistance

: : another super-kirlian?   then capture that aura and bring it here   [pause]   no, send it to sphere dash   let them handle their nemesis and know it for illusion : :

POWER

: : CIVILIZATION : :

The ship was a derelict, but it lived. It had no spin, no gravity, refuse littered its passages, and it drifted without external drive – but deep inside it functioned.

'No one blasted us,' Melody said. 'They think we're dead; no sense wasting valuable energy on a finished hulk.'

She looked into the reactivated globe. The Knyfh cluster charge had brought the ship into the center of the battle area. It was a graveyard; ships and pieces of ships littered space much as the smaller refuse littered the halls.

It had evidently been an internecine struggle. More than half the ships of the original fleets seemed to be here, inert. Yet the battle continued: One group of fifteen ships was looping about for another pass, and on the opposite side another group of eight was maneuvering similarly. The hostages had lost thirty of their forty-five, the home forces twenty-three of their thirty-one. So the loyalists were gaining, yet losing too, for though the difference had closed to seven ships, the ratio had risen to about two to one again. Very soon Andromeda would win, and Segment Etamin would fall.

'We have to do something!' Melody exclaimed. 'We're *not* dead – and we never signaled disablement. We can still fight!'

'We can't orient,' Llume pointed out. 'The lasers may not be sufficiently charged, and the lenses may be too fogged.'

'I'll go out there and change a lens myself if I have to,' Melody said. 'We can shoot from ambush. The enemy will never know what hit it. We might get several – enough to change the balance.'

'We have to give fair warning,' March said.

Melody didn't argue; she was not sure where the ethics were now. 'All right, I'll advertise on the net. They'll know one of the derelicts has come to life, but maybe not which one. If our lasers don't work, they'll never know which one. And if the lasers *do* work . . .'

March smiled. 'That seems fair enough.'

Melody activated the net, hoping it still worked, hoping Captain Mnuhl of Knyfh was still available. 'Lan of Yap calling Mnuhl of Knyfh.'

To her surprise, he answered right away. 'Mnuhl of Knyfh. Provide your location and we shall send a rescue shuttle.'

'Captain, we don't want rescue. We were disabled, but have recovered enough to—'

'Desist,' the Knyfh said curtly.

'Captain, I'm trying to tell you—'

'Our relation is severed if you retain combat status. I am detaching my contingent from the fleet.'

Dismayed, Melody could only ask: '*Why*, Captain?'

Even through the mechanical translation the terrible regret was evident. 'I am no longer free to wage war. Segment Knyfh has fallen to Andromeda.' The connection severed.

Melody sat stunned. Segment Knyfh – fallen! It was one of the strongest segments of the galactic coalition, a leader. She had experienced Knyfh competence and toughness herself. If that segment had been defeated, how many other Milky Way segments survived?

Now another voice cut in. 'Hammer of : : . Melody of Mintaka, we recognize your identity. As admiral of your remaining force, you are entitled to diplomatic courtesy. Surrender your fleet, signal your own position, and we shall harbor you as a prisoner of war. You will be sent to Andromeda and treated with the respect due your aura.'

Melody did not respond. She had no intention of yielding now. Her aura would not serve Andromeda!

'All other segments of Galaxy Milky Way have yielded,' Hammer continued. 'No hope remains for you.'

Melody cut off the net. She did not question Hammer's word. All the rest of the galaxy – fallen! The Service of Termination really *had* been for the Milky Way!

'Why did Captain Mnuhl offer to pick us up if he's out of the fleet?' March asked.

'Noncombative assistance; probably part of the military code,' Melody said. 'The moment he found out we weren't quitting, he shut up, so as not to let us give ourselves away. He's an honorable entity. He doesn't *want* to quit. But he takes orders from his own segment.'

278

'Now that Admiral Hammer knows of your survival,' Llume said, 'he will be alert. You have a most valuable aura, one that Andromeda can use in special ways. He will try to capture you, as Dash did.'

'I have always been desired for my aura,' Melody muttered, remembering again the bitterness of her youth.

The viewglobe showed the Andromedan ships reforming, approaching the derelict area slowly. And it also showed two Atoms detaching from the Milky Wayan group: Captain Mnuhl and the other surviving ship of Knyfh. They could not actually return to their segment; that would take several thousand years. They were simply removing themselves from the battle.

'Can Admiral Hammer give orders to the Atoms now?' March asked.

'No,' Llume answered. 'The Atoms were neither defeated nor taken hostage. They merely become noncombatant.'

'Hammer doesn't need them anyway,' March said. 'He has a fair idea where we are now, and we can't maneuver.'

'Maybe we can take out one or two hostage ships before we go,' Melody said. But she knew it was hopeless. Andromeda had a decisive edge, and Hammer was competent.

'If Knyfh has fallen,' Yael asked, 'why is Mnuhl obeying them? Isn't he a creature of the Milky Way?'

A seemingly naive question – but it struck a chord. Melody reactivated the net. 'Captain Mnuhl, ' she said. 'Your segment is fallen; your loyalty to your galaxy now preempts your obligation to your segment. You are part of the fleet of Galaxy Milky Way. As admiral of that fleet – the only such fleet remaining – I order you to resume hostilities against Andromeda.'

There was a pause. Would this work? How did the military mind adapt to such a situation?

Then Mnuhl responded. 'Accepted,' he said.

Hammer's voice cut in. 'You are a fool, Mnuhl. We have already granted you disengagement status.'

'I renounce it, ' Mnuhl replied. 'So long as leadership exists within the forces of my galaxy, my ultimate loyalty is to it.'

'That leadership shall shortly disappear,' Hammer said grimly. And the globe showed plainly that the Andromedan fleet was orienting on the *Ace of Swords*, ignoring the other derelicts. Melody's notion of finding concealment within the mass of wrecks was illusory – like most of her other bright ideas.

But desperation gave her another inspiration. If she could recover two disengaged ships, what about the *disabled* ships?

'Slammer, will the magnets fight for the Milky Way galaxy?'

Slammed bobbed affirmatively.

'Could magnets reactivate the derelict ships, using the techniques we have worked out here, provided anything remains *to* reactivate?'

Slammer made a complex hum. 'Yes,' Llume translated. 'There are magnets aboard many ships of the fleet, surviving though the flesh entities perished. Those magnets will die in time if the ships are not reactivated. But they cannot act without specific direction.'

It might be enough. 'Llume, you and I are going to transfer to as many of those ships as we can reach,' Melody said. 'We'll check out their condition and tell the magnets there what to do. We'll ambush the enemy from derelicts.'

'But there are no hosts!' Llume protested.

'There are *magnet* hosts.' Melody turned to Slammer. 'I'm going to activate the net. You speak to your kind. Tell them to make themselves receptive as voluntary hosts. Inform them that two female high-Kirlian entities will occupy them and provide directions before shuttling back to this ship – if any shuttles remain operative. The Andromedans will not understand your language soon enough to do them any good; like us, they underestimate the sapience of the magnets. Tell your kind that in this manner we may save them and us all – but that if we fail, they will not suffer any more of a death than had we not tried at all.' She activated the net and left it on BROADCAST for Slammer.

While the magnet hummed, Melody took March aside. 'This is not a *good* chance but it is *some* chance. Once we

280

transfer out, you men seal yourselves tight in the control room and watch the globe. When you see a shuttle or life-boat coming, take it inside if you can, because it will be one of us returning in magnet host for retransfer. Can you handle that?'

'That much,' March agreed, tight-lipped.

'We're safe anyway,' another man said. 'We already had the Service of Termination.'

'The derelicts are pretty close together now,' Melody said. 'We might shuttle directly from one hulk to another, in magnet form, organizing our fleet of ghosts.' Then she thought of something else. 'Did the Knyfh officers evacuate the former hostages – Dash and Tiala and all?'

Llume checked with the computer. 'No. They remain in a sealed hospital room with an individual life-support system.'

'Leave them that way. If one of us reaches a ship with a transfer unit, we might transfer back into those bodies.'

Slammer had finished. Several hums came in on the net, providing the identities of possibly salvageable ships. Melody checked their positions in the globe. 'I think we're in business,' she said with satisfaction.

'We have very little time,' Llume said. 'The Andromedans are drawing near.'

'We may have to distract them with the first couple of ghosts, then skip ahead to set up more,' Melody said. She and Llume and Slammer and Beanball went to the transfer unit in the hold. Again Melody had to help Slammer across the barrier, but now that the magnet had no weight, it was easy. 'Yael will see that you get across next time,' she said to it. 'Maybe we can find a way to break it down so you have free access. You may be best off staying with the transfer unit anyway.'

She showed the magnets how to nudge the transfer control, once she had set it. Little Beanball was just the right size to hit the switch without touching anything else. While they were rehearsing it another magnet showed up. 'Slimmer!' Melody said. 'You couldn't get across the barrier to join the others! It must have been a terrible experience for

281

you.' But at least the little magnet family had been reunited.

Melody oriented the unit on a Solarian derelict in the path of the oncoming ships, and set it on Llume's aura. Llume entered, the Beanball nudged the switch. Then Melody helped the Polarian host out. She was not a zombie. True to her philosophy, Llume had not damaged her low-aura host. 'You and Yael and the magnets have a nice chat while Llume and I are gone,' Melody suggested.

She reset the unit, orienting on the available Mintakan ship, and entered it herself. 'Okay, Beanball,' she said. And privately to her host :'Take care of yourself, child.'

'I love you, Melody,' Yael replied. 'Come back.'

Then Melody was in darkness. She hovered near a metal wall, waiting.

'Hello,' Melody said to her magnet host. 'I am Melody of Mintaka, here to show you what to do. Go to the ship control room.'

The host obeyed immediately. This was a fine body, with a lovely internal heat from burning coal dust and extreme responsiveness in the vicinity of anchored metal. Melody surveyed the situation, getting her bearings. This was a Mintakan ship, but it was every bit as alien to her as the other ships were. She knew the controls would be sonically organized, but in this host it hardly mattered. The question was, could this ship be made to fight?

It was an Atom type, in the same class as the Knyfh ships with a solid nucleus and a magnetically fixed satellite shell. It had been taken hostage, but now the hostages were dead, for a missile had holed it suddenly. It was without air, but it was otherwise serviceable. In fact, since it was loss of personnel rather than destruction of equipment that had derelicted it, this was an excellent prospect for reclamation.

Did it have the missing transfer unit aboard? No. That was a disappointment, but Melody could not complain. Her success so far was fortune enough.

She floated past a dead Mintakan, a confused jumble of pipes and wires and castanets drifting in the hall. Its drum-membranes had burst, its tubes ruptured. Mintakans did not breathe in the sense that Solarians did, but they needed air for their various sonic devices, and decompression was a thorough and awful demise. The sight would have horrified her in her natural body, but sight was not possible in this host; she had instead a magnetic awareness that removed much of her emotional involvement.

The magnets of this ship, the *Six of Atoms*, assembled in the control room, humming with gladness for her presence. Now that she was one of them, she understood that they possessed the complete range of sapient feelings. Much of their emotion was expressed in magnetic fluxes and was therefore not perceived by other creatures, but they were certainly a full-fledged galactic species, deserving of recognition as such.

There were only five of them – all that had been assigned, since the Solarians had been, even in this crisis, jealous of their command over their metallic servants.

Melody flexed her communicatory magnetic fields. Her host was not as intelligent as the sapient norm, but was smart enough for this.

'The enemy ships are passing this ship,' she hummed, and realized that the sonic manifestation was merely a side effect of the intense fields of communication, used for special occasions only. No wonder the magnets had not seemed talkative! 'We shall have to attack them. Your valuable participation shall be rewarded if we are victorious.' She did not go into the matter of hostaging, afraid that would confuse the issue, and did not mention that even if they managed to win this battle and save Segment Etamin, the remainder of the galaxy was already lost. One thing at a time!

The viewscreen was sonic, so she was able to perceive its messages. The enemy ships were almost abreast of the Solarian derelict; had Llume made it there? Would she now actually fight against her own galaxy?

The magnets had better comprehension of the mechanisms of the ship than Melody had hoped. It *was* functional, and they *could* make it work. Quickly Melody organized them, positioning magnets at the key stations, making sure they knew how to respond when she gave the orders. They were natural followers, friendly, willing assistants, wholly likeable.

Suddenly the Solarian derelict fired at the enemy – at virtually point-blank range. The Andromedan fleet had ignored the hulks, concentrating on the *Ace of Swords*, and passed within a thousand miles of the dead Sword. The result was impressive. A Scepter exploded, its missiles detonated by the heat-beam. A Cup sprang a leak.

Quickly the thirteen remaining ships reacted. Admiral Hammer could be caught by surprise, but he was no fool. A missile slammed into the derelict Sword, gouging a great hole in it.

Yet, amazingly, the Sword fired again, scoring on a Disk. The magnets were tough; mere shock or vacuum did not destroy them, and Llume could not be killed easily while in a magnet-host. It was a phenomenal breakthrough in military space tactics; magnet-hosts as ship captains! But then a Cup-cloud enveloped the derelict, fogging its laser lens, and it was through.

However, the enemy fleet, taking evasive action, had now come within range of Melody's ship. They did not yet realize that this was an actual reoccupation of derelicts. Her Atommagnetism reached out and caught two of them, a Sword and a Disk. It did not shake them physically, as the Knyfh weapons did, but induced a powerful vibration in the affected substance that made it ring – literally. Sonic vibration could shake apart a ship.

Meanwhile the eight ships of Mnuhl's command were approaching. The Andromedans, uncertain where the enemy was, were now firing at other derelicts, wasting energy and missiles. They could not have much offensive punch left at this stage. The tide of battle was turning at last!

Then a missile struck Melody's Atom. The concussion was cataclysmic, even to her magnet form. The other shell let go, as its power was interrupted, and the nucleus split like the atom it was.

Melody was hurled into space. The magnet-body was not damaged by this; there was no more difficulty stoking coal dust in the vacuum of space than in the vacuum of the ship, though of course this could not be maintained indefinitely. Her air-vents were self-sealing, and there was an internal gas reserve. When the available combustibles were exhausted, life would fade. In the immediate situation, however, the need was not for air or heat, but for metal: large, anchored metal, for the magnetic field to grab on to. Her host was helpless. There was no hope of retransfer now!

But at least she had arranged to eliminate five more enemy ships. Ten to eight; now Mnuhl had a reasonable chance to win.

Yet what irony, to prevail by the margin of one or two ships. There would soon be a new contingent of hostage transferees from one of the pacified segments, to overwhelm this one. Thus Andromeda would fetch victory even from this defeat. Then on to the dissolution of the Milky Way galaxy, its fundamental energies sucked into the maw of Andromedan civilization.

'God of Hosts—' Melody began, speaking in magnetic fluxes. What use, her prayer, *now*?

A ship loomed close. A magnetic tractor reached out, drawing her in. The impossible had happened – she was being rescued!

It was a Disk. She floated to its center, to the axis of its spin where its null-gravity aperture made docking convenient. How fortunate Captain Mnuhl's fleet had located her before she became irrevocably lost in the immensity of space! The Knyfh must have watched the action, figured out what she had done, and spread his ships to intercept the debris of the fissioning *Six of Atoms*. Mnuhl's species had affinity to the magnets, so he could have been quick to catch on to the magnet broadcast. Even so, to intercept her so neatly amidst a terminal battle – that was either incredible skill or blind luck.

The powerful magnetism brought her inside the lock. This was only the second Disk she ever boarded; it differed from the other types of ships in subtle and unsubtle ways. With her magnet perception it hardly seemed Polarian.

She entered a long outslanting ramp. Here the surfaces were nonmetallic, so that she could not float under her own power; she rolled ignominiously down the incline at increasing velocity. Disk-creatures liked to roll, of course.

The slant leveled, and she halted. There was still no metal near. A powerful generalized magnetic field developed, urging her to a side passage. At last she came to an open chamber, and here she was allowed to come to rest.

'Welcome, Admiral,' a voice said.

Melody extended her perception field, and discovered that what she had heard was a Solarian translation. Beyond the translation machine was a spherical mass with six projecting short axles, a disk-shaped wheel on the end of each. The side wheels were used for locomotion; the bottom one was retracted somewhat, for gyroscopic balance and respiration; and the top one spun rapidly in the air to make the sounds of native speech. This was a high-Kirlian sapient entity.

It was of course no Polarian. This was in fact a ship of Sphere Sador, and this was a Sador host. Both Sador Disks had been taken hostage.

'Hello, Admiral Hammer.' She had, after all, been chained.

Part Three

Master of Andromeda

19

Bog of Jelly

:: *what?* ::

The £ plodded along the channel, her great paws setting down gently: one, two, three. She rotated slowly as she moved, and her mahout spun his wings and rotated in the opposite direction so as to keep facing forward. The elegance in this mode of travel was the hallmark of the planet.

Melody explored the mind of her new host. She had taken it hostage, but did not wish to damage it. This entity was Cnom the £, a new-mature female of gentle disposition. She was on her way to fetch the aromatic Deepwood that only her kind could collect, supervised by the mahout upon her back.

Cnom was more intelligent than her Dash mahout, but lacked the initiative or desire to oppose his will. The Dash were ambitious, organizing, accomplishment-oriented creatures, given to concerns about forthcoming millennia and matters of the distant past, while the £ preferred to take life as it came. Under Dash direction the planet had become the heart of a major Sphere of Andromeda, though it remained primitive. That pleased Cnom, and she was happy to contribute her physical labors to that end.

Melody was not so pleased. 'This is a form of sapient slavery,' she told Cnom. 'My culture disapproves of that.'

'Perhaps you should return to your culture,' the £ suggested amicably.

'I hope to do that. But it is not feasible at the moment.' And Melody explained how she had been captured by a Quadpoint in Milky Way galaxy, and transferred to this planet as prisoner. But by willing herself to arrive elsewhere

289

than intended, she had landed in an unplanned host. 'You see, my galaxy is at war with Andromeda. I regret imposing on you, but it is essential that I recover my freedom.' She did not choose to clarify how important her freedom was; after all, she was not at all sure that she could do anything to save her galaxy now. But she had to keep trying.

How rapidly would the hostages get the energy-transfer equipment set up? How could she prevent it, alone in an alien galaxy?

Yet Flint of Outworld had succeeded, even after he had died in the Hyades. His aura had carried on long enough to neutralize the enemy agent. She was not even dead yet; surely she had a chance!

Cnom marched on, unperturbed by the intrusion of another mind. Melody realized that this was because of the £ relationship with the Dash. An alien personality within the mind was little different from one perched upon the back.

Upon the back. Melody knew she would not be able to do much while the mahout remained. But without the mahout, her host would be deemed 'wild' and subject to restriction until assigned a new mahout. That was the way of this planet.

She looked around. This was easy to do, since Cnom's three eyes were situated on the top, side, and bottom of the main torso. That was so the £ could examine the sky or upper sea, the ground, and the surrounding area for forage and danger – simultaneously. The side-eye brought in a full panoramic view as the body turned; only by closing it could she avoid that information.

The Dash, in contrast, carried all three of his eyes below, as flying creatures related to the world primarily in a downward direction. Of course the Dash no longer flew – not with their wings, anyway. Their brains had grown too large for the necessary economy of body mass. But perched on their £, they still were mainly concerned with a *down* focus.

The surrounding vegetation was luxuriant. Bright translucent feathers caught the sunlight, sending prismatic splays to the lower foliage. Each plant utilized a different wavelength; without the feather-separation, many would wither. Feather-strands overhung the transport-channel, so that rainbow bands of color illuminated it. Dust motes picked it up, making the view ahead and behind a marvel of visual sensation.

Melody had had only the vaguest notion of Andromedan life, but had somehow supposed it must be drab and disciplined, as behooved the militaristic nature of its governing Spheres. This was as lovely as anything she knew in Milky Way. How could a species that resided in beauty like this wish to destroy the beauty of a neighboring galaxy?

Now the channel descended to the swampy level. There was no sharp demarcation; the atmosphere merely thickened. At first this intensified the colors, but then its added refraction interfered, making the rays cross and blend, leaving the pattern vague. The plants thinned and changed. The first bog-floaters appeared, suspended in the viscosity.

The powerful legs of the £ forged on while the Dash furled his wings and dug his claws into the almost impervious hide of her back.

Soon they were into the full swamp. The atmosphere had become jelly, turning gray, then black as its substance denied the light. Melody closed her eyes, Cnom's eyes; they were not needed here and she had other senses. She had nictitating membranes she could use to protect the lenses from the jelly if she did need to look around below. But as the light became useless, sound improved. The jelly transmitted every type of vibration, and the £ skin was hypersensitive to this. Thus she knew the location and often the identity of other entities within the bog, and could communicate with any of them.

This was the true society of the £. Today there were few direct physical threats to these huge creatures, largely because of the efforts of the Dash, who had systematically routed out the nestholes of the major predators and organized efficient alarm procedures. This left the £ free to indulge in intelectual pursuits while performing undemanding menial labors. It was a wholly satisfactory situation, as thought was facilitated by physical exertion. Cnom tapped into vibrations from every side, warming to the camaraderie around her as she plowed on.

'Excellent salt-flavored wood here, enough for five loads,' one of her friends was emanating. No need to give coordinates; the vibrations were excellent locators, and the £ memory was precise.

'Gas bubble rising slowly, toxic,' another warned without alarm. Although entry into such a bubble would be extremely uncomfortable, even fatal, the £ could easily stay clear. Only if a £ were trapped on a narrow branch would there be a real threat. But thanks to this timely warning, the others would route themselves conveniently around the bubble.

'Rendezvous approaches,' another announced. To this there was a wide pattern of response. All knew of the periodic rendezvous, but reminders were constant because of the interest of the occasion. Cnom felt a special thrill, for she had only recently qualified for her first offspring.

'A riddle,' another vibrated. 'Eye opens, sees more than three.'

Instantly Cnom's alert mind pounced on the problem. Her mental paws batted it about, studying it from different angles. Three eyes always saw more than one, unless some special circumstance . . .

'Your top eye encounters a freak beam in the deeps!' a £ vibrated.

'No,' the riddle-giver answered happily.

Still, there was a clue, thought Cnom. *No* eyes were useful in the deep jelly. So one could see as much or as little as three. But how could one see *more* than three?

'A Dash machine-optic!' another guessed.

'No.' The riddle-giver was delighted; one more wrong guess and he would have a social victory.

Another clue, Cnom thought. Not necessarily a £ eye. Perhaps a Dash eye, in the deeps . . .

'Your Dash has fallen asleep!' Cnom vibrated exultantly. 'One of his eyes has opened on a dream, and sees more than exists when he is awake.'

There was a massive general vibration of appreciative mirth: The Dash were the butts of many £ jokes, though

292

there was no malice in this. The Dash pretentions and am-
bitions were foreign to the tolerant £ mind. What vasty
dreams a dull mahout might have as he rode along on a
routine wood-fetching mission!

Cnom had answered the riddle, and scored a point. Her
status had elevated a notch. She felt a pleasant unaffected
pride. She was, Melody realized, a nice entity.

'Spore of predator,' someone else announced.

Now Cnom's pleasure was diminished by alarm. Few predators remained, but those that did were dangerous. They
were jelly swimmers, capable of much faster progress than
the £. Unless this one was located and driven off, it would be
a constant source of nervousness.

'Inform the Dash,' someone vibrated.

'Done. They are now scanning the vicinity with their
machines.' To the £, machines were useless oddities except
on occasions like this.

Cnom relaxed. The Dash machines were not infallible,
but the predator would probably be routed before it did any
damage.

The channel disappeared as the swamp got deeper. Now
Cnom set foot on a large lattice-root. The thing bowed
under her weight, but supported it; such growths were well
anchored and very strong and were buoyed by the jelly. The
root network was the principal highway of the bog, although
only the £ knew how to use it for safe transport to the
favored harvesting sections. One misstep would mean a fall
and descent into unplanned depths, which could mean
injury from too-sudden pressure increase. But the £ did not
misstep, and their slow natural pace gave them time to accommodate to the changes of pressure. Thus this lattice was
a unique and wonderful convenience.

The contour of the bog continued down, but now Cnom
moved on the level, her paws finding firm lodgings on the
wood despite the slippery surrounding jelly. The pads of her
feet molded themselves to the living contours. Her body
narrowed so that a smaller cross-section moved forward
through the jelly despite her constant rotation. Since she had
no rigid interior structure, she could maintain this attitude

without difficulty. Her tentacles helped the jelly pass overhead. The trick was not to oppose the stuff, but to cooperate with it; properly encountered, it provided stability and pleasant skin abrasion, brushing off parasites.

The wood Cnom was headed for was especially deep, near the limit of the mahout's endurance. The Dash were unable to move effectively below the surface of the bog, and their light bony structure could not withstand much pressure. So the £ were very careful.

Melody stepped from branch to branch, working her way down slants. It was especially fine growth Cnom had located: wood with really compelling fragrance, suitable for the most sophisticated building. Scentwood grew slowly from the utter depths; only when it reached this height could it be harvested without unconscionable damage to the mother-tree. The depth tolerance of Dash and the height limitation of the wood was a fortunate coincidence. Perhaps, however, it was no coincidence at all, but rather a symbiotic adaptation, for the wood was vital to Dash civilization on this planet. It was the only sufficient available substance possessing the qualities of weight, insulation, strength, durability, esthetics, and workability necessary to modern architecture. Without it, Dash buildings would collapse. Rock was too heavy for the spongy ground; metal was reserved for space ventures; ceramics tended to fracture when the ground shifted and quivered. And the wood smelled so good! The odor repelled the borers that attacked other vegetative material, while attracting sapient entities.

Melody, from another galaxy, nevertheless found the concept of the wood most attractive. Much of this was because of Cnom's enthusiasm, the source of Melody's information. But it was still a value even when considered objectively, for it was a renewable resource whose natural situation prevented ruinous exploitation. It was a working civilization that was based on wood from the deeps and a firm foundation!

But the Dash had set out to destroy another galaxy merely to achieve more energy. Could it be that the Dash chafed under the natural limits of scentwood?

Cnom halted. In the total darkness of the middle bog, she had sniffed out her cache of lemoncurl scentwood. The latticewood stalks rose past the branch, not touching. Lattice was a vastly different species of wood, never harvested for construction. Access to the bog would be virtually impossible without the lattice. And the bog protected the lattice, which would deteriorate in the open air as it lacked the aroma to fend off infestation.

She reached out carefully with one tentacle, bracing her feet firmly and flattening her body to gain additional purchase against the jelly. This was the delicate part: to break off the top without losing any to the deeps and without overbalancing herself. The Dash mahout helped, tilting his little body to focus all three eyes on the dimly glowing target in a manner Cnom could not, and directing her by appropriate pressures of his claws. His depth perception, even through the jelly, was perfect; membranes shielded his eyes and filtered the lifeglow of the lemoncurl, and trifocal distance gauging was excellent. It was the lack of physical mobility, not lack of perception, that kept the Dash out of the bog when alone.

Cnom's tentacle, unerringly guided by the mahout, touched the tree, curled around it, gripped. She shifted her mass, drawing back, exerting increasing pull, until the trunk began to tick. In a moment it would snap, throwing her off balance, but she was adept, knowing exactly when the breaking point approached, shifting as the tree cracked.

It snapped. She shifted, swung about, shoved hard against the jelly, and recovered her stability. She had the trunk, a fine big section of lemoncurl suitable for the most elegant construction. Another source of pride.

'You could do this pretty well without the mahout,' Melody observed. 'It would have taken you longer to put your first tentacle on the tree, that's all.'

'There would be no point in doing it without the mahout,' Cnom replied. '£ does not need scentwood.'

Unarguable logic! 'Without the Dash, you would be free.'

'We are free now.'

'But you obey their directives.'

'We cooperate with them. We are better off with them than we were without them.'

So it was regarded as a symbiotic relationship, not servitude. The £ was sincere; she had no desire to rid herself of her mahout. She could readily have done so, but that would have restricted her freedom to wander through Dash premises (though she really had no desire to), while the Dash could not penetrate the jellybog alone. It was not the system of Mintaka, but it sufficed for the stellar empire of Dash in Andromeda.

Here in Sphere Dash, according to information gleaned from the hostages, lay the secret of hostage transfer. In fact, this was the very planet of discovery. Obviously the entities of this Sphere, not especially sophisticated otherwise, had stumbled across a functional Ancient site and discovered its secret. If Melody could find out what that secret was, and get the news back to Imperial Outworld before the Andromedans consolidated their victory there ... if Captain Mnuhl had held them off long enough ... well, it was a chance, perhaps the only one remaining for her galaxy.

Yet suppose she *did* learn the technology of hostage transfer? How could that help her galaxy? To all intents and purposes it had already lost. She needed much more than parity now!

'Something is occurring,' another £ vibrated. 'Emergent couples are being halted at periphery of bog.'

Melody knew immediately that this had to concern her. The Dash command was aware of her escape from their net, and was now checking potential hosts. They knew she could not have drifted far from her assigned arrival point, so a saturation testing of the region would reveal her aura.

Still, they obviously had not had a specific tracer on her, or they would have spotted her instantly. There were thousands of potential hosts, all of which had to be checked.

'This is very interesting,' Cnom said. 'You really *are* in demand by Dash.'

'Yes, I really *am*,' Melody agreed. 'The very existence of my galaxy may be at stake. This is why I shall resort to desperate measures in order to preserve my freedom. I must seek and find the key to neutralize the hostage procedure.'

'You would probably find what you seek in the Dash Imperial capital annex,' Cnom said. 'I do not have business there.'

'We may make an exception,' Melody said, 'since I *do* have business there.' She had complete control over the host-body, but had not exerted it, preferring to keep the relationship amicable.

The immediate question was what to do about this search. If she broke ranks and left the route to the woodmill, she would give herself away. So it was better to keep going, hoping she could somehow avoid detection. Mechanical aura analysis was a simple business when aural units were available, but such units were phenomenally complex, not trundled about needlessly. So the verification would be awkward and time-consuming. They might resort to some sort of trick questioning. She could try to thwart that by letting Cnom respond, but then the £ could betray her. Except that the £ did not talk with the Dash.

As the magnets did not talk with the Solarians?

'We do not concern ourselves with Spherical matters,' Cnom explained. 'They are not of sufficient interest, and we cannot travel in space.'

Not physically, and not economically. The £ body was huge, massing many Solarian tons; in fact, they resembled Earth elephants, or the more placid herbivorous dinosaurs of Outworld. A sapient entity had to be small enough to be moved economically via mattermission. A hundred Dash could cross the galaxy with the energy expenditure of a single £.

Transfer, however, was quite different. It cost no more to transfer the aura of a monster than of a mite. Why hadn't the £ gone to space in this fashion?

For two reasons, Cnom's memory informed her. First, the £ had little interest in extraplanetary cultures or desire to experience them, and less desire to vacate their own ideal bodies. Second, Dash controlled the transfer facilities. The £ lacked the incentive to make any effort to change the situation.

'Milk from contented cows,' Melody murmured to herself, drawing on an expression that had spread like Tarotism through the segment but had lost its meaning in the process. Informed scholarly opinion was that cows had been bovine pets connected with a fluid called milk, noted for their placidity. The meaning today was that it was a waste of effort to try to change anything that lacked the desire to be changed.

Melody shook her head, mentally. She had known intellectually that Sphere-level intelligence could exist without the drive toward dominion, but this was the first time she had experienced it personally. How many other sapient species existed in the universe, as deserving of Spherical status as their neighbors, but denied it owing to circumstance?

'We desire space no more than your kind desires the bog,' Cnom pointed out.

An apt parallel. 'Very well,' Melody said. 'I shall not wish for you a lifestyle foreign to your nature. But you should understand that not only my own lifestyle, but the very existence of my kind are being destroyed by Dash and its allies of Andromeda. They are attempting to deprive my galaxy of its energies. All of us will perish. In your terms, it is as though Dash found a way to dry up the entire bog, leaving only a blank hole.'

Horror swept through the £. 'That would be wrong! The bog is vital to our existence!'

'A problem always becomes more serious when it affects your own demesnes,' Melody remarked.

But she got no further rise out of her host. 'Were our bog threatened, we should have to act. But this is not the case.' And Cnom marched on up the channel toward the rarefied jelly that phased into atmosphere, bearing her precious burden of lemoncurl.

As they emerged onto solid land, a Dash mounted on a huge male £ hailed Cnom's mahout. The challenger's triple wings whirled, emitting the controlled vibrations of speech sound. 'Pause, Dash, for inspection.' The £ skin picked up the vibrations and the £ mind comprehended their meaning, but Cnom paid little attention; Dash affairs were not of much interest.

298

Melody, however, listened closely. The moment she was exposed, she would have to act, destroying the inspector and mahout and retreating into the bog. But that could be only a temporary reprieve, and she hoped to escape detection entirely if possible.

—Dismount, enter the aural booth,— the officer said. Now that they were close, Melody was aware of the peculiar Dash speech intonation, a function of the wings. It was sound – but not the kind of sound she normally heard. *Dash* sound.

Then she realized: they had brought a portable Kirlian detector. This was a serious search, all right!

Cnom curled a free tentacle up so that the mahout could perch on it. She lifted the mahout across to the back of the other £, where the box was tied, without ever disturbing her load of lemoncurl. She did not communicate with the other £, because here in the rarefied air her skin could not create a suitable vibration. 'Yes, a problem always becomes more serious when it affects your own demesnes,' Melody remarked. The £ were necessarily mute outside of the jelly, another reason their intelligence was ignored by the Dash.

The mahout emerged from the box. —What is this nuisance about?— he inquired. —My aura's the same as it ever was, and it was verified only a while ago.—

—Imperial matter,— the officer said. Then, his wings whirring confidentially: —Some captive missed the host, and they think she's in one of us.—

— A female? If she were in me, I'd know it!— And the two males whirred together in male humor, the same across the universe with minor variations.

The mahout remounted. —*On*— his claws said by their pressure in Cnom's hide. There was no malice in this; the creature's feet were not strong enough to cause pain to a £.

Cnom resumed her rotary progress.

'But they didn't check *us*!' Melody exclaimed.

'Why should they check a £?'

And Melody realized what had been hidden in her host's mind amid the myriad other facts. The Dash did not regard the £ as true participants in Sphere civilization, though the level of £ intelligence was known. Millennia of experience

299

had demonstrated the £ disinterest in the artifacts of interstellar empire. Thus the £ were ignored, apart from their laboring capacities; they were beasts of burden who never gave away private matters. Male and female Dash routinely copulated upon the backs of their great steeds. Military consultations were held while riding; thus the £ were aware of Dash strategies, but the information never leaked to other Dash.

The hostages aboard the Segment Etamin flagship had treated the magnets in a similar fashion, regarding the magnets as intelligent beasts of burden. Melody had capitalized on this attitude in reviving the derelict ships. Yet she could not conclude that there was anything wrong in this. If some species liked it that way and were mutually satisfied, why not?

But more immediately, it meant that this ingrained cultural conditioning had caused the Dash command to overlook the obvious. *It had not occurred to them that a £ could be a host.*

20

Foiling the Lancer

—I said she escaped us, quadpoint—

:: must I do everything myself? is there no end to your incompetence? after winning the war for you must I chase after the high-kirlian prisoner I forwarded directly to you? how could you bungle such a simple thing as a transfer? ::

—inquire of your quadpoint command in etamin *he* transferred her using captured adapted milky way unit unreliable for an aura of that magnitude—

:: *her?* I had understood it was a male entity ::

—your quadpoint command neglected to inform our local technicians of that modification we provided a male host—

:: so that nemesis who extended the resistance in segment etamin far beyond what it should have been is now loose in andromeda! trace her and kill her! ::

—we cannot do that, quadpoint she is in a special situation not anticipated she occupies a £ host—

:: I have heard of your groundbeasts why should that make any difference? ::

—the covenant prevents direct damage to any £—

:: covenant! surely there are mechanisms! employ them! ::

—the mechanism of proper caution at the outset would have—

:: POWER! ::

—CIVILIZATION—

Cnom deposited her load of fine lemoncurl at the mill, and her mahout received congratulations on its quality and a note of credit on his record. No praise was wasted on the

£, of course, and Cnom neither expected it nor desired it. It was her task to do the work; the intricacies of record-keeping were the responsibility of Dash.

They returned to the bog, following the routine. Melody had to protect her thoughts by clothing them in technical terminology of little interest to her host. She didn't want to reveal her developing strategy. Whatever she decided to do, Cnom was unlikely to see it her way.

One thing was certain: She could not afford to settle into the scentwood-hauling operation indefinitely. Once the vital power started flowing from the Milky Way to Andromeda, this robber-galaxy would become so strong that effective resistance would become impossible. *Now* was the time to act, and Melody was the one to take the action.

The first problem was how to eliminate the mahout, while retaining the freedom to go into the Dash city.

As the jelly thickened, the £ vibrational interchanges resumed. This dialogue was ignored by the mahouts, if they were able to pick it up at all.

'Weak section of lattice,' someone announced. 'Route around it until it strengthens.' And Cnom noted the location carefully, for she did not want the inconvenience of coming upon it accidentally.

'Alien intellect visiting, overlooked by Dash,' Cnom announced. Melody was startled. While she was shielding her own thoughts, she had not been monitoring those of her host. Well, perhaps no harm was done, since the Dash paid no attention to the £ net.

'This explains the search,' another responded. 'Dash does not like alien visitors.'

There was a vibration of general mirth. The ways of the Dash were so quaint. They, who ranged the galaxies, objected to visitors!

'Spoor of predator,' another announced.

'Another?'

'Same one as before. Lancer, large.'

'Were not the Dash notified?'

'They aborted their chase, concentrating on the alien presence.'

'The alien among us.'

'Then let the alien disperse the lancer.'

Melody liked this less and less, but hesitated to speak on her own behalf. For one thing, she wasn't sure the Dash weren't listening; they surely could if they wanted to. The £ would not give her away directly – not intentionally – but she could give herself away. And what was this about fighting a predator?

The vibration of agreement had, it seemed, committed her. Already, by what means she lacked the time to verify, they were routing the predator to her vicinity. She was responsible for its menace, since she had distracted the Dash authorities, even though she was here in Andromeda at Dash instigation. Therefore she must abate the menace. Quite logical and immediate, to a culture that did not concern itself with things distant in place or time. Unexpressed but inherent, was the understanding that if they honored their part by *not* exposing her to the Dash, she must honor hers by dealing with the lancer.

'But how can *I* do anything about this predator?' Melody demanded of her host. 'I don't even know what it is!'

'It will be difficult,' Cnom agreed. 'I could not do it myself. We depend on your alien knowledge.'

It seemed the £ had a stiff requirement for intruders who caused inconvenience! Yet it was fair in its fashion.

They were back near the lemoncurl stand. Abruptly Melody received the vibrations of an approaching creature, a large, smooth one whose passage was too fast and straight to be bound to the latticewood paths. A swimming entity.

Cnom went rigid with terror – and so did the Dash mahout. No help there! Melody took over the body totally, having no choice. She was on her own.

Balancing on the lattice, she oriented on the lancer. She did not face it because she had no face, no fixed aspect of body. She used the sonic vibrations to identify its size, shape, location, and motion. The echoes of its emanations identified the lemoncurl stalks to the side, the neighborhood lattice, and, fuzzily, the more distant branches of latticewood passing above and below this level. It was as good

303

as seeing, better in a way, because she did not have to focus on it all.

The lancer was a sleek, long creature propelled by three threshing fins to the rear and guided by three more along its torso. It was superbly equipped to slide rapidly through the jelly; no other bog denizen could match it. Its front end tapered into a long, hard, deadly spike designed to pierce the globular body of its prey and to suck out the life-juices therein. While it was traveling, that spike sprayed out a thin mist of acid that dissolved the jelly in front, causing it to give way more readily to the thrust of the main torso.

In a flash, Melody's £ memory filled her in on related details. Once the middle layers of the bog had been fraught with terror. The upper section was the domain of the land creatures; only the bottom deeps were secure, for the lancers could not move well there. But the £ could not live in the deeps continuously; their bodies required the release of the upper regions. So their population had been culled in the region of thickest jell, and few lived to old age.

Usually the victims survived the first attack, but an uncomfortable convalescence was required to restore the depleted juices. As most of the necessary food was on land, the £ had to walk up through the bog repeatedly and be subject to repeated attacks by the lancer. The second puncture was more apt to be terminal, and a third almost invariably.

A convalescent £ could not work effectively; therefore the Dash had initiated their bog-safety program, which had been of immense mutual benefit. Far better to haul heavy wood than to suffer the ravages of the lancer!

Melody had thoughts of her own. If the £ were able to direct a lancer to a specific region of the bog, why couldn't they have directed the creatures all the way *out* of the bog, and been free of the menace long ago? And it was strange that so large and fierce a predator should show up now, after a long period of relative quiet. Few dangerous predators were left in this region. They kept mainly to the park bogs elsewhere on the planet where they were not hunted.

But her immediate concern was how to deal with this particular thing. The creature was so large that even this huge

304

body of Cnom's would be severely depleted by the feeding. It would mean a great deal of pain and inconvenience for the host, and would eliminate Melody's chance to go after the secret of hostage transfer. She simply could not afford that!

The lancer was not a sapient; it could not think in civilized terms or master stellar technology. It was merely an animal, a super-predator who had never needed more than its mobility and power. Melody had intelligence, information, and aura, yet what could these avail her against the direct simple thrust of that spike? The lancer could move much faster than she could, and if it happened to miss the first thrust, it would merely circle about and attack again. She could not flee it, and she could not even dodge it well, for she was limited to the narrow lattice branch.

There was no time to consider further. The lancer slid through the jelly, its rigid tubular spike centered on her body. Melody reacted automatically for her own kind: She jumped to the side.

Disaster! She was not in her Mintakan body, where a jump would have lifted her only fractionally amid a ferocious clatter of castanet-feet. She was not in her Solarian host, in which the same effort would have hurled her to the ground. In her present £ host, she went spinning to the side of the lattice branch over-balanced.

The lancer cruised past, one of its stabilizing fins almost brushing her body. She had avoided it, but now she was falling, unable to recover her balance. If only she had flippers to thrust at the jell and pull her through! But that was the mode of the Spican Impact.

She reached out with all three tentacles and caught the adjacent lemoncurl trunk. Still acting on a confused amalgamation of instincts, she clung to that trunk, drawing her body into it.

No good! Her weight was too much. The trunk snapped off, and she resumed her tumble through the jell, clutching the aromatic wood.

Meanwhile the lancer turned smoothly and oriented its lance again. It did not care whether she was on the lattice or off it; it had no need for such support. It angled down, accelerating. Tiny thin bubbles streamed about it as the slipstream of thinned jelly parted.

Melody swung the lemoncurl trunk at it.

Another disaster. She was not anchored, but was slowly dropping through the jell. She had little proper leverage to move so massive an object quickly. Her tentacles were meant for reaching, grasping, drawing in, and holding, not for full-scale manipulation. And the surrounding jell made a rapid sidewise strike impossible. She wrenched a tentacle, and twisted body and trunk in a kind of semicircle that succeeded only in shifting the angle of the descent.

But again this surprised the lancer, who missed her narrowly. Melody suspected that that was about as far as her luck was likely to extend.

She was sliding down on a nether branch. She managed to tilt her log so that it formed a kind of plane. She flattened her torso, adjusting the angle of descent so that she landed on the branch instead of missing it. She had a serviceable tool!

The lancer looped about and down, and charged again. It could play this game as long as she could!

Melody caught her balance and braced herself, still clutching the log in two tentacles. Tool? *Shield!*

As the lancer struck at her with its devastating accuracy, she shoved the log between her body and the spike.

The impact shoved her back along the branch. But she was several times as massive as the predator, and retained her balance. In fact, she had the creature trapped: Its lance had pierced the trunk and stuck there.

But she had counted her victory too soon. The predator reversed its propeller fins and jerked back – and the spike drew free.

Afraid and angry, Melody turned the log endwise and rammed it at the retreating body. Now she had fair purchase for her feet again, and was getting the hang of her weapon. One tentacle hurt, but the spin of her body compensated for this. Like a rod attached to a camshaft, the log struck forward.

The lancer, amazed at this aggressive behavior by its prey, retreated further. Melody continued her advance, trying to jam the log on the spike, so as to nullify the point. Then she might be able to take hold of the creature's slippery body in her tentacles and crush it . . .

But the lancer had had enough. This atypical behavior interfered with its set style of attack; it could not adapt. It curved its long body, revved up its fins, and shot away into the gloom.

'Come back and fight, you coward!' Melody vibrated after it, furious. *She* had not had the option of fleeing! But the creature paid no heed.

Now the vibrations came in from all around. 'The alien has vanquished the lancer!'

'Using a load of scentwood!'

'Astonishing!'

'The lancer is fleeing the region!'

'A double victory for the alien.'

'Triple victory.'

Then a more tremulous vibration, as of an immature £: 'Is that a riddle? What are these victories?'

Melody wondered herself about that, as she picked her way along the lattice route to her former elevation.

'First, she overcame the lancer,' the parent £ explained carefully. 'Next, she concealed her identity from the Dash, who had sent the lancer to identify her. When it fled, it could no longer betray her location; its aural bleeper shows only where it is, alive or dead.'

Melody's feet almost missed their placements. *The Dash had sent the lancer!*

'Third, she eliminated her mahout, so she is now free to range by herself,' the parent concluded.

Eliminated her mahout? She had been planning to do that, but the arrival of the lancer had distracted her. Now her store of host-knowledge provided the explanation. The Dash could not sustain as much pressure as the £ could; the mahout's mind had been damaged by her descent to the lower lattice when she fell from her branch. The mahout lived, but was no longer sapient.

More significant than her personal success, however, was the underlying attitude of the £. They had not betrayed her – but they had not helped her either. They had directed the lancer to her because they considered it to be her responsibility, but they had not burdened her with its significance until the issue had been decided. They had in their fashion put her on trial, and now that she had vindicated herself, they let her have the information she needed.

Melody tried to understand the genesis of this philosophy, but it was, naturally, alien to her. She was left with the conclusion that the £ knew much more of the purposes and mechanisms of the Dash than they advertised, and that £ cooperation was not necessarily passive. She moved among them as a lancer did, not precisely an enemy, but certainly no friend. And the £ had ways to make her behave.

She decided she had better get her business done. It would be better to deal with the Dash, whom she knew to be her enemies, than with the £, whom she did not really understand.

She shifted the log to make it comfortable, taking the strain off her injured tentacle. She moved on to the channel, and out into the thin air. The mahout remained perched on her back, as his claws clenched when at rest; it looked as if he were directing her. That was exactly the way she wanted it. Mahouts often snoozed while their mounts carried on, so his condition hardly mattered, so long as he was there. No one would challenge her while she seemed to be under the direction of the mahout.

Her ruse could not be sustained long, but that hardly mattered, because she had to help her galaxy quickly or it would be too late anyway. So now she had a program of sorts: first, get the hostage secret; then get the information to an entity in authority in Segment Etamin. Then what happened to her didn't matter. Like Flint of Outworld, she could give her life for her galaxy.

She knew the odds were still against her, but they were better odds than before. Her capture by Hammer of Quadpoint had turned out to be a break for her, because she was now much closer to the secret that controlled two galaxies.

She emerged into atmosphere. No mounted Dash challenged her this time; evidently that particular search had been called off. Perhaps they *had* spotted her aura in that prior check, but had chosen to deal with her indirectly. But why?

The question brought the answer: because of the covenant between the species of Dash and £. The one could not deliberately harm the other.

She proceeded to the mill, and the Dash in charge there marked off the load, glancing incuriously at the hole in the wood where the lancer had spiked it. Fortunately he did not try to converse with the mahout, who merely sat on her back. Let the loafer snooze!

Melody started dutifully back toward the bog. But when she was out of sight of the mill, she turned off at right angles and cut through the feather trees toward the path Cnom's information said led to the Dash city. It was no coincidence that the capital was so close, since that was where her intended host was. She had missed her transfer recipient by only a few miles; pinpoint accuracy, considering that it had been an intergalactic effort. But this partial freedom could not last long. No doubt the Dash were even now zeroing in on her again, setting up a way to nab her without hurting her £ host. She had to act first.

She found a new channel and stepped down into it gratefully. The paws of the £ were not hoofs; they were adapted to maintaining lodging on the curved lattice of the bog rather than for tramping down the hard rocks of the dry land. The channels, through concavely curved, were smooth, and the dirt in them was no harder than wood. In addition, their narrow width and curving routes were familiar.

This was a toward-city channel, fortunately. All channels, like all lattice paths, had to be one-way, as there was no room for £ to pass one another. The channels could have been made wider, but that would have destroyed their compatible contours and decreased their similarity to the bog-lattice. This way, their natural contours led them through the refraction feathers with minimum disruption.

She emerged into a clearing. Ahead was the city; a towering mass of wooden spires, quite pretty in its fashion. Melody was reminded of the houses of cards Solarians built. She had entertained herself with some of these during waits aboard the *Ace of Swords*. Each individual card was flimsy, but the buttressed structure assumed a remarkable stability.

She spun closer, concerned lest she be challenged. But though she passed many mounted mahouts as the channels converged, none bothered her. Obviously it was assumed that her own mahout was taking her somewhere on private business.

The splendor of the city did not diminish as she approached it. Trust a bird-species to have uplifting taste in architecture! The wood had been shaped into elegant configurations, with many small passages for Dash to haul themselves through. Though they could no longer actually fly, it was evident that given the proper footing they could propel themselves through the vertical lattice of the buildings with flight-like facility.

Now there was a problem. Obviously the most secret offices of the Dash transfer command would be high up, and it was manifestly impossible for a £ to go there. The merest brush of Cnom's huge body against a lower structure would collapse a section of the city; ascending a tower was out of the question.

Could she locate the spot, then attack the base of the building and bring it down to her level? No, that would destroy her own pretense of anonymity and be pointless. She had to *observe*, not *strike*. It was knowledge she required, not physical victory. For now.

First she had to locate the Kirlian section of town. Her aura and her training had made her super-sensitive to Kirlian emanations; if she got within a reasonable distance of a strong Kirlian source, she would know it. Maybe she would have a chance to transfer to a Dash host and continue her investigation.

Of course her own aura would betray her identity similarly – if the Dash were alert. They should be, since she had twice escaped their net. But perhaps the inherent foolishness of their bureaucracy would help her again. The last thing they should anticipate would be her strike into the heart of the city.

It was a major gamble – but she had to take it.

She moved into the city, which now resembled the land-forest, with buildings in lieu of trees. Even the refraction of light was similar, though here it was done by glass lenses instead of living feathers. This was, her £ memory told her, to prevent the shaded lower passages from becoming musty.

Stalls for £ opened off the sides. Healthy £ preferred to sleep in the bog, but ill or injured ones came here. This also made it convenient for the mahouts, who could indulge themselves in the comfort of the upper regions while their steeds were out of service. No Dash would volunteer to remain in the bog longer than necessary especially not aboard a sick £. For one thing a hurt £ sought the deeps, an area that the Dash could not enter.

Suddenly she picked up the fringe of a strong aura, and moved toward it. High-Kirlian entities were in the vicinity!

She came into an inner chamber. In its center, protected by a sturdy wooden barricade, was a transfer unit. It was not a type she was familiar with. Therefore it must be—

A drape lifted, revealing the snout of a projectile cannon.

—Halt, mahout!— a Dash voice commanded.

A trap! She had half known it, but had taken the risk for the sake of her mission. They had dangled the bait of hostage Transfer before her and lured her in, just as they had done back at the *Ace of Swords* so successfully. Yet what else could she have done?

Perhaps she could bluff an ill-informed Dash . . .

She looked around as if confused, tilting her body to make her addled mahout seem to be directing her.

—Please do not endanger yourself— the Dash said, coming into sight on an upper ledge so that his three eyes focused down on her. —There is no confusion. We have analyzed your aura, and know you for Melody of Mintaka, Etamin, Milky Way.—

Then she knew she was lost.

21

Budding the Mintakan

*report: all fleets secure in milky way galaxy   last
resistance in segment etamin overcome   ready to move on
planets*

:: initiate motion ::

*there will be some delay, as this involves physical propul-
sion and the distances are*

:: do not seek to educate me in elementary physics, ast!
what of the local matter? ::

etamin kirlian agent has just been immobilized

:: immobilized?   *kill* her! ::

*sphere dash assures us that this is not feasible   negoti-
ation is necessary*

:: dash shall shortly be charged with treason!   if they do
not neutralize her quickly I shall ::

POWER

:: just get the job done! ::

—You have been evasive, alien!— the Dash said, his wings
whirring reprovingly. While he talked, a line dropped from a
crane to remove the defunct mahout from her back. —All
we want is the best for you, now that your galaxy is fallen. It
would be a shame to sacrifice an aura like yours. Will you
not now be realistic and join us?—

Melody of course did not answer. But suddenly she
became aware of the specific aura of the Dash. It was a very
strong one, with an intensity of about 175. This was the
entity she had known as Captain Dash Boyd – her lover and
archenemy!

—I perceive you remember me,— Dash observed. —Yes,
what you and I began before can be completed now. Since

my failure in Milky Way I have been recalled and restricted to local duty, with demotion. My aura makes me suitable for important Kirlian work. This was perhaps fortunate, for the regular authorities were bungling the job of locating you. In fact, it is no secret that most of our top leaders are idiots who obtained their positions by factors other than competence; a typical Council Meeting resembles an argument among immature birds. Your own Ministers of Etamin are similar. However, in time of stress competence has a way of manifesting itself, and the Council representative of Sphere : : has been more than adequate in this regard. So we have won the war, and are now merely wrapping up the occupation prior to initiating the energy project. I do not wish to kill you, but capturing you gently was proving difficult, and Leader Quadpoint is becoming obstreperous. But I have given our esteemed leader to understand that once you understand the situation, you will cooperate. You spared my life, and so I attempt to spare yours. Now all you have to do is draw in your aura so that our directional field can encompass it for retransfer to a Dash host. Your present host will not fit within one of our units, so this special arrangement is necessary. All that is necessary is for you to stand astride the unit before you and contract your aura.—

Melody made no move. At least she seemed to have some leverage: They could not remove her from this host without her cooperation, and they did not want to kill her. Probably they could stun her – but then her host would collapse and hurt herself, and it would be a violation of the covenant.

—I realize that I am not especially appealing to you in this body,— Dash continued persuasively. —But it *is* my own, and you are aware of the qualities of my mind and aura. In this lovely female host here – he pointed his wings momentarily at another Dash entity that appeared beside him – you would find me handsome enough. You yourself would be beautiful, as you were in Solarian guise. There would then be no further barrier to our love.—

He was right. His present form *was* unappealing to her, quite apart from her resolution not to mate. But she *did* retain a guilty fascination for him. He had such an attractive aura, and his interest in her seemed sincere. He put a political, practical face on it, but underneath he wanted her for herself. Their auras were nearly equal, they shared an interest in Tarot, and had similar levels of intelligence. Perhaps Flint of Outworld had found a better match, but that was a once-in-a-millennia situation. No male in her lifetime had paid her that compliment (with one exception) and it did move her. She tried to deny that she was still so vulnerable to that kind of flattery, but found she could not.

Then she thought of Skot of Kade, and Gary and March, brave Solarians dying honorably with their fleet. And of Captains Llono the Undulant and Mnuhl of Knyfh and the Drone of the *Deuce of Scepters* sacrificing themselves for their galaxy. And of Yael and Llume and Slammer the magnet and Beanball – yes, even the infant magnet had fought for her! – and she knew she loved them all with a love that was greater than anything available in Sphere Dash. She could not participate in their destruction, no matter what. She was of Galaxy Milky Way, and no personal convenience or lure of aura could alter that. What Andromeda was doing was fundamentally wrong, and she could not support it even tacitly.

—I feared you would require more convincing,— Dash whirred. —Perhaps I can do it yet.—

Another curtain lifted. A strange creature was unveiled. It was composed of strings and tubes and taut diaphragms, as ungainly a thing as Melody could imagine.

Then with a special shock she identified it. 'A Mintakan!' she cried internally. 'My own kind!'

Cnom was surprised and disgusted. 'You look like *that* in your natural form? No wonder you transferred out!'

'It is worse than the Dash,' Melody agreed ruefully. 'A species never recognizes how odd it looks to others until it gets a glance back through transfer. I understand my ancestor Flint was appalled at the sight of naked Solarians when he was in a Polarian host. But every species in the universe has a right to its own existence. That's what I'm fighting to protect.'

314

Cnom subsided, indifferent to the fate of distant Spheres or peculiar creatures.

Melody studied the Mintakan figure more closely. It was an old one, she saw now, with discolored drums, warped strings, and sagging tubing. Hardly a bargain; in fact it seemed near expiration from sheer degeneration. It was female, a spinster, apparently never attractive enough or amenable enough to find a companion for reproduction. It had no Kirlian aura.

—This, in case you did not recognize it,— Dash said, —is not merely a Mintakan host. It is *your* original body.—

Startled, Melody considered the body a third time. Her aura touched it, and sensed the familiarity. This was, indeed, her original shell. She did not know what to feel.

—We have gone to a great deal of energy-expense to arrange things for you,— Dash said. —If you do not wish to occupy a Dash host, you may return to your own. And to ensure your satisfaction, we have also imported a handsome young male of your kind.— And another Mintakan appeared. His strings were taut, his tubing firm.

During all this adventure, Melody had wanted to return to her own body, to retire in peace, contemplating her Tarot cards so as to wrest a few more precious insights from the deck before she expired. She could live for a long time in transfer, over five Solarian years, but eventually she would have to return to her own body to recharge her aura. And if her Mintakan body should die while she was in transfer, her aura would fade out at a hundred times its normal rate. So by capturing her body, the Andromedans had in a very real sense captured *her*. The chains, though subtle, were horribly strong.

The projectile cannon disappeared. —I believe you understand the situation now,— Dash said. —We do not need to threaten your present host, who is of course innocent, being both £ and hostage.—

Another score! Melody had indeed taken the £ hostage, overwhelming her with the immensity of her aura. Cnom did not seem to object, but the principle was the same. Melody was guilty of the offense she fought against.

315

—But you must appreciate now that you have no reasonable escape,— Dash continued inexorably. —If you leave and hide from us again, we shall have to dispatch your body, and you will shortly fade out, wherever you are hiding. That would be an unfortunate waste of the finest aura ever known.—

Was there any way to free her Mintakan body from their clutches? Could she charge to the ledge, knock the body down, grab it and carry it away? No, the risk was too great. The Mintakan body was old and frail; such activity could kill it. And where would she take it? Into the jellybog to drown? In addition, she now perceived that the body was not in the open air, but within a protective shield; obviously the atmosphere of this planet was not suitable. Without the life-support system the Dash were providing, it would die regardless.

On the other foot, if she agreed to reanimate her own body, what then? Could she carry through her campaign to save her galaxy while trapped in an atmosphere bubble, unable to move freely even if she had the physical strength to? Hardly!

—There is an alternative,— Dash said, having allowed her thoughts time to coagulate. —We have chained the lady, but we do not wish to cause her unnecessary discomfort. You can transfer instead to this fine Dash and live in perfect comfort each day, returning to your natural body only during sleep. Thus you will hardly feel your age and infirmity, and can endure so long as your Mintakan body survives. That can be a long time, with the kind of medical care we can provide. We are in effect offering you a greatly extended youth.—

At the expense of her galaxy? Melody knew she could not do it. She remained standing, unable to cooperate, yet also unable to resist. It was an impasse, with the negative power of decision lying with the enemy. They could always kill her, if they so chose.

—I regret the need to force the issue,— Dash said,— but we are under extreme pressure ourselves, and we very much want you with us.—

To help them in their conquest? Hardly! They were accomplishing that nicely without her.

—You see, we can't force you out of your present host,— Dash explained, —and we can't do anything *to* that host, because of the covenant. Should we kill a £, the other £ might stampede. We can't hurt a £ or even detain one unreasonably; our threat with the cannon was a bluff against *you*, not Cnom. So we must convince you to leave the host voluntarily.

—To accomplish this, I shall explain why we need you. This planet is a leading source of Ancient information; sites abound more thickly here than anywhere else in the known universe. From these sites we have rediscovered Kirlian science that has propelled us to the forefront of our Galaxy, and soon the Galactic Cluster too. But more sites remain that are inaccessible to us. They are of the self-destruct variety, a type unknown in your own galaxy, that cannot be penetrated by any entity whose aura is of the wrong type or strength. We *need* the information locked within these sites, for there are many other galaxies in the universe, with many other sapient species. If one of those species should achieve complete Ancient science before we do, they will have the capacity to eliminate us. We cannot afford that risk.

—You have an aura of the family keyed to this generation of sites. The Slash entity you knew as Llume was of this family, but her aura was not strong enough. Your own exceeds two hundred, which we believe more than meets the necessary level. Therefore you and you alone are able to penetrate the ultimate secrets of the Ancients.—

That explained Dash's interest in her from the start. Just as the Andromedans were robbing the Milky Way galaxy of its vital energy, they were taking its best animate potentials. Good, hard business sense.

Many years ago an Andromedan agent had tempted the Milky Way Solarian hero, Flint of the Outworld, with similar logic. She had told him that his own species would have acted much the same as hers had it possessed the opportunity, and she had been right. Yet in the end it was *he* who convinced *her*, though he was the barbarian and she the sophisticated issue of a leading civilization. She had defected to the Milky Way, and parity had returned to the galaxies.

But whatever had happened in the past, she was sure that *Mintaka* would not have sacrificed any galaxies for its own advantage. This ambition of Sphere Dash was wrong, and she could not support any part of it, regardless what happened to her or her Sphere. Better to kill herself, thus depriving the enemy of any possible use of her unique aura.

So she remained silent, though now she knew Dash would not shoot her. Should she try to bargain with him for whatever she could salvage, be it only half or a quarter of the Milky Way? Could she trust him or his Sphere that far?

—I cannot read your mind, precisely,— Dash said. —But I am responsive to the fluxes of your beautiful aura. I believe you are concerned primarily for your galaxy. Tap one foot if I am correct.—

No harm in that. Melody tapped one foot.

—I cannot promise you anything in that regard. But I can say this: If you evoke the secret science of the Ancients for us, we may no longer need the energy of your galaxy to sustain our civilization. Then it would be spared. However, since we do not know what is available in the Ancient sites, this is a gamble.—

A gamble whose terms were all in favor of Sphere Dash. If they won, they had the universe; if they lost, they still had the Milky Way. Yet did she have any better alternative? She could not decide.

Dash took her hesitation for negation, which it probably was. —I dislike coercive measures, but the matter is urgent.—

Melody, perhaps on the verge of acquiescence (and perhaps *not*), now hesitated for another reason. If he could not do anything to her £ host, how could he do anything to *her*? He could only kill her Mintakan body, which would defeat his stated purpose.

—I did some research on Sphere Mintaka,— Dash said. —It was not thorough, for I only recently managed to signal my fleet and get picked up. Marooned in a prison host! For-

318

tunately Hammer of Quadpoint was alert, and caught our crude broadcast.—

So the hostages had adapted the missing transfer unit for regular intergalactic transfer and used it to send Dash Boyd and the others home. Later, it had been used to send her here.

—Forgive me if I overlook the nuances of your culture. But as I understand it, Mintakans are born neuter, turn female at maturity, and male after the first mating. You never mated in your natural body, so spent your life as a female.—

That was close enough. A permanently sexed entity would hardly comprehend the intricacies of triensent sex.

—The sex of your Mintakan body determines the sex of your aura,— Dash continued after a pause. —What do you suppose would happen if the sex of that body should change?—

So that was it! Melody felt peculiar horror. They had a male Mintakan here, who would take the initiative. *They could do it.*

She might kill the male, but that would finish her own body too. And killing them all would not salvage her galaxy. The question she had to answer was whether she could help her galaxy better as a captive female or a free male. She knew the answer.

—You are way ahead of me, I know,— Dash said. —But to be certain we understand each other I will state it openly. There would seem to be two possible consequences of a change in sex in your Mintakan body. One is that your aura would change sex with it. In that case you would be unable to remain in your female £ host, and would have to vacate. Then I believe we would have you, for we control the transfer apparatus and alternate hosts.—

Melody had not thought of that. What would happen to a male aura in a female host? It was impossible to transfer into a host of the opposite sex; only neuter-sexed entities had any option, and even that was uncertain. Would her aura be bounced into the nearest available male host, which was exactly what Dash was ready for? Or would her aura simply be destroyed by the incompatibility of the host? Either way, she was lost.

—Or,— Dash continued, —would your aura fail to change, in which case you would be unable to return to your own body? That seems paradoxical, so I am prepared to gamble on the first prospect. Unless, of course, you elect to cooperate; that would solve all problems.—

No doubt. But Melody still had a galaxy to protect. She would have to gamble. And one part of her mind wondered about the anomaly: What *would* happen? Horrible that it should happen to *her*, but the scientific curiosity . . .

—Well, we proceed,— Dash said. He made a whirring signal with his wings. Music played abruptly. It was a strange harmony, vibrant but incomplete, unlike anything Cnom had ever heard. It was bud music.

Bud music: the compelling sound of a pair of Mintakans in the throes of love. In Sphere Mintaka, mating chambers were soundproofed, to prevent contagion. Otherwise the mating of one couple would trigger compulsive mating by many others within sonic range, and this was not desirable. The decision to mate was supposed to be based on intellectual preference, not sound, but it didn't always happen that way.

The male Mintakan stirred, approaching the old female husk. He had no intellectual preference; the bud music governed him. The female shell, though void of aura, would function. Not even the atmosphere bubbles separated them; Melody saw those two enclosures merge, in their own kind of mating, and form into just one chamber.

No! No! This was the most insidiously hellish rape! Dash had worked out an appallingly effective physical and intellectual torture for her! She would rather suffer anything than this!

Anything except the betrayal of her galaxy – and that was the price. So she could not stop this gruesome exhibit, this ultimate obscenity. But she could not watch it either. She closed her side eye.

But she could not close off the sound, for it came at her sensitive skin (impervious to talons, but responsive to sound) on every side. She tried to turn her attention away from it, and succeeded only in dredging up her painful past.

She had been just two years old when Ariose came. He was a handsome, extremely high-Kirlian sonic male of four, seeming quite mature and cultured. In Solarian terms he would have been thirty-two, she sixteen, each somewhat younger than Dash Boyd and Yael of Dragon, but with a similar set of outlooks. Two was the age of Mintakan blooming, when the tubes first rounded out and the strings became taut, and the diaphragms resonated to every trifling vibration. The age of delight, experiment, ambition, and beauty – and naïveté.

She had all nine feet, by definition the state of female virginity (the concepts were synonymous), of greatest innocence, desirability, and availability. The great majority of adult Mintakans were to some degree male; only once in life was one fully female.

Despite his age, Ariose had eight feet. He had mated only once. She was curious about that, since a male of his talents and presentation should have had opportunity to bud himself all the way down to three feet, had he wanted to. Why had he saved himself for her? She let herself believe that it was her physical beauty and sonic vibrance in intellectual qualities.

Mature Mintakans came at the agreement to bud circumspectly. Often they remained together for life, though there was no legal or moral requirement to do this. It merely reflected the wisdom of their initial decision: truly compatible entities had no need to wander.

Budding was not a casual, multiple performance like the chronic sexual efforts of Solarians, who copulated tens or hundreds of times for every offspring they produced. In fact, it was said in other Spheres that Solarians indulged in sexual activity more for transient personal pleasure than for the extension of the species. Melody knew that was a gross exaggeration; still her impressionable postadolescent mind was intrigued by the amazing concept. How much pleasure *was* there in budding that made it worth the permanent loss of a foot?

321

So when Ariose intimated that he would like to lose one foot with her, she reacted with foolish enthusiasm. She went with him in a brushcar to a mating chamber, and after feeding each other several strands of vermiculate food and absorbing sprays of liquid, they settled down to serious music.

Melody, of course, had never done this before. That was one reason for the system, she theorized. Since a Mintakan did not turn male until completing first budding, and two females could not mate, it guaranteed one experienced partner to show the way. She had heard that Solarians (Sphere Sol was the butt of a wealth of segment humor, perhaps because of its irritating thrust-culture that forced itself into the awareness of dissimilar species) sometimes got together for copulation and *didn't know what to do*. Or the reverse: They copulated without realizing what it was – until an infant Solarian manifested. Of course, such jokes would have been more effective had they had even the slightest credibility.

Ariose started the unique budding music, and Melody followed it without difficulty. As the sound intensified, they approached each other. He raised one clapper-foot invitingly, tapping with the other seven in intricate point and counterpoint. Melody raised one of her own fair feet, and now her eight tapping ones off-balanced his seven, creating a peculiar sensation of incompleteness. Discord and incompleteness were anathema to Mintakans; music had to be *right*.

'Your strings are as tight as steel wires,' Ariose played. 'Your tubes are as round and full as great organ pipes. Your drums are loud and mellow. Your clappers are marvels of precision.'

Oh, such praise! Females, because of their inherent inexperience, were notoriously subject to flattery, and she was no exception. She drew closer, her raised foot seeking his.

'And your aura,' he played. 'Like none ever known before.'

'My aura?' This struck an unmelodious note; females

were not generally praised for their auras. It was akin to praising a Solarian female for her money.

'Did you not know,' he played, 'you have the highest Kirlian aura ever measured – the only one in the Sphere that is higher than mine. I came to bud with you, hoping to produce a super-Kirlian entity . . .'

He wanted her only for her aura! The whole thing had been arranged.

'How long I waited for you to mature, to emerge from drab neuterdom,' Ariose continued, oblivious to the effect his commentary was having. 'The success of such a budding—'

Melody made a discordance so vehement it almost broke her own strings. She swept her foot sidewise, knocking his clapper away.

Ariose, caught by surprise and ready for the budding connection, lost his foot. It flew off and crashed into the wall. His music stopped abruptly.

Then Melody suffered chagrin – for she had castrated him. She had knocked off his bud, unmerged. She fled from the mating chamber.

But the compulsive bud music stayed with her, pressing in from all around, inescapable. Her £ eye opened.

Her youth-budding had been horribly aborted. But the age-budding of her auraless body continued, forced by the compulsion of the recorded music. The male had extended one foot, and the female met it with one of her own. The seven male feet clattered in the imperfect counterpoint to the eight female feet, making the music unfulfilled. *The beats had to match.* Yet were was no eighth foot on the male side free to complete the last pair.

Except for the conjoined foot. Driven by the music, the feet melted together, becoming a single unit. This was the bud. Soon it would flower into a complete immature entity.

Melody closed her £ eye again. She had not fled far from Ariose before some sense penetrated her two-year mentality. So he wanted her for her aura. What, really, was wrong with that? After all, she had wanted him for *his* aura; she merely hadn't said so openly. She could have budded already with

323

some lesser male, but only the high-Kirlian male had really excited her. Normal-level Kirlians were not even aware of aura; it was as though they were blind or deaf, not even able to appreciate what they were missing. *Of course* aura was important; it was the real key to modern civilization. She really had little else to distinguish her. Why let irrelevancies interfere with romance? Ariose had acted with perfect sense. He had formed a conception of his ideal female, based on Kirlian intensity, and had sought that female out. She should have appreciated the enormous honor for what it was.

She returned to the mating chamber, but Ariose was gone. What should she have expected? She had struck off his foot in as callously degrading a gesture as it was possible for one Mintakan to make to another. She had rendered him a male personality with a female number of feet; how could he mate now? Actually, once a Mintakan turned male, he remained so for life, unless he should use up all his feet – unlikely, since then he could not walk – in which case he would be honorably neuter again. But budding required that disparity of feet; two six-footed Mintakans could not mate, even though one were seven-footed in outlook.

She had never seen Ariose again, and never met another like him. His aura had been 190, and she never encountered another close to it. It was as though all high-Kirlian Mintakans avoided her now. Perhaps the music about her had spread. She could hardly blame them! She was lucky Ariose had not pressed a charge of mutilation against her.

She had retreated into her study of Tarot, after a brief apprenticeship with the local Temple of Tarot, and found some solace there. Never again had she been seriously tempted to bud.

There was an abrupt change in the music. Again her eye opened, though she tried to keep it closed. The bud formed from the merged feet had now disconnected from the female's body. Attached to the male, it left him with eight feet; and she now had eight feet also. The beat had equalized. That changed the music.

Then the bud dropped off the male's leg too. The music

stopped. The bud had been formed as a separate entity, incorporating the heredity of each parent. It would, with proper care, grow into a small Mintakan neuter. The miracle of reproduction of the species!

But now Melody's native body had budded. It had become, by the definition of its nature, male.

She, here in the £ host, what was she, now?

She dared not remain here to find out.

22

Crisis of Sex

—it is not merely a matter of the etamin agent, quad-point   it is aposiopesis   if the agent can lead us to—

:: this is ridiculous!   a simple matter of nullifying one captive agent of a defeated galaxy::

—our own agent is working on the matter   there are very great potential rewards—

:: assuming your ancient site can yield us anything we cannot already possess with present technology, to utilize a conscious, dedicated agent of a foreign power to explore it is an exercise in such folly as to make my chisels blunt! are you not aware you are placing our entire program in jeopardy?   I absolutely forbid this!::

—it is too late   the quest has already been initiated—

:: there is something about you slavekeeping creatures, here and in the milky way, that is alien to my comprehension   from certain victory you seek defeat::

Melody whirled back out of the chamber. —You cannot escape! Your body is here!— Dash whirred.

But she crashed out of the doorway, knocking out a supporting post. Part of the upper floor sagged. She bounced to the other side of the hall, bashing in a wooden wall. The aroma of freshly ruptured scentwood surrounded her. Then, venting her inner frustration and uncertainty, she deliberately attacked more posts.

The wood was strong, but was not braced for horizontal impact from such a huge, solid body. The city began to collapse about her. The air was filled with whirrings of panic as thousands of Dash birds were disturbed.

Yet what was this accomplishing, this blind bashing

against those who had conquered her galaxy? Like the shallow entity she had been in youth, she destroyed what affronted her – and maybe did herself the most damage.

She burst out of the city and thundered down a channel toward the bog. Now it seemed the hue and cry was out; other £ were charging after her. What did it matter? She had no body and no galaxy to return to!

Something was funny about the pursuing £. They had no mahouts! Without Dash direction, why should they be chasing her?

No time to wonder! She plunged into the bog. As the atmosphere thickened about her, as the jelly formed and exerted its drag, her first passion faded. What, actually, had happened?

'It is the Rendezvous,' Cnom informed her. 'Your emotion triggered it.'

The Rendezvous: a periodic gathering of the £ in the depths of the bog, for the purpose of acquaintance, decision, and mating. It occurred irregularly, generally when some reason arose. This time Melody was that reason.

Could there be any help for her in the Rendezvous? She did not know. She felt much as she had when the *Ace of Sword*s had been going derelict around her.

The £ continued down the channels, this time avoiding the wooden lattice. The jelly grew thicker, until it seemed impossible to push through it much farther. This was the depth at which the Dash failed. They had dismounted in a hurry when the Rendezvous began. Somehow all £ and Dash had known the moment it started; even the sick £ were hauling themselves along.

But with increasing depth, the jell began to thin, until at last it was the consistency of mere water. Like plasma, Melody thought; the pressure was too great for the jell to maintain its structure.

'Do the Dash know of this lessening of viscosity?' Melody asked Cnom. The question was rhetorical, for she knew Cnom didn't have the answer. What difference did it make anyway? Sub-jelly pressure was fatal to Dash; £ logic pursued the matter no further.

327

No light penetrated here. She was aware of the terrain by its sonic vibrations, and the echoes of the vibrations of the multitude of tramping £. Nevertheless, there was plant life in this gloom. The huge trunks of the assorted deepwoods were rooted here, the scentwoods and the larger nether supports of the lattice. Feather leaves were also present, not as light refractors but as nets to collect edible debris sifting down from above. The jelly held and assimilated most of it – Melody suddenly realized that the jell itself was a form of life – but had wastes of its own that made excellent plant food. The ecology of a planet was always in balance.

Her host-body contracted as the intensifying pressure worked on it, much as the Spican bodies did. The £ were remarkable creatures, capable of adapting rapidly to extremes of environment. It was cold down here, but the sheer mass of her body insulated her.

In the deepest hollow of the bog the £ converged for the Rendezvous. There were thousands of them, but their vibrations became minimal; this was an almost silent meeting.

There were no trees here; a great hollow was clear of all obstructions. Had the £ trampled it out? No, Cnom's memory showed that it had always been here. Yet it was far more than natural processes should account for.

Melody realized that this space was, indeed, artificial. The vibrations from deep below had the signature of dense metal. It seemed to predate Dash civilization. What could it mean?

Then she became aware of the aura, which was so even and unfeatured that she had not recognized it at first. It was not the pulsing, sparkling emanation of a living thing, but the uncanny precision of inanimate aura, such as was used for the transfer of energy. Only one thing could explain it.

It was science of the Ancients.

A thrill ran through her. This was an unspoiled Ancient site! There seemed to be no entry, but the aura identified it positively. Not since the great lusty adventurer Flint – how much he was in her mind, now !– had stumbled on the Hyades site, had a sapient of her galaxy discovered a site of this significance!

And this was in the enemy galaxy.

The Dash could not know about it, or they would have been into it already. They possessed the technology to handle the depth – no, that wasn't it. They *must* know about it, for they had sophisticated Kirlian detectors. But this was the £ demesnes, and the £ did not like aliens among them, even in transfer. The site must be one of the self-destruct variety; the effort to break into it could destroy it and have grievous effect on the contemporary society. So the Dash were balked, and only Melody herself had the aural key, perhaps, to the final secrets of the Ancients!

If she could get into that site . . .

But now the £ had gathered. From among them came the vibrations of their leader; in the crowd she could not identify which body it was, but that did not matter. He called himself Dgab.

'This Rendezvous was triggered by the alien among us, she who defended her right by repulsing the lancer,' he vibrated. 'The Dash put her under pressure of aura, and she fled. We must deal with her first.'

It was uncanny how closely the £ society kept track of her! Melody realized she now had to speak for herself, or the £ would force her back to the Dash lest she disrupt the covenant between the species.

'I am of Galaxy Milky Way,' Melody vibrated. 'The society of Dash is destroying that galaxy, and I must save it if I can. To do this I must enter the Ancient site beneath us.'

'Only Aposiopesis may grant that,' Dgab replied. 'Only when a worthy mating occurs will the portal yield.'

A worthy mating! Was there no way to get away from sex? Her host-memory filled in the background; all £ matings occurred publicly in the center of the Ancient declivity. The aura of the Ancients was the unknowable God, Aposiopesis. Legend had it that when a mating met the approval of the God, he would reveal his secrets to that worthy pair.

Melody seemed to have escaped the sex-change of her Mintakan body. Apparently it was her personal experience that defined her sex. But if she mated now, in this host, she surely *would* change – and have to leave the host. For she could not delegate this to Cnom; the £ knew her, and she herself had to be the one to try to gain access to the site.

What would happen if she were unable to do so? She would probably fade out at an accelerating rate and finally expire, freeing her host. That had happened to Flint of Outworld and his Andromedan mate. Could she afford the risk?

There was no question! 'I will try to please Aposiopesis,' she vibrated. 'If I succeed or if I fail, I will soon be gone from you.'

'Stand at the portal,' Dgab vibrated, and Melody rotated forward until she was in the center of the depression. Here the alien aura was stronger, with an especially focused column; in a living creature it would have approached her own intensity. But there was no living aspect about it, and it spread far wider than any she could imagine from mere flesh and nerves. To think that this remained after three million years! The Ancients, without doubt, had been the ultimate masters of aura!

'Who would breed with this entity?' the leader asked.

No one replied.

'Whom would you choose?' Dgab asked Melody.

'He with the strongest aura,' Melody said immediately. Aura was obviously the key to this site – if there really *were* a key – but this was also a personal preference. She had once scorned love based on aura, and had paid for that mistake with a lifetime's celibacy. Now her body had been brutally freed of that state. Maybe her mating had been preserved for this: the climactic opening of the Ancient site.

Now several £ rotated forward. £ mating was not entirely voluntary; if a suitable partner was needed, he was impressed into service.

They trotted past Melody, each displaying his proboscis according to ritual. Because the £ were rotary – in the Tarot they would surely be represented by the Suit of Disks – their bodies had no fixed projections. But as they had to suck nutrient fluids from the plants, the proboscis unfolded when required.

The first had an aura of about fifty – good, but not at all in

330

Melody's category. The next was better, about seventy. The third was forty.

A dozen paraded by. The highest was just under one hundred. That was quite respectable. Whole planets of entities sometimes did not have any aura higher than that. Still . . .

'Will you, Dgab, also offer yourself?' Melody asked as it occurred to her that a Kirlian-conscious species might elect a high-Kirlian leader.

Dgab emerged from the throne. He was old – as old as Melody herself in her original Mintakan body. He moved slowly, his three legs still strong, but his physical strength diminished. Yet his aura as he approached her was indeed powerful, in the range of 150. Here, perhaps, was a suitable mate!

A new £ whirled down from the outside. His legs were spindly, his body small, and one of his tentacles was missing. 'Allow me,' he vibrated, speaking imperfectly.

'The dead has been animated,' Dgab observed. 'What spirit occupies this body?'

'Dash,' the newcomer vibrated. Actually the designation differed, but this was the way Melody recognized it. 'Alien to you, but mindful of the covenant, I come to settle alien business. By the standard set, I qualify. Perceive my aura.'

Melody found herself in another turmoil of indecision. His aura was 175, certainly the closest to her own she would encounter here. She *had* specified the highest aura. But this was the enemy! Was she to evoke for *him* the secrets of the Ancients?

'No! I do not accept him!' she vibrated angrily. 'He seeks only to nullify me, to destroy my galaxy!'

'I meet the specifications,' Dash replied. 'I come to save her galaxy from the destruction that otherwise is certain – but that is irrelevant to these proceedings. I *qualify*.'

'Agreed,' Dgab decided, stepping back toward his favored anonymity in the crowd.

'I *don't* agree!' Melody vibrated. 'Come near me, bird, and I kill you!'

'Let the aliens decide between themselves,' Dgab decided.

Dash approached. 'I seek only the blessing of Ap-

331

osiopesis,' he said, 'for the good of the universe, your galaxy included.'

What amazing persistence! He had thrown himself into an unsuitable host and was risking his life by intruding among hostile £, when he could have simply destroyed her own £ host by some subterfuge and been done with it. While he really *did* want the Ancient science – he wanted Melody, too. He retained all those admirable traits of intelligence, aura, and courage that had attracted her to him despite her knowledge of what he was. Yet – 'I cannot trust you!'

'Why not merely knock off my foot?' he inquired, stepping nearer.

He knew! He had found out about her past, and now he taunted her with it.

She could feel his aura, the strongest she had encountered in the better part of her lifetime. She had been bemused by that aura once, and thought she loved him – until he had tried to kill her. Until he had sexually tortured her aged Mintakan body. Until – but it had never been possible!

She poised herself for combat, but had no effective weapons. The £ were huge, but not normally aggressive. They could only bang against each other, not really hurting. If only she had that trunk of scentwood!

Well, then, she would bang! She launched herself at him – but the water slowed her body. Dash met her with a lunge, his proboscis unfolding. It jabbed deeply into her torso, like the thrust of a lancer, plunging all the way into her liquid core.

She could have cried out – had she a mouth and air system. She had been caught by surprise, undone! But before she could reorient, she felt, instead of pain, a slow warm, rich, growing pleasure.

Dash had not wounded her – he was mating with her! Mere puncture did not hurt the £; it was the loss of core substance. There were similarities to the way they had mated in their Solarian bodies, but also differences. In each case the male used an erectile member to penetrate the body of the female, and through this member the juices of copulation flowed. The difference was that here there was no prepared

332

aperture in the female; the male made his own. And the flow through the proboscis was two-way.

She was caught up in the developing ecstasy of the exchange. Dash was her enemy, symbol of all that she fought – yet he was a fine configuration of an aura and a bold, smart, intriguing male. He pursued his objectives as rigorously as she pursued hers. He had animated a defunct £ body – an extraordinary step for a Dash to take! – merely to join her in this. It was hard to condemn that.

His tube inside her sucked out the liquid core, depleting her. But this was a gentle, wholly exhilarating release, not the brute rupture the lancer's attack would have been. Then the flow reversed, and her fluid was pumped back through the conduit, mixed with his own, doubling the volume. The pleasure as she swelled was double what it had been.

Then he withdrew, and the puncture closed after him, bringing on the climax-completion – the most exquisite sensation yet. Now the dual fluids were within her – the pool for the formation of new life, possessed of the twin genetic patterns and of its nacent aura. Like the Solarian process, parturition was not immediate; it would take time for the new entity to take shape from that pool, to develop and finally break out.

So she had not yet completed procreation. Only the mating had been effected thus far, but she was – gravid. The process was inevitable. And with it, she would turn male, and have to leave her host. The commitment had been made at last.

And she was not sorry. All her long life she had waited for this, and now it was complete, though she die. The ghost of her past had been extirpated.

Suddenly the impersonal machine aura around them changed. The surface beneath their feet began to sink.

'Aposiopesis!' someone vibrated. 'Our God accepts!'

For the Ancient site was opening .·.. after three million years.

23

Ancient of Days

—the day of reckoning may be on the wing   aposiopesis
wakes—

'A-PO-SI-O-PE-SIS!' the massed vibration cried. 'A-po-SI-
O-PE-sis! A-po-SI-O-PE-sis!'

'God of Hosts!' Melody cried to herself as she sank.

'And so we win,' Dash vibrated gently. Melody realized
what sounded strange about him: In this host, he did not
speak with the Dash inflection. 'Because we are meant for
each other, and the Ancients found us worthy.'

'The Ancients merely required sufficiently high aura,'
Melody replied. 'They make no moral judgments.'

'How can we be sure?' he asked. 'To them, aura itself may
be a state of morality.' And she could not answer.

The platform moved well below the floor of the bog, descending on a slant. Melody watched the feet of the standing
£ rise out of sight. All knew this was a historic event,
a three-million-year breakthrough. Aposiopesis had
answered.

Below the opening, the well widened. Melody detected the
vibrations of a counterweight rising. As their platform
dropped lower, it spiraled outward, and the counterweight
spiraled inward, rising to fill the hole above. It was a giant
sophisticated airlock!

As the valve screwed closed in its fashion, the water
drained away and gas filled the chamber. Melody, in a non-
breathing host, could not analyze its type, but she was
certain it was an inert substance, probably to protect
the intricate mechanisms of the Ancients. Three million

years – and still operative! What greater wonder could there be?

Yet Melody was not so bemused by the mating and admittance as to forget her priorities. Dash was still her enemy, and in no case could she allow him to emerge with the secret science of the Ancients. Surely he would not permit her to use it to save her galaxy, either. Their battle had not yet been concluded.

Already she felt the stirrings of masculinity within her, of aggression. This host was becoming uncomfortable. She had to do what she had to do before she lost her identity.

But it was also possible that neither one of them would escape this site. The machinery had chosen whom to admit; why should it not choose whom to release? Melody doubted she could get out on her own.

Melody looked around her. Huge as her present host was, this site was large in proportion. It was as if it had been constructed to accommodate £ alone. And that was impossible, because—

Why was it impossible? The Ancients, according to the best modern research, had vanished approximately three million years before, from all across the galaxies. That was a long time ago, in terms of civilization, but a relatively short span geologically and paleontologically. There had been £ that long ago, and Mintakans, and Solarians, and all the rest. The fact was that the Ancients had been contemporaries of all the major modern sapients before these species developed highly organized technological cultures. It was almost as though the Ancients had to vacate before the modern cultures could rise, as the dinosaurs of Sphere Sol had passed (in most places) before the contemporary mammals, and the subsonic monsters of Mintaka before the sonics of Melody's own species.

But there the parallel broke down. The modern species were superior to the ancient ones. The small mammals had better brains and were physically better articulated than the large reptiles. The Ancients, on the other hand, had been superior to the moderns – so far ahead that even three million years later the gap had not been closed. No shift of

335

galactic climate could have dislodged *them*. Their disappearance had not enabled more progressive cultures to arise; it had allowed *inferior* ones to take over the galactic cluster.

Had there been any doubt of that, the mere experience of this site would have dissipated it. What a mechanism!

She could not talk to Dash, for now they were in gas and the skin vibrations did not work. Had the £ been able to communicate linguistically in atmosphere, their relation with the Dash would have been entirely different.

Yet it was as though this site had been made with the £, not the Dash, in mind. It was at the bottom of the jellybog, where Dash could not readily go, and its gargantuan scale and mode of entry were suitable only for £. But when this was built, the £ had been primitive creatures. Only in the past hundred thousand Solarian years – twelve thousand *real* years – had their society ripened. Unless the Ancients had anticipated – but that was preposterous. Why should the Ancients have *cared* about the future of the £? Or about *any* of the modern cultures?

If by some chance of indecipherable logic the Ancients' like gods, *had* cared about the then-primitive species of the galaxies, they would have done better to dismantle their sophisticated outposts. For it was the occasional discoveries of functioning Ancient sites that had triggered the phenomenal intergalactic wars, wreaking havoc among Spheres and segments. Without transfer technology – which seemed to stem entirely from Ancient science, as far as technological archaeologists had been able to determine – the Spheres would have continued regressing at the Fringes, and therefore been unable to make effective war against their neighbors. There would have been continuing peace, instead of the monstrous uncertainties of contemporary war.

Why, then, had the Ancients left these sites so carefully preserved from degeneration? If not for the species to follow, for whom?

And she realized: *for the return of the Ancients themselves!*

She spun about, looking for an exit, but of course there was none. The plug had sealed the hole above, and now the platform had stopped its descent. They stood in a chamber like the bottom of a spiral oubliette, a deep well widest at the base. And the circular wall was fading out.

It thinned into vapor, then vanished entirely, and they stood in a broad plaza. The vista extended on every side so far that her nonfocusing eyes could not see its end. This was no room; this was a city!

Beside her, Dash had to be as bemused as she. Never in all known history of the two galaxies had such a thing been discovered. This planet had numerous Ancient sites, but they were broken-down relics, with few real artifacts. This – this was Aposiopesis Revealed!

This was surely the home base of the Ancient culture. It would take a planetary task force of specialists many years to explore the secrets of this amazing metropolis. Whoever came to comprehend it would control the universe!

Melody felt a chill. Who could investigate this – except Sphere Dash? *She* could not; she could hardly hold on to this female host.

Better that they both perish here, never emerging!

They had not moved from their platform. Where would they go? There was so much here that they could get lost if they attempted to wander. There had to be some point of reference, some way to orient.

Suddenly from the distance came a machine. At first it seemed formless, but then she saw a large screen on it, like a spaceship viewer. Of course: a communication device!

Dash was paying close attention, she knew. The screen – actually a viewglobe – stopped a short distance away. Then an image appeared on it, shifting and chaotic. First it resembled a £, then a Dash. Disorganized sounds were manifested, and there was a peculiar medley of odors. A Solarian biped wavered and faded.

Suddenly Melody caught on. She concentrated – and the figure firmed into the Queen of Energy card of the Cluster Tarot. The lovely bare-mammaried Solarian female, chained to the rock by the restless sea, her hair blowing out in the ocean wind.

Dash's body quivered. He saw it too! The chained lady

resembled Yael of Dragon. whom he surely recognized.

This was an animation globe, similar to those used by the Temples of Tarot, whose images were defined by the imaginations of the viewers. Flint of Outworld had encountered such a device in the Hyades site, and used it to evoke the formulas that brought parity to the intergalactic scene. Too bad that site had been destroyed; later expeditions had never been able to make sense of the rubble. But this time, *this* time . . .

Dash was already at work on it. A disciplined series of pictures appeared on the screen: Sphere Dash entities. No – these were merely his animations of the Ancients. Not knowing their actual nature, he rendered them in his own image. But the message was what counted. He was trying to fathom the ultimate secret of these mysterious people, and thus gain some hint of their technology. Otherwise he would not even know what questions to ask, just as a creature of a civilization of three thousand years ago would not have known how to ask for Transfer. Had such knowledge been offered. As of course it *had* been, via these same sites.

Melody watched. It gave her time to wrestle with her own problems of host-rejection and Galaxy-salvation. Maybe there would be some key here.

Dash did an excellent job of zeroing in on the later stages of Ancient history. The network was extremely complex, because the Ancients had spanned the entire cluster – some twenty assorted galaxies and fragments. It had been the most extensive Empire ever known, with no Spherical regression. How had they managed that?

Expertly, Dash located the key lines. Slowly the mechanisms of the Ancient disappearance emerged. There had been no invasion from any other galactic cluster; the Ancients were supreme. No devastating pandemic, no holocaustic war, no precipitous decline in the reproduction rate. They simply . . . resigned. They shut down their myriad bases carefully, returned to their home, and . . . faded out. Trillions of sapients disappeared from the universe.

Why?

Dash swiveled his eye to meet her gaze. On this they were

united: The rationale of the Ancients remained as confusing as ever.

He returned to the animation, questing for the reason, not the fact. This time he centered on it faster.

And as the rationale came clear, Dash and Melody stared and listened and experienced with mounting incredulity and horror.

Suddenly the animation cut off. Melody wasn't certain which one of them had terminated it; it could have been either. Far better never to have known this terrible Ancient secret! Aposiopesis indeed!

Melody blanked it from her mind. She had no intention of letting her own culture die, no matter what the alien psychology of the Ancients had been. Through Ancient science she could certainly redeem her galaxy.

The problem was how to get what she needed without giving it first to Sphere Dash. No doubt she could learn from this globe how to build invincible spaceships that would conquer a galaxy, jumping from Sphere to Sphere by inanimate aural transfer – but Sphere Dash would build them first. She could discover how to mattermit whole planets across millions of light years, using minimal power – but Sphere Dash would do it first.

What possible secret could she learn that would save her galaxy – without being subject to prior nullification by the enemy?

She tried to concentrate. But the progression of pregnancy in her host was affecting her. She *had* mated; she was turning male. Her whole aura was reacting with the knowledge, suffering hostile incompatibility. It was a peculiar, awkward sensation; soon she would simply *have* to leave, no matter what.

If only she could arrange to put Dash in a similar situation, to force him to vacate any hostage he took. If it were only possible to make hostaging itself impossible, so that only voluntary hosting could occur. The Andromedan effort would collapse, and Milky Way would be forever secure.

More than that: She would have to do it retroactively, so

that the damage already done could be undone. For Galaxy Milky Way had already fallen.

Then it came to her. There was one secret Dash could not counter even if he shared it.

This site was not merely informational. It was the key. Flint of Outworld had discovered that the Hyades site was one big transfer unit, controlled by thought. This £ site had to be another.

In moments Dash would catch on, for he was not stupid, and he was almost as fiercely motivated as she was. She had to act *now*.

'Oh Aposiopesis, God of the days of the Ancients,' she thought, couching it as a prayer because that was what, in essence, it was. The intensity of her need made it so. 'Modify your transfer mechanism. Make every hostage entity dominate the invading aura – wherever transfer is used.' Her internal verbilizations were crude; the essence was her will. 'Let the host-aura dominate, regardless.'

But Dash had now understood the situation. He emanated a blast of negation that fuzzed the image in the globe; Melody's thought could not get through.

She fought him with her fading aura. Already it was down to his level; her own hostile discordance was phasing her out. She was 175 and declining; soon he would be stronger. *Stop the hostaging!* she willed.

The picture changed back and forth. Light and dark thrust against each other, symbolic of her aura and his, evenly matched, neither prevailing. But slowly, inevitably, the darkness gained, absorbing more of the globe.

Desperate, Melody cast about for some device, some insight that would help her. *Her galaxy depended on her success!* But the picture kept darkening. She hit him with aural : : blows, but he absorbed them; she set a $^0_0$ trap, but he avoided it. He was thoroughly experienced in aural combat, and she could not overcome him.

Better to destroy the whole site than to give him this victory. That was what Flint had done.

She sent a blast of despairing hate at the globe – and it puffed into vapor.

Amazed, she stared at the fading wisps of smoke. Beside her, Dash was unmoving, as surprised as she. Could the machine itself have been an illusion of animation?

The answer came: *Yes!* This was the nature of animation. Their thoughts not only animated the pictures of the globe, they *were* the globe. And the entire city. All that really existed here was the oubliette – and the animation transfer unit and bank of information that surrounded it. Which was worth more than any city.

Melody acted immediately. Under her guidance, the entire city exploded ferociously. The acrid odor of destruction was painful. The site seemed to be collapsing, burying them.

And while Dash stood confused by the sheer threat and fury of the falling buildings and leaping flames, not certain how much was real, not yet aware that it was merely the dissolution of the animation, Melody thrust forward her overwhelming thought-urge-prayer: *reverse hostaging!*

And her world dissolved.

24

Milk of Way

COUNCIL INITIATED   PARTICIPATING $* - / :: {}^{0}_{0}$
—aposiopesis has spoken—
andromeda is fallen
/the lady is chained/
${}^{0}_{0}$ the monster strikes ${}^{0}_{0}$
:: shame! ::
CONCURRENCE

Melody opened his eyes and sat up. His body felt stiff, and he had a headache, but he could function.

He licked his lips. The flesh was raw, and one or two front teeth were missing. 'Mush have veen some fight!' he muttered.

He was in a round room. He was clothed – a Solarian affectation. Next to him several other Solarian males and one female lay on pallets. Melody recognized them: They were the hostages that had taken over the *Ace of Swords* of the fleet of Segment Etamin. He knew them only by their hostage identities: Hath of Conquest, Tiala of Oceana, all of the entities he had unsuccessfully tried to salvage from Andromedan domination. All were there except Captain Dash Boyd.

For *he* was Captain Boyd! Melody had changed sex, and animated a male host. He must have had the subconscious desire to return here to the Segment Etamin fleet, and the Ancient unit had picked up that wish and transferred him here. What miracles of science the Ancients had!

But what of his main intent, to abolish hostaging? Now *he* governed another hostage body! Well, he might still be able to do something.

He drew upon his host-memory information and ascertained that this was a chamber within a Disk of Sador. The host-mind, unconscious at the time, had no memory of being brought here, but Melody was able to figure it out by reference to the older memories. Victorious Admiral Hammer of : : must have boarded the derelict *Ace of Swords* and salvaged all useful equipment, especially the serviceable hosts. He evidently knew enough about magnets and magnetism to handle Slammer and his companions, too.

Melody, in control of this body without Hammer's knowledge, could do some damage, maybe even taking over the ship. Then . . .

He went to a water nozzle and activated it. A jet of cold, refreshing fluid spurted into his face. Sador didn't worry about the inefficiency of such mechanisms; the surplus water was reclaimed, and an automatic cutoff prevented the device from operating in null-gravity conditions. Sador was a huge, degenerate Sphere; creature comforts had intruded on many of the military vessels. He was feeling better already.

He touched the door-button, and the round door opened. This ship was of course designed for globular, wheeled Sadorians; push-buttons were satisfactory, but not pull-levers. It was no problem for this bipedal, twin-handed host, however.

Melody emerged into a great central level, with ramps leading up and down. The wheeled creatures preferred the open range. But within the ordered physical system was chaos. The Sadors were hunched, unmoving; their wheels drawn in, as though in shock. He walked among them, unchallenged.

What had happened? This whole ship was non-functioning!

'Captain!' a Solarian voice called.

Melody turned, his human ear orienting on the sound – his *two* ears; they gave him an immediate sense of direction. He spied a screened cell containing two men. 'Skot! March!' he exclaimed, concentrating so as to avoid slurring his words. Those teeth were a problem!

343

'Well, half right,' March said, satisfied. 'But – who are you?'

Melody smiled. 'You may have some trouble believing this, so I'll come at it obliquely. I'm not the Andromedan. Remember the Service of Termination?'

March's eyes widened. 'Captain Boyd wouldn't know about that! Only—'

'Only Melody of Mintaka could know,' Skot put in. 'Feel that aura!'

How did Skot know about that? He hadn't been there! Melody leaned closer, probing for the man's aura – and it was not Skot of Kade. Yet it was familiar . . .

March glanced across at him. 'Maybe such things aren't significant to you, Slammer, but I can't feel the aura, and Melody is a female. She can't—'

'*Slammer?*' Melody demanded.

Skot's head nodded. 'Admiral Hammer didn't trust me in my natural body, so he transferred me to this ungainly thing. Poor Beanball is locked into another cell with my body; he must think I'm dead.'

'But Skot – what—?'

'He is gone,' Slammer said. 'His ship was blasted. This is an empty host.'

Add Skot of Kade to the growing list of entities to mourn! If only he hadn't insisted on going on that mission . . .

'We've been getting to know each other,' March said. 'Slammer's a nice guy; I never realized how smart the magnets were. But just now all hell broke loose. The hostages keeled over, then you came out. Who *are* you really?'

'The anti-hostage mechanism!' Melody exclaimed. 'It *worked*!'

Quickly Melody explained about his effort at the Ancient site in Andromeda. 'Transfer is instant,' he concluded. 'And so is this, it seems. I animated this host because the original personality is gone, so there is no host-mind to preempt it, and I am male, now.' He explained about that as he activated the cell-release.

March shook his head in amazement. 'I thought meeting a

344

magnet in human form was the limit; now I have to get used to a beautiful girl in male-captain form.'

'I never was a beautiful girl,' Melody said. 'That was merely my host, Yael of Dragon.'

March nodded thoughtfully. 'I'd like to know – her.' Then he remembered something. 'What was the Ancient secret? Why did they suicide, and why were you so horrified, even after three million years?'

'Aposiopesis,' Melody said succinctly.

'What does *that* mean?'

'I will never tell,' Melody said with absolute seriousness. 'If the truth were known, much of the drive of our own contemporary civilization would dissipate. We might, like them, give up. I don't *think* we would, but we *might*. I refuse to gamble on it – and I doubt Dash Boyd will gamble either.' Then he returned to the business at hand. 'Admiral Hammer and all the other hostages must have been nullified; that's why they collapsed. Their host-minds may have been taken over, but it's too soon to – you know how the hostages suppress their hosts, even destroying them . . .'

'Then we'd better get control of this ship fast,' March said. 'Because pretty soon those hostages may be back on their wheels, if their hosts are really dead or dying. We'd better herd them into these cells until we're sure.'

'Yes,' Melody agreed.

But already the Sador hosts were moving. A large one rolled up. Melody reached for a weapon, but found he had none, so waited alertly.

'I am Rollo of Sador,' he said formally. 'Former Rotary Officer of this ship. I now control the aura of Hammer of : :, though I am very weak.'

Could he believe him? It might be that Hammer was pretending to have succumbed. But that would have been pointless. If he retained control, he should act to assert control of the ship. It was possible that the : : had not repressed his host-aura as viciously as some, so that Rollo remained sane. If so, Hammer was not only competent, but pretty decent for an Andromedan. Melody decided that the risk was worthwhile. Apparently the human auras had faded out

345

only after the oppressive Andromedan auras had departed, as though beaten into such dependency they were helpless without alien support. But there was a difference between individuals, and there could, indeed, be native host-personalities to take over. Those who were mad would now plunge their erstwhile masters into hell; those who had been treated more kindly would respond in kind.

He did not know what a Rotary Officer was in Sadorian terms, but since Sador was a circular culture like Polaris it seemed appropriate. It was probably equivalent to Captain.

'I am Melody of Mintaka, temporary Admiral of the Etamin fleet,' he replied. 'I believe we have won the war by recovering all hostages. But we shall have to take stock and reorganize.'

'My guest aura informs me that there is one you will wish to meet,' Rollo said. 'A companion of the Milk of Way. Please wheel along this vector.'

Melody hesitated again, but decided to go along. 'Free all prisoners and ascertain their identities,' he told March. 'See if you can locate Slammer's natural body. Be alert.'

March nodded. 'Yes, sir.' He knew as well as Melody did that the situation remained highly flexible; some hostages might remain in power. But due care should suffice.

Melody was sure that a similar confusion existed all over the Milky Way galaxy as the counterhostage impulse took effect. But out of this chaos would emerge victory, the salvation of his galaxy. Again he marveled: What powers the Ancients had, yet how carefully guarded!

Melody accompanied the Sador to another level of the ship. Here, alone in a cell, sat a breathtakingly lovely woman in a simple, ragged dress. Her hair was long and brown, her features even, and her body lithe yet full-fleshed. There were some bruises on her, as if she had suffered a beating in the past few days, and one leg was bandaged. But these imperfections seemed only to enhance the general splendor of her person. Melody had never seen such beauty in a Solarian female before, and it did something to him. He experienced a nascent urgency.

Rollo's wheel whirred. 'The situation has changed,' he said. 'Here is a friend.'

The girl looked up, her glance cold. 'Forget it, Hammer,' she snapped. 'Dash and I aren't on the same side any more. You know that.'

Melody came close to the cell-screen. His aura interacted with that of the prisoner. The two auras were amazingly similar. 'Llume!' he exclaimed. 'In Yael's body!'

Startled, the girl jumped to her feet, her breasts bouncing. God of Hosts! Melody thought. Every motion she makes – I wish I could take her and– 'That aura! So like my own, but so strong – impossible!'

'I depart,' Rollo whirred discreetly. 'The cell is open.'

'You can't govern Yael's body,' Melody said. 'The hostage reversal–'

'Hammer transferred me,' Llume said. 'He was very smart about neutralizing potential troublemakers without further killing. But I did not dominate the host. I have had enough of hostaging,' She paused, then spoke again, in a different manner. 'That's right. Llume refused to take over, but her aura was so like Melody's – maybe not her aura, because I can't feel aura, really, but anyway there was something about her – well, I told her to go ahead and use my body. It hardly made any difference, here in jail with all our friends dead.'

'Yael,' Melody said. 'Don't you know me?'

The girl squinted. 'Something Llume's thinking . . . you're not Dash . . . someone else, like Flint of Outworld . . .'

Melody laughed explosively, male-fashion. 'Yes, very like Flint of Outworld – now! I am Melody.'

The pretty mouth dropped open. 'You *couldn't* be!' Then: 'Unless–'

'Yes. I mated in Andromeda, and then had the Ancients reverse the hostaging. Shall I remind you about the dinosaur you tried to tame as a child, or the *Four Swords* poem that–'

'Nobody knows that!' Yael exclaimed.

Melody smiled, opened the cell, and spread his arms. Yael hesitated, evidently listening to what Llume was telling her.

Then her eyes teared. She stepped forward and fell into his embrace.

Melody became acutely aware of the formidable physical female charms Yael possessed, and began to comprehend what had never been quite clear before. He had, in his female aspect, employed those charms in a mercenary manner, not really understanding why they created the response they did. Now, with those full soft breasts touching him, that slender, exquisitely contoured torso against him – this was not a game! The response, the sheer *need* – he wanted to grasp, hold, squeeze, kiss, penetrate. Those smooth round legs, that shaped posterior . . .

But there was something else. More than the merely physical, compelling as that was. 'Do you know why I never had much interest in mating, despite inhabiting a body so well designed for it?' he asked them. 'I mean, apart from the Mintakan complication, and my age, and the war . . .'

'Do you know why I defected to your side?' Llume asked in return.

'For a pair of bright entities, you two are pretty dumb,' Yael said. 'You always were in love with each other, but you couldn't admit it because you were both female, and two different species at that.'

Melody and Llume looked at each other, realizing it was true. 'I was also in love with you, Yael,' Melody said. 'That was even more complicated.'

The lovely eyes returned her gaze. 'Yes . . .'

'The situation has changed,' Melody said, bending to kiss them.

Epilogue

The counterhostage measure was effective. The Andromedan thrust collapsed. Because the governing Spheres of that galaxy depended heavily on hostaging, for a time there was anarchy. No transfer aura could dominate a host; it could only visit. If a voluntary host objected to any measure taken by its transfer entity, the will of the host prevailed.

Gradually a new philosophy of transfer evolved, in which hosts participated equally in all activities. Government in both galaxies became more responsive to the will of lesser auras. In fact, the archaic concept of 'democracy' had to be revived and applied. The Spherical governments were replaced by responsive administrations who promised never again to practice or tolerate energy theft.

Melody of Mintaka never told the secret of the Ancients, and neither did his erstwhile lover of Dash. The fabulous site of Planet £ remained sealed. Melody, after some pleasant dalliance with his friends Llume and Yael, retired to his own aged body and his own Sphere. He contemplated his Tarot, finding new insights there, until he expired shortly thereafter. He seemed satisfied, and not much concerned with the fact that his name had already been entered in the annals of two galaxies, parallel to those of Flint of Outworld, Brother Paul of Tarot, and other historic figures in the folklore of cluster civilization.

In Galaxy Andromeda, Melody was honored in his female form, represented in the Queen of Energy or Thirteen of Wands card of Tarot. But it was mooted privately that the name of the lovely chained lady was Andromeda, as the Solarian mythology had said all along, and that the name of the sea monster was Melody.

The host-entity, Yael of Dragon, was retired with honor and granted a Society of Hosts pension. The young guard who had discovered the first hostage of Outworld, March (the name originated as a code, but he elected to retain it), was feted regally and offered anything in the Segment he might desire. He chose Yael. They married and carved out a pleasant ranch in backvine Outworld, and their children had a pet dinosaur.

Slammer the magnet recovered his body and son. The magnets were granted civilized status, and developed a considerable fleet of spaceships, as they were well suited to economical space travel, requiring neither atmosphere nor gravity on any regular basis. In due course Sphere Magnet joined Segment Etamin, and contributed its first representative to Segment government: an entity by the name of Beanball.

Galaxy Andromeda, having twice erred by casting lascivious desires on the energy of her neighbor, was now chained. For a thousand Solarian years she was contemptuously reviled by sapient species elsewhere in the galactic cluster. The cultures of Spheres $*$ — $/$ $::$ and ^o_o stagnated, and not merely at their regressive Fringes. Their need for massive new energy had been critical, and remained so; civilization could not be maintained at its prior level.

But the mystery of the Ancients remained hidden. Slowly, inevitably, the level of civilization in the cluster declined, for the available energy was being depleted. It seemed that modern sapients were doomed never to approach the technological level of the Ancients, let alone to comprehend the secret of the Ancients' demise.

Suddenly, the greatest threat of all: the Space Amoeba. It threatened to engulf the entire cluster. There was only one possible way to oppose it: to achieve the immediate breakthrough of complete Ancient science. Under this imperative, a new figure appeared in Cluster history.

This was an entity of lowly, oppressed Sphere Slash of Andromeda, who sought to fulfill the plea of his ancestral kin Llume that Sphere Slash redeem its honor. He possessed the third and greatest of the phenomenal auras. His Kirlian rating was 236, and in certain respects his adventure was to be the most remarkable of the three. He was known colloquially by his twin professions: Herald the Healer.

His thrust into history was the Kirlian Quest.

THE WORLD'S GREATEST SCIENCE FICTION
AUTHORS NOW AVAILABLE IN PANTHER BOOKS

Robert Silverberg

Tower of Glass	60p	☐
Recalled to Life	50p	☐
A Time of Changes	50p	☐

Poul Anderson

Fire Time	75p	☐
Orbit Unlimited	60p	☐
Long Way Home	50p	☐
The Corridors of Time	50p	☐
Time and Stars	50p	☐
After Doomsday	50p	☐
Star Fox	40p	☐
Trader to the Stars	35p	☐

Philip José Farmer

The Stone God Awakens	80p	☐
Time's Last Gift	50p	☐
Traitor to the Living	85p	☐
To Your Scattered Bodies Go	85p	☐
The Fabulous Riverboat	85p	☐
Strange Relations	35p	☐

All these books are available at your local bookshop or newsagent, or can be ordered direct from the publisher. Just tick the titles you want and fill in the form below.

Name...

Address..

....

Write to Panther Cash Sales, PO Box 11, Falmouth, Cornwall TR10 9EN.
Please enclose remittance to the value of the cover price plus:

UK: 22p for the first book plus 10p per copy for each additional book ordered to a maximum charge of 82p.

BFPO and EIRE: 22p for the first book plus 10p per copy for the next 6 books, thereafter 3p per book.

OVERSEAS: 30p for the first book and 10p for each additional book.
Granada Publishing reserve the right to show new retail prices on covers, which may differ from those previously advertised in the text or elsewhere.